TRUST NO ONE

A ***CONOR THORN*** NOVEL

GLENN DYER

TRUST NO ONE

A ***CONOR THORN*** *NOVEL*

GLENN DYER

TMR PRESS, LLC

ALSO BY THE AUTHOR

The Torch Betrayal

The Ultra Betrayal

The Unquiet Genius

TMR PRESS, LLC
2057 MAHRE DRIVE
PARK CITY, UTAH 84098

Trust No One is a work of fiction. References to real people, events, incidents, organizations, or locales are intended to provide a sense of authenticity. All other characters, and all incidents and dialogue, are drawn from the author's imagination or are used fictitiously.

TRUST NO ONE A Conor Thorn Novel (Book 4)

First Edition

ISBN
979-8-9887961-0-7 (ebook)
979-8-9887961-1-4 (paperback)
979-8-9887961-2-1 (hardback)

Printed in the United States of America

Cover and Interior Design: JD Smith Design
Edited by: Gretchen Stelter and Kimberly Hunt of Revision Division
Author Photo: Terry Moffitt

You can grab a free short story that pits Winston Churchill against the leader of the Soviet Union, Joseph Stalin, when you join my newsletter. You'll also get the Prologue and Chapter One of *The Torch Betrayal*, the first book in the Conor Thorn Series, and notice of upcoming releases, promotions, and personal updates.

Sign up today at:

WWW.GLENNDYER.NET/SUBSCRIBE

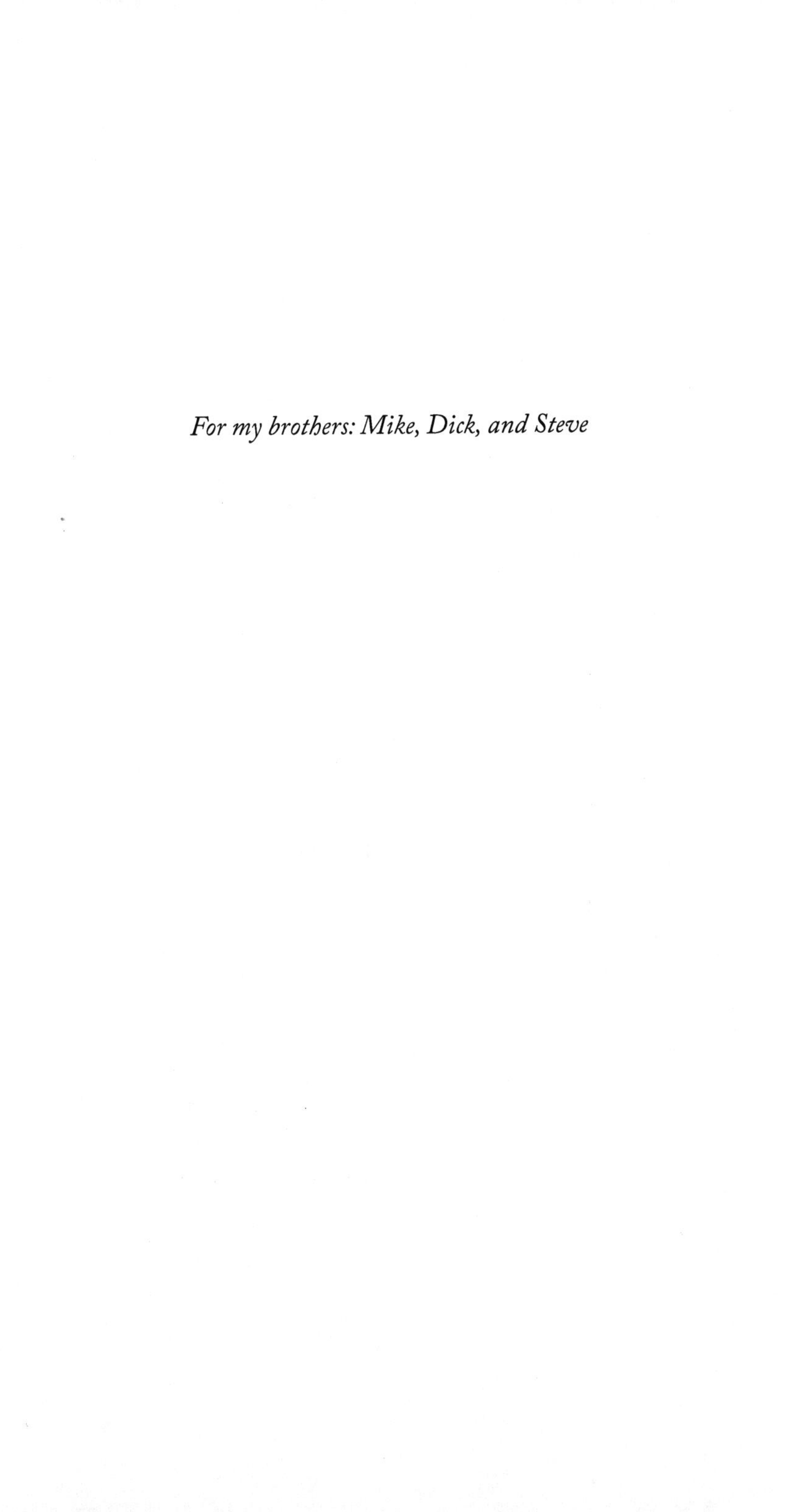

For my brothers: Mike, Dick, and Steve

"If you know the enemy and know yourself, you need not fear the result of a hundred battles. If you know yourself but not the enemy, for every victory gained you will also suffer a defeat. If you know neither the enemy nor yourself, you will succumb in every battle."

—Sun Tzu, The Art of War

PROLOGUE

0810 Hours, Friday, December 25, 1942
Basilique Notre Dame d'Afrique, Algiers

"Trust no one." His mother's words were all too familiar. "Trust no one," she repeated. "Not your friends, nor your compatriots. You do not know their inner thoughts. Their fears. Their eager willingness to betray. No, Michel, trust no one. Do you—"

Michel Chrétien cut short his mother's voice with a hand gesture that swatted at the dank, tepid air in the basilica's crypt. There wasn't time for her forewarnings. He felt sure he hadn't been followed. Michel had quickened his pace and had chosen a more direct route to the basilica, cutting several minutes off his usual serpentine travels through the alleys and souk of Algiers. Having the archive in his possession rattled his nerves more than he expected. The weathered satchel contained the records of the Group of Five, the men who successfully conspired to assassinate one of the leading traitors of France, Admiral Jean François Darlan, High Commissioner of France for North and West Africa. The traitor had betrayed his last Frenchman.

"There, move that stone to the side," his mother whispered. She was a longtime cook in the Carmelite convent adjacent to the basilica. She pointed to a pockmarked sandstone block sitting atop a low stone wall that ran the length of the crypt, dividing it into two equal sections. She lifted an oil-fed lantern, shedding more light in a twenty-foot radius. "Under it, there should be enough room for the satchel."

Michel laid the satchel to the side and, with the heels of his hands, shoved the heavy stone aside. The edge of the damp stone crumbled at his touch. When the stone had slid two inches, the low grinding sound was replaced by a high-pitched hissing. A bulbous rat scampered into the darkness, leaving Michel and his mother stumbling backward and gasping for air.

"*Merde*," Michel blurted. Shit.

"Michel, please, no profane language. Not here."

Michel shook his head. "Watch out for his friends," he said. "And lift the lantern so I can see inside."

She did as he asked, and Michel peered inside the hole beneath the stone. Satisfied, he shoved it farther to the side.

"Are you going to tell me what is inside the satchel?" Not waiting for an answer, she said, "Does it have anything to do with the murder of the admiral?" Michel lowered the satchel into the dark hollow, struggling at first to fit it in the confined space.

"It is better that you do not know. You never were a believable liar, *maman*." His mother started to say something, but he hushed her. Michel pushed the stone back into place, took his mother's hand, and led her to the door to the stairs. They climbed the stairs back to the nave on ground level, Michel's mother breathing heavily as they ascended. On the last step, Michel squeezed his mother's hand and brought his other hand to his lips. He pointed at the door and whispered, "Voices, *maman*."

Michel slowly cracked open the thick oak door and looked into the foyer of the basilica. There were five men—all wearing the uniform of the local police. One, who was a head taller than the rest, barked orders at the others. Michel softly closed the door and held up his hand with his fingers spread wide. "It's Captain Roget," he said in barely a whisper. His mother began muttering, but he couldn't make out what she was saying. After she made the sign of the cross, he grabbed her upper arm. "There's another way out of the crypt, correct?"

His mother looked down the stairs, then back at her son. "Yes, another stairway," she said, her voice hushed. "At the far end. It goes up to the sacristy behind the altar. In the sacristy, there is a door that blends in with the wall and is difficult to see. It is behind the small desk and leads to another stairway, which takes you to a walkway high up in the apse that surrounds the altar. Stay low behind the balustrade and be very quiet. Sound…it…"

"I know, *maman*. Sound carries. Wait here for a minute, then go talk to them." He snatched the lantern from his mother and descended the stairs.

As he ran the length of the crypt, Michel started perspiring. He considered dropping his wool coat but thought better of it. When he got outside, he would need it. He reached the end of the crypt that lay below the altar and dome, stopped, and caught his breath. When he had been given the assignment to deliver the group's archive to a secure place, he'd expressed disappointment that he was not given a more important task. When they'd pulled straws as to who would shoot the traitor Darlan, the honor had gone to his friend, the monarchist and anti-Vichyite Fernand Bonnier de la Chappelle. In the aftermath, he was not told of his friend's situation. Was he alive? Was he dead or just sitting in a cell awaiting the release the group's leaders said would come once they found themselves in positions of influence?

Michel cursed his underestimation of the danger that his task held for him. He should have taken more time to lose the police or their informants on his way there. His impatience could cost him his life. A price he was willing to pay for his country—but not now.

He calmed his breathing and strained to detect any voices or movement from the other end of the crypt. The sooty smoke wafting up from the lantern triggered an urge to cough, which he fought back. Hearing nothing, he entered the stairway. He stood in the pitch-black, running his right hand down the wall for a light switch and finding nothing but a moist, chalky smut. After swiping the left wall produced the same result, he extended his right foot to locate the first step. Fighting off a network of cobwebs on his climb, he reached the door to the sacristy. He put an ear to the door and, hearing nothing, cracked it open.

He stepped into an empty sacristy save an oversized oak armoire, its doors left open, and a petite writing desk and a wooden chair. The air in the room was infused with a heavy mustiness tinged with the scent of incense. He closed the door to the crypt with a soft touch, rushed to the writing desk, and pulled it off the wall four or so inches—just enough to squeeze through the door hidden behind it. Before he closed the door, he tried to pull the desk back as close to the door as possible. Looking up, he was relieved to see the uppermost area of the two flights of stairs bathed in dingy sunlight. Michel scaled the stairs rapidly, stumbling several times, the last leaving a gash on his shin. Reaching the top of the second flight, he felt blood trickle down his leg into his shoe.

He placed the lantern on the top step, removed his coat, and pushed on a flimsy door, two and a half feet wide, that opened out onto a walkway just wide enough for the door to fully open. It ran along the inside of the basilica's apse, a semi-domed roof that enveloped the altar, which lay one hundred feet below. Between the altar and the curved wall of the apse was the towering crucifix. The upright post and crosspiece were unusually narrow. From his vantage point, the upright post looked no more than three inches in width.

The thigh-high marble balustrade's top rested on a row of lathe-turned balusters that provided near-ample refuge from the authorities searching for him below. Two sets of three stained glass windows hung below a massive painting that filled the surface of the half-dome. It depicted two separate groups of people, some kneeling, others standing, all looking skyward to the Virgin Mary holding the baby Jesus in her lap.

Several voices reverberated inside the basilica's nave. One was shouting orders to move into the nave and search every pew, confessional, and sacristy. Another voice, much softer, was a voice of a sobbing woman. His *maman*.

From a prone position on the walkway, he peered between two balusters and tracked the movement of two policemen as they made their way toward the altar, searching each pew in their path. He could no longer hear voices and wondered what exactly that meant. Was his mother safe? Had she been taken from the basilica and put under arrest, he wondered. He watched the two officers complete their search of the pews, then rush toward the altar area. One officer prowled around the altar as if he was looking for a secret compartment. Michel lost sight of the other officer.

He wrestled with the idea that he was trapped on the walkway. Michel would fight his way past his pursuers with all his strength if they decided to head up the stairs. He slowed his breathing so that he could detect any movement on the stairway. The marble floor felt cool. It soothed the scabs that had formed after he and his compatriots had scored their chests with the Cross of Lorraine. A symbol of their patriotism and loyalty to their country and each other.

For several moments, he heard nothing, and his nerves calmed as he gazed through the balusters down at the crucifix. His mother would have told him to pray. Especially now. His lips started to move just as the door to the stairway slammed into the wall, missing his head by inches.

Michel gasped for air, turned his head toward the door, and saw a single coffee-colored shoe, its leather scuffed and cracked. The laces frayed and faded. He pushed back with his hands, but they slipped on the floor. The officer, panting heavily, didn't move. He must have been as startled to see Michel as Michel was to see him. But the officer, his facial features droopy, recovered quickly. He leaned over the balustrade and directed a shout down toward the nave.

Michel was on his knees. He rose to his feet and reached his right hand out to the top railing to gain leverage. He rushed the officer, hoping the advanced age of the overweight policeman would give him an advantage. Michel had to get past the officer and head back down the stairs before anyone below could respond. That meant he had only seconds to move, no more.

The officer lunged and blocked the door, then threw a punch that connected with the bridge of Michel's nose; starlight washed over his vision as he stumbled backward. The officer grabbed Michel's shirt before he fell to the floor.

"Get back down on your knees and hands behind your head. Do it or I will shoot," the officer sputtered but produced no gun as he spoke. The beats between his words signaled that he was still winded from his climb. Michel had to get away. He pulled back. His shirt ripped open, exposing his chest.

The back of Michel's legs smashed into the sturdy balustrade, his shoes slipping on the marble floor. His arms spread like wings as he tried to regain some lost balance, but his right shoe slipped off the walkway—then his left shoe followed. For a second, he sat atop the railing. The officer's grip on his shirt kept him seated on the rail.

Michel barely heard the officer whisper, "The cross."

Their eyes met for a moment. Then his shirt ripped again. In that second, Michel knew he was done.

As he plummeted toward the floor behind the altar, he saw the officer leaning over the railing, his mouth agape.

When he hit the upright post of the crucifix, Michel grunted and reached up toward the painting of the Virgin Mary, the fingers of his hand closing into a fist. Then he gave in to the pain.

CHAPTER ONE

2115 Hours, Monday, January 4, 1943
Hôtel Saint-George, rue Michelet, Algiers

Conor Thorn sat at the end of the bar mumbling swear words to himself. He cursed his difficulty in processing the events of the day. Those who had occupied stools near him had disappeared, leaving him alone at the end of the counter. He ordered another Jameson and surveyed the other patrons using the mirror behind the bar. The last time he had been there, about three weeks ago, he and Emily had enjoyed a few rounds after they'd returned from their mission to keep the Italian physicist Ettore Majorana from falling into the hands of the Nazis. Failing to convince Majorana—who had spent the last four years in a Carthusian monastery—to join the Allied effort to beat the Germans in the development of the atomic bomb, he and Emily had arrived at a compromise with the brilliant physicist: let him disappear. After they staged his death. Rest in peace, Ettore. Their compromise had an unintended consequence. It got Conor's ass sacked from the OSS.

His head was still spinning. He monitored the entrance to the bar, looking for any friendly face. He preferred one in particular—Emily. His wife of nine days, ten hours, and—he squinted at his watch—twelve minutes. But he had no idea where she was. Somewhere between England and North Africa, he guessed, doing the bidding of Prime Minister Churchill.

Aah, shit!

When he first set eyes on Lieutenant Stevens, Colonel Eddy's aide, his shoulders slumped. Eddy was Conor's boss and ran the Tangier OSS office where Conor was first assigned. Eddy had shifted to Algiers as the Allies moved eastward across North Africa. There was a noise in Conor's head; he was sure it was the sound of shit hitting the fan. Conor glimpsed a red-faced lieutenant in a British uniform trailing Stevens into the bar, muttering something about a cock-up. Stevens had stirred up a potential hornet's nest when Conor and Emily had returned from Italy with the news that Majorana was dead. Gossip had reached them that Jack Waddon's copilot had blabbered something about a stop that Conor had convinced Waddon to make before he flew to Algiers in his PBY-5 to drop off Conor and Emily.

The first stop had been so they could drop off Ettore Majorana and Father Sean Sullivan, a Thorn family friend from their days in Dublin, so the two men could catch a neutral-flagged steamer to South America. Colonel Eddy had challenged Conor and Emily on the veracity of their final mission report, but when Conor and Emily pressed the point that he wouldn't have agreed to help with the Allied atomic weapons program—in fact, he might have taken steps to sabotage it—Eddy backed off. But not before leaving doubt in the air about whether he truly bought in to their story. As it turned out, he didn't. Neither did Colonel Donovan, Eddy and Conor's boss.

"Thorn." Stevens shook his head like a judge scolding a truant. "I'd be drinking, too, if I just got my ass handed to me." The Brit lieutenant tugged at Stevens's sleeve, prompting Stevens to wheel around and snarl at the man. "I said we are done. Now leave!" Stevens, his eyelids droopy from drink, turned back to Conor. "I have business with my friend, Thorn." The Brit flexed his jaw muscles and stretched his neck in anger. In so doing, it revealed a mark on his neck. *A stain or a birthmark, one of those port-wine stains,* Conor thought. After the Brit stormed off, Stevens took the stool next to Conor, who decided he didn't need any shit from this weasel and started to slide off his stool. Stevens grabbed his arm and held him in place. "Stay. Let me buy you a going away...aah, *I just got shitcanned* drink." A glassy-eyed Stevens grinned. "So what is it you Irish assholes drink? Anything, right?"

"You are one annoying little shit, Stevens. Like a gnat buzzing in someone's ear. You need to be swatted."

"Aw, come on, you can do better than that. Spin me some bullshit just like you did for Eddy," Stevens said, slapping Conor on his back and spilling some of his Jameson on the bar. "Oops, we can't have that. Let me get the mick another drink." He signaled the bartender.

Conor knew, if he didn't leave then, this scene wasn't going to play out peacefully. He didn't need the added trouble staying there would create by letting Stevens push his buttons.

Stevens leaned toward Conor, stopping inches from his ear, and whispered. *Aah shit. A little added trouble won't kill me.* Conor pushed away from the bar, his stool screeching as it scraped the floor. Stevens again grabbed his arm, but this time Conor spun toward him and planted his right hand on Stevens's face, shoving him backward and sending him crashing to the floor. Conor turned to leave when someone in the bar shouted, "Watch it!"

Conor turned back but only managed a half turn when a punch from Stevens glanced off his right shoulder and landed on the side of his head, pummeling his ear. Conor shook his head as ringing reverberated in his ear.

Conor turned and riveted a stony stare on the red-faced Stevens two feet away, a stupid grin on his face. A Jameson-fueled rage started to boil. Enough crap rained down on him earlier that day. And he had to sit there and take it. He didn't need any shit from this pain in the ass. He did take the first punch, after all. Conor swept his left arm up in a blocking move, which spooked Stevens, then he delivered a solid right upper cut to Stevens's stomach. The blow sent Stevens staggering backward gasping for air. Conor wasn't done.

He closed the distance and delivered two rapid left jabs that sent Stevens's head back and forth like a speed bag. His jabs set up what Conor wanted to be the last blow, a right hook to his jaw. Stevens's head rocked hard to the side, and he dropped to the floor like a sack of Jersey corn. Conor, taking in his handiwork, heard the scuffling of feet behind him—*patrons heading for the exit*, he thought. A blow to the back of Conor's head led to the explosion of stars in his eyes as he fell forward, his forehead rapidly closing the distance with the rounded edge of the hard oak bar. Then darkness came.

#

0600 Hours, Tuesday, January 5, 1943
Maison Blanche Airfield, Algiers

Conor stirred. His head was pounding like the bass drum in the US Naval Academy marching band. When he opened his eyes, one person stared back at him. The facial features were out of focus, as if he were looking through cheesecloth. He blinked. The onlooker's mouth began to flap. He sat up, but his head almost exploded. A hand pushed him back. The cheesecloth dissolved, and he could see someone smiling at him. Given the slow shake of his head, Captain Jack Waddon was not pleased to see him.

"You are one lucky bastard, Conor," Waddon said.

Conor looked around and recognized that he was back aboard Waddon's Consolidated PBY-5 Catalina, the ship that had taken him, Emily, and Father Sean Sullivan to Italy on their mission to snatch Ettore Majorana. "What did you say?" He could barely hear his own words. "What the hell happened?" He reached for his throbbing forehead and felt a knot the size of a billiard ball. The surface of his forehead radiated a low heat.

"You were introduced to a blackjack swung by one angry MP, that's what happened," Waddon said. "As far as being lucky, well, that's because Commander Butcher saved your butt. Told the MP that he'd take it up with Colonel Eddy himself and see that you, being nonmilitary, would exit the theater as soon as he could arrange transport."

Conor rolled over onto his right side. The two men were in the plane's compartment forward of the waist gunner's area and aft of the flight engineer's compartment. He reached for the back of his head and discovered a lump where the blackjack had ambushed him. "Stevens?"

"Hauled out of there to the field hospital. Out cold. Like you were."

Conor groaned.

"Here," Waddon said as he handed him a damp handkerchief.

Conor spied white gauze peeking out from under Waddon's left sleeve. Waddon had been wounded three weeks prior when his PBY approached the beach near Anzio to exfiltrate Conor, Emily, Sean Sullivan, and Ettore Majorana.

"How's the arm?"

Waddon waved off the question. "On the mend. Already back in the left seat."

Conor nodded, then held up the handkerchief. "What's this for?"

"Your ear. There's some dried blood. Stevens must have landed at least one blow."

Conor took the handkerchief and dabbed at his right ear, loosening some dried flakes but also coming away with some fresh blood. The bass drummer in his head pounded away. His head had seen better days.

"So you dragged my ass here after Butcher saved it?"

"Yep. Me and DiLazzaro. We thought you had some lead bars in your pockets. You were a load getting you in here." Seaman Eugene DiLazzaro was one of Waddon's crew and had wound up part of Conor's team that went ashore at Anzio. The New Jersey–born Italian American had handled himself like a pro, particularly when the shooting started.

Conor's stomach roiled. Bile crept upward. A mixture of oil, perspiration, fuel, and grease hung in the air, fanning the flames of his nausea. "Jack, do you have a bucket? I don't feel too good."

"Conor, don't you lose it in my ship," Waddon said, scurrying forward in search of something to keep his Catalina puke-free. Conor wondered what did the most damage: the blow to the back of his head from the blackjack or the oak bar that gave no quarter when his head collided with it. Waddon returned with a collapsible canvas bucket and shoved it into Conor's hands. "Here, and don't miss."

Conor leaned over the side of the bunk and let loose a stream of vomit that filled the bottom two inches of the bucket. When he finally felt he had no more to give, he handed it to Waddon and lay back. "So you just happened to be in the area when the action started?"

"Hey, I was thirsty." Waddon went aft and tossed the bucket's contents out through the open starboard-side blister. He returned and sat across from Conor on the port-side bunk. "When I approached the bar's entrance, I saw Butcher coming from the other direction. We were about ten feet from the bar when we heard a massive crash. That must have been Stevens doing a back flop on the backbar. Two MPs were already there. We saw one lower the boom from just inside the doorway. We both cringed when your head hit the bar."

"Well, thanks for the sympathetic cringes. Then what?"

"I already told you. Don't you remember?"

Conor shook his head and felt the pain surge as if his brain were bouncing around inside his skull.

"Like I said, Butcher jumped in, threw Ike's name around a bit, and eventually, the MPs backed down. He told them to get Stevens to the field hospital and told me to take care of you, but not to go far. That he needed to see you when you got put back together. He wanted me to get this to you." Waddon handed over a note.

Conor unfolded the paper. It was short and sweet. He folded the note and put it in his pants pocket, then settled back to let the whitecaps in his stomach calm down.

"Well, you going to let me in on it or not?"

"He wants to know why Donovan shitcanned me."

CHAPTER TWO

0715 Hours, Tuesday, January 5, 1943
Hôtel Saint-George, rue Michelet, Algiers

After the first outburst, the only sound in the cramped meeting room was the clinking of coffee cups as they were shakily returned to their saucers, spilling some contents. Commander Harry Butcher observed several cigarettes were snuffed out in ashtrays, and the attendees sat ramrod straight in their seats, hoping their careers weren't about to be cut short or redirected to some backwater post.

"I have learned..." General Eisenhower, Supreme Commander Allied Expeditionary Force of the North African Theater of Operations (NATOUSA), paused to take a deep drag on his cigarette. He didn't exhale before he began speaking again. "That there is a strong possibility that the OSS and the SOE may have been involved in some way with the people behind the assassination of Admiral Darlan." Ike's voice was still an octave lower and a bit raspy from fighting the flu bug he had been skirmishing with ever since they arrived in North Africa.

Butcher had concluded that spending as much time as they did in the bone-chillingly damp caves of Gibraltar, on the days leading up to D-Day of Operation Torch, had done it. Ike gazed around the table, staring at each person intently for a two-count before moving to the next stone-faced officer. Bill Donovan, head of the Office of Strategic Services (OSS), the fledgling espionage organization founded merely seven months earlier, sat motionless, returning Ike's steely gaze.

Brigadier Colin Gubbins, the assistant director of Britain's Special Operations Executive (SOE), Churchill's tool to "set Europe ablaze," furrowed his brow as he stroked his neatly trimmed mustache. Colonel Douglas Dodds-Parker, a senior SOE officer for most of the SOE's time in North Africa, had his eyes on his boss—*looking for a sense as to how to react*, thought Butcher. Colonel Bill Eddy, right-hand man to Donovan and a grizzled World War I marine veteran whose main expertise was centered on the Arab world, sat back, staring at his lit cigarette. Eddy's unruffled demeanor impressed Butcher—or maybe the man was just hard of hearing.

A somewhat calmer Ike sat back. "I sent General Smith to meet with General Bergeret, who, you should know, is now the deputy high commissioner for French North Africa. This is what I told him to tell Bergeret." Ike leaned forward and crushed his cigarette with his thumb, nearly tipping the ashtray over. "I told him to report that if it becomes clear that the OSS or the SOE were involved in the plot, I am going to resign."

The only sound that Butcher registered was Ike's wheezy breathing. No one dared to look at anyone but Ike. "If that happened on my watch, I deserve to be sent back Stateside, pronto." Ike picked up a pack of Lucky Strikes and fished the last one out, then, in a snap, crushed the pack in his hand. The men around the table jerked like they had been stuck in the rear with a hatpin. "Anything I should know, gentlemen?"

The attendees jostled in the seats, exchanging furtive glances. Butcher knew that there was not one among them who wanted to see Ike leave his command. All knew the disruption in the chain of command would probably put Allied planning for the invasion of Sicily, Operation Husky, behind schedule for many months. The room remained quiet.

"We are done here." Four words voiced, in no uncertain terms, his anger and disappointment.

As the room emptied, Butcher sought out Colonel Eddy. "I need a minute."

"Fine," Eddy said, just three steps behind the exiting Donovan.

A khaki-uniformed aide entered the room, moving against the tide of attendees taking their leave. He had a flimsy in his hand, folded in half. He handed it to Eddy, who took his time reading it before handing it back to the aide. "Wait for me outside. I won't be long." Eddy turned to Butcher but abruptly turned back to the aide. "And, Heugle, I'll respond to Jacqueline myself. As soon as I think of what I'm going to say." He turned his attention to Butcher. "Commander, I'm all ears."

CHAPTER THREE

0800 Hours, Tuesday, January 5, 1943
Banque Worms, rue Childebert, Lyon

Pierre Laurent's two guests were involved in a discussion that ran tangentially along the lines of what he brought them together to discuss—recent wartime developments that impacted the *Synarchique*'s goals of aligning the future of France with the new economic world order created by a victorious Third Reich. Otto Abetz, Germany's ambassador to État *Français,* the French State, and Emil Bardet, an officer of Worms et Cie, Worms & Company, rehashed a deal that a Romanian oil refinery—owned by the bank—struck with Germany to provide fuel for a top-secret rocket program. Laurent's unsettled mind was elsewhere—namely in his bathroom just prior to his guest's arrival. There, he'd witnessed the reappearance of blood in his urine. A reminder that his prostate cancer was a relentless scourge. One that might soon take his life.

"Pierre…Pierre, are you with us?" It was Bardet. Laurent's opinion of his fellow officer had evolved since the hostilities began. Once considered by Laurent a staunch supporter of his and the *Synarchique*'s ambitions, Bardet's reputation had taken some punishment after the Allies' successful campaign in North Africa. He was heard, by more than one technocrat, to have expressed some growing doubts about the establishment of the new economic order so sought after by the movement. "Did you hear what I asked?"

"Aah, no, Emil. Please forgive me. What did you say?"

"Otto and I want to know what the other members think of this deal we have been discussing. Is it not looked upon favorably?"

Laurent took in Abetz. The fortyish, blonde-haired German with dark, piercing eyes was someone Laurent was careful not to put a great deal of trust in. Since the Nazis occupied Vichy France, just days after the start of the Allied invasion of North Africa, his stature in the halls of the German Foreign Office had diminished. Ribbentrop no longer needed to coddle and cajole the troublesome Vichyites. Diplomacy was no longer the order of the day, as the Germans did what they wanted. Laurent knew well that a successfully completed deal to provide fuel for the German weapons project, helpfully orchestrated by Abetz, would go far in restoring his reputation within the Foreign Office or, more importantly, with Ribbentrop himself.

Laurent directed his response, not to his questioner but to Abetz, who leaned forward in his club chair, his hands clasped tightly together. "While the per-liter factor is much less than what was requested"—Laurent paused and took in Abetz's eyes as they widened in anticipation of the rest of his response—"this arrangement is seen by our members as a major milestone in setting the stage for the Third Reich's ultimate victory."

Abetz released a long-held breath.

"Ambassador Abetz's deft assistance in the negotiation process was critical to its success," Laurent said. "I will make sure that Prime Minister Laval is well aware of this."

Abetz sat back and crossed his legs. "Is he still in contact with Foreign Minister von Ribbentrop, Pierre? I ask that, if he is, a favorable report received by the foreign minister will place me in a more advantageous position to help the *Synarchique*'s ultimate goals."

"Yes, Otto. I agree. Where Laval stands with the foreign minister, I cannot speak to. Daily events seem to have a dramatic effect on attitudes and decision-making in both our governments. We can only hope."

Bardet started to speak, but Abetz's raised hand shut him down. "I have not shared some key facets of the program, Pierre. Trust me when I say that this weapons program will bring the English to their knees. And future development in the program will have the Americans rethinking their foolish decision to come to the aid of their past oppressors."

Laurent smiled and offered a curt nod. All he could think of was the blood in his urine.

CHAPTER FOUR

0815 Hours, Tuesday, January 5, 1943
No. 10 Downing Street, London

The unlit Romeo y Julieta dangled from Churchill's mouth as he surveyed the breakfast tray that his housekeeper just delivered. Looking for any abnormalities and finding none, he plucked the cigar from his mouth, took a fork, and stabbed at a sausage link. He finished the full English breakfast before he polished off the leftover steak from the previous evening. The silver tray, which featured a round cutout to accommodate his ample belly, also had space for a glass of Pol Roger champagne, a rack of toast, and a petite jar of preserves. After a generous swallow of champagne, he fired up his cigar with a long match, filling the space around his head with heavy blue-gray smoke.

He grabbed the *Times* that he had been reading and picked up where he left off—an article devoted to the victims from a recent bombing of Lewisham. When he finished, he tossed the broadsheet to his left, where it landed on the oriental rug. The sharp noise of air whipping through the pages rattled Jock, his marmalade-colored cat that slept at the foot of the twin bed. Jock flew off the bed and slipped out the door that had just opened, revealing Clementine, Churchill's wife of close to thirty-five years. His spouse sported a royal-blue wool crepe dress and had her hair under the tight wraps of a robin's-egg-blue scarf, except for three tufts of silver-gray hair that rested softly on her forehead. She wore the set of pearls that he'd bought her to mark their thirtieth wedding anniversary.

"Winston, you know Mr. Sawyers detests your habit of tossing your newspaper on the floor," Clementine said.

"You are wrong, Clemmy," Churchill said, relighting the dormant cigar. "He detests having to bend over to pick them up."

"You are incorrigible, I swear." She scooped up the broadsheet, folded it, and placed it in Jock's recently vacated spot. "So tell me, when do you leave for Casablanca? Is it still to be in two days?"

"Yes, yes. In two days. I look forward immensely to seeing Franklin again. There is much to discuss. Or I should say, much to negotiate with our American allies. However, I do not look forward to the seemingly endless hours in the *Commando*." Churchill named the Consolidated B-24 VLR (Very Long Range) Liberator himself, employing a touch of tongue-in- cheek.

"Have you seen any weather reports for your route?"

"No, my dear. I'll leave that up to my trusted crew." Churchill picked up a slice of toast and spread plum preserves across it when his valet, Frank Sawyers, entered the room.

"Prime Minister, this just arrived for you. I was told it was of the utmost importance." Sawyers handed over the cream envelope and grabbed the newspaper from the foot of the bed before heading out. Churchill winked at his wife as he opened the letter with a knife. He moved his lips ever so slightly, grunting several times as he read the contents.

"Well, that news was totally unexpected," Churchill said, tossing the letter on his tray. He finished his glass of Pol Roger champagne and cleared his throat.

Clementine waited. When several quiet seconds passed, she cocked her head and raised her eyebrows. Churchill knew what that meant.

"It's from Hambro." Sir Charles Hambro was the head of daily operations of the SOE and worked closely with Bill Donovan, head of the OSS. "Apparently, General Eisenhower has threatened to resign his command if it is found that either the OSS or the SOE was involved in the assassination of Admiral Darlan."

"Oh, my word. That seems quite drastic." Churchill grunted, signaling his agreement. He turned his head to gaze out the window at the light rain that coated the windows. "Were they?"

"Were they what?" Churchill said, continuing to stare out the window.

"Were they involved? The OSS or the SOE?"

"I have no earthly idea, Clemmy." He picked up his glass, saw that it was empty, and replaced it roughly on the tray, dislodging a slice of toast from the rack. He turned to his wife and chuckled. "That said, I am quite tickled that the little man is gone. He was a thorn in the side of our relationship with the Americans."

Clementine nodded. "But General Eisenhower can't be serious…can he?"

"My dear wife, I have never known Ike to be anything but."

#

2115 Hours, Tuesday, January 5, 1943
Anfa Hotel, Casablanca

Emily stepped off the short set of stairs from the twin engine C-47 Dakota and moved to the side to allow the other members of the prime minister's Casablanca conference advance team to exit the aircraft. Her bones ached. Or was it, she wondered, the muscles attached to her bones that were responsible for her incessant discomfort? The flight from Gibraltar to Cazes Airfield was much shorter than the first leg of their journey, Tempsford to Gibraltar. After touching down at the Rock, the twenty-four passengers weren't allowed to leave the plane for any reason to eliminate the possibility that someone would let their ultimate destination slip out. After a swift refueling, they were on their way to French Morocco.

The metal seats that ran down both sides of the transport provided no comfort, only an overabundance of misery. The luggage and crates of typewriters, phones, and various office necessities that were lashed down in the aisle kept anyone from seeking the comfort of stretching their legs.

Emily took a deep breath, noting the absence of the familiar ocean scent that was so prevalent during her and Conor's brief honeymoon at her mother's home in Southend-on-Sea. As there was no detectable breeze, she assumed they were farther from the coast than she'd thought.

As some semblance of relief returned to her legs, she spied Detective Inspector Walter Thompson, the prime minister's bodyguard, who had been sent ahead to meet with General Patton regarding conference security. He huddled with another man whom Emily couldn't identify because the broad-shouldered Thompson blocked her view. It was when Thompson turned back and looked at Emily that she saw the other man was Claude Dansey, Colonel Z, sometimes just Z, MI6 Chief Stewart Menzies's deputy, also known as C.

She wasn't sure whether Dansey knew her, but he was quite familiar to her. Dansey was known in many quarters for his strong, general dislike for Americans—and from inside MI6 as being vindictive and a troublemaker. He had been involved in British intelligence since the turn of the century. Thompson headed to the terminal, leaving Dansey alone. Emily started to follow Thompson and several others, who were the last to deplane, when Colonel Z shouted her name.

Emily stopped and turned. Dansey, wearing a blue pin-striped suit, shirt, and tie, with a raincoat draped over his arm, stepped toward her. His features came into clearer view. Most prominent were the round tortoiseshell glasses he wore that seemed too small for his broad face. His hairline had receded, and what remained was a short gray stubble.

"You are Emily Bright, are you not?"

Emily started to reply but stopped a beat. "I'm Emily Bright-Thorn…Mr. Dansey."

"Yes…I am aware that you married that…American." His tone was awash with disappointment. "One of Donovan's men."

"Yes, sir." Emily waited for Dansey to speak, but he just stood there, staring at her. "Was there something you wanted, sir?" Emily expected something like a change in assignment, but what she heard was totally unexpected.

"You have been relieved of your position at MI6."

Emily's lips parted.

"As soon as that plane refuels, it will take you to Algiers." His tone was flat, like he was ordering dinner at his favorite gentlemen's club in London. "From there you will take the next available flight back to London. I will wait here with you while the plane refuels."

Emily felt her face flush with anger. "Questioning? Regarding what precisely? Does it concern my time working for the prime minister?" Her questions were mounting, but Z made no attempt to interrupt the flow with answers. "By whose order am I relieved? Surely, I am owed an answer to that question."

"Your last question I will answer—the prime minister himself. With full knowledge of C."

Emily was thunderstruck. Her anger matched her confusion, but a sense of dread outmatched both feelings. *Ettore. It's all because of Ettore.*

CHAPTER FIVE

0830 Hours, Tuesday, January 5, 1943
Hôtel Saint-George, rue Michelet, Algiers

With purpose, Commander Harry Butcher entered the corner suite that served as Ike's office. He found the general in a heavy olive-green sweater sitting in his desk chair that he had pulled up to the small fireplace, which crackled and spit as he dictated a situation report for the Casablanca conference. The Saint-George had no heat save a few fireplaces found here and there in the hotel. Ike looked up from the Dictaphone when he heard Butcher enter. Butcher took note of Ike's bloodshot eyes, which he hadn't noticed during their earlier meeting, when Ike put the rival Allied intelligence services on notice.

Butcher was eager to report on the information that he collected from a reluctant Colonel Eddy. Before he'd sought out Ike, Butcher had taken a brief coffee break after the Eddy meeting to recall the details of the conversation and fine-tune some of his thoughts.

"Donovan looked pretty tense in there. More than the others. Any reason for that?" Butcher asked.

"He's got a lot on his plate. Just like your boss," Eddy said.

"Not just those two. We all do."

"True. But Donovan has people back home taking potshots at him and the OSS. They say he's spending too much money, running a reckless operation. General Strong...he's the loudest voice. He wants to absorb the entire OSS into Army G-2. And that doesn't sit well with Wild Bill one iota. Donovan realizes that any screwup blamed on the OSS will mean more voices raised against him. This Darlan situation certainly doesn't help, timing-wise." Eddy lit up a Chesterfield and offered Butcher one. He accepted, and they both took a moment to read each other.

"He told Ike when they were one-on-one, the day after Christmas, that he wasn't aware of any OSS involvement in the assassination. So what is he worried about?" Butcher said.

"Frankly, he's worried some people aren't telling him the full story," Eddy said, taking a deep drag on his cigarette.

"That includes you, Bill?"

Eddy blew a lungful of his Chesterfield in Butcher's face. "I'll ignore that question." Butcher touched a nerve.

"What else, Bill?"

"Well, he's not so sure about the SOE. He knows they aren't always forthcoming when dealing with him. Hell, Donovan's not forthcoming…completely…when he's dealing with the SOE." Eddy snorted and shook his head. "Part of the game, Harry."

"So you say," Butcher said, taking a pull from his cigarette, studying Eddy as he did.

"And there's…" Eddy stopped, and he tapped an ash onto the floor.

"And there's…what?" Butcher took a deep pull on the Chesterfield.

"I had just reported to him, before the Ike meeting, that this so-called group of conspirators had an archive, according to a well-placed source of mine—a collection of documents with names, dates, assignments, a bunch of material."

Butcher forced a thick stream of smoke out of his nostrils. *Evidence of the individuals involved*, he thought. *Organizations as well.* "And where is this archive?"

Eddy stared at him. "It's missing."

Butcher said nothing.

"We've got feelers out. With dollars attached. We'll see what we catch," Eddy said.

"Will you let me know? About the feelers?" Butcher asked, knowing full well that he would have to track Eddy down again and drag it out of him.

"Sure, Harry. I'll let you in on it." Eddy extinguished his smoke in the ashtray and stood. Butcher heard his wooden leg creak. The leg resulted from wounds the grizzled marine had received during the First World War.

Butcher had almost said thanks when he thought of one more question. "Tell me, what the hell is going on with Conor Thorn? I saw..." Butcher started to mention the bar scene but held back. "I mean, I heard some scuttlebutt."

Eddy's look of surprise came across to Butcher as sincere. But he wasn't always an expert judge of sincerity. *Just ask his wife.* "Thorn? What did you hear?"

"That he lost his job. Kicked to the curb. By you guys." Butcher waited as Eddy, his head tilted downward, seemed unsure what to say.

"That's not something I can discuss. Inside OSS business."

"But you're not denying it?"

A slight hesitation. "Nor confirming it."

"So he's an intelligence agent...without portfolio?"

Before Eddy turned to leave, he said, "Back off, Harry."

Butcher finished his coffee, confident he had remembered accurately the key parts of their conversation. He waited a few more minutes, deciding to get a half cup more of the thick brew to help smooth out a proposal for the general in his mind.

Ten minutes later, after Butcher related his conversation with Eddy, Ike firmly replaced the microphone into the cradle of the Dictaphone, muttering something under his raspy breath. Butcher caught only one word: *archive*. "Eddy. How well do you know him? You trust him?"

"General, I know no reason not to. At least he's not given me one reason yet."

Ike rose and stood closer to the fire. He reached toward the flames and rubbed his hands together. Without turning to face Butcher, he said, "If they—and I mean the OSS—somehow get their hands on this archive and its contents prove their involvement, or the SOE's, we'll never hear about it. Wouldn't you agree?"

A phrase came to Butcher, *honor among thieves*. Then a slight retooling popped into his head. *Honor among spies.* "I agree, General. They're in survival mode."

Ike turned to Butcher. Ike's forehead was gleaming with sweat. "Maybe I am too. I made a promise to Bergeret, after all."

Ike took his seat and stared into the fire. The general looked beaten. "General, give me a few more minutes of your time. I have a plan to propose."

CHAPTER SIX

0835 Hours, Tuesday, January 5, 1943
DuBois Home/Office, 5th Arrondissement, Lyon

He nearly didn't make it to the toilet. When he did, his stomach spewed forth a foul bile that made his eyes water. Dr. René Fitzgerald DuBois was still bent over, letting the remnants of vomit drain from his mouth when his mother, Sarah, came up behind him.

"René, what is wrong? You…you never get sick," she said.

DuBois wiped his mouth with the back of his hand and stood. "My last patient," he said, moving to the sink to wash his hands. "I was called to the Hôtel Terminus to see someone. It was…it was very alarming to see."

Sarah placed her hand on his shoulder. "René, more… Tell me more."

DuBois detected a tinge of her New Jersey accent, what was left after spending the last four years in Lyon. It always resurfaced when she was agitated. He dried his hands and turned to her. "Barbie—I finally met him. The doctor who normally attended his prisoners was in Marseille. So I was called." Klaus Barbie's name had been whispered among the residents of Lyon ever since May of the prior year when he arrived as chief of the Gestapo. DuBois turned to look at his image in the mirror. His face was chalky white. "The prisoner, a woman from Alsace, was barely alive. Beaten for what looked like hours, given that some of the blood around her ears and nose had dried. Yet there was plenty of fresh blood. Barbie said neighbors, who claimed she was a radio operator for the Resistance, turned her in."

"Nazis…they are monsters. You can't help them. You must refuse the next time."

"I think that would be unwise, Mother. For you and me."

Sarah shook her head. "I'm surprised that devil Barbie called for a doctor. They say many have died at his hand."

"He wanted to keep the young woman alive for some reason. He said that he was close. Barbie used those exact words. *I am close.* He wanted the location of her radio."

DuBois stepped around his mother and left the bathroom. She followed him into his office, which also served as the main patient examination room. He sat behind his desk, swiveled in his chair, and stared out the rain-streaked bay window at the courtyard one floor below. The covered passageway that led out to the street was still cloaked in darkness. On either side of the courtyard, from their windows, tenants on the third floor had tossed trash, which had been dispersed by a cyclonic wind to the corners of the courtyard. Sarah took a seat in one of the two armchairs in front of the desk.

"I couldn't get over my shock when I first entered the room. It was like a laboratory for torture." He turned around and set his elbows on the desk and buried his face in his hands. "There was a tub filled with ice and water. There was a truck battery with cables attached. Whips hung on the walls along with an array of other tools—ball-peen hammers, pliers, ice picks. My God, the stench was awful. The smell of feces was overpowering."

"Did you get the name of the prisoner? Maybe I can reach out to her family."

"No. It would be too dangerous for you to get involved." She nodded, but DuBois saw his mother take on an all-too-familiar look—placative, almost condescending. She would say yes but ignore his warnings. He had been aware for the past year that his mother was assisting Jews leave France for the safety of Spain, Portugal, the United States. She kept it from him because he shared his late father's views about Jews and the control they had of the major institutions in France, the United States, and in most European countries. He did not confront her, nor she him, both not wanting to trigger arguments similar to those she had with his father, Raymond, a born-and-bred Lyonnais. But like many children, he had kept secrets from his parents.

"René, pour me a glass." Sarah pointed to the tray with a decanter of water and glasses that sat on the edge of his desk. As he poured, he watched her knead her hands.

"The tingling. It has returned?" DuBois asked, handing her a glass.

Sarah didn't answer before she emptied the glass with a swift series of swallows. "Yes. For the past couple of days. Mostly in my hands. My feet, not so much." She handed the glass back to him, and he refilled it, then placed it before her. She fixed her gaze on it for a moment, then grabbed it and drained it just as quickly as the first.

"You need to do a better job managing your stress…and your diet. You're eating too much cheese. I've told you this many times over."

"Not now, René."

"When did you take your last insulin injection?"

"I don't remember. A few days ago, I think."

"It does you no good if you are forgetting to take it. I go to much trouble to secure the insulin. Much trouble."

"For which I am grateful, René," Sarah said, drawing out the words but leaving out *I've said this many times.* Her response never varied when he mentioned his efforts to help her manage her diabetes.

DuBois rose from his chair abruptly, startling her. "I have to see Pierre. He is not well."

His mother's face contorted into a painful look of disgust. "Aah, Laurent. Why do you continue to treat that fascist? He is a piece of shit. Cares for no one but himself and the other technocrats."

"You know why. I promised Father that I would pick up with his care when he died." Raymond DuBois had been Pierre Laurent's primary doctor ever since the DuBois's return to Lyon in 1938. Laurent had paid Raymond handsomely because of Raymond's expertise in the treatment of prostate cancer. And he continued to pay well when René took over his care from his late father.

Laurent had twisted DuBois's arm for months to convince him

to join the ranks of the shadowy *Synarchique*. Feigning an initial lack of interest, he finally agreed, unknown to his mother. Laurent used DuBois's father's membership as one reason for his son to join. France needed to align itself wisely if it was to survive the war as a leader in Europe. Laurent's argument had convinced René. "Besides, Mother, he is one of the few patients who actually pay their bills. You could say it keeps this household in cheese."

Sarah scoffed and left the office, mumbling under her breath.

CHAPTER SEVEN

1000 Hours, Tuesday, January 5, 1943
Maison Blanche Airfield, Algiers

Emily was grateful she was the sole passenger on the flight to Algiers. It allowed her the privacy to shed a few tears and let fly a few choice expletives, not directed at those who jettisoned her from MI6 but at herself and Conor for decisions they made. By the time the flight approached the airfield, she had decided that she was going to track down Buckmaster, head of the SOE's F Section. With her command of the French language and her training and experience, she was sure it wouldn't take much to convince him she could become one of his most prized agents.

It did not surprise her to find that there was no one to greet her when she disembarked from the C-47 Dakota. Maybe word had reached the staff at the airfield that she was not to be touched, like a live wire. Across the tarmac, she spotted a PBY-5, its wings secured to the ground by thick tie-downs. The PBY appeared to be undergoing some repairs, given the sets of metal stairs that led to the top side of the port wing. She could barely make out the dark lettering on the port-side fuselage, just forward of the plane's wing struts: *14-P-11*. It was Captain Waddon's ship. One on which she and Conor, along with Sean, had spent some harrowing moments what seemed like a year ago.

She sighted a tall officer in a waist-length leather jacket with his combination cap pulled down low, carrying a tray coming from the direction of the airfield's terminal. As the two converged on the PBY, she was pleased to see that it was Jack Waddon. The tray contained some flatbread and a couple cups of coffee.

"Well, I'll be damned. Emily Bright." Waddon stopped ten feet short of the port-side blister and stood there, his broad, bright smile a welcome sight for the emotionally reeling Emily.

"Captain Waddon. Thank God for a friendly face. And how did you know I hadn't eaten in twelve hours?"

"What's mine is yours, Emily. Step inside my humble abode. There's someone I'd like you to meet."

Emily tilted her head and almost asked the obvious question, but Waddon had already taken two steps up the ladder hanging from the blister opening and handed the tray to someone inside. He slid across the blister's sill and then extended his hand to Emily, who stood on the bottom rung of the ladder. Once aboard the dimly lit aircraft, she heard a familiar voice, one that made her stomach flutter.

"Hello, beautiful. I thought I might see you soon." Conor stood in the waist gunner's compartment, holding the tray. The nasty plum-sized lump on his forehead stole her attention almost immediately. "Sit down and let's swap stories."

#

After asking Jack to give them some time to brief each other, Conor struggled to pull his recollection of the meeting with Donovan and Eddy into some coherent report, given the headache hammering away inside his head. He started slow, choosing his words deliberately.

"Conor, you're not making sense. You...you sound confused. Just how hard did you get hit?" Conor stared at her. "Conor, answer me."

Conor shook his head, hoping for some relief from the thick fog inside his head. "Donovan flat-out told me—" The squeal of brakes just outside the thin skin of the fuselage made both of them snap their heads around. Conor stumbled down the catwalk into the waist gunner's compartment. The port-side blister was open, and he heard Waddon's voice. There was another voice giving a rapid report. Conor stuck his head out of the blister with Emily just behind him. He couldn't make out who the new arrival was with the moonlight being screened by low-flying clouds, but it only took a few words to make it clear that Eugene DiLazzaro had just shown up. And he looked like he had news.

"What's going on, Jack?" Conor asked.

Waddon turned to Conor and Emily with a grim face. "It's not good, Conor. Stevens, they just found his body at some café—"

"The Coq Hardi. In an alley in the back. He was stabbed. Bled out before they could get him to the field hospital," Eugene said, getting out of his jeep. "It gets worse." Eugene looked at Waddon, who gave a quick nod. "A buddy of mine...he says they're looking for someone—you, Conor."

Emily drew in a quick breath and jerked her head toward Conor. "Let's start this debriefing again. From the beginning, and get to the part about Stevens in due haste, please."

CHAPTER EIGHT

1000 Hours, Tuesday, January 5, 1943
Vieux Lyon, 5th Arrondissement, Lyon

DuBois decided to forgo taking his Peugeot to Laurent's home, even though he had ample gas rationing coupons by way of Laurent given his standing and connections. Instead, he felt a walk to help exorcise the gruesome images from his visit to the Hôtel Terminus was the treatment he needed. Head down and his coat collar pulled up close to his ears to fend off a blustery morning, he turned off Place de la Baleine onto rue Saint-Jean and confronted an even stiffer, chillier wind.

He was the only one headed north on the granite cobblestone street. Several people, mostly elderly, headed in the opposite direction. Some were unsteady, as the wind seemed to push them along at a brisk pace. The face of the young, battered woman flashed past his eyes, replaced just as swiftly by the ruddy, puffy-faced Barbie. DuBois fought off the lingering sound of shoes sticking to the blood-soaked floor. Outside the hotel, he'd found a puddle in a nearby gutter and took five minutes to soak and scrape clean the blood from his soles.

DuBois looked up from the cobblestones and found himself ten yards from the entrance of Chez Francine, one of the preferred cafés and brothels of Wehrmacht officers since the Nazis took control of Vichy France. He slowed his pace. It was in the spring of the previous year that he had sat outside the café at the invitation of a reporter for the *Washington Times-Herald*, Jacob LaFleur. At least, that's who he said he worked for.

His interest that day was in DuBois's patient, Pierre Laurent. A specific focus of his questioning was Laurent and his association with the *Synarchique*, an association shared with the DuBois family. LaFleur's proposal of information in exchange for payment was at first a shock. He remembered asking LaFleur if he paid all his sources, which received no reply, just a shrug followed by eyes being averted. DuBois explained he would only provide information on Laurent and his *Synarchique* activities if LaFleur could have his newspaper use its Washington connections to arrange travel visas to America for him and his ailing mother, an American citizen.

"That's not the business we're in, Doctor," he remembered him saying.

"Aah, but you are in the business of paying informants to spy on their patients." Again, a shrug. LaFleur left him sitting in the café after telling him to think about his proposal.

Instead of doing what LaFleur asked, DuBois went straight to the lone official British presence in Lyon, the British Trade and Investment Office. DuBois did not consider himself in the least naive, so he concluded that there was more going on in the office than simply the British government running interference for British corporations still doing business in what was left of free France. There, Peter Selborne, a high-level official, took an interest in him. Initially, Selborne told him given the great influx of refugees from Norway, Denmark, and the Netherlands, he would not be able to act on his and his mother's behalf in securing travel visas to England.

DuBois left disappointed but not surprised. It shocked him, however, when Selborne showed up at his office several weeks later in June with more or less the same offer that LaFleur originally presented. Spy on Laurent, his Synarchist cronies, and their Nazi contacts for at least four months and in exchange, he would arrange for travel visas to England, traveling through Spain, then Portugal. But Sarah, his Jew-loving mother, refused to go. Then the Nazis came. They were no longer unoccupied. He never knew what happened to Selborne, but he knew that he took the offer of travel visas with him.

As DuBois drew even to the entrance to Chez Francine, he spotted the waiter, who had served him and LaFleur months before, smoking a cigarette just outside the doorway. He glared at DuBois intently, then his medical bag, as he passed by. DuBois glimpsed through the slightly fogged-up window at a table with three Wehrmacht officers laughing heartily at the expense of a teenage busboy. One pudgy officer threw a soiled napkin in the boy's face, which drew even more raucous laughter. He pressed on.

#

1015 Hours, Tuesday, January 5, 1943
Home of Pierre Laurent, Vieux Lyon, 5th Arrondissement, Lyon

As was normal, Laurent's butler, a graying seventy-year-old of short stature, greeted him at the front door to the stately house with a dour, jowly face.

"Dr. DuBois. You are early," the butler said. He did not open the door wide to let DuBois pass; instead, DuBois thought he was waiting for an explanation for his early arrival.

"I walked this time, François. I didn't know how long it would take." His answer must have been satisfactory because the butler stepped back and fully opened the black lacquered door.

"He is meeting with close associates presently. And there is someone else waiting to see him. Someone who did not make prior arrangements," François said, making no effort to strip his words of disdain. "He's a priest. A rather nervous one."

"Hopefully not here to perform the last rites," DuBois said, adding a smile to signal his attempt at dark humor. François's wide eyes were his signal that he did not appreciate the attempt. "I'll show myself up. I am sure you are busy with affairs of the house." DuBois didn't wait for François's usual protestation and scampered up the staircase to the second floor.

DuBois walked down the carpeted hallway to a double door at the end and entered the outer office. The first sight he took in was a man dressed in a black cassock that extended down to the top of his brown, highly polished shoes. He was standing with his back to DuBois, his ear up against the seam between the two pocket doors to Laurent's office. DuBois cleared his throat. The startled priest turned abruptly and faced him. The red-faced cleric cleared his own throat and moved away from the door.

"Who are you?" the jumpy priest asked.

DuBois admired the tactic of taking the offensive when caught in a compromising position. "I could ask you the same."

"I am Abbé Robert Alves. My parishioner, Pierre Laurent's mother, asked me to check on the health of her son." The priest lowered his gaze to DuBois's medical bag, then back to DuBois. "You...you must be his doctor?" It sounded more like a question than a statement to DuBois.

"Yes. I have an appointment to see Monsieur Laurent..." DuBois said, stealing a look at his watch, "in five minutes."

The priest responded with a nod, then moved to a window and stared out. A moment later, Laurent and three other men exited the office. The smiling Laurent looked as if he were about to introduce his guests to DuBois, but he suddenly altered his demeanor when he saw the priest by the window. Laurent's shoulders sagged. Then he whispered something to his guests that DuBois couldn't hear. It must have been a brief goodbye because the men took their leave with much haste. Laurent took a step toward the priest, who matched the stride, hand outstretched. Laurent's hand remained at his side.

"Tell my mother that I am in expert hands here with Dr. DuBois and that she needs to stop sending emissaries to check on my health. Now, please leave and let the good doctor do his examination." Laurent spun on his heels with great speed, surprising DuBois, and headed back to his office, with DuBois several steps behind. DuBois took one last look over his shoulder and watched the priest clench his jaw, with both hands balled up in fists.

#

Laurent closed the pocket doors, turned, and looked at DuBois. He took a deep breath and expelled it deliberately. "My mother, she never stops talking about that priest. Thinks he walks on water. I've told her only Jesus Christ can do that. Not his minions." Laurent headed for his desk, slipping his suit coat off as he made his way. DuBois rummaged through his medical bag and pulled out his stethoscope and a file.

Laurent draped his jacket on the back of his chair and headed over to a long red leather couch that sat beneath a hulking painting. A creation of Eugène Delacroix, it was called *Liberty Leading the People.* The famous painting commemorated the Revolution of 1830, which brought the reign of King Charles X to an inglorious end. Laurent had told him it was a reproduction. But an excellent one, Laurent would always add. Laurent lay down on the couch after taking off his shoes. DuBois went about taking vital signs, while Laurent went on about an upcoming meeting.

"And Ambassador Abetz will bring along a special guest, René. SS-Obergruppenführer Karl Oberg."

"And who is this Nazi?"

"René, please, do not show disrespect."

"I am not. He is a Nazi, isn't he?"

"Yes, of course. A very important German officer," Laurent said, wagging a finger at DuBois. "He is in charge of all German police forces in France, including the *Sicherheitsdienst* and the Gestapo. A good man to know, René."

DuBois nodded as he listened to Laurent's heart. DuBois placed his index finger across his lips to silence his patient. When he pulled his stethoscope from under Laurent's undershirt, Laurent started in immediately. "He is the top German official in charge of their anti-Jewish policies and"—Laurent touched DuBois's left forearm and leaned closer—"the campaign against the Resistance." Nodding, Laurent leaned back. "According to Abetz, he speaks to Himmler every day. As I said, very important."

"And the reason for his visit?" DuBois asked, pulling up Laurent's pant legs to examine the swelling around his ankles.

"Abetz says he does not know. It's the first time he's been to Lyon since the occupation." DuBois nodded as if absorbed in his examination. Laurent continued. "But I am most excited about the bank's new arrangement to provide fuel from our refinery in Romania to the Reich."

DuBois raised his eyebrows. "Pierre, congratulations. Tanks and submarines are thirsty weapons."

"*Non, non, non.* This is a special fuel for a new weapon. Something powerful and very secret." Laurent pursed his lips. "I should not have mentioned it. Please, René, tell no one."

"Of course, Pierre. You are my patient. You are in trusted hands."

Laurent sighed. "Yes, I know. Now if I could just get my mother to stop mothering."

CHAPTER NINE

1130 Hours, Tuesday, January 5, 1943
Hôtel Saint-George, rue Michelet, Algiers

Seaman DiLazzaro dropped Conor and Emily off at the entrance to the hotel, which was crawling with uniformed American and British personnel—officers and enlisted—and male Arab hotel staff, who scurried about trying to manage the ebb and flow of personnel. Some of the Arab men were clad in black, tailored uniform pants with an embroidered shirt and red chechias made of tightly woven felted camel hair atop their heads. The bellboys and porters wore loose, colorfully decorated pants that ran to midcalf. None of the Arabs were smiling. But then Conor noticed that none of the enlisted men were either.

"That's our boy." The MP had a deep, booming voice that complemented his heft. It carried across the lobby Conor and Emily had just entered. The MP moved toward Conor, the mostly uniformed crowd in the lobby parting like the Red Sea. There was someone trailing the MP that Conor couldn't make out given the MP's size. Conor stopped, Emily a step behind him.

"This can't be good," Conor said.

The MP stopped two feet from Conor. Then the second uniformed man stepped from behind the MP, beaming. "Ask and you shall receive. Thanks so much for coming to me. It saves both of us some time. We are so busy tracking down bad guys, you see."

"Always aim to please, Major," Conor said.

"That's what I like to hear. And who's this young lady?"

"I'm Emily Bright-Thorn. Major..."

"Major Campbell Stewart. I'm with military police. Commander Butcher asked us to look into an incident even though it involves a civilian. You, Thorn. I considered it a request from General Eisenhower himself. We're very interested in getting some answers from...your husband, I take it?"

"That would be correct, Major Stewart."

"One happy family. How 'bout that." He turned his attention back to Conor, who was surprised by how fast his dislike for the major took hold. "Why don't you allow our friendly military policeman, Lieutenant Johnston, to escort you over to that office behind the hotel desk so we can have a private conversation. And Emily, join us, unless you have something better to do." Stewart nodded at Johnston, who put a vise grip on Conor's upper arm and headed for the office.

"You wouldn't be the MP who clobbered me on the back of the head last night, would you?" Conor said, noticing that his booming headache had returned, along with some nausea.

"That would be me. And don't look for any apologies, Thorn." Conor detected a Midwestern accent and pinned him as a farm boy, one that, given the rock-hard grip on his arm, had a hobby of juggling bales of hay.

Stewart shooed two middle-aged Arab clerks from the tiny office and took a seat behind one of two metal desks. Johnston directed Conor into the other desk's chair, minus a gentle touch, and stood behind him. Emily stood in the corner, folded her arms, and stared at Stewart. If her eyes could fire bullets, they would have riddled Stewart with holes.

"You've heard about your friend Stevens?" Stewart said.

"Word has reached me." Conor flexed his arm, hoping to restore the blood flow.

"Where were you early this morning? Around one in the morning."

"Sacked out in a PBY out at the airfield." Conor pointed over his shoulder with his thumb. "Sleeping off the effects of this guy's sneak attack on my head," Conor said, adding a tilt of his head toward Johnston.

"Why would I believe you…the guy twenty or so people saw throwing Stevens over the bar into a shelf of booze bottles?" Stewart leaned his head back and looked down the ridge of his nose at Conor.

"Don't."

"Don't what?"

"Don't believe me. Talk to Captain Jack Waddon. It's his ship I was sacked out in. He's the one who took me out of the bar. He stayed on board with me, since I wasn't exactly feeling good."

Stewart looked up at Johnston. "That right?"

"The part about taking him out of the bar? Yep." That booming voice again. Johnston, it seemed, didn't have an inside voice. "Don't know about the other part."

"We'll check in with this Waddon fella."

"What is the time of death, Major?" Emily said.

Stewart, without turning his head, locked his gaze on Emily. "Around two hours after the dustup in the bar." Stewart turned to face Emily straight on.

"I'm sure that Captain Waddon, being the stellar officer he is, will back up Conor's story. He's a man of impeccable honesty."

"Yeah, well…he sounds like a saint." Stewart turned back to Conor. "Was Stevens alone?"

"I don't remember everything about that night. Some of it comes and goes, thanks to Johnston. The bar was crowded…a lot of uniforms. I had a few, in case that news hasn't hit your desk."

Stewart rose and approached Conor. He pulled up alongside, bent down, and drew close to Conor's ear. "I'm after someone who has been knocking off Allied personnel indiscriminately." Stewart's breath warmed his ear. "Someone who's not just your plain killer. Someone with problems. In-the-head problems."

"What the hell are you—"

"I'm looking for someone with cock issues," Stewart said, prompting Conor to jerk his head back. "I have multiple victims. All with mutilated cocks. There's some guy out there who's, like I said, got problems in the head." Stewart straightened and stared at Conor.

"What makes you think it's a man? That's pretty crazy to think—"

"A lot more men around here than women, or hadn't you noticed?"

"Listen, I've told you all I remember. If I remember more, I'll get word to you."

Stewart nodded slowly. "In the meantime—"

"Don't leave town," Conor said. Stewart sneered, disliking being interrupted as much as he liked interrupting, Conor guessed. Both turned back to the others. No one moved or said anything. So Conor did the honors. "Where did they find the body?"

Stewart landed his left butt cheek on the edge of the desk, pulled a pack of Luckys from his breast pocket, and flipped it over in his hand. He waited a few beats before responding, probably mulling over whether he should fill in any relevant information. "He was in the field hospital." He stopped flipping the pack of cigarettes. "Because you broke his jaw," Stewart said in a raised voice. He tossed the Luckys on the desk. "He insisted on getting discharged. Said he had a meeting he had to go to. When they protested, he just got up and left." Stewart rose and picked up the pack. "So, tell me. What pushed you to get into it with Stevens?"

Conor considered not answering but decided there might be benefits if he did. "He said something I didn't like."

"And what would that be?" Stewart said.

Conor stood. "He said something very nasty about…her." He turned to Emily. She greeted him with a smile.

CHAPTER TEN

1145 Hours, Tuesday, January 5, 1943
Jardin Archéologique, Vieux Lyon, 5th Arrondissement, Lyon

The image of the battered, bloodied, and unconscious wireless operator that he treated at Hôtel Terminus would come into focus, then drift away. A cycle of images of her slumped, nearly naked body repeated itself several times as DuBois walked from Laurent's home on his way to the One-Eight, the brothel owned by Germaine Gilbert. The repetition of the images made his heart race, so DuBois slowed his pace as he traveled down the rue Mandelot, the street that ran along the Jardin Archéologique, which was once the location of a fifth-century cathedral. A flock of sparrows pecked at the frozen ground in between what remained of the foundation and the low walls of the church.

He turned onto the rue Saint-Etienne and headed toward the Fontaine Saint-Jean in the middle of Place Saint-Jean, a vast plaza that fronted the Cathedral Saint-Jean Baptiste. He stopped at the fountain and placed his black medical bag, which had belonged to his father, on the curb. He craned his neck to take in the patinated, bronze statues of John the Baptist as he baptized Jesus, whose arms were folded across his chest in a pose of someone who had given himself over. To further calm his racing heart, he took a seat on the narrow stone step that encircled the base of the statues. He glanced over at the cathedral and watched parishioners exiting after Mass through the tall faded red double doors. Several were milling about shaking hands and chatting. The air was chilled, so no one stayed long. Only a handful lingered and chatted among themselves.

A calmer DuBois stood and was about to set off for the One-Eight when a black Citroën pulled up to the fountain. A rear door opened, cigarette smoke billowed out, and a voice from inside called out to him in heavily accented French. A German accent. Before he slid into the back seat, he surveyed Place Saint-Jean. There was a gaggle of people quite a distance away, huddled in a far corner. Turning back toward the cathedral, he noticed that the group of churchgoers had thinned down to two people: a young man and a woman. The man was unfamiliar to him, but the woman was not—it was Suzanne. One of Gilbert's most loyal girls. She was staring at DuBois. The man with her was older and of a slight build. A relative? DuBois walked away from the Citroën, the voice from inside louder this time. "Get in the car. Now."

He stopped. "I am being watched," DuBois said over his shoulder. He took a step and heard the car surge ahead and stop, its brakes squealing.

"You worry too much. Get in."

DuBois turned around and slipped inside the car, but not before taking another glance at the front steps of the cathedral. The couple was still there. Still staring at him.

"Is this wise? Everyone knows that Gestapo and the Abwehr all drive these damn black Citroëns," DuBois said, placing his medical bag on the seat between him and Bleicher.

Sergeant Hugo Bleicher scoffed. "Dr. DuBois. You are always so skittish. Look at this as a favor to you. If anyone doubts your loyalty to the Resistance, just tell them that the Abwehr is suspicious of you and that you have been questioned…and let go."

The bespectacled and burly Bleicher, code-named Colonel Henri, wore his signature long black leather coat and a burgundy beret that no Lyonnais would dare be seen in. He even wore it in the summer, which was the season when they'd first met in Paris. DuBois had been dissatisfied with the subordinate role he'd held within the *Synarchique*.

He'd wanted to do more to ensure the outcome of the war in favor of the Nazis and the leaders of the *Synarchique*. Bleicher and his superior, Colonel Fredrich Rudolf, listened to DuBois intently, then asked a series of questions about the activities of the Resistance in the Lyon area. DuBois provided several names of some who were known to him. When it seemed there was nothing more to discuss, they asked him to wait outside the office while they conferred. Then Bleicher came out and told him to get a room in the hotel that the Abwehr had commandeered as their headquarters. They would meet again the next morning.

That next morning, Rudolf held the floor. When he asked DuBois to work for the Abwehr, a chill ran up his spine. They would pay handsomely for information like names and descriptions of people associated with the French Resistance in the Lyon area, including people associated with the Heckler Network, specifically someone called Marie Monin. He described this woman as someone who had eluded them for quite some time, causing great frustration within the Abwehr and the Gestapo. They believed she was an agent of the SOE, possibly a Canadian. While Rudolf talked, Bleicher, his hands joined just beneath his chin, fingertips pressed firmly together, studied DuBois raptly, as if he were trying to interpret any physical reaction.

When DuBois agreed to work for the Abwehr, a very pleased Rudolf rose and extended his hand across his desk. DuBois rose also and shook the offered hand. "Sergeant Bleicher will be your contact. He will explain everything to you. Your code name is Columbia. It will require several days to run you through some basic training in ways to communicate, meet, and...things of the spying game. You listen carefully to what he has to say. It may very well save your life, *Herr* DuBois."

Sitting next to Bleicher, now in the back of the idling Citroën, he wondered what Rudolf would have thought about the way his subordinate approached him. It seemed reckless.

"I have heard little from you, René. Now what would the reason be for that?" Bleicher said, flicking cigarette ash out the cracked open window.

"I am busy. Very much so." DuBois peered out the rear door's window across the Place Saint-Jean and noticed Sophie and her friend head toward the River Saône. Before disappearing from view, Sophie turned and took in another glimpse of the Citroën.

DuBois turned to face Bleicher. "I have made inroads in my relationship with Dr. Russier, the brothel's doctor. This has given me access to Germaine Gilbert. My list of members of Heckler is growing."

"Excellent, Doctor. Colonel Rudolf will be pleased that we are getting closer to shutting down the entire network. But he has made it clear we will not wait much longer."

"I understand. I am headed over to the One-Eight now. There is talk that new contacts are arriving from England. I do not know any details. Once I do, I will use the normal method to notify you."

"That is good. The madam..."

"Gilbert."

"Yes. She has been allowed to operate for too long."

DuBois knew well that Gilbert's time in Lyon was running out. It was the prior month that DuBois alerted the madam that a meeting she planned to attend would be raided by the Gestapo. News of the raid came from a Gestapo agent who was delirious under a light anesthetic while DuBois pulled some bullet fragments from his shoulder. The warning had allowed Gilbert's trust in him to take root and grow.

"And there's some news from Laurent. Karl Oberg is coming to Lyon. Were you aware?"

Bleicher was quick to sneer at the mention of Oberg. The mistrust between the Abwehr and the Gestapo was not to be underestimated, Bleicher once told him. The Abwehr was more interested in counterintelligence work, not police work. It was a grim dance that the Abwehr found itself engaged in. Instead of banging on doors, arresting, then torturing arrestees, they preferred to live and work among them, to know them to a point where they trusted the Abwehr men, and then quietly roll them up at the most opportune moment—or turn them, a practice Bleicher preferred. *Funkspiel.* Radio game—the act of transmitting controlled information, bogus or misleading, over a captured agent's radio set. Radio counterintelligence.

"Yes, yes. The obergruppenführer must have grown tired of his usual haunts in Paris and is looking for new conquests. Business is looking up for Lyon's brothels." Bleicher laughed and tossed out his cigarette through the window crack. As he rolled the window up, he turned to DuBois. "Maybe he'll fit in a visit to the One-Eight." Bleicher paused. "Maybe some photos of the old man with his pants around his ankles could be arranged?" It took DuBois a moment to realize that Bleicher was making a serious inquiry.

"I will certainly discuss that with Madam Gilbert."

"Aah, good. That will delight Colonel Rudolf. They are, you know, at each other's throats quite often."

DuBois thought Bleicher laughed then—it was the first time he'd heard it. It was an odd laugh. It sounded more like the trilling of a cat. The memory of the sound would stick with him for the rest of the day.

CHAPTER ELEVEN

1140 Hours, Tuesday, January 5, 1943
Barberousse Prison, Algiers

Charles Brunel was lying on his straw mattress when the rust-colored metal Judas window slid open. Brunel rose and leaned on the cold metal door, his hands on either side of the half-foot square opening. The sleepy-eyed jailer, heavily bearded and smelling like everything he had eaten in the last month, muttered one word—"visitor"—then retreated to the wall across from his cell to watch the exchange. His assistant, the fiftyish French Algerian, who he'd hired when he'd first arrived in Algiers in late October, gripped the bottom of the window with both hands and pleaded once more for help.

"He has disappeared. No one knows where he could have gone." Alain Chrétien spoke in a soft voice, one that seemed weakened by his repeated pleading. "I have been to all the city's jails, the hospitals. I have visited all his friends in the Corps francs d'Afrique, even those that conspired for months—on what, I cannot say."

Since he had first arrived from France on business for his company, Trans Huile, his assistant had never displayed such persistence while working for him. Intent on building a pipeline for vegetable oil from the fertile lands of West Africa to Algiers for export to France, he traveled freely given his close connections to cooperative high-level officials in the Vichy government. But it was those very connections to officials, who had introduced him to high-placed Nazi officers, that led the Vichy police—at the request of the Americans—to arrest him and his son, Antoine, as Nazi spies a month after the Allied invasion of North Africa. It was unwise to have extended their stay in the capital city, instead of heading to Spanish Morocco as he had planned.

"Alain, look at me. I sit behind locked iron doors. How do you think I can help you find your son? I have no genie in a bottle to grant my wish to flee this hellhole."

"But, monsieur, you told me you know many important people here and...and in France. You also told me that some of these people are in your debt. Maybe, if I could contact them for you, I could convince them to—"

"Stop. Please stop, Alain. It is useless. Those people you speak of were of no help to me in keeping my wife from being taken to an internment camp. It could be worse for your son. He could be Jewish, like my wife. The Americans think I am a Nazi spy. The Nazis think I work for the Allies." Brunel returned to his flimsy mattress, lay back, rested his head against the crumbling wall, and closed his eyes.

Alain, ignoring Brunel's pleading, pressed on. "Michel, he went to the basilica and saw his mother, a housekeeper for the sisters at the convent next door. He was there..." Alain turned to look at the guard. He turned back and, in an even lower voice, continued. "Michel was there to hide the archive...records of his group's recent activities on behalf of the monarchists." Brunel sat up at the mention of monarchists. "My wife, she told me that the police, they arrived while she and Michel were hiding the archive. They searched the basilica. Michel told her to talk to the police while he tried to escape.

They took her outside and held her under guard for over an hour. Then they told her to return home and to remain there. They said nothing about Michel. So I think he outwitted these policemen and is in hiding. But we have heard nothing. Not one word from him or his friends. You must have someone who can help. You...you yourself said that you have many friends."

"Alain, are you finished? The lights will go out in a few minutes. You must leave." Alain was done speaking. He leaned his head against the cell door. Brunel looked up and saw he was shedding tears. He couldn't help himself or his own son. Yet the mention of monarchists struck a nerve. His legs weak from a lack of exercise, he struggled up from his mattress and pulled up opposite Alain. "Your son, his friends, were they involved in Darlan's assassination?" Brunel whispered. "Were they plotting against Darlan and his administration?"

Brunel knew that many Frenchmen, including those born in Algeria, thought Darlan to be a traitor to France. Darlan had many who wanted him gone. Including the British. After the Americans did a deal with Darlan just after the initial invasion, many Americans decried the agreement, agreeing with the British and many others that Darlan was a self-dealing opportunist. Alain's tears ceased. His eyes settled on the bloodstained concrete floor inside the cell.

"He told me very little. Just that he was a part of the Corps francs d'Afrique. They were led by Henri d'Astier de la Vigerie. Yes, they were monarchists and anti-Vichyites. I warned Michel that he was in danger if he continued to associate with them. He told his mother they had received some training in warfare from the British and the Americans. Training for what, he never told me or his mother." Brunel nodded but remained silent while he thought. Alain seemed to take Brunel's silence as a sign of interest, given the wide-eyed expression on his tear-streaked face.

"What are you thinking, monsieur? Do you have an idea? Something you could do?"

Brunel grabbed the bottom of the Judas window and drew closer to Alain. "My son, he has been told that they will release him tomorrow. He will need travel papers to move about…under a false name. Use Charles Lewis." Charles thought using his first name and Antoine's mother's maiden name would be easier for his son to remember. "Meet him at the Café Coq Hardi at nine. Listen to him and do what he tells you. He will have the money for the travel papers. Take him to the basilica and find the archive. He will…use them to bargain with the Vichy police officials for information about your son."

"*Alhamdulilah. Alhamdulilah,*" praise be to God, Alain said in an uplifted tone. The guard woke and looked at him. "I will do as you say. I will ask no questions." Alain's tears resumed.

Brunel returned to his straw mattress and thought that praising God wouldn't be enough to guarantee the success of his nascent plan.

CHAPTER TWELVE

1230 Hours, Tuesday, January 5, 1943
The One-Eight, 5th Arrondissement, Lyon

Vieux Lyon, Old Lyon, consistently surprised DuBois. No matter how often he traveled through the oldest district of Lyon, he discovered a traboule he had never come across before. The city was famous for its traboules, the name derived from the Latin *trans-ambulare*, meaning to pass through, which, his father said, numbered over one hundred. Dating back to the Middle Ages, the narrow corridors serpentined through buildings and courtyards, connecting one street with another, allowing people—mainly poor people and weavers in the centuries-old silk industry—access to the River Saône to collect their drinking water. Besides such access, the traboules provided cover to anyone who wanted to travel about unnoticed.

Today, it was DuBois who wanted to travel through the ancient district unnoticed by the Gestapo and their police lackeys. The Gestapo was, when they operated in the Vieux Lyon on their own, at a great disadvantage—one exploited at that very moment as DuBois traveled through the *Longue Traboule*, one of the longest traboules in Vieux Lyon. It connected the rue Saint-Jean with rue du Bœuff. DuBois was much more sensitive about being seen as he traveled to the One-Eight, the brothel owned by Germaine. Not because of what most of Lyon knew went on there, but because of what few knew went on there.

As he navigated the Vieux Lyon, his thoughts returned to the unexpected meeting with Bleicher. The cavalier and flaunting demeanor of the Abwehr agent unsettled him. Meeting in the open was fueled by Bleicher's bluster, which seemed to be boundless.

The thirty-seven-year-old Germaine Gilbert, known for her teeming sexual magnetism, wasn't the least bit shy about playing the role of madam. She relished donning furs, silks, and copious amounts of jewels. The brunette's apartment on the top of the unremarkable four-story building that was home to the One-Eight, where she would hold evening gatherings replete with caviar and champagne, was resplendently decorated with tapestries and abstract artwork. Among the plush furniture and deep pile rugs were several chests filled with gold coins.

And there were her cats. DuBois never knew how many. One was a favorite of Germaine's. It was a coal-black cat she called Baker. Germaine played Josephine Baker's music incessantly during the soirees she hosted. The cat Baker was an unusually loyal companion. More loyal than DuBois ever knew a feline to be. She would obediently follow Germaine down the street on her frequent early-morning walks in the Vieux Lyon.

DuBois knocked twice, then twice again, the required signal for a friend of Germaine's. Seconds later, he heard the rattling of locks and deadbolts. The door swung open, and he saw Louis, Germaine's bodyguard, beside the door. Germaine was huddled together with Dr. Paul Russier on a cranberry-hued felt settee, a half-empty champagne flute in her hand. Concern creased her forehead. After dismissing Louis, she motioned DuBois to take a seat on an identical settee opposite hers. The floor-to-ceiling gold-threaded brocade drapes blocked windows that, prior to the German occupation of Vichy France, had usually been open, providing a view of the red-tiled rooftops that extended toward the River Saône.

After polite greetings, Russier lit up Gauloises for both him and Germaine and offered one to DuBois, which he declined. The burnt-rubber smell emanating from the lit Gauloises was one DuBois never got used to. Russier was the gynecologist of choice of Lyon's *filles de joie*—prostitutes. He was a fleshy-faced man in his fifties who proudly sported a debonair mustache and wire-rimmed glasses that magnified the size of his eyes.

"Is everything…all right? You both look worried," DuBois said.

Germaine waved off his question. "It is nothing unusual, René. Don't be concerned."

"It's just one of the girls. A Gestapo thug roughed her up last night and is refusing to work," Russier added.

"Was it Sophie?" he blurted, unable to mask his concern.

Germaine let out a stream of gray smoke and giggled. "Heavens no. That one can take care of herself. But the others, they are always at risk."

DuBois released a breath and sat back on the settee.

Germaine eyed him through the smoky haze that separated them. "René, your concern is sweet. But I've told you. One man cannot take her. She is not wired that way. You must accept this about her."

DuBois nodded and lowered his head. His thoughts shifted to the one night they were together. DuBois had consumed several drinks that Sophie offered to relax what she considered being a "highly stressed client." He had bristled at the label. The sex they engaged in was blissfully engrossing and exciting but also not prolonged. They spent much time talking—and that night, he'd talked too much. His feelings about the Jews slipped out, and with his tongue thick due to drink and his mind dulled, he struggled to convey his utter despondency and rage over his young wife being run over by a Jewish butcher the prior year. He held the entire Jewish race responsible. The world's heartaches laid at the feet of the Jews, he told her.

Sophie would have none of it. Deep down, he knew, the soft-hearted Sophie felt sorrow for his loss, but there would have been no acceptable explanation, drink or no drink, why it was right for him to condemn an entire race. As far as any future relationship was concerned, it died that night.

"What news do you bring us, René?" Germaine asked, rising from the settee. She reached for a sweating bottle nestled in an ice bucket and poured herself another glass of champagne.

"It's Laurent." He delivered a brief report on Laurent's information about a visit to Lyon by the Nazi Oberg. His report elicited a reaction that was different from the responses to his previous reports. Silence. Exchanged glances. Averted eyes. Germaine's shaky hand spilled her champagne. He waited for her to say something. She drained her flute.

"Are there reasons for this visit?" Germaine said.

"None were stated."

Germaine nodded, quickly composed herself, and retook her seat next to Russier. "I have received word from London. It seems that I have been successful in convincing F Section you would be the perfect person to rebuild Réseau Gloria."

"Actually, she convinced Marie Monin who then convinced F Section," Russier added.

Germaine's news floored DuBois. Réseau Gloria was the Paris-based network infiltrated by the Abwehr and decimated August of the prior year. Bleicher had been jubilant when it shut down. He never mentioned who exactly infiltrated the network, only saying that they rounded up over eighty members and deported them to Mauthausen and Buchenwald. It was not lost on DuBois that he was the new Bleicher infiltrator, hoping to do the same thing to Réseau Heckler.

"I am caught completely off guard," DuBois stammered. "I had no idea that you were having conversations about me with Marie." Monin—he learned after she escaped Lyon to Spain the prior November, slipping through the fingers of the Gestapo's Klaus Barbie—was Virginia Hall. A wily and extremely brave, yet cautious agent who continued to confound the Nazis for months while she built up the Heckler Network and the myriad services it offered to the Resistance movement. DuBois never met her. But one evening Germaine told him that Hall had, unknown to DuBois, watched him work on a downed Royal Air Force pilot at their makeshift infirmary in the rear of a silk shop in the Vieux Lyon.

"René, you underestimate your contributions to the Resistance. You will be hard to replace, but we shall survive," Gilbert said, lighting a new Gauloises with the tip of the nearly spent one. The last word that rolled off her lips—*survive*—echoed in DuBois's head.

"Germaine, I cannot leave. You know my mother has made it clear that she must stay here in Lyon. I will not go to Paris without her."

Germaine's head bobbed before he finished, as if she never doubted what his response would be. "You aren't going to Paris. At least at first. They want you in London to go through some training in wireless operations, recruitment, and other disciplines. And as far as Sarah's position, I made that clear. Trust me. The response I received was that they would send someone to convince her to leave."

"That seems quite ridiculous. If I can't convince her—"

"There is more, René," Russier said. "This unnamed person apparently has a relationship with your mother that goes back years. That is all we have been told." Russier sat forward, his elbows resting on his knees. "And there is another reason for your trip to London." Russier glanced at Germaine, who nodded. "Operatives up north sent us documents—photos, maps—of a major Nazi fortification project. They come to us from a group of scout masters and youth leaders up north."

DuBois's head was spinning with the information coming at him. "What project?"

"The Germans refer to it as the 'Atlantic Wall.' They are building it along the northern French coast. This information must get into the hands of the Allies so they can properly plan the invasion that we all know will soon come."

DuBois stood and beat a tight circular path in the deep Persian rug. They watched him. He stepped toward Germaine and held out two fingers. She passed him a Gauloises and Russier offered him a light. He took a deep drag and resumed his pacing, wondering what Bleicher's reaction would be.

CHAPTER THIRTEEN

1200 Hours, Tuesday, January 5, 1943
Hôtel Saint-George, rue Michelet, Algiers

In one hallway that jutted off the lobby like a bicycle spoke off a wheel hub, Conor stopped and looked at Emily. "Ready for this?"

"I don't know how I could be. We have no idea what the commander wants."

"But we have some idea, right?" Conor said.

"A complete shot in the dark. And you know it." Emily, looking like she got little sleep last night aboard Waddon's PBY given her red eyes, pushed past Conor and headed down the narrow-tiled hallway, her low-heeled pumps tapping out a determined cadence. Conor fell in and pulled up the rear, having trouble walking in a straight line. Something he was glad Emily didn't witness. When they arrived at a corner suite of offices, a beefy, thick-necked staff sergeant with a bulging waistline immediately redirected them to the hotel's pool.

"The commander is waiting for you there. He said it would be more private. Follow me." Which they did, back down the hallway, through the lobby, and a right turn back outside onto a sprawling pool deck devoid of any hotel staff or servicemen, except for Commander Harry Butcher, who sat at a glass-topped table in a wicker chair just ten feet from an empty pool that had turned into a massive receptacle for trash and dead palm fronds from the trees that rimmed the deck. Conor spied an old man wearing a tattered gray coat and a soiled scarf wrapped tightly around his head. He swung a rudimentary, handmade broom across the bottom of the empty pool, coaxing some rotting fronds into a pile. A grunt accompanied each swing of the broom.

"Thanks, Billings," Butcher said. He motioned for Conor and Emily to take a seat at the table. "See if you can track down a pot of joe for us. I think my guests could use it." Billings took his leave, and Conor and Emily settled in. "Thanks for coming. Emily, I'm glad you caught up to your husband. I wanted to get a chance to rope you in on something along with Conor."

"Rope me in…Commander, what is it with you Americans and your cowboy references?" Emily cracked a smile. "Conor once told me I was a slowpoke. I had no clue what he was talking about."

Butcher smirked. "I get that from my wife too. Too many Western serials growing up, I guess. You know—"

"Commander, why are we here?" Conor said. "We should be out at the airfield, trying to hitch a ride back to England."

Butcher frowned, surprised by Conor's interruption. "By all means, let's get into it. What got Donovan and Menzies so riled up that they bounced you two? I want to hear it from you both directly."

Conor looked at Emily, having trouble recalling the run-through they did back at the PBY. "Results, Commander. They didn't like the results from our last mission."

"It was their prerogative to…*bounce* us, as you say," Emily said.

"What results were they looking for?"

"We can't get too deep into it," Conor said. "There's classified intelligence involved. Just say, results fell short, which, according to Colonel Eddy, caused a crisis of trust."

"I suppose that was not so dissimilar to C's position, Commander," Emily said as Billings returned carrying a tray with a carafe and three mugs.

Conor, closest to the tray, got a whiff of the strong brew. Butcher poured.

"I'm surprised by the outcome. I understand, according to Colonel Eddy, that you both performed quite successfully on your second mission together. And given your…results…in Rome recovering the directives of Operation Torch just days before D-Day, I would think you both built up some…hmm…goodwill."

"Commander, in the navy, if your ship performs poorly, you got shot up, or you grounded Uncle Sam's property, you became the owner of a desk back in Washington or Pearl, no matter how many days of operating screwup free." Conor grabbed his mug and handed one to Emily.

Butcher nodded. "Well, I can say this. You both pulled my butt out of the fire by finding that missing page from the general's diary." Butcher, as Eisenhower's aide, oversaw the compilation of documents to be used for Ike's wartime diary. One that the commanding general would use after the war to write a book. When the page with the directives for Operation Torch from General Marshall, chief of staff for the US Army, went missing, the clock was ticking and Conor and Emily were assigned to find it before it could end up in Nazi hands. That led them to a spy in Churchill's Cabinet, Henry Longworth, and the eventual recovery of the document. Lives saved. Top-shelf results. "So what's next?" Butcher asked.

Emily sighed and put her mug down. Conor watched her. The redness in her eyes had vanished. There was some color in her cheeks. *She is a beauty*, he thought. "We regroup back in London. I am thinking of approaching the SOE, since MI6 has made it clear they no longer want my services."

Conor shot a look at Emily. *That wasn't in the script.*

"Conor, and you?" Butcher said.

"Not sure, Commander." Conor fumbled for a more complete answer. "Maybe the FBI. Maybe I'll offer my expertise to Federal Shipbuilding, back in New Jersey. They're building some new destroyers. Other than that…" Conor lost his focus and didn't know what to add so he stopped talking. Emily was staring at him now. New Jersey or the FBI wasn't in the script either.

Butcher nodded and drained his coffee. "I have a problem. Actually, the Allies have a problem. Want to hear about it?"

Without looking at Emily, Conor said, "I suspect your problem is why we're here, so have at it, Commander."

Butcher refilled his mug and slid his chair closer to the table. "With the assassination of Admiral Darlan, we thought that a big problem for us—or really for General Eisenhower—had been solved. Don't misunderstand me, we were prepared to continue to work with him, regardless of how the British and American press felt. We were committed to live with the deal we made with him." Butcher took a slug of coffee. "As much of a shock as the assassination was, what was more shocking to the general was the rumor that the OSS and the SOE were involved in some way."

Butcher pushed away from the table and zeroed in on Conor, then Emily. Neither betrayed much of a reaction except for sharing a sideways glance. Butcher also didn't betray any response to their nonreaction. "The problem I spoke of involves the general. He has gone on record that if it turns out to be true that either organization was involved…" He pushed his mug aside and folded his hands, laying them on the table as if he were about to dispense a final judgment. "He would resign."

This time, Conor reacted. His lips parted slightly and with eyebrows raised, he darted a look at Emily. She held a hand over her mouth.

"The resignation of the commanding general at this point would be disastrous. He's developed an uncanny ability to get everyone headed in the same direction. Early on, it was like herding cats. Cats that had egos the size of Manhattan. A change now would set back Allied progress in this theater many months."

"Then there's the French," Conor said. "Any proof of OSS or SOE involvement would destroy the fragile relationship between the French and the US and the British. The Nazis would pay to see that happen."

"So you can see that there's a great deal at stake for the Allies."

"I don't disagree, Commander," Emily said. "I'm sure Conor doesn't either. But it's not clear to me why you bring this to our attention. Conor has been severed from the OSS, and I have lost my standing in British intelligence."

"Which makes you both the right people to look into something for the general and me." Butcher sported a thin-lipped smile, seemingly pleased with where the conversation was going. "I learned from Colonel Eddy that the group of people involved in the assassination had compiled an archive of documents concerning their activities. Eddy confided to me that Bill Donovan is extremely concerned about what may be in the archive. Eddy also mentioned that Dodds-Parker, the head of the SOE's

Massingham base near Algiers, shares those concerns. You see, General Eisenhower has also threatened to boot both spy outfits out of this theater of operation if they were involved. Conor, from what I hear about what's going on between General Strong's G-2 and the OSS, your old boss can't afford a black eye like that."

Conor was aware of the whispers about Strong wanting to absorb the OSS into army intelligence, citing the reckless mismanagement of the organization. It was Donovan's strong personal relationship with the president that kept Strong at bay. "I don't get it. Either they were involved or they weren't," he said.

"Well, either way—"

"I'm assuming that someone asked the question," Emily said.

"Yes, but...the general is very hesitant to believe their answers. They have too much to lose."

Conor pushed his mug aside. "Commander, why are we here?"

Butcher pursed his lips. Before he continued, Conor noticed that the grunting from the old man in the pool had ceased and the dust had settled.

"Commander..." Conor tilted his head toward the pool and the idle sweeper.

Butcher took in the pool scene, then turned back. "We're okay. According to Billings, that one is deaf as a post. A mute too." Butcher cleared his throat and narrowed his gaze on Conor and Emily. "Find the archive. We need to know if there is any mention of either organization's involvement."

Well, that request isn't much of a surprise. But what came next was.

"If you locate the archive and the content reveals no involvement in the planning by the Allies, then the general will pull some strings to get you, Conor, back in the navy or the OSS and you, Emily, back with MI6 with no loss in standing."

The thought that he could return to the navy was something Conor had never contemplated. That just didn't happen. But wartime changed many things. Conor gauged Emily's reaction, which looked positive given her wide eyes. He looked back at Butcher. "Assuming we find this archive, which is a big assumption, what if there's proof that there was some involvement?"

"Well, Ike won't be in a position to do anything for either of you. He'll be on his way back to the States, looking for a job."

"But would he follow through with banning the OSS and SOE from the Med theater?"

Butcher took in the pool deck surroundings. "If he says he will...he will. But we don't want that, right?"

Conor and Emily exchanged *what the hell does that mean* looks. "Commander, could you—"

"I'm saying destroy the archive. Report that it couldn't be found."

"Lie?" Emily asked.

"You could put it that way."

"What if the archive has no proof of involvement?" Emily said.

"Bring it back and we'll share it with the French. Case closed."

Conor leaned in. "What if we can't locate it?"

"Not an option, I'm afraid."

Conor sat back.

"As a last resort, you'll report that you did find the archive, no involvement was noted, but that you had to destroy the archive because of the threat that it would fall into the wrong hands."

Conor thought back to their last mission. Truths were bent way out of shape when it came to explaining what happened to Ettore Majorana. They did the right thing. Putting a gun to Majorana's head to force him to work with the Allies would have been morally and strategically wrong.

"If you agree to look for the archive, you need to know there's a deadline."

Conor hated deadlines. People made stupid mistakes trying to meet or beat deadlines.

"Why?" Emily asked.

"General Eisenhower, if he is to step down, wants to give General Marshall some time to pick his replacement. That person will need time to pull together his team." Conor raised his hand. Butcher held his up to stifle him. "And there's Sicily. The next general to take this command will need time to put his stamp on Operation Husky."

It all made sense to Conor. Too much sense. "What's the deadline?"

"Friday the fifteenth."

"That's ten days. We're talking about a *needle in a haystack* situation here, Commander," Conor said.

"I…correction…we realize that. But that's all he's given us. General Eisenhower is headed to a high-level meeting on the fifteenth. He will meet with General Marshall, among others. He's dug his heels in on the deadline, I'm afraid."

Conor remembered Emily mentioning something about a summit of sorts to take place somewhere in Morocco. Plenty of brass, British and American. Possibly French as well. Ike wasn't the type to resign via a letter or a cable. He would do it in person. *And*, Conor thought, *he'd want this Darlan mess behind him one way or another. Butcher would too.*

"I wish there were more time. But I'll pull out all the stops for you. I'll give you a letter from General Eisenhower that will pave your way around Algiers. Outside of North Africa, you'll have to make do. Just like the both of you have done in Italy and Sweden."

Butcher sat back in his chair. His pitch was done.

Conor and Emily shared the look of two people who were force-fed an intelligence dump through a wide-mouth funnel in record time. And while he couldn't speak for Emily, it was making Conor nauseous.

CHAPTER FOURTEEN

1210 Hours, Tuesday, January 5, 1943
Barberousse Prison, Algiers

Antoine Brunel, standing just outside the open cell door, slipped the jailer a two-franc note. "Thank you, Claude. I just need a few minutes with my father."

Claude—Charles Brunel hadn't taken the time to learn the jailer's name—grunted, held up his spread-fingered hand—signaling he had five minutes—and left the door to Charles's cell open. He stood in the middle of the fifteen-foot-wide hallway, gluing his eyes on the father and son as they sat on the bunk. Antoine, a foot taller than his father, had most of his mother's facial features. Something Charles was thankful for. But he had Charles's blue eyes, his most striking facial characteristic. Today, Charles noticed that Antoine's eyes were red-rimmed. Charles's eyes were, most likely, of similar coloring as sleeping in the prison was virtually impossible.

Antoine handed his father a book. It was from a writer his wife—his *second* wife—and Antoine's mother had mentioned the last time they were together. "Claude passed me this book. It's quite good. Especially if you ever wanted to fly," Antoine said. The cover of *Wind, Sand and Stars* depicted a single-engine monoplane on a steep dive earthward. The author's name was in capital letters at the bottom: *ANTOINE DE SAINT EXUPÉRY.* As he'd told his wife, Marie, he preferred to read books related to business-building and biographies of the titans of business. Dismayed, as she often was with him, she had just shaken her head.

"I'll try it. Something to help time pass."

Antoine nodded. "I tried to pry some information out of the prison administrator about your situation. He had none. I'm not sure if he is keeping something from me to spite me or if he is being truthful."

"I would lay some francs on the former." Charles put the book aside and was about to speak when Antoine stood and took in the cell's environs.

"At least you have your own cell. I couldn't bear another day sharing a cell with the three ghastly Algerians. All murder suspects. All most likely guilty." Antoine's eyes settled on the corner of the space, where a two-foot square piece of badly warped Saharan cypress covered a hole in the concrete floor. The warped edges of the cover kept it from lying flat, where it would have trapped some of the noxious stink from the human waste below. "*Dégueulasse.*" Revolting. "This has been nothing short of a nightmare," Antoine said, retaking his seat beside his father.

"But you are leaving the nightmare. I think my past is more complicated for the authorities to delve into. If they are even trying."

"Who filled their ears with the nonsense that you are a Nazi spy? Do you have any idea?"

"Antoine, after all these years, I have made many enemies. It would be a waste of time to dwell on that question."

The jailer poked his head in the cell and barked, "*Trois.*" Three. Both men flinched.

Charles took a deep breath. "Antoine, I have a mission for you. Possibly, if you are successful, it may lead to the release of your mother." Antoine drew close. Charles could feel his warm breath on his face. News that the Germans had arrested Marie and sent her to the Merignac internment camp just days before their own arrest in early December had crushed both men.

His travels to Algiers and French Morocco the week before the Allied invasion of North Africa must have created strong suspicions among his Nazi contacts that he was conspiring with the Allies. Suspicions that triggered the arrest of his Jewish wife.

"Alain Chrétien, when he was here last, told me about an archive that the plotters of the Darlan assassination kept. Apparently, his son has hidden it in the Basilique Notre Dame d'Afrique. It may contain information about who was involved in the assassination. Alain tells me that there was some involvement by Americans and the British. If this is so, that information will be of great value to the Nazis. The release of which would do much harm to the relations with the French. It would weaken the resolve of the French to fight side by side with the Allies."

Antoine looked at his father, whose blue eyes bored into him.

"After they release you, meet Alain at the Café Coq Hardi. Tell him to take you to where his son hid the archive at the basilica that night. He will have travel papers for you in the name of Charles Lewis."

Antoine raised his eyebrows at the mention of the blended name.

"Pay him one thousand francs from the money we hid before our arrest. He believes you will use the archive as leverage to get information about his missing son. Instead, you will need to find a way to get to Marseille. That is the busiest port. Stay away from anyone in authority here in Algiers. It's too dangerous. Do you understand?"

Antoine's head bobbed.

Charles patted his son on the shoulder. "When you arrive in Marseille, seek out the *préfet régional*. His name is François Leclerc." Charles reached under his mattress and pulled out two lightly soiled envelopes and passed one to him. "Give him this letter. He will lend assistance in getting you to Lyon. Take the rest of the hidden money. You'll need it for bribes, food, whatnot. Once in Lyon, meet with Pierre Laurent. And give him…this letter." The second envelope was more soiled than the first. "Listen to me."

Charles explained that Laurent owed him a great debt. One that he wanted to collect. He wanted Laurent—in exchange for the archive, which would put the Nazis in debt to Laurent—to convince his Nazi contacts to release his wife and arrange for travel for the both of them to a neutral country. "Once you are safe, you will send Laurent a cable telling him where the archive is hidden… somewhere in Lyon." Antoine nodded cautiously as Charles went on. "If Laurent balks at your terms, the letter says that you will leak information about claims of bank fraud, loans made to nonexistent people, that I helped cover up. And last, you will make claims that Laurent is in a leadership role in the *Synarchique*."

Antoine's jaw dropped. Charles had schooled Antoine in the mysterious workings of the powerful *Synarchique*. Men who willingly threw in with the Nazis to ensure their own lucrative future once the war ended in Nazi Germany's favor.

"Father, what is to keep Laurent from having me arrested before I can make these threats public?"

"The letter to Laurent says that we have put the damning information in the hands of someone. That someone is François Leclerc. It's all in the letter to him. If this someone does not hear from you, the information will be released to the police." Antoine shifted his gaze from his father to the far wall. When Antoine began biting his lower lip, Charles knew doubts were settling in. "Antoine, my son, we have much leverage. But you must locate the archive and get to Laurent."

"What if I can't find the archive? What if it contains no such information about the Americans or British?"

Charles detected anxiousness in Antoine's rapid delivery and held up both hands in a calming gesture. "The threat to expose the fraud and his involvement in the *Synarchique* should be enough to convince Laurent to act on your mother's behalf. If he refuses…" Charles hung his head. "Then Pierre Laurent may very well find himself in a hellhole like me."

"*C'est l'heure!*" It's time! Claude's bark was louder this time, but neither man flinched.

CHAPTER FIFTEEN

1215 Hours, Tuesday, January 5, 1943
Hôtel Terminus, Gestapo Headquarters, Lyon

Klaus Barbie, chief of Section IV Intelligence and Gestapo in Lyon, hadn't seen Obergruppenführer Oberg since the gathering in Paris in May of the previous year on the occasion of Reinhard Heydrich's visit to the City of Light. The chief of the Reich Security Main Office's (RSHA) primary purpose for the visit was to initiate the transfer of overseeing French Jews from the French to the Nazis.

French defiance and general unrest had gotten out of hand. Troop train derailments, sabotage, and assassinations were on the rise, and something needed to be done. Heydrich, accompanied by Adolf Eichmann, the SS officer in charge of Jewish policy, met with Oberg and his second-in-command, Standartenführer Helmut Knochen. When Heydrich expressed his rage over the seemingly uncontainable disastrous nature of daily life in and around Paris, Oberg and Knochen let the shit roll downhill. They made it clear to the attending officers with the rank of hauptsturmführer and above that it wasn't just a Paris problem, but the swelling of the ranks of the Resistance and the growing boldness of their attacks was also a problem in the now-occupied part of France that was overseen by the Vichy government.

They focused the more scathing reprimands on missing quotas of slave labor for German factories. More French Jews, as well as foreign Jews who had sought safety in France, needed to be rounded up and shipped to factories in Germany and annexed lands. It was clarified to be a top priority for all units of the *Sicherheitsdienst* (SD), SS, and the Gestapo. A swift current of shit flowed downhill that day. Not even a visit to Le Sphinx, a brothel taken over by the Wehrmacht, sufficed to take the ringing out of Barbie's ears.

When Oberg entered Barbie's lushly carpeted third-floor office in the Hôtel Terminus, there was a confused sneer on his face as if he didn't expect Barbie to be there, in his own office. Barbie, back straight and eyes locked on his perplexed superior, stood beside his desk, the one he had stolen from the chief of Lyon's police department's office when he first arrived in Lyon.

"The Hôtel Terminus. A suitable name, don't you think, Barbie?" Oberg, bespectacled and in a sharply tailored, fresh-looking uniform, gripped a pair of black leather gloves in his right hand and headed directly to Barbie's desk chair. Once seated, he tossed his gloves on the desk, lifted his feet, and dropped his gleaming black boots on the desk, making enough noise that it brought Barbie's adjutant to the door. Barbie held him there with a raised hand.

"Coffee, sir?"

"Yes, with a shot of schnapps. And a cigar. I must have left mine in Paris."

Barbie nodded at his adjutant, who left with all speed. "I trust your trip was uneventful?"

"It was quite horrible. Turbulence. There was much turbulence. The pilot refused my order to fly above the turbulence. I have already reported him to his commanding officer, who begged me not to share my anger with Göring. I agreed but...I've changed my mind. I plan to contact Göring as soon as I return to Paris." Barbie's adjutant returned with a tray loaded down with fine china cups and saucers from the hotel's collection, two apéritif glasses of schnapps, and a Cuban cigar from Barbie's personal collection, one of his remaining few.

Oberg plucked the cigar from the tray, sniffed the barrel and placed it between his thin blue-tinged lips, and motioned the adjutant to light it. Before leaving, the adjutant placed one cup of coffee and a glass of schnapps on the front edge of the desk within reach of his superior. Barbie made no move to either offering.

Oberg took a series of puffs to ensure the cigar was fully lit. Once satisfied, he turned his attention to Barbie. "There is the matter of your last progress report," Oberg said, his words making their way through a gauzy haze of blue smoke. "Or should I say, the lack of demonstrable progress? Tell me." Oberg paused and tapped ash into the saucer. "Why are you having such difficulty? It seems simple to me. Round up the Jews, shove them into a cattle car, and head them eastward. Auschwitz is starving for Jews, Barbie. And besides your declining quota numbers, there has been little success in taming the local Resistance."

Barbie was about to respond when Oberg took a quick puff and then smiled in a strange way, as if to say *none of what I said can be true, can it?* Barbie tried but couldn't take his eyes off Oberg's teeth. In their previous and only other meeting, Barbie had been too distant to notice such a detail. They were filed down to stubs, or they never developed beyond the size of baby teeth. Their yellow tint completed the peculiar image.

"The numbers of Jews have increased in the past week. You will see even more impressive increases in the next few weeks. We have shifted our focus to the activities of the UGIF." Barbie halted when the confused look reappeared on Oberg's face. "The Union Générale des Israélites de France." The expression didn't leave his face. "They were created by the Vichy regime after we requested—"

"Don't patronize me, Barbie. They locate and classify the Jews in France. They do the laborious work, so we don't have to." Another short puff and an exhale through his nostrils. Barbie thought Oberg found deep pleasure in the cigar given that his eyes gently closed and remained so for several moments.

"I don't trust the French-Jewish bourgeoisie. They say they represent Jews before public authorities in matters of welfare assistance. But they are nothing but a funnel for Jews escaping to Spain and Switzerland. They collaborate with the Resistance," Barbie said, picking up the cup of the now-tepid coffee.

"This is disappointing. Why have you not shut it down?" Oberg removed his feet from the desktop and snatched the glass of schnapps in a blur of movement. Barbie paused, which gave Oberg an opening. Barbie cursed his hesitation. "Your refusal to act is not unlike your fumbling of the Marie Monin fiasco. You grossly underestimated the woman."

There it was. It took a mere five minutes for Oberg to bring up the most disappointing chapter in Barbie's service to the Reich. The escape of the most troublesome SOE agent in southern France. Marie Monin, the limping lady. She had a natural instinct for spying. She also had what seemed a bottomless reservoir of good luck. Her eventual escape, just when he was so close to closing in, was a black mark on his otherwise impressive career in intelligence gathering on behalf of Nazi Germany. That's what he preferred to call it—intelligence gathering, by whatever means necessary.

"Plans are in the works," Barbie said. "They have smart people in charge. My aim is to capture as many Jews in one action as possible and be rid of them in a decisive blow."

"*Ach*, you wait too long. That was the problem with Monin. Plan, plan, plan. Then poof, she's gone." The disgust in Oberg's voice was unambiguous. "You remind me of someone." Barbie waited for the insult. "In fact, he's someone I brought with me. Another officer of the Reich who has failed miserably. Someone like yourself who must show the confidence the führer placed in you was not a mistake. You both need to redeem yourselves."

"Sir?" Barbie repeated the word *redeem* under his breath.

"Go and invite our guest—your new associate—in and I will make introductions."

Barbie didn't move.

"Go," Oberg said, his jowly face tightened in anger.

Barbie rose and went to the office door and opened it. Standing at attention was an SS-sturmbannführer with close-cropped blonde hair combed straight back. He tucked his cap under his tightly clenched left arm. But two characteristics stole Barbie's attention—the eye patch and a severely deformed ear. Barbie looked closer and realized that it wasn't actually deformed—it was missing.

Barbie stood aside, and the major stepped into the office. Barbie shut the door and headed back to the desk, the major close behind. Oberg signaled both to take seats. "This is Sturmbannführer Kurt Eklof. It appears that Schellenberg no longer wants him and has pawned him off on me. He said it had something to do with a failed mission in Sweden. I asked for details, but Schellenberg remained tight-lipped, as he is known for being. So I am pawning him off on you." Barbie cut his gaze sideways and saw Eklof's upper body stiffen. "It would seem that you both need to impress me."

Oberg stood and made a mess of extinguishing his cigar in the saucer. "Set up a meeting with your senior staff for tomorrow. I want to express my disappointment to them because I can't trust you to do that." Oberg set his cap on his head firmly with two hands and smiled, revealing two rows of stubby teeth. The smile resembled one given by someone who had just passed along a bag of shit. Oberg came around the desk and stopped.

Barbie rose, followed by Eklof.

Oberg opened his mouth as if struck by a thought. "Yes, it almost slipped my mind. How careless of me. It has come to my attention that the Abwehr has been working with a priest—Abbé Alves is his name. I am unaware of his first name. He's an Alsatian who seems to have chosen the wrong calling. This priest has been effective in gaining the trust of some members of the Resistance here in Lyon. He was involved in bringing down the Gloria Network. Pry him away from the Abwehr. They will just waste the priest's talents."

CHAPTER SIXTEEN

1230 Hours, Tuesday, January 5, 1943
Hôtel Saint-George, rue Michelet, Algiers

Conor and Emily returned to the table from the far side of the pool deck, where they mulled over Butcher's offer. They retook their seats as Butcher, sitting cross-legged and lighting up a Philip Morris cigarette, eyed the couple expectantly through a shroud of smoke.

"Before we answer, can you go back to General Eisenhower and ask for more time?" Conor asked.

Butcher scratched the back of his neck and followed with the longest exhale Conor had ever witnessed. Like he was holding his own breath as well as Eisenhower's. "What you're talking about is moving the timeline for this upcoming conference. Not possible. It's out of his hands."

"We had to ask, Commander," Emily said.

"We're in," Conor said.

"Not that we know where we'd even begin, but we're willing to help," Emily added.

Butcher cracked a broad smile. "Well, I have some ideas." Before he could continue, a gust kicked up some of the severed palm fronds that littered the deck and dispersed the pile of cigarette ashes from Butcher's shallow white triangular Martini ashtray. The unfazed Butcher reached for the carafe and poured himself another cup of coffee. "You've got to get to some people who were involved. Murphy let us know that two Frenchmen, Henri d'Astier de la Vigerie and a priest that d'Astier is very close to named Pierre Marie Cordier, have been arrested. They are interned at Barberousse Prison."

"And who is Murphy?" Emily said.

"Robert Murphy. He's been FDR's personal representative in North Africa since 1940. Murphy was deeply involved in determining who we could depend on for assistance and when from the Free French in the lead-up to the invasion. He knows all the key players from Casablanca to Algiers. That includes d'Astier. Murphy knows that d'Astier was a member of what Murphy calls the Group of Five. D'Astier was a monarchist who wanted to install Henri, Comte de Paris, as the new head of a provisional French government. He's the head of the House of Orléans, pretender to the throne, as Henry VII. Darlan was never their guy, and Murphy's convinced they were involved in the assassination at some level. Maybe at the top."

"Did they know the assassin de la Chapelle?" Conor asked.

"According to Murphy, chances are very good."

"Anyone else spring to mind?" Emily said.

"Yes. One who worked for Colonel Eddy by the name of Carleton Coon."

"I know Coon. From my stint in Tangier. Another field archaeologist working with Eddy along with Chester Booth."

"No. He's a racial anthropologist. Not that the difference matters."

Conor was not one of Booth's favorite people. His complaints about Conor's recklessness were primarily responsible for getting Conor booted from Tangier back in October. Coon, on the other hand, got along with Conor. They had similar operational styles. Coon was willing to try just about anything to make life for the Germans in Tangier as shitty as possible. Conor knew that Coon was not above keeping Eddy in the dark when it made sense. "Where's Coon now?" Conor said.

"Eddy sent him out of Algiers to a place called Cape Serrat, right after the Darlan assassination." *Might things in Algiers have gotten too hot for Coon? If so, what was the reason?*

Butcher thumbed his all-but-spent Philip Morris deep into the

Martini ashtray. "This has me real worried. Both Coon and a captain Michael Gubbins were involved in some training of members of the pro-Gaullist Corps francs d'Afrique. Coon pulled this unit together as a sort of commando outfit."

Emily flinched. "You said Gubbins? Son of Colin Gubbins, number two in the SOE?"

"The same."

Emily's shoulders slumped and she gave Conor a furtive glance.

"Commander, you paint a pretty bleak picture," Conor said, fighting back a wave of nausea. He wanted to ask if General Eisenhower had packed his bags yet, but he held back.

"We know. I almost told Ike to start packing his bags."

Conor swallowed a slight gasp at Butcher's admission.

"That's all the intel I can give you at this point." Conor and Emily nodded. "But there is one more thing. Since you also are persona non grata as far as Allied Force Headquarters is concerned, I have made arrangements to have someone work with you. Someone to…facilitate your investigation. Grease the skids, so to speak. He's attached to General Ryder's 34th Infantry as an intelligence officer."

"You mean he's a parole officer?"

"Or a babysitter, Commander?" Emily chimed in.

"A facilitator. A skid greaser. Like I said." Butcher rose. "I'll send him in so you three can get acquainted." Butcher bolted from the pool deck, done with fielding back talk from the personae non gratae still seated at the table. A minute later, a tall, gangly army captain walked across the pool deck in long strides, digging his bootheels into the concrete.

"Captain Simon Simmons. And let's get this straight from the very start: I'm damn pissed that they handed me this chickenshit assignment. I don't work well with women unless they can get me some damn coffee and type some damn reports."

Conor gaped at Emily who had a half-bemused, half-shocked look on her face.

"And I especially don't enjoy hanging around anyone who washed out of any military service, including the pansy-assed navy."

Conor had enough. He stood, the backs of his knees sending

his wicker chair sliding across the deck. Emily stood just as quickly and intercepted Conor on his path to Simmons. "Captain, I'm Emily Bright. I don't get damn coffee and I'm a terrible typist." She paused so she could push Conor off with her open right hand. "No, believe it or not, I'm a very good typist. Maybe a little rusty since I began working undercover for MI6. Oh, and Conor, that's him who you insulted, was, to use your terminology, washed out of the navy on false charges admitted to by his former commanding officer. He was… Conor, would the term 'railroaded' be appropriate?"

Conor made no effort to mask his smirk. "Appropriate as shit, Emily."

"And has Prime Minister Churchill shaken your hand not once, but twice, to thank you for demonstrating some…ballsy behavior on behalf of the Allies?"

Simmons looked like he had just been pummeled by Joe Lewis in his prime.

"Wow." Conor tilted his head at his wife, asking the voiceless question, *are you done?* When she nodded, he nodded. *Now that's why I love this woman.*

Simmons looked crestfallen. "Listen, don't get me—"

"You're right. I don't get you." Conor cracked a smart-ass smile. "We'll need to split up, Captain." Conor turned to Emily. "You and Simmons head to the prison. Spend some time with this d'Astier and his priestly friend. I'll get Butcher to make arrangements to get me to Cape Serrat by the fastest means possible." Conor gave a quick thought to Jack Waddon and his PBY, and whether its port engine repairs had been completed. He then turned his attention back to Simmons and reeled off several orders. "We'll need some sidearms. One Colt M1911A1 and a M1903 for me and one Walther PPK for Emily. I want ten extra mags for each gun. Also, we both want Fairbairn-Sykes knives. We'll need a full set of civilian clothes. No skirts or dresses for Emily. Also, boots and a wool cap for me and a…fedora-style hat for Emily. Oh, and I want two flashlights, a blackjack, some tins of food."

Simmons was about to say something, but Conor closed him down with a shake of his head that said *nope, not done*. "And…five grenades…each, along with some plastic explosives, time pencils, detonators, and delay-action fuses. Find two musette bags, like a haversack—something a Frenchman would carry." Conor paused. "You need to locate a suitcase radio for trips outside of Algiers. An SSTR1 would do. Or the British version, a Type 3 Mark II (B2). Any questions?"

Simmons stammered, but before any comprehensible words emerged, Butcher and Colonel Eddy marched onto the pool deck, spoiling a truly memorable moment.

Between the two, Eddy was the one who had a full head of steam. Butcher placed a hand on his shoulder to slow him down, but Eddy pulled free. Butcher, a pace behind the charging Eddy, looked at Conor and slowly shook his head. A warning?

"Thorn," Eddy shouted. "I want all of it. Every second of your beef in the bar with Stevens. Or you're not going anywhere but to a dark hole in some forsaken Algerian prison."

"Hello, Colonel," Conor said in a dulcet tone, hoping to calm the charged-up Eddy. As Conor dove into the details of his and Emily's earlier encounter with Captain Stewart, Eddy and Butcher remained standing. Eddy wasn't happy that Conor couldn't recall many details about the dustup with Stevens, but Eddy seemed to run out of steam as Conor got to the end of the explanation as to his whereabouts later that night.

"It wasn't me, Colonel. We didn't like each other, but I have to say, there was more bullshit coming at me from Stevens's direction than at him from me." Conor let his words sink in. "It's no secret that he had beefs with others, Colonel."

Eddy had been shifting from one leg to the other during Conor's testimony, spending less time on his artificial right leg. He moved to the table and took a seat, with Butcher joining him. "Yeah, he had beefs with others. I knew that…but…we've got enough crap to deal with here. We don't need to add a murder to the list."

"I get it, Colonel."

Emily shot Conor a glance and nodded to the pool deck exit.

Good idea. "Any other questions, Colonel?" Conor asked.

Eddy shook his head. "As long as you've given me the low-down…all of it…no, nothing else." Eddy slumped in his chair. Butcher offered him a Philip Morris, which Eddy accepted.

Conor took one step toward the exit when the word of the

day popped into his head—*beefs*. "Aah, there is one more thing, Colonel. Stevens had someone with him when he entered the bar. My mind has been pretty foggy these past few days." An understatement for sure. His head had been pounding away like the pistons in a V-12 Packard engine. "It was a British lieutenant." That late recollection sparked a startled look from Emily, as well as Eddy, who sat up in his chair and snubbed out his cigarette. "The Brit wanted to talk to Stevens, but he wasn't playing along. He was too interested in bending my ear."

"Talk about what?" The question from Emily surprised Conor.

"No way of knowing. Stevens shut the lieutenant down pretty quick. Then the lieutenant just left the bar."

"Did he have a name?" Eddy asked.

"Not that I heard."

"Could you give us a description?" Butcher said.

"Listen, I was in a sour mood, and I think you all know the reason, and that led to downing a few Jamesons. The blow to my head makes it—"

"Conor, a description," Butcher said.

"Facial features, I didn't zero in on. But something came back to me. He did have a dark port-wine stain."

"What?" Eddy said. "You mean on his tunic?"

"No. A port-wine stain on his neck. It ran under the collar of his shirt."

CHAPTER SEVENTEEN

0815 Hours, Wednesday, January 6, 1943
OSS Headquarters, London

Charles Jocelyn Hambro, chief of the SOE, sported his perpetual frown when he was shown into David Bruce's office. His pasty and pudgy face looked as if it hadn't been exposed to the sun since the Nazis invaded Poland.

"Where's Donovan? I was told he would be here," Hambro said, his tone agitated. Obviously Hambro still had his knickers in a bunch at not being able to host the meeting at No. 54 Baker Street. Hambro tossed his trench coat over the back of a chair to the left of Bruce, who sat at the head of a long conference table. There were three empty chairs at the table, two to Bruce's right and one at the end of the table.

"Stuck in Algiers. Nasty weather in the western Med. He told me to tell you he would contact you as soon as he touched down at Tempsford." Bruce wasn't going to tell him that Donovan also told him to have the meeting recorded. Bruce didn't have to ask why. Trust in the spy business was never in substantial supply.

Hambro grunted in what Bruce thought was Hambro's sign of resignation. Bruce hit the intercom button just to his right and instructed Joan, his assistant, to bring a pot of coffee and a pitcher of water. "And, Joan, see if you can find me a pack of cigarettes." Bruce looked at Hambro, who was looking at his watch. "Charles, need anything?"

"Yes, for this blasted meeting to get going," Hambro shot back.

"That's it, Joan. Thanks." Bruce shifted in his seat to face more directly the seemingly put-out Hambro. "Can't well start without your people…Buckmaster and Atkins…can we?"

Hambro again responded with a grunt, a measure softer this time.

Colonel Maurice Buckmaster was the head of the SOE's F Section, whose primary responsibility was to recruit and train agents to be dropped into France to assist the Resistance. The Romanian-born Vera Atkins handled the housekeeping for Buckmaster, minding the details attached to each agent's deployment.

"They'll be here in short order," Hambro said, adding a dismissive flick of his wrist. Hambro leaned toward Bruce. "Does she have any idea what this is about?"

"Not from us. I can tell you that." Joan entered the office with a tray laden with the asked-for pot of coffee and a tall glass pitcher of water. A pack of Camels sat in an ashtray along with Bruce's Zippo lighter.

Joan set the tray near Bruce's left elbow and leaned toward his ear. "Your guests have arrived. The younger woman appears to be quite nervous. Shall I bring them in?"

"Yes, of course," Hambro said before Bruce could form the words. Bruce nodded at Joan, who cocked an eyebrow as she turned to leave. "Joan, there will be one other…guest. A Miss Hall. We will let you know when to let her in."

A moment later, Buckmaster entered at a brisk pace, dressed in a brown British Army uniform belted at the waist and adorned with a small service ribbon whose significance was lost on Bruce. Atkins followed close behind dressed in a similarly colored uniform, a calf-length skirt and single-breasted tunic, heavy flesh-colored stockings, and sensible black clunky shoes. Her thin lips were a slash of red. She made no eye contact with Bruce or the fidgety Hambro.

Pulling up the rear was a woman of medium height with blazing-red hair, her lustrous skin the second feature that caught Bruce's eye. He saw no resemblance to her brother. Her full, perfectly shaped lips were coated in a muted red. To Bruce, she showed no signs of nervousness. *A talented actress*, Bruce thought. An excellent trait for what lay ahead.

Buckmaster and Atkins took seats to Bruce's right, leaving the seat at the end of the table for the redhead, who slipped into the chair and brushed an errant lock of hair from the side of her face.

Bruce locked his gaze on the redhead. "I assume that Colonel Buckmaster and Miss Atkins have introduced themselves." Bruce extended his arm toward Hambro. "This is Charles Hambro. He heads up the SOE. Charles, this is Maggie Thorn. One of our newer and…quite promising agents." She seemed to appreciate Bruce's introduction given the lip-curling smile Maggie displayed.

Hambro's gaze took in Maggie. Both Buckmaster and Atkins had eyes drilled into files laid out before them.

"Let's get to it, shall we, David?" Hambro said, resetting himself in his chair. Hambro was about to follow up on his question, but Bruce made an exaggerated effort to clear his throat, which shut the impatient spymaster down.

"Maggie, your training has wrapped up, I hear?"

"Yes, sir. Or as far as I've been told. I do have questions that don't always get answered."

Bruce did a good job of stifling a laugh. "We plucked Maggie out of the ranks of the hundreds of journalists who seem to have taken over London." Bruce looked around the table and quickly realized that his quip didn't register with the Brits.

"Well aware, David. Well aware," Hambro said.

Bruce gave his throat a genuine clearing and nervously straightened the knot of his tie. "Maggie, the OSS had every intention of sending you to Algiers in the next week. From there, you were going to be infiltrated into France. We have an agreement with our SOE friends that the OSS can't initiate operations from English soil, so we have to—"

"David, please. No inside business," Hambro said, his eyes exploring the surface of the table, then stealing a look at his watch.

"What if we all agree to stop dancing with each other? Tell me why I'm here. I have two more days here in London before I ship out. And I'm told that I may not see London, or any other place outside of France, ever again. So let's get on with it." Maggie sat back, folded her arms, and waited.

Bruce held back a smirk. The others made no such effort to mask their surprise. He wondered just what Mrs. Thorn fed her kids when they were growing up. "Yes, shall we?"

Hambro, recovered from Maggie's bluster, looked at Buckmaster and rolled his hand, prompting the blue-eyed spymaster to get on with it.

"We have asked, and have been granted, permission by Colonel Donovan to have you seconded to the SOE for an urgent mission."

Maggie looked at Bruce for a corroborative signal.

Bruce nodded, then turned back to Buckmaster.

"But first, a few questions to confirm what we know about you," Buckmaster said.

Maggie sat up and placed her folded hands in front of her.

"You attended Columbia University from 1935 to 1939." Buckmaster looked up from his file.

"Yes."

"While attending Columbia, you met and became…hmm… involved with a René Fitzgerald DuBois."

"Involved." Maggie snorted. "You Brits. So proper." The Brits at the table all exchanged exasperated looks and squirmed a tad in their seats. "We dated. Steadily. Until he left with his parents after he graduated from medical school. To Lyon, if I remember. But I'm sure that's in that file of yours."

"It is. And Lyon is correct," Buckmaster said, closing his file as he turned to Atkins.

"When he left with his parents, how did the two of you… handle his decision to return to France?" Atkins said. "Was it—"

"Amicable?" Maggie shifted her gaze to the bank of windows that overlooked Grosvenor Street. "Let's just say he broke it off. There were tears. Mine actually." She returned her gaze to Atkins. "Ever been in love, Miss Atkins?" Atkins's face flushed. She looked down at her file. "After he and his parents left, I focused on studies. Went over to France for two semesters. And, no. I never sought him out." Maggie paused, looking lost in a thought. "I couldn't help but feel that his father forced René to return with them. Sarah, his mother, who I loved dearly, seemed to be of the opinion that he should be allowed to make up his own mind."

A glassy-eyed Maggie hesitated. "He broke it off." Another

pause while she took a breath. "Anyway, I had a year left and... time moves on." Maggie cleared her thick throat. "Enough about me." Her face lit up. "Anyone else abandoned by the love of their life?"

More squirming gave Bruce an opening, and he took it. "Maggie, DuBois has been working for the French Resistance for almost a year. A high-level operative in France recommended DuBois to the SOE as someone who could rebuild a Resistance network in Paris."

"Miss Thorn, the need for a vibrant and effective network in Paris is crucial," Hambro said. "We have agreed with the recommendation and need to get DuBois more fully trained and in place as soon as possible." Maggie stiffened. Her attention was fully locked on Hambro. "Our need to get him out of France and to London has coincided with one other necessity."

"The Heckler Network, based in Lyon, has received some intelligence that we need to get out of France now," Bruce said. He shot a look at Hambro and received a curt shake of the head. "She needs to know, Charles."

"Damn right I do," Maggie blurted.

Hambro flicked his wrist in defeat.

"The intelligence is a series of photos and maps of a massive Nazi project consisting of fortifications along the northern French coast. The Atlantic Wall," Bruce said. "The inevitable invasion of northern France will depend on an effective Resistance network in Paris *and* detailed intelligence as to what to expect on the beaches when D-Day comes around."

"Okay," Maggie said, drawing out the word.

"We need to get DuBois out of France for training. Now," Buckmaster said. "And he'll be carrying the Atlantic Wall intelligence."

"Come on. I'm not dumb. Just send a Lysander or a Mosquito and get him out. Or have him get to the border with Spain and have some partisans get him over the Pyrenees."

"He won't leave Lyon without his mother. And she won't leave," Buckmaster said.

The room went silent. Bruce couldn't even hear anyone breathing. Maybe his guests were holding their breaths like he was.

"Sarah won't come? Really? She told me once that she didn't really like France. Just one Frenchman, and that was Raymond, her husband. She's a Jersey girl, just like me."

"We've learned that she has been helping Jews get out of France. She has become even more involved since the Germans invaded Vichy France back in November," Atkins said.

Maggie grinned and sat back. She shook her head, freeing a ringlet of red hair that swooped down across her forehead. "What a pistol, that woman. Gotta love her."

"We're sending you over to bring René, the intelligence, and his mother out. We're counting on your close relationship with Sarah to make that happen. You need to convince Sarah that, while her work is important, what her son will be trained to do is more important. Can you do that, Maggie?" Bruce asked. "And bring out the Atlantic Wall intel?"

"That's what you trained me for. I think it's about time you got something for your money. Don't you?" Maggie pushed herself away from the table. She must have thought her closing statement would have been an excellent way to end the meeting. Instead of smiles and *atta girls*, all she got were stares and long, sorry-looking faces, a perfect prelude to the delivery of bad news.

"Maggie, we're not done. There's one more assignment we need to discuss," Bruce said, reluctance resonating in his voice.

Maggie surveyed the room, all eyes riveted on her. "Well, out with it."

Hambro slapped the table with an open hand, sparking flinches from the others, except Maggie. "Excellent," Hambro roared. Bruce noted the complete lack of hesitancy in the Brit's voice. Hambro handled the background of the Abwehr agent called Abbé Robert Alves, including the havoc he wreaked on Resistance operations in France. Buckmaster delved into details concerning the interaction between Virginia Hall and the priest, specifically how he wormed himself into her and other high-level Resistance members' confidence and how he, then unbeknownst to Virginia, betrayed agents associated with Virginia. Buckmaster reported that Alves was principally responsible for shutting down the Gloria Network in Paris, the network that the SOE now wanted René DuBois to reconstitute. The Nazis arrested members of the network and sent them to camps after intensive interrogations. The revelations seemed to shock Maggie.

"Not like the priests I know back in New Jersey," Maggie said. "Not even close." She asked no questions, just took it all in.

"You are to kill this spy at the first opportunity." All eyes were on Maggie, straining to detect any hesitation. Maggie took several deep breaths. "Maggie?" Hambro said.

Then it was Bruce's turn. "Maggie. Any questions?"

"No...no questions."

"Excellent," Hambro said again, exchanging glances of approval with Buckmaster and Atkins. Bruce sat quietly, his gaze locked on Maggie's stunned face.

Hambro turned to Bruce. "Let's have Virginia spend some time with *our* new agent, David." He spun around to take in Maggie. "Virginia Hall, I'm sure you've heard of her exploits in France. She'll brief you on her dealings with DuBois and the Resistance's activities in and around Lyon. Ask all the questions you can think of. Don't be shy. Vera here will sit with you both. Take it all in." Hambro pushed back from the table, followed by Buckmaster and Bruce. "Oh, lastly, you'll leave tonight. There's no time to waste. You understand, I'm sure."

"No time to waste," Maggie echoed, her voice shaky. "How'd you know that was my motto?"

#

When Virginia Hall entered the room, Maggie and Atkins were standing at the rain-streaked window, cups of coffee in hand, chatting about the weather in France. Maggie turned at the sound of a greeting. The statuesque Hall slid a green felt hat with a prominent, high-peaked crown from her head and snapped it twice to rid it of raindrops. Hall fashioned her slightly muted reddish hair in a short bob, parted on the right. The ends were faintly curled, most likely from the damp weather, Maggie surmised. Hall smiled at the two women.

"Do I smell the delectable presence of...coffee? Not that awful ersatz coffee...no, no, no, I should not even call it coffee.

It's nothing close to it. It has made me hate the sight of acorns." Atkins moved to the pot of coffee and filled a cup. When she handed it to Hall, they gave each other a light hug, Hall holding the cup with an outstretched arm, careful not to spill a drop of the precious brew. "Hello, Vera. So nice to see you. And this must be Margaret Thorn."

Maggie approached Hall and extended her hand. Hall's hand was calloused and still damp from the elements outside. "Actually, it's Maguire, Virginia." That got the reaction Maggie was used to seeing. Hall cut her a sideways glance and raised an eyebrow. "My mother's maiden name was Maguire. She always wanted to use it as a first name. She lost that battle twice, but my father didn't stand a chance when I was born." Hall giggled. "But when it came to what I was going to be called, he won out. So to my family and friends, it's Maggie."

"I love that story, Maggie. I truly do. Now let's sit and get to business. I know you don't have much time."

After taking their seats, Maggie and Atkins opposite Hall, Atkins pried a cigarette from a box of Senior Service cigarettes, lit it with a silver dented Parker lighter, and started the briefing. "The biography she'll be using was developed by the OSS for the mission she was going to be sent on. There's no time for us to change it. It would be too dangerous."

"Agreed," Hall said, draining her coffee. "And what is her new identity?" Atkins started to reply but was stopped by Hall's raised hand. Hall just looked at Maggie.

"My name is Elisé Carré. I am unmarried. The daughter of Marie and André Carré. Both deceased. I am an only child." Maggie fought off the feeling that her dry mouth had been covered in sandpaper. She took a sip of her coffee.

"They were lifelong residents of Rouen. They died in 1942 in an Allied bombing raid. Their daughter, Elisé, went missing," Atkins added, earning a nod from Hall.

"And?" Hall said, helping herself to another cup of coffee.

"I am working in a dressmaker's shop in Paris. I live in a back room of the shop…alone."

"This checks out. The OSS arranged through some French staff who used to work at the American Embassy to employ and put Elisé up," Atkins said. "We've gone over all her documents. They aren't as good as ours, but given the lack of time, they'll pass muster."

"And your French?" The question got an immediate *tsk* from Atkins.

"I think it's damn good, but I guess Vera here doesn't agree."

"In the report from your OSS handler, there's a comment about your New Jersey accent."

"Ha, I've heard something like that before. They told me that my Baltimore accent would get me killed. But I proved them wrong," Hall said, adding a dismissive wave of her hand. "You're being sent to Lyon. And the reason for a Parisian to travel to Lyon?"

Atkins passed a file stamped *TOP SECRET* to Maggie. "Elisé Carré has been sent to Lyon to deliver a dress to Sarah DuBois. We have the dress at Baker Street."

"What about—"

"Yes, Virginia, we changed all the labels. I've double-checked it myself." Hall nodded. "We have produced Paris-to-Lyon train tickets and found someone who resembles and will be dressed like Elisé. She will be seen boarding the train to Lyon at the Paris Nord Station." Atkins turned to Maggie. "All train stations in Paris are crawling with Gestapo and the Vichy police." She turned back to Hall. "The look-alike will slip off the train at Écully, the last stop before Lyon."

Virginia, her cup clutched between her hands, had been staring at its cooling contents while Atkins walked them through the subterfuge. She raised her gaze. "Well done, Vera." Maggie and Atkins met her gaze but did not speak. "I suppose now is a good time to talk about…the priest. Abbé Robert Alves."

Hall recounted how she had played and replayed all her dealings with Alves over in her head countless times since her escape from France in November. "Being duped…betrayed by the priest…was a dark moment in my life," Hall said.

She drew in a deep breath and took the next ten minutes to brief Maggie, starting with Dr. Paul Russier, her trusted friend, fellow Resistance member, and close associate of Hall's dear friend, Germaine Gilbert, the operator of the One-Eight. She explained that Russier, being a deeply religious Catholic, was so trusting of

Alves that, after numerous attempts to convince Hall of Alves's fidelity, she acquiesced. Germaine saw no signs of trouble. Virginia fought back the feeling that continued to nag her about Alves. Priests in the Resistance weren't a novel thing. In fact, given their added freedom to move about to tend to their parishioners, they made effective couriers and informants. They were never asked to betray the secrets heard in the confessional. Yet she was sure that some did, in an indirect way.

"Is Gilbert aware of Alves's duplicity?" Maggie asked.

"No," Hall said. Maggie didn't hide her look of puzzlement.

"F Section didn't want to alert Gilbert for fear of a leak. We didn't want Alves to run if he thought we were onto him," Atkins said.

"He's a cancer that must be cut out as soon as possible," Hall said. She peered into Maggie's green eyes, seeming to search for something. Maybe a sign of a solid resolve. Maggie hoped she saw it.

"I understand. It will be done, Virginia. Trust me."

Virginia let out a long breath, as if she had been holding it for a long moment. "Thank you…Elisé." Virginia smiled, her back straighter. "Let me share some fieldcraft tips with you, some things that the OSS might not have schooled you on. First…" Hall noticed Maggie glance about the office for a pen and paper.

"No. Don't write these down. Just be mindful of them." Hall pushed aside her cup. "Never daydream. Always know someone is watching you, especially a beautiful woman such as you. Don't be overly alarmed if you feel, at the outset, unnervingly conspicuous, like you have a sign hanging around your neck that says *I just arrived from England.*"

Maggie made mental notes of the myriad things Hall went through. Some were never mentioned by her OSS handlers.

"Never mention *Angleterre*, England, in conversation. Always use the phrase *domicile*. Home."

Maggie nodded. Her focus on Hall was unshakable.

"Being American, crossing the street won't be a problem." Maggie's pinched face communicated her confusion. "We lost one agent, an Englishman, who forgot the French drove on the right side of the road. A sharp-eyed Gestapo agent picked him up after he walked out in front of an oncoming car.

"Clean your plate. Use the bread to soak up every last ounce of gravy. Eat like a Frenchman," Hall proclaimed, waving her index finger in the air. "Do you smoke?"

"Yes. Especially when I drink."

"Oh, well, while you are in the field, you drink sparingly. Only to fit in. Never to excess. Listening?"

"Yes, Virginia. I get it. Loose lips."

"Yes. As far as smoking goes, Frenchwomen do not smoke in cafés, on the street...in public places. Remember that. When you are among fellow Resistance members, you can smoke. Also, tobacco is rationed, so cigarettes are almost impossible to come by... legally. Buying from the black market isn't wise as it will arouse suspicion. Anyway, few people have the resources to do so. What you should do as soon as you get to Lyon is to start stub snatching."

Maggie made another face. "Explain."

"If you see a stub of a somewhat-spent cigarette, pick it up and save it in a napkin or something else like an envelope. It's become an unshakable habit of many Frenchmen. Do it to fit in." Hall sat back and tilted her head toward the ceiling. Maybe searching for another piece of fieldcraft.

"Virginia, anything else?" Atkins asked.

"Yes. Vera, you'll check her wallet for litter?"

"Of course." Atkins turned to Maggie. "We will make sure that your wallet and purse will have nothing that can be traced back to England or America. No snaps of family. Except for Marie and André, your parents."

Hall settled her gaze on Maggie. "My, your green eyes sparkle. You will turn many heads in France." Hall leaned in and, in a soft voice, said, "When you're questioned, and you will be at some point, do not be afraid to use your beauty to...distract. It can be an effective weapon." The room fell quiet. "Questions?"

Maggie hesitated, but her curiosity won out. "What would you have done if they caught you?"

The stern, serious look on Hall's face melted. "Yes. A question easy to answer. But so difficult to act upon." Hall stood and grabbed her rakish-looking hat from the table. She put it on, pulling the front brim down low over her forehead. "Take your pill." Hall handed her a silver heart-shaped locket on a thick chain.

Maggie opened the locket and saw a close-cropped picture of her mother, Bridget. *How the hell did they find a picture of Mom?* She was about to verbalize her thought when Hall continued.

"Behind the picture is your pill. Keep the locket under your blouse. If taking the pill is not possible, steel yourself, Elisé Carré. And take your secrets with you."

CHAPTER EIGHTEEN

0900 Hours, Wednesday, January 6, 1943
Cape Serrat, Tunisia

From the right seat in the cockpit of the PBY-5, Conor followed the desolate northeast coastline of Algeria, followed by the similar-looking northwest coastline of Tunisia as they made their way eastward to Cape Serrat. Butcher's last-minute wrangling of a ride to Conor's destination came together in little time. The SOE station at Cape Serrat desperately needed to resupply, so much so that they left Maison Blanche Airfield with only five of its normal crew of nine, due to cases of dysentery, including its regular pilot, Jack Waddon.

Conor was glad his friend Eugene DiLazzaro, the PBY's bow gunner, was healthy and made the trip. Waddon's new copilot, Lieutenant Jimmy "Beans" Turley, a proud son of Boston's Back Bay, was ticked off that he was still ordered to make the resupply trip to the cape without a full crew. After the flight engineer, a sergeant they called Pork because he and Turley were so tight, went through the preflight checklist with Beans, he offered the copilot's seat to Conor. Not necessarily a thoughtful gesture, but one that got Conor out of his way. Being in the cockpit actually soothed his nerves. He didn't have any of the ginger pills that Emily usually carried to help quell his stomach acids, which churned whenever he was airborne.

Beans wasn't too talkative on the trip. After an initial "Who the damn hell are you," his first words to Conor through the headset didn't occur until they were twenty minutes out from Cape Serrat. "So you gonna tell me what's so damn important that we have to taxi your butt to this godforsaken place?"

"No can do, Lieutenant. Wish I could, but if it's worth anything, I hate being in the dark too."

"Nope, that's not worth much."

Conor laughed at Beans's level of directness. Glib people weren't his favorites. "So, Beans, tell me how experienced you are with getting this bird on the beach, then off it. That has to be a little tricky, right?"

"If the tidal dope we got back at Maison Blanche is accurate, we shouldn't have any issues," Beans said, easing back on the PBY's throttles. "Surf will be a bit high and somewhat rough. But we've seen worse."

Just as Beans finished with the throttle adjustment, Conor heard it. He slipped the right can of his headset off his ear and listened. Beans started to elaborate, but Conor held out his left arm to quiet him. Five seconds of listening calmed him.

"What?" Beans asked.

"Sorry, thought I heard a few misfires...pistons misfiring. But I guess not. Sorry."

"No problem. But it's what we have a flight engineer for. And he's pretty good."

"Right. Got it." Conor looked at his watch. "Should land in about five, right?"

"About that." Beans grabbed his throat mic. "Eugene, dig out a spare roll of toilet paper. Not the army-issue stuff. Give me the soft roll we got from my navy buddy."

"You got it, Lieutenant. You feeling okay?" Eugene DiLazzaro asked.

"Yeah, yeah, just thinking ahead."

Beans was right; there were no surprises on landing. He carefully pulled back on the throttles so as to let the ship softly make landfall nose first. Surf was calm. The beach absent of any obstacles save for the rusting hulk of a small coastal steamer. Conor spied a lone man, an Arab given his clothing, pulling in a fishing net fifty yards east of the PBY. About the same distance from the PBY in the opposite direction was a single-masted sailboat resting on its starboard side. The scarred port-side hull didn't look like it had met a paintbrush since the twenties.

The two Pratt & Whitney engines spun down, and the crew piled out of the PBY. Conor fought through a dizzy spell as he slid through the starboard side cupola. Four men, all with beaming smiles plastered on their faces and Lee-Enfield rifles slung over their shoulders, emerged from a rise seventy-five yards from the water's edge. They trotted down a narrow sandy path carved into the rise that was covered with a low-growing green scrub. Conor could tell that none of the men were Carleton Coon.

"I'm going to head up to the lighthouse and take care of some business. I'll make it as quick as I can." Conor grabbed his musette bag. "And, Beans, I have no way of knowing for sure, but I may have a guest to take back with us."

"Suit yourself. I'll be here with my crew making sure that they don't drop any supplies into the drink."

Conor made his way past the crew as they began to loosen the tie-downs that kept the cargo in place during flight, then slipped through the port-side cupola and splashed down into a two-foot-deep swirling, foamy surf. The four men, with at least two weeks of beard growth and without the benefit of a bath as far as Conor could tell, were chatting among themselves, all four Brits. "Hi, gents, I'm looking for Carleton Coon. Any chance he's hanging around somewhere?"

All the men seemed to groan in unison. "You mean Crazy Coon?" the youngest-looking one said, prompting a slap on his back from the one who looked the oldest.

"Who are you?" the old Brit said.

"Just checking in with him. Can't share much more than that."

"He's up at the lighthouse."

"Making mule turd bombs," the younger one chimed in, causing a ripple of laughter even from the older one in the bunch.

"Well, that's something I have to see," Conor said as he sloshed his way out of the surf toward the path.

It took Conor a solid five minutes to reach the crest of the rise. When he did, a bit winded from treading in the soft sand, he took in the sight of a two-hundred-foot-tall circular lighthouse, its white paint faded and flaking. There was an equally faded red stripe, about four feet wide, that encircled the structure halfway up. The plot also included a large metal building with wide double doors that looked like it could accommodate large trucks.

Another structure, a shed with an adjoining corral, held two donkeys and three mules. Two of the mules were having a contest as to which one could bray the loudest. What caught and held Conor's attention the longest was a one-and-a-half-ton Chevy truck, *late thirties*, he thought, sitting in a far corner of the expansive yard. All the tires were flat. The wood stakes that formed the sides of the truck's bed were smoldering. Fire had already consumed the canvas canopy. The driver's side door was ajar, hanging on one of its two hinges.

"Who the bleedin' hell are you?"

The mules' braying contest masked the sound of someone coming up behind him. He turned and stared at a bushy-haired, mustachioed man with intense eyes, dressed in a scruffy British captain's uniform. Coon. He was gnawing on a short dark-colored stick. He noticed Conor staring at it.

"It's just a miswak." Coon pulled the miswak from his mouth and held it like it was a Lucky Strike. "I forgot to pack my toothbrush." *A bit rushed leaving Algiers*, Conor thought. "The locals have been using these twigs to clean teeth for seven thousand years." Coon eyeballed Conor up, then down, studying him like he was an anthropological specimen. "What's in the pack? Anything I need to be worried about?"

"Not unless you're bothered by extra drawers and a couple pair of socks. Oh, I didn't forget *my* toothbrush." Conor made a mental note to get to the bottom of why Coon was dressed as a captain in the British Army. "Who the bleedin' hell am I? You were born in Massachusetts. But you sound like a foulmouthed Englishman."

"Hanging around these guys will do that to you. I still didn't get your name...Yank."

"Conor Thorn. I used to work with Colonel Eddy. I think you also know Chester Booth. We worked together...for a time."

"Yeah...Thorn. I heard that Chester the molester wasn't a fan of yours." Coon reinserted the miswak and proceeded to scrape his front teeth. "That...?" Conor couldn't make out his last word or words, given the scraping action.

"If you're asking if that's true, I'd have to say…yeah. But, it's pretty mutual." Conor and Booth never got along. He was too cautious. Conor was too unpredictable. He called Conor a "reckless cowboy." Oil and water. "Chester was a little too…sedate for me. A marriage not meant to be."

That brought a smile to Coon's face. He pulled out the miswak and pointed it at Conor. "Sedate. Ha. Chester pissed his pants too often to be an effective agent. So we're on the same page there, I guess."

Conor waved at the smoldering Chevy. "You saw some action, it seems."

Coon shrugged a shoulder. "Yeah, the Chev hit a land mine the Italians laid on the approach road. Used the mules to tow it here. Used it for a little demolition training. Trying to keep my new mates from killing each other over the boredom. The Italians are land-mine crazy. They lay them at night. Then the locals find them and mark them with sticks so their kids and goats don't trip them." Coon nodded at the lighthouse. "Let's go have a seat and maybe you'll tell me what the bleedin' hell you want."

Once inside the lighthouse, they headed up a steep stairway along the chalky interior wall, passed a spacious circular room that was set up as a barracks, and, after climbing up one more set of stairs, entered a smaller room furnished like a classroom. Three windows the size of Conor's head restricted the amount of sunlight in the dimly lit room. The air was stuffy and tainted with a mix of sour scents, as if it had been taken in and exhaled many times. There were three narrow tables about six feet long and a myriad of chairs spread haphazardly about. Conor noted a chalkboard with roughly drawn diagrams that, after a quick glance, he couldn't make sense of except a sketch that looked like a pile of dung.

They each pulled a chair up to one table. Conor noticed that a *Trevor* had carved a smart-assed greeting on the surface. Something that featured the word *cock*, which prompted a fleeting thought about Major Stewart telling him he was looking for someone with cock issues.

"Need any coffee?"

"No. Not right now," Conor said, wanting to move things along.

"Good. Because it's god-awful. Save your gut the damage it would wreak. So, what do you want, Conor Thorn?"

Conor jumped to it and laid out a fairly complete picture to Coon, who hadn't heard about Eisenhower's claim that he would resign if the SOE or the OSS were involved in the assassination of Darlan. He wasn't surprised to hear that Ike also threatened to boot both the OSS and SOE out of North Africa if that happened.

"Admiral fucking Darlan," Coon said before sucking in a deep breath and blowing it through puffed-out cheeks. He ran a hand through his thick unkempt hair. "You couldn't trust the guy. No one knew each morning when he rolled out of bed which way he was leaning or whose pocket his hand was in."

"So, safe to say, you don't miss the admiral?"

Coon squinted at Conor and gave him a long stare. "So, safe to say, you're here to see if I had anything to do with the assassination?"

"Safe to say, yes."

"You said you used to work with Bill Eddy. You must have some pull if you got on that PBY. Just who do you work for?"

"General Eisenhower." Conor was fine with the slight inaccuracy. He had no proof the general knew he and Emily were dealing with his aide. Aides kept things from their superiors all the time. And threw their names around to get things done. If he had to lay money down...well, he wouldn't.

"Donovan talk to you about me?"

Conor was interested in why Coon asked that question. He didn't have a quick answer, so he played dumb and gave Coon a razor-thin smile.

Coon bit. "So, he probably told you about the proposal I made to him."

"I've heard about it." Conor felt his face heat up as he fidgeted in his chair.

"The concept of wet work...you know the term, right?"

"Sure," Conor said, drawing the word out. "Operations that, umm, draw blood. As in assassinations."

Coon's eyes lit up and he leaned into the table. "In the paper I gave to Donovan, I stated that the world was becoming a much smaller place. Governments and big businesses are becoming so closely intertwined that one rotten apple, say a fascist dictator of one major country, can spoil the whole bunch. For example"—Coon sat with a rigid spine, glancing about the room as if he were back at Harvard giving a lecture to some pimply faced anthropology students—"if there was an elite corps of assassins in 1933, trained to recognize the potential danger of political movements, they would have come to the conclusion that Hitler and his goons represented a deep political danger to the rest of the world. And… taken the necessary action by…" A beat. "Spilling their blood." Another beat, a trace longer. "Performing wet work."

When Conor considered the news about atrocities perpetrated on Europe's Jews, the highjacking of neighboring governments and annexing of their land at the point of a Mauser, he realized he wouldn't need any high-level arm-twisting to get him to join such an outfit. But there was something about the look in Coon's eyes, coupled with the sights and feel of the lighthouse base operation, that made him feel that special ops in the North African theater were like the Wild West. "A tool of statecraft," Conor said.

"Precisely." Coon beamed like he had just broken through to a struggling student. Coon pushed away from the table and stood. "We need to play dirty, Thorn. No more gentlemanly tit for tat. I've been a big proponent for hostage taking. Take someone of value, ask for something of value for their return. But…" Coon's voice trailed off. He went to the blackboard and picked up a piece of chalk, then turned back to Conor. "Our cousins in the SOE have no mixed feelings about these types of things. Their national interest is always top of mind." Conor didn't doubt the truth behind that statement. "They, according to Brooks Richards, the chap who heads up the operation here, feared that Darlan would set up a fascist regime in North Africa over time. And that would mean danger to the Allies' overall strategy."

"Sounds like you're implying that they were knee-deep in the… wet work."

"I can see where you could come to that conclusion." Coon turned back to the blackboard and drew a foot-high letter *N*. "I'm just rambling a bit. There was a point during the training we were doing at Aïn Taya that the Brits became cautious and… suspicious. They smelled something that I didn't. If you off the little admiral, the French might kick up a dust storm. The SOE quietly pulled back when they got a strong sense that the corps francs were getting involved in dangerous politics, as opposed to the single-minded idea of killing Nazis."

"So that leaves you or, more accurately, the OSS. Were you involved in the Darlan wet work?"

Coon turned back to the blackboard and drew the letter *O*, firmly adding the period, snapping the chalk in half. "NO." Coon tossed the remaining piece of chalk into the gutter below the chalkboard. "But the more precise answer is…tangentially."

"Meaning you were in on the planning?"

"Now that's a firm *no*. Gubbins and I—he's an SOE chap. We trained some wet-behind-the-ears French boys in the corps francs—weapons training, bomb making, that sort of thing."

"You said the SOE pulled back when they got nervous about French politics. But you stayed?"

"Yes, I did," Coon said in a sheepish manner as he retook his seat at the table.

Conor leaned forward and rested his elbows on his knees. "What can you tell me about an archive or a batch of documents the people involved compiled? Ever hear anything about that?"

Coon showed no hint of surprise at the question. Like he had been waiting for it all along. "First I'm hearing about that. But listen, Thorn. I made it clear to Bill Donovan that me and Gubbins didn't know any of those people were involved in the assassination in any way." Coon ran his index finger back and forth over his graying mustache. "That's the most important thing to take back to Ike." Coon cracked his neck, first one way, then the other. "Don't you think?"

Conor rose and gave Coon a stony look. *Someone should write a book about this guy.* "I think—"

Before Conor could say Coon was right, the sound of an explosion made both men jump.

By the time they sprinted down to the beach, Eugene, Beans Turley, and two other members of the PBY crew were hauling the lifeless body of the flight engineer out from a section of scrub bush. A few feet behind them, a fourth member, who was dry heaving, carried the flight engineer's severed right leg. It was dripping blood over his boots. The young boy, no more than nineteen years old, stopped and vomited in the sand.

"He said he had to go real bad," Beans said, his voice faltering as he tried to tamp down the shock. "I had just taken a dump. I told him exactly where to go and to follow my footsteps. But…" Beans took a gulp of air. Conor, Coon, the four Brits, and the PBY crew just stood there, eyes glued on Beans's buddy, Pork. "End… of…story."

"If you're done unloading, you better get out of here," Coon said, running his hand through his hair. "The Italians will snoop around, wondering what they caught in their net." As if they were waiting for their cue, small arms gunfire erupted from a grove of cork trees on the starboard hillside.

Pfft. Pfft. Pfft. Rounds drilled into the ground a handful of yards from the area around the PBY. *Pfft. Pfft.*

The four Brits dove into the sand and returned fire into the low scrub oak and cork trees. Turley yelled at his crew to board. Conor pulled his Colt from his shoulder holster as Coon mimicked his action, unseating a long-barreled Colt Woodsman. The blueish steel glinted in the sunlight.

Pfft. Pfft.

"See ya, Thorn. We'll hold these buggers off. You better—"

"I'm sure you could use some help from those twin .30s in the nose turret." Conor turned to Turley. "Right, Beans?"

Without answering, Turley turned to Eugene, who was slipping over the edge of the starboard cupola. "DiLazzaro, you man the .30s, and, Lakin, take the starboard .50 and give these guys cover." Turley nodded at Conor and boarded, just behind Eugene. Conor and Coon took up positions flanking the four Brits on the beach twenty yards from the nose of the PBY. Before they could scoop out enough sand to partially screen themselves, Eugene's M1919 .30s opened up, spitting fire at the muzzle flashes coming from the groves of scrub oak. The starboard .50 joined in, raking the tree grove.

Conor spotted movement in the row of cork trees twenty yards from the front edge of the hillside's vegetation and fired a few rounds. A camouflaged Italian, with sprigs of cork tree branches sprouting from his helmet, dropped into the undergrowth. He zeroed in on another cork tree and fired another string of rounds.

When his Colt ran dry, he swore as he reloaded. He released another full magazine into the base of the line of cork trees. The sound of his last shot was drowned out by the sound of the Pratt

& Whitneys as they stuttered, coughed, then caught, sending up a cloud of thick exhaust into the air. The PBY's guns ceased firing. Lakin screamed at him to board. The gunfire from the hillside had diminished to single shots separated by elongated pauses. Conor rose into a crouch and sand crabbed over to Coon, who was reloading another magazine into his Woodsman.

"You should ask for some Brownings next time you send in a shopping list," Conor yelled over the sound of the PBY's engines.

"Ha, I'd really like a couple of M4 Shermans." Conor slapped Coon on the back and hightailed it to the PBY. He joined Eugene and two other crew members in pushing the PBY off the soft bed of sand, almost slipping into the surf when another wave of dizziness hit him. After mounting the short ladder up to the cupola, he turned and took in the view of the beach. Coon and his Brit friends were getting to their feet. Conor waved. Coon responded with a shit-eating grin and a sloppy salute.

CHAPTER NINETEEN

0930 Hours, Wednesday, January 6, 1943
Barberousse Prison, Algiers

"Jailer, take this woman away. Immediately!" With a wrist flip, the metal plate of food spun toward the Judas window and clanged against the frame before dropping to the floor. A thin oily, soupy stock dripped down Emily's face. She took one step away from the cell door and wiped the cold gruel-like meal from her eyes with her index fingers. Captain Simmons handed her a handkerchief.

"Hey, buster. Calm the hell down." Simmons turned to the jailer, a droopy-eyed bearded fellow who leaned against the wall across from Henri d'Astier de la Vigerie's cell. "Tell this felon to drop the tough-guy act." The jailer responded with an apathetic gesture, arms slightly outstretched and palms skyward. "Do something!" Simmons shouted. Which apparently was the signal the jailer took to fold his arms and close his flaccid eyes.

"It's all right, Captain. I wouldn't be—"

"You damn British, you have the audacity to insinuate that I and my compatriots had anything to do with the killing of Admiral Darlan." D'Astier's flushed face filled the Judas window. He appeared to be tall, given his stoop to level his face with the window. His dark eyes flashed with anger.

"Then why are you on that side of the door and I'm out here? Someone must think there's enough evidence to have you and your friend Cordier locked up," Emily said as she finished mopping the gruel from her face, thinking how lucky she was the jail didn't provide hot food to their prisoners.

"We had nothing to do with this…this murder. You and your British and American friends know this. Murphy knows this." Behind her, Emily heard some other prisoner pound on their door and start shouting something about sleep. She darted a look to her right and watched the jailer approach a door across the hallway and one down from d'Astier's cell. Simmons followed the jailer. "You and your people are such blatant hypocrites. Your Churchill and his military leaders have wanted Darlan out of the way for months. Just so your anointed choice for the leader of the Free French, de Gaulle, could mount the throne."

"Interesting comment coming from someone who wanted a traditional monarchy led by the Comte de Paris to ascend to the leadership of France." As a part of Butcher's briefing, Emily and Conor learned that d'Astier, before the war, had been a member of *La Cagoule*, the Cowl. A group that employed violence to bring down France's leftist Popular Front government. Besides being widely known as a devout Catholic, he was also acknowledged by American officials like Robert Murphy, President Roosevelt's personal representative to French North Africa, as a consummate conspirator.

D'Astier organized teams of Vichy resistors to stage a coup in the city of Algiers as D-Day of Operation Torch arrived. His groups, comprising many young men from the Corps francs d'Afrique—including the assassin Fernand Bonnier de la Chapelle—seized the telephone exchange, radio station, the governor's house, and arrested Admiral Darlan and General Alphonse Juin, the commander of all Vichy troops in North Africa. Emily had no trouble understanding why d'Astier was livid about his arrest. Betrayal always left a sour taste.

Emily's mention of d'Astier's background as a monarchist seemed to siphon off some of his red-hot anger. He pushed off the cell door and started pacing in a tight circle, his head hanging low. "There's talk that the people responsible had a dossier or archive that contained important papers…maybe plans with names and dates."

D'Astier stopped pacing and his head snapped up. "Who told

you of such nonsense?" He turned toward Emily and, two quick steps later, was at the door again, hands wrapped tightly on the sill of the Judas window. "Why would plotters, whoever they are, keep such documents? What a foolish thing to do. It's…it's almost laughable."

"You and your men who took over key facilities when the Allies invaded North Africa…didn't you keep records? Names, dates, assignments?"

D'Astier stood erect. Emily could only see the lower half of his face as he stroked his chin. "Yes, of course. We considered ourselves an army. We had to be organized." He stooped down again. The angry redness in his face had vanished.

"The plotters who assassinated Darlan also had to be organized. Trained. Instilled with discipline," Emily said.

D'Astier's forehead lay on his left arm, which rested across the top of the window, his eyes unfocused. "I assume, since they were successful, that would be true," he said with little trace of conviction.

"So it's not so…laughable."

D'Astier's eyes snapped into focus. "I have nothing else to say to you. Your people, and the Americans, betrayed me and those who made it possible to capture Algiers with little to no bloodshed. Something else that is not so laughable."

Emily called the jailer over to her and asked to see Abbé Cordier, the friend and confessor of d'Astier.

"No, no, no."

In French, Emily asked why. The jailer, about to close the Judas window to d'Astier's cell, turned to Emily and muttered that Cordier was being questioned by the police. As the Judas window slid shut, Emily caught a glimpse of d'Astier's ashen face.

As the jailer led Emily and Simmons out, she asked Simmons what the commotion across the hall was about.

He poked his thumb toward the jailer. "He said it was another person rounded up after the assassination. A bigwig French businessman. The guy was asking about his son, who was also arrested."

Emily asked the jailer the identity of the prisoner across the hall. He looked over his shoulder and gave the international sign for remuneration, a rubbing of the index finger and thumb. "My son...his tenth birthday has arrived. I can't disappoint him."

Emily looked at Simmons.

"Really? This is part of greasing the skids?"

"A perfect example."

Simmons peeled off an American five-dollar bill, the currency in great demand since the invasion, and stuffed it in the awaiting jailer's palm.

The jailer mentioned the name Charles Brunel in unrefined French and repeated what Simmons had already mentioned. He said his son was *chanceux*. Lucky.

"*Pourquoi si chanceux?*" Why so lucky? Emily watched the jailer fold the bill into a tiny square and shove it deep into his front pocket.

"*Il a* été *libéré.*" He has been freed.

CHAPTER TWENTY

0930 Hours, Wednesday, January 6, 1943
Café Coq Hardi, La Vigerie, Algiers

Antoine Brunel held the soup spoon near his lips, careful not to spill one drop of its contents, to take in another sniff of the sweet and fragrant onion soup. With closed eyes, he savored the last spoonful as it slipped down his throat. The clatter of his spoon in the soup plate caused the customers at nearby tables to cease conversing and shoot displeased looks his way.

He sat there waiting for the waiter to bring his next course, chicken confit with a side order of *frites*, which drew a protest from the waiter because it was only offered for dinner. The waiter had marched back to the kitchen, nose high in the air, after Brunel threatened to complain to the manager. He pulled a Gitanes from a nearly empty pack, lit it, and silently bemoaned the thought of his father having to suffer through another tasteless and foul-smelling plate of muck that was classified as food at the prison.

The thought of his father's early refusals to even touch the offerings made him think about the years that his father taunted him for being an overweight child. *Grassouillet.* Plump cheeks. That was what his father would call him. In front of his friends and his father's friends. In front of anyone. Even his mother began to use the term. But her tone was softer, loving even. After calling him *grassouillet*, she would follow up with kisses on his cheeks and end with a peck on his nose. The warm hug that would always follow went a long way toward lessening his low self-esteem. When he turned thirteen, a growing fascination with cycling turned a chubby adolescent into a slim sinewy teen. He consumed copious amounts of fruits, vegetables, meats, milk, and cheese, but his persistent approach to his new undertaking turned the massive number of calories into muscle. But the name stuck, which confused new acquaintances. A confusion that he occasionally would clear up, if he took a liking to the person, especially a girl. But it was the change in his father's appraisal of him that he was most proud of. His father took great interest in all his physical exploits, which filled Antoine with a powerful pride.

Brunel snuffed out his Gitanes when the chicken confit arrived, and he admonished, a little too loudly, the waiter for not bringing the *frites*. When the waiter finally fetched them, he also brought a peace offering: two glasses of champagne.

"My apologies, sir. Please accept this fine wine as recompense for you and...your guest." He stepped aside, and like a bullfighter in the ring, a slight turn of his body followed by a flourish of his arm revealed a man of short stature.

"Alain. You're late. I was hungry, so I ordered," Brunel said, his gaze settling on the plate now before him.

"I have no appetite, monsieur." Alain Chrétien took a seat with his back to the door and conveyed his indifference by smiling politely and placing his ruby-red fez on the table directly in front of him. Next to the fez, Alain placed a folded newspaper. Brunel glanced at the newspaper, then at Alain. Brunel tipped his chin toward the newspaper and received a quick nod of recognition. He forked a mouthful of *frites* as he watched Alain take in the café's clientele.

Brunel recognized some of the businessmen at the surrounding tables. Some who had, prior to the Allied invasion, told him and his father that they would be honored to do business with them, mentioning that their connections to the Vichy government and to key business figures in Nazi Germany would set them apart from their competition. Brunel was quite sure they mentioned their long-standing Allied connections to their gullible prospective customers.

A young worker clearing tables in the front of the café dropped a tray of dirty dishes, startling the seated patrons, who turned to take in the scene. Antoine seized the opportunity to take an envelope with French francs from his breast pocket and slip it under the newspaper. When Alain turned back, Brunel tapped the newspaper with his knife. Alain nodded again, this time with a more pronounced effort.

As the buzz in the café returned to normal, Alain, slouched and looking drained, pushed his glass of champagne aside. There were beads of sweat, three orderly rows, forming on the surface of his brow. "Is it safe to talk here?"

"As long as you don't shout," Brunel said. Alain didn't catch humor in his reply. Over Alain's shoulder, Brunel eyed a battered Citroën skid to a stop just outside the café's entrance. He couldn't make out the driver because of the passenger who was hanging precariously out of the window, both hands operating a camera with an impressively sized lens. It was clearly snapping away at the occupants of the café. Brunel slid his face slightly to his left, hoping the head of his guest, Alain, blocked the camera's view in time. The barrage of blaring horns that erupted moments after the Citroën stopped increased until the coupe finally pulled away from the curb, the passenger still hanging halfway out the window.

"Tonight, take me to the basilica."

A despondent look washed over Alain's face. "Can we talk of my son and what you can do?"

"No. First, we speak about my business."

A pause as Alain's expression signaled his disappointment.

"You know where it is hidden, correct?"

"Yes." Alain's response was almost lost among the babel of voices in the café.

"Just you and me. Do not bring your wife. Understand?"

"She was arrested. Taken last night."

"By whom?"

"Captain Roget." Alain swiped his forehead, then wiped his hand on his chest, leaving a smear of sweat on his tattered beige coat. "They won't let me see her."

Brunel lowered an empty fork and studied Alain. A sheen of sweat began to reform on his forehead. "What do they want?" Then it hit him. "They know about the archive?"

"I am sure they do. They know everything. From their spies," Alain said, making the motion of spitting on the floor.

Brunel spotted three uniformed police officers entering the café. They took over a vacant table just inside the entrance. One officer facing Brunel made no effort to mask his interest in Brunel and his guest. The two other officers chatted and lit up cigarettes. Two tables closest to them emptied, making plain to all those who watched that they held no warm feelings toward the policemen. The waiter approached their table with two ashtrays. One officer held up four fingers and said something inaudible, which sent the waiter away.

Another table emptied and the patrons headed for the front door. Before they could exit, they hurriedly stepped aside to make way for another police officer, this one higher ranking given his uniform's insignia. He had an athletic build, wide shoulders, and sported a neatly trimmed mustache. He shouted, "Écartez-vous." Step aside. He held a woman, a careworn and desiccated woman, with a slight widow's hump, tight by the upper arm. The officer and his captive headed straight to Brunel's table. Alain noticed Brunel staring at the front of the café and turned toward the commotion.

"*Liliane*!"

"Who is he?"

"Roget. He—" The words perished on Alain's tongue when Roget and Alain's wife arrived at the table.

"Alain…Alain," she said, her voice brittle and raspy, as if it hadn't tasted water in days. "Michel…have you found him?"

Alain hushed his wife and turned to face Roget directly.

"He's dead." Roget yanked the woman's arm toward a chair, and she hit the seat with the sound of a sack of laundry hitting the floor. "We caught him performing subversive acts." Roget's hand disappeared inside his tunic, and he pulled out a note card, dropping it onto the table. He glared at Alain. "You can claim the body at that address. If you do not do so within the next two hours, the government will bury it in an unmarked grave outside of the city's limits."

Alain's face, drained of its color, lost what little tautness it possessed, while his wife's posture seemed to surrender to gravity. She hung her head, chin on her chest, whimpering.

Roget shifted his gaze to Brunel. "And who are you?"

Antoine thought about not responding, then considered delivering a false name. Truth won out. "Antoine. Antoine Brunel."

"Aah, Brunel's son." Roget stroked his mustache with the side of his index finger. "When were you released?"

"Just this morning." Alain grabbed his wife's hand and stroked it. The only effect was to raise the sound of her sobbing.

"What are you still doing in Algiers?"

"Waiting for my father to be released."

Roget smirked. "You may be waiting a long time. Quite possibly until the war has ended. The Americans think your father works for the Nazis." Roget leaned down and tapped the note he dropped earlier on the table. "Two hours." He lurched to his left and strutted to the table with the three other policemen, where a cup of coffee awaited him.

The waiter returned to Brunel's table. No one spoke, each processing news none of them wanted to hear. "Will there be anything else more—"

The air-splitting sound of a motorcycle engine filled the café, swallowing the waiter's last words. The motorcycle, both driver and passenger wearing head scarves, screeched to a stop in front of the café. They pointed long-barreled handguns at the café's interior. Multiple shots rang out. Brunel glimpsed the waiter returning fire from the rear corner of the café.

Screaming patrons dove to the floor, some colliding with one another. Tables toppled, followed by the sound of smashing glass. Brunel grabbed Liliane's arm and yanked her to the floor. He fell on top of her and heard her grunt. At the sound of the motorcycle speeding off, Brunel raised his head and surveyed the room.

Thick-throated moans replaced the patron's screams. Then a stillness came over the scene. The tables that weren't overturned held toppled glassware and half-eaten pastries. One patron was slumped over, his head resting in a pool of dark liquid. The table that hosted the four police officers had tumbled over. He saw three officers draped in their chairs like puppets that had finished their show. Roget emerged from under the table; he looked dazed as his head moved on a swivel, taking in the carnage.

Brunel rose to a crouch. Alain was still seated in his chair—a bullet hole in the back of his head and much of his face blown away by the exiting bullet.

Brunel stood, swiped the newspaper from the table, pulled Liliane off the floor, and dragged, then carried the woman out of the café through the kitchen. He needed to get out of Algiers before the hell that was the police rained down on the city.

#

0930 Hours, Wednesday, January 6, 1943
Ria Bar, 2nd Arrondissement, Lyon

Major Kurt Eklof, the son of two devoted Catholics, loathed the priest sitting next to him. While he had no time for the medieval machinations the Vatican used to control the minds of their followers, it turned his stomach that a *man of God* possessed mistresses and hoarded currency, precious jewels, and priceless artwork according to the information the Gestapo had gleaned from their plants who worked for the Abwehr in Paris. Abbé Robert Alves fidgeted in his seat in the back of the Citroën like a man plagued by irksome insects.

"*Sich beruhigen.*"

"Calm down?" Alves sputtered.

"He just wants to talk to you."

"Why won't you tell me what he wants?"

"Because he didn't tell me." A lie. Eklof knew why his superior, Klaus Barbie, wanted to see the scheming man of God—to turn him against his employer. To co-op his services. It would come down to money. It always came down to money with these types of people. Men of the cloth were, after all, men.

They weren't like him. Service to a victorious Reich was recompense enough. That and a cushy position in the postwar Third Reich. As long as there were no more failures attributed to him. The escape of Conor Thorn and Bright after they destroyed intelligence that the traitor Gunnar Lind planned to sell to Lina Stuben, his incompetent SD superior, was a blot on his record. A record that, up to that point, was spotless and quite impressive—his ten kills as a Luftwaffe pilot in the North African campaign qualified him as an ace. The award of the War Order of the German Cross was an achievement that few men of the Reich could claim. The pride he experienced receiving the award was doused by losing an eye at the hand of a hysterical prostitute during a British attack on his air base in Libya. It was the darkest day of his life. One he had fruitlessly tried to forget.

"Where are you taking me?"

"The Ria Bar." Eklof gave the priest a sideways glance, looking for any sign that he knew of the name. It was a favorite haunt of the Gestapo, owned by a former madam who made a killing off Wehrmacht and Gestapo officers just after the occupation of Vichy France. Seeing no sign, Eklof slumped in his seat and habitually repositioned his leather eye patch as they sped down the rue Auguste Comte.

As they approached the intersection of rue Sainte-Hélène, the driver pulled onto the sidewalk bordering the dormant patio of the Ria Bar. Tables and chairs stacked and stored along the front wall blocked a full view of the street from the inside. The driver opened the rear door, and Eklof and Alves slid out and took a moment on the sidewalk. Eklof smoothed the front of his uniform tunic and reset his service cap, while Alves squinted through the sunlight up and down the rue Auguste Comte. Hatless, Alves tamed his hair, which swirled in the light breeze blowing southward down the narrow street.

Eklof snapped off orders to the driver to man the front door and not let anyone inside. Eklof entered first, Alves at his heels. A woman, heavily made up and smoking a cigarette in an ivory holder, leaned at the far end of a six-seat mahogany bar that ran along a brick wall. Shelves stacked with glasses and bottles ran the length of the wall. A wrought-iron staircase positioned in the corner ran up to the next floor, where Eklof knew the owner's office shared the floor with her apartment. There were two patrons, a middle-aged man and a much younger woman, seated at a table next to a staircase that led to a low-ceilinged loft overlooking the front room. They stared broodingly at Eklof as their cigarettes billowed smoke up toward the loft.

"Pay your bill and leave," Eklof said in what he thought was a bridled tone. When the couple didn't move, he unbridled it. "*Tout de suite!*" Now!

The couple hastily withdrew after slapping some coins on the bar, drawing a withering look from the woman leaning on the bar.

"I will have no business if you persist in scaring away my customers, Major Eklof." The woman's voice was low and harsh, as if it was fighting its way through years of cigarette tar. "He's in the back room. Alone. Waiting for you and your special guest."

Eklof removed his service cap and directed a half nod in her direction. "My thanks, madam."

The door to the back room was somewhat ajar, emitting a dim light. Eklof pushed through and stood aside as the priest followed him in. The room held eight tables spread out along the walls, which were covered with heavy brocaded curtains. An additional four tables took up the center of the room. The heavy scent surrounded them—cigarette smoke mixed with a mustiness that seemed to radiate from the curtains. At a middle table along the back wall sat an SD officer in a steel-gray-and-green uniform, Hauptsturmführer Klaus Barbie. His pinched face sported two-day stubble; his cobalt-blue eyes provided a beacon as Eklof and Alves traversed the dimly lit room.

"Aah, finally, the man of the cloth," Barbie said in faux relief. The fingers of his right hand took the form of a pistol, and he aimed at a chair on the opposite side of the table. "Sit." The command was unmistakably hostile. Alves took the seat, not once unlocking his gaze from Barbie. Eklof took up a position behind and to the left of Alves. "I have known a few Alsatians in my time. None of them impressed me. In fact, they all seemed to be untrustworthy." Alsace-Lorraine was a prize that exchanged hands several times in the past between Prussia and France, then Germany and France as recently as 1940.

Barbie waited for a reply to his baited appraisal. When Alves wouldn't bite, he threw another line. "Do you consider yourself French or German?"

"I am a naturalized German citizen, by decree of the German government. Which I am sure you already knew."

Eklof noted the corners of Barbie's mouth curled faintly. Barbie did know. "Yes, of course. I also am aware that you, a priest, have not one mistress...but two." Barbie shook his head slowly and shamefully. "As a child growing up in a Catholic household, I once had thoughts of joining the priesthood. That you dare to indulge in romantic relations galls me. Yet it also indicates that you are someone to be wary of. Someone who pursues whatever he wants, God be damned." When Alves shifted in his chair, Barbie waited for the man to settle. "Strasbourg. I never liked it. I found it to be dirty and its people unpleasant. Wouldn't you agree?"

"I have never been there." A pause. "It is wartime. Most cities are dirty. Authorities have conscripted all the men." Another pause, longer this time. "What is it you want from me? Some form of absolution?"

Barbie roared with laughter, something Eklof hadn't witnessed before. Barbie stole a glance at Eklof, who chuckled weakly. "Absolution. That, my priestly friend, is something that *you* should be in steady search of...before it is too late. No, no. Here's what I want. And what you will give me." Barbie leaned against the table, spread his arms out wide, and settled his hands on the surface, fingers spread like the talons of an eagle.

Barbie, with an economical number of words, laid out his demands to a flustered Alves: whatever information he uncovered in his skulking about Lyon concerning the Resistance's activities, membership, structure, and whereabouts must be provided to Barbie first. Barbie added a demand for news of hidden Jews and those who assisted them. "The Abwehr cares little about the Jewish problem. A weakness exhibited from the top down," Barbie said, a hint of contempt in his tenor. He added that one week later, Alves could then pass along the intelligence, with some key exclusions, to his Abwehr handlers. But payments received by Alves from the Abwehr must be split between Alves and Barbie. This bit of personal gain from the priest's activities surprised Eklof, who was even more caught off guard that Barbie mentioned it in front of him.

Alves, during Barbie's discourse, bunched up his cassock in each hand, freed the soft black material, then began the process again as he glared at Barbie. "Now, as an illustration of your understanding, tell me something the Abwehr does not know. Nothing trivial, mind you. Something...of a high grade."

Alves slumped forward; his head bowed slightly. Eklof saw a bead of sweat trickle down the priest's left cheek. "I have been made privy to something about a woman. She is well connected. She is not French." Barbie's eyes narrowed, zeroed in on Eklof, then moved back to Alves, who seemed to register Barbie's disappointment. Alves sat up straighter and cleared his thick throat. "She is helping Jews make their way to Spain and Switzerland. She has someone…I don't yet know whom…who produces false papers."

"Aah. That is not very…specific. Way too vague to satisfy me. You need to do better."

"I need time." Alves paused. "I have some sources."

"Then I suggest you get a move on. You will find that I am not a patient man. Quite the opposite, wouldn't you say, Eklof?"

CHAPTER TWENTY-ONE

1500 Hours, Wednesday, January 6, 1943
Hôtel Saint-George, rue Michelet, Algiers

Emily caught a whiff of the coffee before she saw Staff Sergeant Billings show up with the pot and two mugs. She had been waiting for Commander Butcher for five minutes out on the pool deck when Billings arrived. Before he could place the coffeepot and mugs on the glass table, Butcher appeared behind him.

As Butcher, dressed in his naval khaki service dress uniform, stepped around Billings and pulled out a chair, Emily saw a familiar look. It was a look that she had seen while working in the underground war rooms back in London—the look that said someone had some top-flight gossip.

"Thorn's upstairs in his room," Billings said. "Seems to have a bit of a sour stomach. Said he wanted to puke in private." Butcher sent a stony glare Billings's way. "Apologies, miss. He's under the weather. Said he'd be down soon."

"Thanks, Sergeant. Get him out here as soon as he comes down. And find out where Simmons has escaped to. I want him back here. And find a bottle of Jameson. Two glasses. But don't make a show of it."

"Yes, sir." Billings cracked a smile and turned to leave but broke step and turned back. "Commander, you know Simmons isn't too happy with his assignment. He might try to go around you."

Butcher looked at Emily—cocked an eyebrow as if to say *excuse the boy.* "Thanks for the heads-up, Sergeant." Billings gave a *got it* nod and took his leave. "That young man is always looking out for me."

"From what I hear, sergeants will win the war for the Allies, Commander."

"Well, someone has to."

Emily wondered why the call for Irish whiskey and waited for the reason to reveal itself, even though, at that moment, she'd have preferred a brimming cup of hot coffee. "Emily, General Eisenhower received word this morning from London. Startling news. It came through British Naval Intelligence. Someone by the name of Lieutenant Ian Fleming." Butcher poured two mugs of coffee and slid one across to Emily, who ignored the offering, her anticipation trumping her coffee desires. "Your brother...he's alive."

Richard. Alive?

Emily had to break eye contact with Butcher and repeat in her head what he just told her. A horrible joke if Butcher had been misled. But she knew her dear friend Ian wasn't that cruel. Looking back at Butcher, she said, "But the prime minister himself said that he succumbed to his wounds back in October. How could this..."

"SNAFU, Emily." *Situation normal, all fouled up. Could this be another mistake?* "Another shipmate with the last name Bright. This one went by the name Dick Bright. So the death was recorded as R. Bright."

Rest in peace, Dick Bright. Richard was an officer on board the *Rochester Castle* sailing in a convoy to Malta during Operation Pedestal. It was attacked, like most ships in the convoy, but was one of the few merchant ships to make it through to the starving and beleaguered island. Richard was two years her senior. He never shied away from his duties as a big brother. He protected her, educated her as to the ways of the world, and of course, ignored her whenever she dispensed her opinions about the girls from Southend-on-Sea who clamored for even a hello from her striking brother with robin's-egg-blue eyes.

"Your brother somehow lost his identification papers and his merchant navy identification pendant. He was in a coma for some time and...well, it took a while to figure out who he was."

"Where is he? Still on Malta?"

"The word we received had no mention of that."

"Is he…in one piece?"

Butcher drew in a breath and expelled it gradually. "He's on a long road, Emily. Severe burns to his face and hands. He was helping crew from the engine room to the top deck."

Billings strode up to the table, laid out two shot glasses, and poured the caramel-colored liquid in them, starting with Emily's. She grabbed hers before Billings finished pouring Butcher's and downed it. When she lowered her head and placed the glass on the table, tears rolled down her cheeks. Billings didn't need to be told what to do. This time she held up the glass and waited for Butcher to match the movement.

"To Richard Bright," Butcher said.

"Hear, hear," Emily added. The clink of glasses was followed by two shots of Jameson sliding down eagerly awaiting throats.

"Now, tell me about this guy d'Astier."

"Commander, before I get into that, what can you tell me about a Charles Brunel?"

#

"You look like shit, Thorn."

"Well, that's good. It matches perfectly with how I feel." Conor, leaning against the lobby wall, knew that his raging headache had something to do with his roiling stomach. A one-two punch that was close to seeing him flat on his back on the lobby floor. Staff Sergeant Billings had finished telling him where Emily was, but his throbbing head kept him from making sense of the man's answer. "Where did you say she was?"

"I said she was with Commander Butcher…out on the pool deck. He wanted to be briefed. He's gonna want to see you too." The collar of Billings's uniform blouse had soaked up a healthy amount of perspiration despite the cool January air in the lobby. He leaned into Conor as if he were a dentist about to ask him to open his mouth. "Should I call a doc? You don't—"

"We've already established I look like shit. Tell Butcher I'll see him in a few minutes." Conor pried himself from the wall and brushed passed Billings.

"Where are you going?"

Without looking back, Conor said, "To my room, so I can puke in privacy." He pulled up when he remembered his Colt. Turning to Billings, he said, "Sergeant, I gave all my spare mags to the pilot as a tip for the ride out to Cape Serrat. I could use some replacements. Can you scrounge some up?" Billings nodded and Conor headed up to his room.

Upon entering, he tossed his coat onto the bed but missed. Not pausing to pick it up, he shuffled over to the small writing desk on the wall opposite the bed and placed his shoulder holster with his Colt and soggy musette bag on it. He thought about sitting on the wooden spindle chair but decided he needed some gastronomical relief.

He headed to the bathroom. When he shoved open the frosted-glass-paned door, it bounced against the wall. The beaded curtain on the inside of the door rustled and clicked as the beads glanced off the glass. The relentless pounding in his head worsened when he bent over the toilet to vomit. When his heaves came up dry, he straightened, which brought on a spell of dizziness. He left the bathroom and shuffled over to the bed, kicked his coat aside, and sat.

A series of deep breaths had a minor calming effect on his nausea but did little for the pounding headache. He lay back, his feet still on the floor, and shut his eyes, which produced a sense that the room was spinning. He gripped the bed's blanket in each fist and held on, hoping the sensation would pass. It didn't. He decided not to fight it. He let the room spin. And spin.

Only an hour into his watch, the Morning Watch, 0400 to 0800 hours, Conor's feet already ached. And it wasn't even close to the end of his day. The pitching deck of the four-piper plowing through the swells of the North Atlantic only added to the discomfort. The messenger wound through the seven-man crew stationed in the bridge and handed Conor, the OOD, officer of the deck, a steaming mug of coffee. As he thanked the messenger, his eyes settled on the lettering on the side of the weighty handleless mug. Bold lettering circled the outer edges of the seal depicting an eagle with wings swept wide over a three-masted sailing ship:

DEPARTMENT OF THE NAVY * UNITED STATES OF AMERICA. *Below the seal was the ship's name: USS* Reuben James.

After another look at the surging sea as it washed over the flush decks of the Clemson class destroyer, he set his mug on the chart table and headed toward the aft section of the bridge, past the captain's emergency cabin, to the ladder leading down to the port-side radio room. "Mr. Pearce, you have the conn," he said to the junior OOD. Entering the radio room, he became instantly annoyed that the room had yet to go to red-light status.

"Hooker, why haven't you shifted to red? That should have happened hours ago."

Ensign Hooker, a doppelgänger of the actor Andy Rooney and fresh out of the academy, stammered like he usually did before summoning a clipped, "Yes, sir."

After asking for and receiving a status report, Conor exited and made his way back up the ladder to the bridge. During routine underway steaming, the cramped space held seven personnel, including the OOD. The messenger stood nearby, his eyes glued on the OOD. The radar operator, Seaman Altman, was seated behind his scope with the telegraph operator patting the radarman on the back and mussing what hair wasn't covered by his headset.

"What's going on here?"

"Altman, sir. It's his birthday today," the sailor said.

"That right, Altman?" Conor said as the telegraph operator returned to his station.

"Yes, sir. October thirty-first. It's always a lucky day for me. Plenty of good things fall in my lap on this day."

"How old, Altman?" Conor asked.

"That would be twenty-one, sir. Drinkin' age where I come from."

"Well, congratulations. First beer in Liverpool is on me," Conor said, drawing a couple of whoops from the two plotters.

The entire aft section of the bridge superstructure was open to the elements, so the temperature was just a few degrees lower than the outside temperature. He blew hot breath into his cupped hands as he studied the plot board. In his head, he called off the names of all the ships that formed convoy HX 156, including the US Navy task unit 4.1.3 that met up with the convoy on October 24. He was about to complete the names of the six US destroyers in the task unit when a seaman assigned to the radio room, inches short of five feet, his head practically swallowed up by his helmet, shoved a clipboard into his hand. "Message from the commodore, sir. They're picking up German chatter via HuffDuff."

Conor read the message but had difficulty with the numbers. They appeared to be switching places. He handed the clipboard back to the seaman. "Read it."

The seaman brought the clipboard up two inches from his nose. "Likely detection of U-boat. Bearing zero seven nine degrees, range ten to fifteen miles." He handed the clipboard back to Conor and snatched a pencil from behind his ear. Conor signed for the message.

Conor picked up the 1MC. "Captain to the bridge...captain to the bridge." He slammed the handset back into the cradle. "Sound general quarters...all ahead full..." Conor ran through more orders, all rushing around his head like a swarm of angry wasps. The bridge crew watching...waiting. "All ahead full. Right full rudder...come to zero seven zero degrees."

The lee helmsman snapped to, followed by the telegraph operator rapidly ringing up the ordered bell. The sound of the engine room confirming the order rang through the bridge. Reuben James *heaved to port, and the steel deck under his feet vibrated, easing some of his foot discomfort. He stepped toward the bridge windscreen, but his legs were leaden, uncooperative, as if immersed in vats of molasses. Was it a full minute later before he reached the windscreen?*

He raised his binoculars to his eyes. Sunrise was still two hours off. Ice rimmed the edges of the windscreen, the wipers struggling as they scraped the surface of the glass. Thick ice coated the barrel and splinter shield of the forward four-inch gun. The claxon rang throughout the ship. The messenger shoved a helmet and life vest into his hand. Conor looked up. His men trained their eyes on him, young eyes, frightened eyes.

"Torpedo...torpedo. Bearing two zero zero degrees, range...range four hundred."

"Right full rudder," Conor ordered, but in a voice he didn't recognize. He struggled into his life vest. He had to get out to the starboard-side bridgewing. There he could assess, form a plan. Save the ship. His legs were no less heavy. It seemed like the entire bridge crew was on his back, welding his feet to the steel deck. He must get to the wing...to assess.

"Orders, sir?"

Why…so…heavy?

"Orders, sir?" A shout this time.

To his right, with a pitch of the ship, his mug slipped off the table and shattered on the deck.

Conor's eyes shot open. His fists had a stranglehold on the blanket. His shirt was damp with sweat. He felt a rivulet of blood dribble down his chin from a bit lip. *Orders. They want orders. I have to—*

The door lock was rattling. He heard voices in the hallway. Two men. He couldn't nail down the language; they were attempting to whisper but doing a piss-poor job of it. Conor loosened his grip on the blanket and rose from the bed. Two quick steps and he was at the door. Whoever was there still fiddled with the lock. He took a step toward the desk to grab his Colt when the door sprang open. Standing there were two beefy men, one kneeling and the other standing over him, looking surprised to find someone inside the room.

"What can I do for you fellas?" Conor's faux cheery inflection did little to tamp down his rising alarm about the two circus strongmen in front of him. Both men exchanged a *you or me* look. The one standing advanced, landing both meaty hands on Conor's chest, driving him into the room toward the bed. Conor landed on the bed with a bounce. No surprise to Conor, he pulled a switchblade from his sleeve and flicked it open with a snap of his wrist.

Conor started to rise, but the man wasn't interested in seeing that happen, so he shoved Conor back on the bed, where he bounced again on the mattress before settling within arm's reach of the side table. The goon, a younger man with a small head and a dried, scaly, reptilian face that looked way out of proportion to his hulking body, raised his right leg and placed his foot on the bed, inches from Conor's left leg. He bent downward and inserted the tip of his knife into Conor's left nostril. His circus partner, an older man with a round face and a wild beard, standing two paces behind Snake Face, found it funny and laughed. *Move fast and hard.*

Conor raised his left leg and planted his boot in Snake Face's groin, shoving him backward into the chest of his partner. Both goons hit the floor next to the open door like a bag of bricks.

Conor stretched for the water pitcher. Feeling the cool enamel handle, Conor sprang from the bed and swung the pitcher, pummeling the side of the rising Snake Face's head. The goon fell back into his partner's lap. *One down.*

Round Face shoved Snake Face to the side and leaped at Conor. Sunlight glinting off the knife in his hand. Before Round Face could bring his knife to bear, Conor lowered his shoulder and drove it into his attacker's midsection. He pumped his legs like Packard pistons, his momentum carrying both of them toward the wall. Round Face's back slammed into the wall; air rushed from his lungs. Conor heard the knife hit the floor but couldn't locate it. For a moment, the goon was stunned.

Conor rushed toward the desk for his Colt. He reached for the holster and yanked the Colt out as he heard Round Face take steps toward him. Conor turned to the sound of the footsteps with the Colt raised in his right hand. The rushing goon's left arm flailed in a wide arc; his fist slammed into the base of Conor's right hand, dislodging the Colt. It clattered to the floor and landed on one of his duffel bags. Another wide arcing arm came at Conor. The goon's knife slashed across his body. In an instant, Conor felt blood trickle down his chest.

Round Face gazed at his handiwork and smiled. His arms were spread wide, and his legs spread under him a shoulder length apart like a linebacker waiting for a charging running back. Conor unleashed another groin kick; the goon's smile vanished. Conor grabbed the spindle-back chair and slammed it into the gasping goon's head. The seat broke free and hit the floor at the same time as his knife. Round Face fell to his knees, and his forehead slammed into the floor. Conor dropped what was left of the chair and grabbed a nib-tipped pen that sat in a toppled inkwell on the desk.

In a swooping move with his right arm, he planted the pen deep into the left side of Round Face's neck inches below the ear. Blood spurted, instantly filling Conor's nostrils with the coppery smell. Conor lunged for the knife and kicked it under the bed, then stepped over the swooning goon to reclaim the Colt. It was time to get some answers. Round Face pushed off the floor and turned toward Conor. He was dazed but was able to pull the pen from his neck. Then the smile returned. Not the reaction Conor expected since he was the guy with the gun. Conor hesitated. That was a mistake.

Conor opened his mouth and then heard it—a grunt, the type of sound that came with extreme exertion. Something hard, unforgiving, slammed into the side of his head. Stars exploded in his eyes. As he slipped into a darkness worthy of the name, he saw the enameled water pitcher land on the floor.

#

Emily heard the dull heavy sound of something hitting the floor. When she burst through the open door, two huge heavily breathing men were looming over Conor's body. One had a bloodstain coating the collar of his blue jacket. Conor's shirt was also soaked with blood. The startled men looked at Emily, then each other, before they both bolted for the door. The man with the bloodstained jacket took the lead and drove a shoulder into Emily's chest, sending her crashing to the floor. Her head hit the floor, stunning her momentarily. She heard the pounding of heavy footfalls as the two men raced down the hallway.

The smell of blood mixed with sweat hit her. She rolled onto her side and propped herself on her elbow. She struggled to her feet and shuffled to Conor, slipping as her shoes skimmed through someone's blood on the tile floor. She ripped his shirt open and searched for stab wounds but only found a shallow knife slash across his chest. She silently thanked God for small favors. Then cursed him for the shitty job God did watching out for Conor.

CHAPTER TWENTY-TWO

1930 Hours, Wednesday, January 6, 1943
Maillot Hospital, Algiers

When Emily returned to Conor's room, a carafe of water in hand, she was surprised to see a thickset man in a white knee-length coat at the foot of his bed, his long blizzard-white hair a frizzled mess. He was talking in a low tone to the nurse who was applying a copious amount of mercurochrome to the knife slash carved on the still-unconscious Conor's chest. When the white coat took notice of Emily, he turned and brushed past her, leaving in his wake the astringent scent of isopropyl alcohol.

Emily placed the carafe on a small enameled bedside table just as the nurse, a heavyset woman who sported a beaten-down, haggard look, finished applying the burnt orange–red antiseptic.

"Who was that man?" Emily asked in French.

The nurse capped the bottle and placed it on a tray on the table beside the bed, then stood and stretched her shoulders, grunting at the end of the stretch. "Dr. Tolstoy, the lead surgeon here. He was the doctor who tended to Admiral Darlan when he was brought here…after they shot him."

Emily tried to detect some hint of which way her loyalties skewed but found none, her fatigue masking any anti-Allied feelings she might have held.

Emily watched the nurse waddle-step out of the room, her concerns rising that Conor still lay there, unconscious, the side of his head still swollen. Periodic flinches and half-formed words that sounded like grunts were the only signs of life. Her euphoria upon learning that Richard was alive had vanished in a flash when she came upon Conor's bruised and bloodied body. She dipped her forefinger into the carafe and slid it softly across Conor's lips, which twitched faintly. Emily leaned in and, inches away from his ear, whispered, "Come back, Conor. Open those blue eyes."

Conor's breathing was shallow but steady. A second pass of her dripping finger produced something better—heavy lids fluttering, then rising to half-mast.

"Aah, there you are. You decided to join me. I was getting a bit lonesome, you know."

Conor turned his head and stared vacantly at her for a long, drawn-out moment, as if time slowed. "Em, where am I?" Conor reached for the side of his head. His eyelids fluttered again.

"Hospital. Those men, they gave you a beating."

"What men?"

"Conor…really?"

Conor's face screwed up. He looked at his chest. "I…I remember that smell. It's…it's—"

"Mercurochrome. Something to fight an infection."

Conor studied the gash across his chest, then stared at her again. "What men?"

"I can't believe you don't remember." Conor continued to stare at her.

"What men?"

"Two hulking men. I didn't get a thorough look at them. Things happened quickly."

"Right. I think I remember a piece of it. I was sleeping, dreaming actually. I heard a noise and I went to the door. They were trying to pick the door lock—I think. Not sure… Conors voice trailed off. He brought his hands up to his face and held them there for a moment, then dropped them to his sides. Those goons…I dont think they were run-of-the-mill thieves.

"What makes you think that?"

"If they were thieves, they would have hightailed it as soon as I opened the door. No, they were looking for something." He paused. "The archive?"

"If they were, my arrival kept them from searching for it. Maybe they were looking for you."

Conor looked at the slash across his chest again. "I'm sure your showing up kept them from slitting my throat." Conor closed his eyes so tight that it seemed they were being swallowed up into his sockets. "Any chance you can get your hands on some aspirin? The pounding in my head won't back off."

She nodded and left his bedside and ventured out into the hall, then returned with a bottle of aspirin and handed him two. "Repeated blows to the head will do that."

"Give me four."

She tipped out two more and handed those over.

Conor tossed the four tablets into his mouth and chased them with the glass of water Emily handed him. "Em, I've been thinking. You know that pro–Free French and anti-Vichy sentiments run hot in Algiers. There weren't many tears shed by members of those groups when Darlan was assassinated. But it reminds me of another message that was sent our way not long ago. That time it was meant for both of us."

Conor recapped the night they were walking down the Victoria Embankment, just after a dinner with his father, Jack; his sister, Maggie; and Bobby Heugle. He and Emily had spent a good part of the day verbally fencing with Henry Longworth, a member of Churchill's War Cabinet, about his involvement in the disappearance of General Eisenhower's missing diary page. A speeding Rover had jumped the curb and come close to running them both down. "When I suggested to you that I took the attempt to take us out as a sign that we had to be getting close to finding out what happened to the missing diary page, you called me—"

"A madman. Yes, there's absolutely no forgetting that night." She took Conor's hand in both of hers and, with a warm smile, added, "When we hit the ground, if I remember correctly, you wound up on top of me. And you took your damn time getting off."

"Getting off? You shoved me off."

"Well, that's what you get for taking liberties."

"Back in the States, we call it—"

Emily squeezed his hand firmly as if to say *don't say it*. "I don't care to know. It probably has something to do with cowboys and the Wild West." They both fell silent, but she didn't let go of his hand. Emily knew, lying on the Victoria Embankment on her back that night, with Conor staring deep into her eyes, that he was going to play a central role in the rest of her days. *A role,* Emily thought, *he is perfectly suited for.* "Tell me about the dream you had before the attack. You did say dream and not a nightmare, right?"

"I did. But it might have been a nightmare. I can't recall much of it. Little, in fact."

"Well, that doesn't color in very much."

"All I remember is that I had…trouble…moving. I was on a ship. That's it." Conor looked past Emily, his eyes darting about, focusing on nothing in particular.

Conor pulled his hand from hers.

She waited a heartbeat. "If it's too painful…" Emily said, the rest of her words dying on her tongue.

Conor closed his eyes. "No. That's all I remember. I was on a ship… Conors voice wavered. He slowly shook his head. He seemed to be overcome by a heavy sadness. Yes…on a ship. That's it." He looked up at her. "I'll take two more aspirin."

"It will take more than that to get your sorry ass discharged from this Mediterranean resort."

Conor's head snapped up. Filling the doorway was the six-foot athletic frame of Bobby Heugle, garrison cap clasped in his right hand. Conor's best of best friends. His face sported a wide toothy smile as he approached Emily's side of the bed. They hugged warmly. He quickly peered over at the doorway, then back at Conor. "Eddy told me to steer clear of you. For what reason…well, that remains a mystery. But when I heard you got manhandled by some local talent, I had to come see my buddy."

"We heard you were still in the area, Bobby. You qualify for the left seat in a PBY yet?" Conor asked, referring to Conor and Emily's recent exfiltration from Italy with the Italian scientist Ettore Majorana. Against orders from Colonel Eddy, Bobby had hitched a ride on Jack Waddon's PBY and helped pull Conor, Emily, and Father Sean Sullivan, along with their prized scientist, off the Anzio beach. Bobby had a role in all their assignments, with the mission to Sweden the prior November almost killing Conor's longtime friend.

"Nah. Eddy's got me too busy. You know, espionage stuff."

"What kind of stuff?" Emily asked.

"Well, between us girls, resupply missions into Corsica."

"You're kidding," Conor said.

"Nope. The first mission was back in December. A unit established a radio network and supplied the local maquis with guns and other supplies of the nasty nature. The road to Berlin goes through France, my friend. We are working on something bigger than Corsica right now. Destination France for some lucky bastard."

"When you say resupply missions to Corsica, are they by air or sea?" Emily said.

"Listen, I already said too much. Let's just say we used some sewer pipe sailors and the *Casabianca*," Bobby said.

Emily, fully confused, looked at Conor. "Sewer pipe—"

"Right here, Commander." Commander Butcher was led into the room by the squat weary nurse, who took her leave without taking note that her patient had regained consciousness. Directly behind the commander was a tall US Army major. The thin-faced dark-haired major had a Roman nose, thin and sharp.

"You're alive…and awake. Good to see," Butcher said, approaching the foot of the bed. Conor introduced Bobby to Butcher. "Yes. One of Colonel Eddy's men. I've heard of you. The three of you seem to work well together. Does Colonel Eddy know you're here?"

"I was just leaving, Commander. I had to make sure Conor was in one piece." With that, Bobby almost sprinted from the room, flashing a thumbs-up to Conor and Emily just as he crossed the threshold.

Butcher tilted his head toward the major, who stood to his left, a black valise in his hand. "This is Major Tompkins, MD. I don't trust the Algerian medics." Major Tompkins gave Emily and Conor each a nod as he sidled up to the bed; his eyes shifted to the gash across Conor's chest.

"That's a story to tell your kids." Tompkins smiled but let it dissolve when Butcher cleared his throat. "Right, any discomfort from the—"

"None. The red stuff stings a bit. But I'm fine." Tompkins dug into his bag, pulled out a stethoscope, and listened to Conor's heart. With no facial reaction to reveal what he heard, he then looked into Conor's eyes. He grunted, reached into his bag, and pulled out an ophthalmoscope, a silver flashlight-sized device he used to look more intently into Conor's eyes. After shifting the device to the second eye, he emitted another grunt.

"So give me a theory as to who and why you've been singled out for a beating," Butcher said.

Conor pushed himself up against the bed's wrought-iron headboard. "At first, Commander, I thought it was a simple robbery. Now...I think they came for me and the archive. And if Emily hadn't arrived when she did, I'd be on a cold slab by now."

"Commander, someone or some group must know what we're up to. They must feel threatened," Emily said.

"How would they have any knowledge of what you two have been doing?"

"There's plenty of people in Algiers who would sell any piece of information at the drop of a hat. Maybe someone at the hotel overheard conversations or snuck a glimpse of notes, orders," Conor said.

"This operation has a tight lid on it. But, I believe Emily is right. And the beating goes the distance in proving that," Butcher said.

"How's the head?" the doctor asked.

"Not happy. It's punishing me for some reason."

"Maybe for letting it come into contact with extremely hard objects?"

"Maybe."

"He's taken four aspirin in the last ten minutes, and he's asked for more," Emily said.

Conor gave her an accusatory look.

Tompkins nodded as if things made sense to him. "Eat much?"

"My stomach seems to be completely uninterested. It's more concerned with churning and stewing in its own acids."

Tompkins nodded. "How's your memory? Any issues remembering things?"

"No more than—"

"He has little recollection as to what put him here, Doctor," Emily said, trying to mask her exasperation.

"Any dizzy spells. You steady on your feet?"

Conor looked at Emily. She tilted her head toward Conor. Waiting for a lie.

"Yeah, some. But it doesn't last long."

"Okay. Another clear sign that your brain is scrambled." Tompkins stowed away his tools and snapped the clasp to his black bag shut. "Given what the commander here has told me and our brief conversation, I'd say you have one helluva concussion." He waited for any reaction and only received a handful of rapidly exchanged glances from his audience. "Your brain has bounced around inside your melon like a rubber ball against a brick wall. And that's not good. Your brain needs a rest, big time. Without it, you won't be worth much in the field, not that I have any idea what you're expected to do." He turned to the commander. "This guy should stay right where he is or...if you think he needs better care and supervision, he needs to be under my care at the nearest field hospital. Your call, Commander."

"Thanks, Doc. Let me have a few minutes with Conor and Emily. Wait outside, if you don't mind." Butcher placed his combination hat at the foot of the bed and leaned on the footboard as Tompkins shut the door behind him. "I need to pull you out of the game, Conor. You need rest. Emily—"

"Commander, you and I know that isn't going to happen. With all due respect, let's not waste any time banging that back and forth." Conor eyed Emily as if looking for moral support.

"Did you not listen to the doctor?" Emily said, noting Conor's icy glare.

"Conor, Captain Simmons will have Emily's back. In the meantime, you need—"

"Nope. Like I said, not going to happen. Now the best use of the last few minutes that I plan on spending in this bed would be Emily getting me updated on her questioning of d'Astier. After which I will do the same concerning my encounter with Carleton Coon."

Emily shared a look with Butcher, both knowing that the clock was ticking, and Conor wasn't going to allow anyone to pull him off the field of play. A pouty-faced Butcher gave Emily an almost imperceptible nod, signaling his surrender to Conor's stonewalling.

Emily, well aware of what the outcome was going to be, jumped into an overview of her conversation with d'Astier. After Conor expressed his lack of surprise at the outcome, he took the next five minutes to share some brief points about his time with Coon.

"He's like no one I've ever met. A little squirrelly, but that man has some interesting ideas about how to work in the shadows. Long story short, while he did some training of the young kids in the corps francs, he said he had no hand in the assassination. He couldn't speak for the SOE though." Conor looked at Emily and held out his hand, palm up.

She tapped two more aspirin tablets into it and passed the water glass to him.

"That leaves us right about where we started," Butcher said.

"Commander, I haven't briefed Conor on our talk about Charles Brunel. I think, based on what you told me, we might want to spend some time with him before we figure out where to turn next. There's something about him, his contacts, and his circle of friends that might yield something."

"Who the hell is this Brunel?" Conor asked.

"I'll brief you on the way to Barberousse Prison." Emily turned to Butcher. "We'll seek you out when we return so we can plan our next steps."

"All right. Nothing to lose…except time. But make it quick. I'll have Simmons meet you outside the hospital. Again, don't waste time if Brunel clams up."

"Understood, Commander," Emily said.

Butcher snapped up his combination hat and turned to the door, but pulled up. "Emily, get a chance to tell Conor about your news?"

"News? Hope it's good. More bad news is only going to stoke the storm in my gut."

Emily cracked a grin. "It's about my brother, Richard."

Conor cocked his head. "But he's—"

"Alive. Quite alive," Emily said.

"Well, I'll be damned."

"Conor, there's something I never told you about Richard. Something I don't want you to share with anyone."

CHAPTER TWENTY-THREE

0930 Hours, Thursday, January 7, 1943
Barberousse Prison, Algiers

"So, Richard and this Catherine's baby makes you an aunt. How do you feel about that?" Conor shouted at Emily above the roar of the canvas-topped jeep as they sped down the boulevard that hugged the northwestern wall of El Kettar Cemetery. A grumpy Captain Simmons occupied the back seat, struggling to stay somewhat erect as Conor wove through the maze of streets from the Maillot Hospital to the Barberousse Prison.

Emily shook her head while pointing to her ears.

Conor eased off the accelerator and repeated the question.

"I haven't the foggiest." She paused. "I mean I haven't focused on me. I've been trying to dredge up some background on Catherine. I do remember that she was always very flirty."

"You gotta admit, that news was a real shocker."

"What are you two talking about?" Simmons asked.

Conor reapplied pressure to the accelerator, raising the howl of the jeep's four-cylinder engine. Emily met his sideways glance and made sure he saw her giving him a shameful shake of the head. With the remaining time on the road to the prison to question Charles Brunel, Conor gave some thought to the briefing that Emily gave him on her discussion with Butcher regarding Brunel. He focused on the one thing Butcher said that Emily homed in on.

Just before Charles Brunel and his son, Antoine, were arrested, they had met with General François d'Astier de la Vigerie, a top emissary of General de Gaulle and the brother of Henri, also an internee of Barberousse Prison. Butcher mentioned that General d'Astier de la Vigerie left Algiers just days before the Darlan assassination. Conor worried it would take days to peel back the onion that represented the intrigues between the Darlan camp and the followers of de Gaulle. Days they didn't have.

A chilly rain fell as they approached the entrance to the prison. Before they got out of the jeep, Emily pulled on Conor's sleeve. "Before we talk to Brunel, I want to chat with the guard, the one I talked to on my last visit. He should be on duty."

"Do we really have time?"

"I think it will be worth our while."

"Why?"

"Can we, please, get on with this sideshow?" Simmons pleaded from the rear.

Conor's head swiveled toward the man. "Captain, cut us some slack, all right? Why don't you run ahead and—"

"Grease the skids?" Simmons said.

Conor shook his head, thinking they should have left Simmons behind. "The guard you and Emily saw. Tell them we need to see him. Do that and we'll finish putting together our plan of attack," Conor said.

Emily slipped out of the jeep to let the grumbling Simmons out and then hopped back in. "So you were saying?" Conor continued.

"The guard, he seemed to be willing, if shown some motivation, to talk. He doesn't appear to be very observant, but that's precisely what I think he is."

"Motivation?"

"American currency. Last visit, in exchange for money for a birthday gift for his son, he told me about Brunel's son being released. The sight of American dollars caused his eyes to shine with delight."

"He has a son…hmm." The visage of Carleton Coon popped into his still-pounding head. "This guard have a name?"

"I was remiss in not asking for it. We know what he looks like. That should be enough."

"Okay, you take the lead with your friend, but when…or *if* I butt in, take my lead."

Emily started to speak, but Conor's hasty exit from the jeep silenced her.

A guard dropped them off at what appeared to be a kitchen or galley used by the prison staff, who, at that time, were all deployed elsewhere. Several tables were placed haphazardly in the center of a room. Along the wall opposite the door to the galley was a long rough-hewn table whose surface was speckled with food stains and burn marks. A single platter sat on the table, which held nothing but the crumbs from some cake, now vanished. They took seats at one table and waited for Emily's guard friend to arrive.

"This place stinks to high heaven, worse than the last time," Simmons said and was promptly ignored by Conor and Emily. "We're not going to be here long, are we?" The question went unanswered as the guard, droopy faced with a bushy gray beard, strode into the galley. Simmons motioned the droopy-faced guard to take a seat.

If he was nervous, the guard didn't give it away. He couldn't take his eyes off Emily, quite possibly expecting another payday. Emily spoke first, her French a bit halting. "What is your name?"

The guard finally took in the sight of Conor, then Simmons, then looked back at Emily. They weren't nervous glances but the look of someone trying to figure out his next chess move. "*Pourquoi?*"

Emily paused, as if formulating her French response. "*Car*… because, I would like to become…friends."

The guard snorted. He drew his left hand across his upper lip, beaded with sweat. "There are no friends inside this place." He dragged his hand across his chest to cleanse it. "My name is Claude. What do you want? I am due back on watch."

"When I was here last, you mentioned that Monsieur Brunel's son had been freed."

"*Oui.*"

"But beyond that, you struck me as someone who is…quite observant. Someone who doesn't miss much."

"*Non.*" Claude's bearing seemed to relax. "They think I can't hear. Or don't care what they say."

"Is there anything you can tell me about conversations between Monsieur Brunel and his son that you heard?"

The guard puffed up his chest like he was ready to take a stand to defend his family's honor. "There might be. But I couldn't—"

"We have taken your son." Conor stared at Claude. His interruption startled both Emily and Simmons. "Tell him," he said without looking at Emily. She paused. Conor glanced at Emily and saw a light go on in her eyes. When she repeated the claim in French, the guard's chest deflated.

"*Mon fils?*"

"*Oui*," Conor said. He turned to Emily. "And if he wants to see him again, he needs to answer all our questions. And fill in whatever we don't know. The more information, and we will verify it, the sooner he will see his son. And as a special gift, some American cash to buy...hard-to-find items on the black market."

The guard didn't waste any time in responding. "What is it you want to know?"

"Who has been here to visit Monsieur Brunel?" Emily said.

"From the outside, just one person. His assistant. Someone named Alain Chrétien. He wanted Brunel's help to find his missing son."

"Did he say what the circumstances were surrounding his son's disappearance?" Emily said.

Claude's pinched brow told Conor he didn't understand the question. "Ask him who Chrétien's son was and what did he do."

Emily translated the question and received a shrug as an answer. "What did Brunel and his son talk about?" Emily said.

"The father, he's the cheap one...that angers me because some say he is a rich man with a château in France. We Algerians—"

"Claude." Emily touched the guard's forearm, which made him flinch. She pointed to her watch. "Brunel and his son, what did they talk about?"

Claude set his gaze on Conor. "They are up to something. They have a plan. If I tell you what it is, you will let my son go?"

"He will, Claude. I will make sure of it," Emily said. With that assurance, Claude spilled his guts. Emily was challenged in keeping up with the deluge of information he laid out for them. There were words that stood out to Conor, and based on Emily's reaction, they hit her the same way. *Le archive...Marseille...a port administrator named Leclerc...Lyon...Laurent.* When Claude mentioned a secret group called the *Synarchique*, it rang a bell. It wasn't the first time he had heard of the group.

His father, Jack, had taken Conor to meet with their family friend, Bill Donovan, shortly after he resigned his commission from the US Navy. Jack thought Conor would be a good fit for Donovan's new espionage organization, the office of the Coordinator of Information, the precursor to the OSS. Conor remembered that Donovan was in a foul mood that day. He complained to Jack that FDR had yet to respond to three reports his department had compiled on a group he called the Synarchy. It comprised powerful technocrats, mainly bankers and industrialists, who wanted to preserve their power by supporting and collaborating with the Nazis, who they felt would ultimately succeed in dominating Europe.

Three minutes later, Claude ran out of words. Conor shot Emily a sharp nod, rose, and patted Claude on the shoulder. "*Merci*, Claude. *Merci*." Conor looked at Simmons, who had been studying his shoes for most of the questioning. "Give this man a Jackson."

"What? Are you kidding me? Twenty bucks? The guy could buy a herd of goats for a twenty."

"Quit your bellyaching. He led us to something and saved us a lot of time."

Simmons dug out his wallet and passed a twenty-dollar bill to the wide-eyed guard.

"*Mon fils?*" My son?

Emily reassured Claude, adding her own back pat. "*Nous ne l'avons jamais pris.*" We never took him.

#

At first, Charles Brunel would answer no questions, nor would he indicate he had any idea why Conor and Emily were even outside his cell door. When Emily brought up the guard Claude and a smattering of what he revealed to them, Brunel's response was a terse, "Who's Claude?"

Conor leaned into Brunel's view through the Judas window.

"The guard, Brunel," Conor said. "The guy who looks like he doesn't give a shit but has big ears, as they say. He doesn't like you, by the way."

Brunel's eyes narrowed, and he stared contemptuously at Conor. Conor stood aside and let Emily step up to take her swings. "Tell us about the plan you discussed with your son. The one that involved a secret archive, friends in Lyon, and deals for the release of your wife."

Conor took a peek through the small opening and witnessed Brunel lose what little color he had in his face. "We have it on solid authority that you're on your way back to the States with the branding that you're a Nazi stooge," Conor said. "Your buddy-buddy act with Nazi officials finally caught the attention of the wrong people. The FBI, according to our source, is on their way over here to pack you up and get you to the States posthaste." Brunel's jaw slackened. "Whatever you and your son have cooked up won't get off the ground." Conor watched Brunel turn from the window and take a seat on his bed. He picked up a book, the only one Conor saw in the cell, and began to fan through the pages.

"A good report from us might help your cause, Charles," Emily said. "Where was your son going to pick up the archive? Here in Algiers? How was he going to get to France?"

Brunel moved in a flash, hurling the book at the door. It sailed through the Judas window, slid across the stone floor, and stopped at Simmons's feet where he leaned against the far wall.

"Hmm, *Wind, Sand and Stars*. Good book. Read it at the academy. Did you like it?" Conor said.

Brunel stood and shuffled to the door. With his face framed by the window, he seemed to be choosing his words with care.

"Go ahead, say it," Conor taunted.

"There are powerful people in France who have much to gain… and much to lose. Those people will…" Brunel didn't finish his thought and backed away.

"Will what, Charles?" Emily said.

Conor, with a tilt of his head, motioned to Emily that they were done.

CHAPTER TWENTY-FOUR

1030 Hours, Thursday, January 7, 1943
Abwehr Headquarters, Hôtel Lutetia, Paris

The set of three glass doors that led to the balcony on the top floor of the Left Bank hotel channeled beams of dusty sunlight onto the oriental rug in the suite occupied by Colonel Friedrich Rudolf, Hugo Bleicher's superior officer and chief of Abwehr Section III F. When Bleicher entered the suite, he found Rudolf like he often did, annoyed, peeved.

Bleicher was well aware that the suite and the entire hotel was, while elegant in a muted way, another reminder that the Abwehr was, once again, outmaneuvered by Oberg, the Höherer SS-und Polizeiführer, head of the SS and police in France including the SD and Gestapo. Rudolf would often rehash his complaint that Oberg and his rabble of underlings moved more speedily than the Abwehr in requisitioning the finer hotels on the Right Bank, such as the famous Ritz, the George V, and the Crillon. This morning was no different.

"It rankles me, Hugo…you know this… When I ask for a simple glass of wine, to be told there is only beer and champagne is galling." Rudolf slammed his hand on his heavily lacquered walnut desk. "This is France, dammit! Where is the fucking wine?" Rudolf was about to set off on his well-worn theory that the owners of the hotel had hidden most of their wine stock, except for a hundred or so cases of their worst vintages, somewhere in the hotel.

Somewhere as yet undiscovered by the aristocratic Abwehr officers housed in the hotel's 233 rooms, who, according to Rudolf, didn't want to get their hands too dirty in their search efforts.

Bleicher could repeat the diatribe almost word for word. But Bleicher put on his most serious faux-concerned face to short-circuit his superior's well-worn rant. "What is it, Sergeant? You look as if you have received disconcerting news. Is it from our friends across the river?"

Bleicher shook his head. "Colonel, I took the liberty to have Abbé Alves join us this morning. I feel that your expertise at formulating probing questions would be exactly what is called for when dealing with this…troublesome and untrustworthy asset." Bleicher noticed his deferential approach had hit its mark. How Rudolf didn't see through his blatant attempts to manipulate his superior officer mystified him.

"What trouble has he caused this time?"

"We have seen our agent with Gestapo officers in Lyon. Klaus Barbie, namely."

"And we know this how?"

"Our informants inside their headquarters, sir. They are reliable." Rudolf's pinched brow told Bleicher that his superior had mentally made the leap to the logic that if the Abwehr had informants inside the Gestapo, the Gestapo had theirs inside the Abwehr. A reality that Bleicher hoped the colonel would leave for another time.

"These reliable informants…did they provide any information as to the reasons for this subterfuge?"

"*Nein.*"

"Has he been seen at Avenue Foch?" Bleicher expected the question regarding whether Alves had been seen in or around the Paris headquarters for the SS and Gestapo.

"Thus far, *nein*," Bleicher said, realizing that he was not fully confident in his response. Obergruppenführer Oberg's massive staff had requisitioned three adjoined sizable buildings along Avenue Foch. It was practically impossible to watch all the entrances and exits to their headquarters.

Rudolf emitted a low groan, then spun around in his chair to gaze out the doors to the terrace behind his desk. With only the top of his balding head visible, Bleicher could hear Rudolf mumble something indecipherable. Bleicher was about to ask if he was ready to engage the priest when Rudolf spun back around. "Have the godless scoundrel shown in. But know this: I have little patience for double-dealing."

"Depend on me for having the needed patience, sir." Bleicher picked up the phone on the corner of the desk and ordered the corporal to show in Alves. "I am convinced that our relationship with Alves will yield results."

"I will remember your words, Sergeant."

Bleicher kept his gaze anchored on Rudolf to take in his reaction to Alves. It was as he expected. Rudolf's lips parted and his mouth slackened as the priest, dressed in a finely tailored double-breasted dark-blue suit, a matching trilby in his hand, entered the suite. The appearance of Alves dressed as a wealthy self-assured French businessman had likewise shocked Bleicher. Someone or something had bestowed a jolt of confidence in the man of God.

"I have already given my report to Sergeant Bleicher," Alves said as soon as he crossed the threshold of the suite, which compounded Rudolf's shock. "A face-to-face meeting with you means you are pleased with my report or that I have...disappointed you." Alves made for one of the two Louis XIV–style chairs in front of Rudolf's desk.

"I assure you that you have not pleased me." Alves pulled up suddenly, his left hand on the back of the chair. "The fact is, our level...my level of distrust in you appears to be mounting."

"Oh, why is that, Colonel?" Alves seemed to have a second thought about taking a chair.

"You work for the Abwehr. For me and Sergeant Bleicher. You do not work for the Gestapo."

"Aah, it appears you have eyes and ears in Lyon. Why is it you Germans seem to wage a silent battle against your own? Are you not all for the Third Reich?" Alves took a seat, his bluster further antagonizing the red-faced Rudolf. Bleicher remained standing.

"What did Barbie want with you?"

"He wanted to recruit me. I'm sure that does not surprise you."

"And when you said that you work for the Abwehr, for me, what did he say to you?"

Alves chuckled. "He said why not work for both of you."

"Go on."

"I told him I cannot serve two masters." Bleicher squelched a laugh at that response. "I further told him that if he was so interested in what information I pass along to you, he should…just ask you. You are on the same side, after all."

Bleicher watched Rudolf's anger simmer as his superior sat back, his face obscured by folded hands. A handful of heartbeats later, Rudolf sat up and waved off Alves's last remark. "What progress have you made infiltrating the Heckler Network? Thus far, you have provided so few names. This network must be rolled up now. You seem to be dawdling. Why is that?"

"Simply put, these people are cautious. They have sealed me off from their larger planning meetings. Building their trust in me will take time. As I have said many times to Sergeant Bleicher."

Rudolf gave Bleicher a sideways glance, then stood. "I tire of this. You have twenty-four hours. If you cannot provide a full list of the key members of that network within that time, I will cut you off. No more handsome payments. No more blind eyes to your black-market dealings, your trafficking in stolen artwork. No more," Rudolf said, pounding his desk with each resounding *no*. "And while we're at it, Germany's ambassador to the Vatican will hear about and see evidence of your unholy skulduggery. But I can't help but think that will not faze you one iota. Now, off with you and heed my words. Twenty-four hours!"

CHAPTER TWENTY-FIVE

1045 Hours, Thursday, January 7, 1943
El Kettar Cemetery, Algiers

The two-lane avenue ran along a ten-foot concrete wall that showed ample signs of erosion. Conor noticed, in some sections, a greenish mold-like color reaching up from the ground to a point a foot from the top. There were rusted metal signs haphazardly spaced, calling out the location of El Kettar Cemetery. Spread out just as randomly were heavily robed men leading lumbering, slow-footed donkeys loaded down with firewood and goods from the casbah east of their location.

The road, still wet from an early-morning rain, stretched out ahead of them. Puddles still pockmarked the surface every twenty feet or so. Passing military vehicles of all types occasionally sprayed the interior of the jeep as they sped by, causing Conor to release a string of profanity that, he was sure, Emily was not used to hearing, given the stony stare she sent his way each time.

Conor quieted down when his side mirror revealed that a beat-up lime-green Renault, its windshield cracked and caked with dust, appeared to be following them. Conor looked away and focused on the traffic that sped along the avenue, most traveling in the opposite direction. Another look in the mirror depicted a clear, vehicle-free road for at least half a mile behind them. He glanced at Emily in the passenger seat, swallowed up by her washed-out pea-green waistcoat. "I swear I thought we were being followed.

But as soon as I convinced myself, poof, they vanished." Conor downshifted from third gear to second, the resulting engine growl prompting a mumble from Simmons in the rear seat that he couldn't make out.

Conor eyed Emily with a side glance as she pulled out her Walther, released the magazine, checked it, then slammed it back in with her palm.

"You see something?"

She leaned in toward Conor. "This is still a war zone. Need I remind you that two brutes recently made a punching bag out of you?"

"Ouch. That wasn't kind." He settled into his canvas-covered seat and wondered what their next move was. A feeling of dread overcame him and made itself comfortable inside his still-aching head. As they passed the last US Army deuce and a half in a long convoy, Conor fastened his eyes on Emily. Words formed in his mind but died on his tongue.

The front grill of a car rammed the driver's side of the jeep. It was the Renault. Its right bug-eyed headlight slammed into his elbow. Emily's upper torso dangled over the side of the jeep, her legs still planted in the footwell. She reached for the steering wheel to break the outward force of the collision.

The Renault's momentum bulldozed the lighter jeep toward a gated entrance. The jeep's right-side tires caught the edge of a low curb, and the Renault, gunning its engine, rammed the jeep, depositing it on its right side, completely blocking the cemetery's entrance. Emily and Simmons hit the ground hard. Conor heard their grunts over the engines of both vehicles as he fell on top of Emily, producing a low groan, this one muffled by his body. The two musette bags stored at Emily's feet tumbled out of the jeep and fell alongside the entangled couple. Simmons emitted a low moan that was mixed with a gurgling sound. Steam from under the hoods of both vehicles hovered over the mass of entangled metal.

Conor grabbed both musette bags with his left hand and pushed off the ground with his right, shooting into a crouch. He brushed a wisp of hair from Emily's face, which was scrunched up like a prizefighter going in for a kill. "Let's move…inside the graveyard."

Emily matched his crouch. He handed one of the musette bags to her. "Five grenades. Use them wisely."

Emily moved through the cemetery entrance.

Before he followed her, a glance at Simmons told him he was in bad shape. Blood surged from his nose and mouth. Conor grabbed him by the lapels and dragged him inside the cemetery. Along the interior wall, a line of overgrown leafless shrubs sat two feet high. He dragged Simmons behind the row of shrubs and covered him with the leaves. "We'll be back. Be quiet," Conor said just above a whisper. And then, like a sprinter springing from the blocks, he bolted from the wall to a row of three-foot-tall bleached-white headstones about twenty-five yards distant and ten rows deep, where Emily was hunkered.

"You okay?" Conor said.

"Fine. Maybe a bruised hip. What about Simmons?"

"He needs a doc. Now. But we have other problems to deal with first."

A banging sound behind Conor made him throw a look toward the wrecked jeep. He saw that its size fit just the width of the entrance, making ingress impossible unless he climbed over the jeep's carcass. Which was what whoever had been in the Renault was doing. Conor wished he'd gotten a head count. He knew a car that size could hold five. Two the size of the circus thugs who introduced themselves to him the day before in the front seat and maybe three more skinny guys in the rear. Conor liked skinny guys.

Conor stepped around the headstone, crouched, pulled a grenade from his bag, yanked the safety pin. He rolled it like he was sending a bowling ball down an alley toward the upended jeep just as two men in dark clothing crested it. The grenade came to a rest among shards of glass from the smashed windshield a half foot from the front passenger seat. The detonation drove the two climbers in the air back toward their own wrecked sedan. Whether they were merely stunned or wounded more severely, Conor had no way of knowing. He turned to rejoin Emily. Before he even got close, Emily let three rounds loose just over Conor's head. As they passed over him, the air pressure around him rapidly changed, like he had instantly been dropped into a cave. Conor reached Emily's position and crumpled to the ground beside her.

"What were you shooting at…besides me?"

"Didn't you see them?" Emily said in a high-pitched voice. "Those two men…they were the ones who beat you."

Conor shook his head. "Son of a bitch." He rotated his jaw a few times to flex his ear canals. "Did you get one?"

"Couldn't tell. Did you get a look at the inside of the car? How many were inside?"

"No. Could be two, could be five."

"There's got to be another way out of this place."

"No. We have to stand our ground. Simmons is still alive. Rough shape but alive. Can't leave him."

The sound of squealing metal and shattering glass filled the air as the jeep tumbled into the cemetery grounds and landed on its top, the wheels up in the air. It was thirty seconds later that the two hulking men climbed over the jeep.

"Are those the—"

"Yep. And look at what they're carrying."

Emily stole a peek around the headstone. "Where would they get Thompson machine guns?"

"The black market must be thriving since the invasion. I'm sure the US Army doesn't miss a couple of Thompsons."

"So what now? Split up and outflank them?"

"Yeah, it's the only way we get out of this fucked-up mess. We have to put these grenades to good use," Conor said. Grenades. They made an impression wherever they went. And they were easy to carry. *What's not to like?*

Before Conor could reach into his bag, two more men scaled the jeep. This time, they were Conor's favorite type—skinny guys. And more good news. They didn't have the big boy Thompsons. "Four. We can handle that," Conor said, pulling himself close to Emily. "So here's a plan. You stay here. Keep these goons busy. Fall back if you have to. I'll circle to the left, scale the wall, and drop down onto the street to hit them from behind. I'll take my extra mags and three of my grenades. That leaves you with your supply and one extra from mine."

As Emily was about to offer her two cents, a quick burst from a Thompson strafed the tops of headstones twenty feet behind their position, spewing chips and chunks of stone in all directions. "But you have to keep these guys busy while I head to the wall. Can you handle that?"

"As I don't have a better plan, I guess I'll have to. But keep your head down. When I fire, move. Or after a grenade blast. I'll make sure their heads are down." Conor nodded as Emily peered over the headstone. "They've taken up positions behind the first row of graves. On the count of three, I'll toss the first grenade. Wait for the blast, then move."

Another burst from a Thompson reminded them that their pursuers were still out there. "Get ready," Emily said, pulling out a grenade. She counted off, then sent the fragmentation grenade flying in a high arc toward the front gate. Conor waited, then sprang just as the grenade detonated. He made it as far as twenty yards before the hulks returned fire with their Thompsons. Squatted behind a headstone that had lost its top half due to deterioration, he readied for another sprint.

Conor decided that he'd make it to the wall in his next run. When he heard Emily open fire with her Walther, he rose and sprinted toward the outer wall. Return fire erupted, silencing the Walther, but he made it to the wall's base. He looked down the length of it in the direction of the gate and saw the prone shape of Simmons's body. He was doing a good impression of a dead guy—at least Conor hoped it was an impression.

He dragged over a fallen headstone and propped it up against the wall to give him a toehold about eighteen inches off the ground. With the sound of the next grenade, Conor hoisted himself up. Both hands landed in what felt like chalky mush. Years of the elements had softened the texture of the wall. He swung his right leg over and straddled it. Before he could pull his left leg over the top, a rush of vertigo hit him. Then the wall gave way.

A mixture of sand, dirt, stones, and bits of concrete cascaded down to the street, with Conor riding it like a wave. He slammed into the ground butt first, but the force of his landing sent his upper body backward, his head speeding toward the street. It hit with a crunch. A starburst filled his vision. A familiar sensation now. There were words that came and went—scrambled brain, the doc said. Yeah, his brain was doing a jitterbug inside his head. As he lay there, dazed and disoriented, he heard the distant sound of gunfire, single rounds intermingled with short machine-gun bursts.

He fought off the brain fog and headed for the scene of the collision. A Renault sedan sat perpendicular to the out-of-action jeep. The front end folded like an accordion. The driver, his face bloodied, was slumped over the steering wheel, his eyes open, staring at nothing. Conor looked over the jeep's chassis and spotted four men, two oversized and two rail-thin, huddled behind a row of headstones. All had their backs to Conor.

Perfect. Well, not perfect—not with his head pounding like a blacksmith hammering iron. He felt his body temperature rise along with the acid in his stomach. The four entrenched attackers launched a full broadside on Emily's position. Through foggy vision, he saw the headstones flanking Emily's position disintegrate under the withering fire. Conor struggled for some clarity. After the thugs unleashed the last barrage, he saw the two skinny attackers laugh as they hid behind their headstones. Conor reached into his musette bag and pulled out two grenades, fumbling one. *Shit. Shit. Shit.* His delay gave the group time to respond in unison. He reached down to retrieve the errant grenade as another of Emily's exploded.

The goons, grouped close together, simplified targeting. He rose and pitched two grenades and followed with five rounds from his Colt as the grenades landed two feet from their position. His rounds found two targets, one hulk and one skinny guy, before the grenades took care of the remaining two. When the cloud of dirt and bits of gravestones thinned out, four bodies lay motionless in grotesque positions. All four were facedown, bleeding from noses and ears. Limbs of three bent at unnatural angles. The fourth, Round Face, had his head twisted to the left.

Conor approached to get a closer look, his Colt held tight in his right hand. Emily popped up from behind a headstone and approached from the other direction. The hulks from the hotel were lying side by side. Snake Face had a trickle of blood that ran from his left ear, down his face, across a sharp jawline, and down his neck, past a bulging Adam's apple.

He stripped Snake Face of his Thompson and slung it over his left shoulder. He bent down to strip Round Face of his Thompson and then stretched out his arm to hand it off to Emily.

The hand, or that's what Conor thought it was, tightened its grip around his right ankle. A heartbeat later, his right foot was yanked forward, and he tumbled backward. He hit the ground with force, feeling the Thompson dig into his back.

The round-faced hulk rose to his knees. Conor lifted his head. It felt like he was lifting an anvil. He spotted the blurred figure of Emily lowering into a crouch, trying to bring the Thompson to bear on the hulk, but she fumbled with the machine gun's sling tangled around her hand. Her mouth moved, but all Conor could hear was the high-pitched ringing in his head.

The hulk was on him, gripping Conor's right hand with two massive hands, wrenching his wrist up, then down to free the Colt. Conor raised his right knee and drove it just below the rib cage into the hulk's left kidney. The grip on his wrist loosened but didn't release. Conor repeated the motion and threw in a sweeping left cross that found the hulk's jaw, freeing his wrist from the hulk's grip. Round Face collapsed to the ground, landing on his right side, his jaw aligned three inches right of center.

Conor, welcoming the end to the battle, struggled to his feet and for mere seconds took his eyes off Round Face. The knife in the hulk's hand was a shocker. The stream of .45-caliber ACP rounds from Emily's Thompson was slightly less of one.

CHAPTER TWENTY-SIX

1315 Hours, Thursday, January 7, 1943
Algiers Waterfront

The pallid winter sun was no match for the biting wind that whipped around Antoine Brunel like a family of miniature cyclones. He traveled past the Great Mosque, grappling with the problem of how he would make his way to Marseille. He carried a small red-trimmed tweed suitcase containing three changes of clothes that concealed the archive. When the expansive waterfront came into full view, the number and variety of ships that lay at anchor in the Bay of Algiers startled him. He wondered if there were similar scenes being witnessed in Oran and Casablanca.

Out in the bay, the wind churned up the water's surface, creating a chop that produced whitecaps. Nestled in the crook between the docks and a long meandering quay that stretched out into the bay was a cluster of feluccas tied up, hull to hull. At least twenty in number. The single-masted wooden sailing boats were a major mode of transport in the eastern Mediterranean. A mode that was not a feasible choice to make the transit of over four hundred miles to Marseille.

As he drew closer to the water, he detected the smell of rotting fish, exhaust from the dozens of trucks and other vehicles operating along the waterfront, and smoke swirling upward from several fires set in fifty-gallon drums that warmed dockworkers up and down the waterfront. The northernmost section of the quay wall loomed over the landscape of the feluccas as they danced in the water on the swells, a layer of detritus surrounding the boats like a carpet. Articles of clothing, empty bottles, skeletons of dead fish, splintered wood from shipping pallets, and other trash of myriad colors floated on the surface, trapped by the tide that locked them in the tighter confines of the harbor.

All but three of the fleet of feluccas were crewless. One was tied up just below the position Brunel took on the wall. A lone bearded figure sat on the gunwale facing in his direction, continuously puffing on a cigarette like he was running out of time to finish it. Older in years, he wore a waist-length heavy coat and a scarf wrapped tightly around his head with longish strands of graying hair escaping the scarf. There were three neat piles of rope, all in a tight coil, sitting at his feet. He paid no attention to Brunel.

Brunel set down his suitcase at his feet. "I don't suppose your boat would make a trip across the Mediterranean this time of year?" he said in French, his hands cupped around his mouth. The old man continued to ignore him as he flicked his spent butt into the water's rubbish-rich surface. Brunel raised his cupped hands again but stopped when he saw the old man make a motion with his first two fingers as if he were smoking another cigarette. Brunel returned the gesture with a look of confusion, which prompted the old man to repeat the motion with greater urgency.

"Aah," Brunel said to himself as he dug a spare pack of Gitanes from inside his coat and dropped it down to the old man. The pack bounced in his open hand, then settled into its firm grasp. The old man pumped the pack, pulled a cigarette from it, and, in one smooth motion, flipped it into his mouth. He patted his pockets and then stared back at Brunel as if to say *got a light*? Brunel pulled a lighter from his side pocket and carefully tossed it down to the old man. Brunel once again raised his hands to communicate with him but stopped when he looked back up at him.

"It would be a death wish. The sea is not to be tampered with this time of the year." The old man's voice was high-pitched, squeaky.

"But it looks like you have just come back from a voyage. Am I wrong?"

The old man picked a speck of tobacco from his tongue and

flicked it into the air. "You are. I come to my boat this time of year to get away from my wife."

Brunel laughed. "I need to secure passage to Marseille. As soon as possible. I must get back to see my dying mother."

The old man looked down at the three coiled piles of rope, nodding for two long, deep drags on his Gitanes, then looked up, pointing to the south. "The *Cadiz*. She sails under the Spanish flag. Mostly Spanish crew. She is two days behind her departure date. Headed to Marseille. Do you speak the language?"

Brunel nodded excitedly and turned to take in the view just to the south. He spied at least three dozen ship superstructures. Massive praying mantis–like cranes loading and offloading cargo in a choreographed ballet. He turned back to the old man and nodded.

"They are delivering a load of vegetable oil and cork. They have need of crew members. At least according to the second officer who came by yesterday."

Brunel's shoulders drooped. He envisioned being a passenger, not a working crewman. "I have no experience as a seaman."

The old man responded with a shameful shake of his head. "You can wash dishes, can't you? Move a mop around a deck?"

Brunel responded with another nod, followed by a wave of his hand as he turned south and began a trot to find the *Cadiz*.

Soon after he located the single-stack *Cadiz* tied along the quay in the Agha Basin, it began belching billows of inky black smoke. The gangplank was manned on each side by a dockworker on the quay with the same number of *Cadiz* crewmen on the top deck, waiting for the signal to disengage it from the ship. Without a word to the dockworkers on the quay, he sprinted up the gangplank, his breathing sounding like a dog in a heavy pant.

The story he recited to the second officer was greater in detail than the one he told the old man. The lack of sufficient crewmen seemed to outweigh any concerns about his identification papers and transit paperwork he had received from Alain Chrétien. For the most part, the second officer's questions centered around what tasks Brunel could take on. At first, little to no trepidations were raised about a dying mother, which served to calm Brunel's anxieties, given he hadn't worked out all the details of his cover story.

When the gangway was pried away from the ship, Brunel let out a slow breath. "Where should I—"

"Senor Lewis, I believe this...this story about a dying mother. It sounds...plausible. Your papers are in order. But..." The officer closed the distance between them, throwing off the mixed scent of body odor and wine. "I cannot guarantee that the agents who will greet the ship in Marseille, German and French, will find it as believable as me. You see, we are desperate. They are not. You may not be allowed on French soil. Is that risk understood?"

To Brunel, it was all understood. To see the Germans release his mother from their internment camp, he would jump ship once it arrived in Marseille if he was forced to.

CHAPTER TWENTY-SEVEN

1500 Hours, Thursday, January 7, 1943
The One-Eight, 5th Arrondissement, Lyon

Eklof enjoyed being early. The whores weren't haggard and worn-out as they would be later in the evening. Not that he would have asked much of them. Not since his run-in with the SAS, the British Special Air Service unit in Libya two years prior that left him less of a man than he once was. Yet he found there were other avenues to carnal pleasure.

The interior of the One-Eight was so much more ostentatious than the interiors of the brothels in Stockholm, the site of his last posting. What they did share were the overpowering scents of perfume, one fighting another for supremacy. The atmosphere almost made Eklof's eyes water. On the street side of the main floor of the One-Eight was the parlor, the primary gathering place for clientele. The spacious area's most striking features were the vaulted ceilings with encased mirrors. Vibrant reds and blues of the plush furniture and soft fabric wall coverings saturated and overwhelmed the space.

Eklof found the painted ceramic friezes depicting naked women in erotic scenes pleasing. But the panels depicting centaurs mingling with dancing, harp-playing nymphs were overdone and gaudy in Eklof's mind, as were the images of fauns, half-human and half-goat figures, leering at scantily clad women. One such figure had lifted the hem of a flowing diaphanous gown and peered underneath.

Most annoying to Eklof was the music emanating from a phonograph that sat on a table to the side of the wide archway to the parlor off the foyer. The shrill tinny voice belonged to the American *negerin*, so loved by the self-indulgent French. Josephine Baker's voice was too much for him. He stalked his way to the phonograph and pulled the arm from the disc; the abrupt silence captured the attention of the handful of customers, most of them Wehrmacht officers.

There was a kidney-shaped intricately tiled bar in a similar shade as the azure couches that dotted the floor of the parlor. Bottles of champagne were lined up on the bar like a chorus line. But it was the woman standing beside the bottles who truly caught his eye. Blonde, a slight frame, a graceful neck adorned by a three-string pearl necklace, her lips a lush red, almost the color of fresh blood. She was looking at Eklof. But this one wasn't staring at him because of his eye patch. She took him in as a whole man.

He tossed his service cap onto the bar. He pointed to a bottle of Moët & Chandon champagne, confirming that the madam had black-market connections. The blonde filled a coupe with a skill that impressed him. She never once took her eyes off him as she tilted the bottle for the exact length of time to produce the perfect pour.

"What is your name?" Eklof said.

With the knobbed stem of the champagne coupe nestled between her index and middle fingers, the blonde slid the glass across the bar toward Eklof. He didn't touch it. He wouldn't until the whore answered his question. His disapproving look produced a name.

"Sophie. My last name will mean nothing to you."

Eklof lifted the coupe to his lips and sipped. "You're correct on that point. And if you prove to be unskilled in your trade, your first name will mean nothing to me as well."

"Touché, Major." Sophie smirked. "I have had no complaints."

"Maybe they just haven't reached your ears." Sophie cocked an eyebrow at his response. "What is your specialty, if I may ask?"

"Major, let's say that…I follow orders."

It was Eklof's turn to smirk. They spent the next thirty minutes polishing off two bottles of champagne. Eklof actually did the drinking; Sophie performed the role of the fawning, attentive purveyor of sympathy and adulation. Their banter mainly pranced around topics of sexual pleasure, the level of directness reaching new heights with each emptied coupe. A Wehrmacht major replaced the Baker disc with a different selection. This time, the music was more attuned to German tastes. The familiar voice of Ilse Werner singing "*Mein Herz hat heut*" replaced the indecipherable murmuring in the parlor. Eklof perceived an uplift in spirits of the German officers as their voices joined Werner's in the ballad.

Eklof had just about had enough of the verbal foreplay when a surprise visitor entered the parlor. Through the mirror behind the bar, Eklof spied Abbé Alves in the archway, like a doctor entering the leper colony, surveying the flock of sinners. His dull black cassock was in gross conflict with the rich hues that adorned the parlor. In his hands, he spun his black three-peaked biretta.

The priest, not seeing Eklof—or having a mind to ignore him—set off toward two women, both dressed in frilly undergarments and silk hosiery. He stopped, then seemed to decide to head to the back of the parlor, toward individual rooms where business was conducted. "Alves!" Eklof shouted above the singalong.

Alves pulled up and looked over at Eklof and Sophie. Eklof motioned him over to the bar with a beckoning finger.

Alves at first hesitated, like most people when they first came upon him. He traipsed over to the couple, his biretta notched into the crook of his arm. "Major Eklof, good evening." Alves nodded a greeting to Sophie, whose expression appeared as someone who just came face-to-face with a debt collector.

"Are you on a soul-saving mission? Or could it be something… else?"

"Something else? What do you mean?"

"Come, come, Alves. We know your interests transcend those of normal priests," Eklof said.

Sophie's expression remained unchanged.

"I visit occasionally. Madam Gilbert has full knowledge and has given me full approval."

"Such a mistake." Eklof turned to Sophie. "Don't you think, my dear?" Sophie's look of disdain piqued Eklof's interest. He made a note to question her about Alves—as long as the champagne allowed his buzzing head to remember. "Why let a fox into the henhouse?"

Alves had had enough. He bowed stiffly and turned to leave the parlor.

"Should I take the opportunity to remind you of your…non-priestly obligations to the Gestapo?"

Alves stopped, turned, then placed his biretta atop his head. "No need, Major. No need. May God bless you and all who are here," Alves said, sweeping his hand in the sign of the cross.

Eklof turned to Sophie and grabbed another bottle of Moët & Chandon. Sophie grabbed his free hand and led him back to her room.

Her boudoir was expansive. A spacious canopied bed covered in a dark cherry-red sheet with two long pillows at the head. The sheet was taut, showing not a ripple, which pleased Eklof. The floor was covered in a thick Persian rug, the walls concealed behind wide tapestries depicting Egyptian women with slaves lounging at their feet. Between the tapestries were heavy brocade curtains interlaced with threads of gold and silver.

Eklof, seated in an armless chair covered in black velvet, asked Sophie twice to undress. When she started to after the first order, he stopped her. "No, no, no. Not like you are readying for bed, but in a manner to titillate."

"Yes, Major. I understand." She complied, and for the next five minutes, she slowly, seductively, revealed her luminescent skin, pronounced curves, and small uplifted breasts. "Shall I undress you, Major?"

His smile was his answer. She made slow movements to undress him. He helped where she was unfamiliar with his uniform's belting accessories. But she managed quite well. She ran her petite hand, the skin of which was a talcy translucent, across his forearm, sending a chill down his back. She stopped before removing his underwear.

"Major, it would be helpful if you told me what pleases you."

Eklof's head swam from the champagne and from memories of what used to please him. Before his experience in Libya over two years ago. When he was a complete man. The young Libyan whore, who made a weapon out of a spoon to gouge his eye from its socket while he battled SAS troops, had a frame and features similar to this Sophie. This was the point in these encounters where he treaded cautiously, protectively. His pondering confused Sophie.

"I want you to lick my ear."

Sophie gave him a look of what Eklof thought was surprise, but it was fleeting, for it turned to one of curiosity. "Men have asked me to do many…different things. Some by your fellow officers. But, you must admit, Major, your request is…unusual." Eklof ignored the judgment. He was pleased she didn't laugh at his request. "Do you expect me to—"

"My right ear. That will do." Sophie exhaled in what looked like relief. "I will spare you from asking the obvious. I lost my left ear in a battle for the Reich. As you can see, I do not question sacrifice for my country." Eklof thought of his pledge to kill the first American he came across to avenge himself for Conor Thorn ripping his ear off in Sweden, just before Thorn slipped out of his hands.

The whore stood and stared. Whether or not she was aware of it, her hands covered her breasts.

"Sit on my lap. While you lick my ear, you must do two things. Grind your hips against my groin." Eklof searched for a reaction. Seeing none, he continued. "I need you to add some…how shall I put it? Auditory urgings."

She uncovered her breasts. "I'm sorry. What do you mean?"

"I require filthy talk. Is that clear enough?" Eklof shook his head, annoyed he had to spell it out for this Frenchwoman.

"Yes, Major. May I suggest a glass of schnapps before we begin? It will…make you relax." Eklof nodded, which sent Sophie scurrying to a heavily lacquered two-door cabinet beside the bed. She bent over to retrieve a bottle, giving Eklof a full view of what he no longer could enjoy.

She pulled out a short glass along with a bottle. He heard her fill the glass, or so he guessed, as her back blocked his vision. Eklof rose and padded softly toward Sophie. He wrapped his left arm around her neck, grazing the pearls she had left on. She stiffened. He looked down at the top of the cabinet. A glass with a finger of schnapps sat in the middle of the table. In her right hand was a vial, less than an inch long, capped with a small cork. It was empty.

"What is that?"

Sophie tried to turn toward him. He clamped down his left arm around her neck. Eklof asked again, knowing the answer. He loosened his hold and waited a beat. She didn't answer. He felt tears roll off her cheeks onto his forearm. He retightened his grip. "We've heard of such cases. Whores drugging German officers only to have their possessions searched for intelligence to be passed on to the Resistance. It is your misfortune that I can hold my liquor. Take both glasses and finish them."

"I don't like schnapps." Her words were carried on weak breath.

He spun her around. The pearl necklace flew from her neck and landed on the cabinet, spewing pearls in all directions like the sparks of a holiday sparkler. Eyes filled with terror looked back at him. He threw her on the bed. Before she stopped bouncing, he poured the glass of schnapps on her naked body. She pushed away toward the wall. He grabbed her feet with both hands and pulled her back. She screamed, the shrill, high-pitched sound readily absorbed by the lush impenetrable tapestries and drapes. As was the beating he administered to the lovely young conspirator.

CHAPTER TWENTY-EIGHT

1545 Hours, Thursday, January 7, 1943
79th Station Hospital, Algiers

Conor's head felt like it was at the last stage before it was about to split in half. He took up a guard-like position outside the requisitioned two-story stucco-faced warehouse that served as the newly established US Army hospital. He left Emily sitting beside Simmons's bed, mainly because he didn't want to answer any more questions from doctors and nurses about why he looked like he had just run through a meat grinder. His reply, that he looked better than Simmons, didn't score any points with the staff, so he quietly took his act outside.

The sound of the jeep's engine as it approached told Conor that the driver didn't realize that the vehicle had a third gear. The high-pitched roar of the engine would have woken up any hospital patient lucky enough to have been catching some sack time. But the look on Commander Butcher's face had another message for Conor. He didn't care about sleeping patients. His entire face froze in a demonic stare when he saw it was Conor standing outside the entrance. Butcher had one leg outside of the jeep as it skidded to a stop three feet from Conor.

"What the hell happened? Ike is banging around HQ like there's a hornet's nest in his pants."

"It sounds like you got some of the story. What *do* you know, so I don't wind up reporting yesterday's news?"

"Robert Murphy had a visit from General Bergeret, whose head looked like the top of the Mount Vesuvius volcano. He was spittin' mad. It seems he and his provisional government don't take too kindly to an American and a Brit blowing up half of the most revered and holy cemeteries in Algeria. Good God, Conor. As if relations with our French friends weren't rocky to begin with, this just makes—"

"Commander, here's the bad news. The two goons who used me as a punching bag were leaders of the cemetery attack. I hate to say it, but I think there's a leak somewhere on your staff."

Butcher's jaw dropped and his face flushed. "That can't be. I just won't believe it. The staff...they've been with the general since he first arrived in the theater. I'd put my life in their hands."

Then it hit Conor. "How did Billings know the old man sweeping out the pool was deaf and mute?"

"I...I don't know. I never asked him." Butcher's eyes widened like he had just spotted a heavenly spirit. "You think someone lied to Billings?"

"I think there are plenty of locals selling whatever they can get their hands on. Including Allied intelligence and gossip. But the bigger question is...who's the buyer?"

"Or worse yet, who are the buyers?" Butcher said.

"We can all lay our money on the fact that someone isn't too keen on us finding that archive, Commander."

That statement slowed Butcher's train. He leaned against the front fender of the jeep and took off his combination cap, wiping his head with his handkerchief and letting his hand linger on his neck. He made a face like someone who just wanted to lie down and forget the last few years of his life. "You look okay. What about Emily and Simmons?"

"Emily's fine. Ears ringing a bit from the grenade show. Simmons...well, he took a hard hit when the goon squad rammed us...went flying and hit the wall pretty hard. Emily's keeping an eye on him."

"And he thought this was a chickenshit assignment," Butcher said, shaking his head. "Let's go have a quick look and then you and Emily can tell me where the hell this circus has left us, besides holding our you-know-what."

When Butcher entered the expansive ground floor of the ward, Conor, a step behind him and to the side, saw Simmons push himself up toward the head of the bed with his left arm. He was at attention—as much as anyone with a busted shoulder and arm could have been. Emily handed Simmons a cup of water.

"Commander. I'm sorry I couldn't keep these guys out of trouble. Those guys came out of nowhere. I swear."

"Relax, Captain. Not much you could have done from what I've heard."

Simmons slumped against the single pillow behind his back. "I can tell you that if Conor had left me in the street, those guys would have made quick work of me. He saved my life. Maybe General Eisenhower should know that."

Emily had a hard time wrestling the smile from her face.

"I'll make sure of it, Captain. Now, when you get out of here, I want a full report. For my eyes only. Is that clear?"

Simmons nodded and downed his water.

Butcher looked at Emily, then Conor, and motioned to the exit with a tilt of his head. The three of them gathered around the jeep's hood, Butcher at the front with Conor and Emily flanking the sides of the still-cooling vehicle. Butcher rested his hands, knuckles down, on the hood and leaned on his fists. "Tell me you learned something helpful at the prison." *Butcher's words almost have a pleading ring to them,* Conor thought.

"We learned nothing from Brunel, except that he thinks whatever he and his son are up to will help them somehow," Emily said.

"He must have the goods on someone, Commander. Something that gives him leverage. It sounds like the archive might be that leverage. But like Emily says, he was a waste of our time. But—"

"But? What else?" Butcher said, sounding like a young kid asking if there were more birthday gifts to unwrap.

"A prison guard was another matter," Emily said. "Namely, the guard who seems to have had a meaningful amount of exposure to Brunel and his son, who, by the way, was released yesterday." Butcher looked at Emily expectantly and motioned rapidly with his hand for her to continue. "Brunel's son, Antoine, was to meet at a café with Brunel's assistant, who was to give him false travel papers."

"He expects to leave North Africa? How?"

"No idea," Conor said. Conor and Emily took rapid-fire turns revealing what they learned from the guard at the prison.

"Commander, we have to assume that the son has already claimed the archive that was hidden in the Notre Dame Basilica," Emily said.

"And is headed to Lyon," Conor added.

Butcher rubbed the back of his neck and let his hand rest there for a few moments, then he leaned on the jeep's hood. "So, am I wrong to say that we aren't one hundred percent sure the son has left Algiers? Do we know the name on the papers?"

"No, you're not wrong. And no, we don't know the name he'd be traveling under," Conor said.

"But I did get a description from the guard," Emily said.

"Holy smokes," Butcher said as a morose minute-long silence crept in and around the three of them. "All right, the next move is to pull Robert Murphy into this. He has the best connections and relationships with General Bergeret and the police in Algeria. We need to know if the son has skipped town or not."

"What if he has, Commander?" Emily asked.

Butcher stepped around the front of the jeep and had a leg up into the driver's side before he responded. "Then we make travel plans for you two. Destination, Marseille." Butcher's butt hit the driver's seat. "Get in and hang on. It's going to be a bumpy ride."

CHAPTER TWENTY-NINE

1600 Hours, Thursday, January 7, 1943
DuBois Home/Office, 5th Arrondissement, Lyon

Dr. René DuBois pushed away from his desk and swiveled in his chair to face the three-sided bay window that looked out over the courtyard. He stood, parted the chintz drapes, and pulled down the shades of the window on the far left, then right. He raised the middle window shade so that it revealed the entire window, then turned on the double brass candelabra and removed its black oval-shaped parchment shade. And waited. If there were any Resistance members or transiting Allied airmen in need of medical attention, his light and shade signal would be his beacon.

His nurse, Lucie Villard, entered. The slender woman with boyish hips moved about the office quietly. Moonfaced with deep-set cobalt eyes, Villard had been his father's loyal assistant for the last ten years of his life. DuBois's mother appreciated nothing that Villard brought to the job, notably her loyalty, suspicious that Villard's loyalty was more accurately driven by an emotional and physical attraction. Of course, his mother's feelings on the subject were always discounted in a flurry of harsh words from his father.

The forty-five-year-old nurse, whose hair still showed blonde-tinged signs of her constant pre-occupation bleaching, finished wiping off the examination table and straightening his desk's surface. The latter task always annoyed DuBois. When he first mentioned that her flitting about his desk was unnecessary, she responded first in silence. Apparently forming a reply, which she then delivered as if she were reprimanding a child.

"Will there be anything else, Doctor? Oh, before I forget, the rats in the courtyard. We need more strychnine. They seem to be multiplying. Will you pick some up?"

"Yes. Certainly. Before you leave, will you please check the cabinets in the storeroom and take a quick inventory of supplies? It's something we haven't done in some time."

"We, Doctor? You mean I haven't done an inventory," Villard said in her typical end-of-the-day, *I've been on my feet all day* tone.

"Lucie, I have offered to help many times, but you refuse to even let me enter the storeroom."

"Of course, and as I've said many times, I never let your father worry about the inventory of supplies either. So you are in good company, Doctor." Villard whirled about and trudged off to the storeroom nestled under the stairway that led to the second floor.

DuBois could have written the script of their back-and-forth from memory of similar scenes that had played out since he took over his father's practice. The other more familiar script dealt with Villard's constant pressure to romantically link her daughter, Aimée, to DuBois, ever since his wife tragically died. Those conversations were most uncomfortable for both of them.

He settled back in his chair, laced his hands behind his head, and closed his eyes. DuBois was playing a dangerous game; he was like a circus tightrope walker—if he fell, he would blow the cover that kept him in growing regard with the Resistance, namely Germaine Gilbert, and would be exposed as a double agent plying his trade on behalf of the German Abwehr. The vision of looking down from the tightrope into a dark abyss sapped his much-needed concentration when a knock at the door to the foyer interrupted him.

DuBois approached the door but stopped short of reaching for the handle. "I'm sorry. The office is closed. Come back tomorrow."

His request was met with silence at first, then two mumbling voices. Then, in a louder voice, "But it is my stomach. I can't keep anything down." DuBois silently mimicked the expected reply as it was spoken, then opened the door. Standing before him was a Resistance member called Yves, a fabric travel bag slung over his shoulder. The squat pudgy-faced man was in his late forties with longish gray hair hanging down over a broad creased forehead. His nose, flattened at its end, spread across half his upper lip. The man's eyes were blue and bright. DuBois knew Yves wasn't his real name. The men shared a mutual distrust, which DuBois couldn't pinpoint the origins of. Behind him was a blonde emerald-green-eyed woman, exactly a head taller than Yves and years younger. Draped on her shoulders was another woman, her head hanging down, her vivid red hair obscuring her face. DuBois stood aside and waved them in. Before closing the door, he stole a glance at the empty courtyard and covered passageway that led to the street.

Yves helped the young woman lay the redhead on the exam table. DuBois washed his hands in a basin on a small table behind his desk. As he did, he glanced over at the unconscious woman and couldn't make out any obvious wounds. He picked up a linen tea towel, dried his hands, and approached the examination table. "What happened to her?"

Yves cupped his hands and, through puffed cheeks, blew warm breath into them. "They dropped her outside of town. Landed in a tree. Then the Germans arrived. We couldn't get to her until they moved on. It took a while."

DuBois nodded and reached for the clump of red hair that covered her face. There were tiny pieces of twigs lodged in the clump. When he brushed her hair free from her face, DuBois's jaw slackened. Maggie Thorn was the last person he ever expected to see again.

CHAPTER THIRTY

1615 Hours, Thursday, January 7, 1943
Dressmaker's Shop, Algiers

Jemond Lavigne Dupont hadn't been back to the shop since two days before Darlan's assassination. That day, the air in the back room was electrified, powered by the realization that their plans were about to be enacted. The Group of Five had sat around a worktable strewn with several bolts of richly colored fabric. Slivers of fabric fibers floated in the air as the group discussed the plan that was to be initiated on Christmas Eve, the agreed-upon date for the demise of the French admiral who would finally pay for his double-dealing and penchant for his past collaborations with the Nazis.

Dupont glanced at his watch. The single exposed light bulb hanging above the worktable did little to reveal the time on the watch's face. He had to raise his wrist inches from his eyes to see that his confidant and fellow Group of Five member, Julien Tremblay, was late. Again.

The winded Tremblay slipped into the back room two minutes later, peeking through the doorway to the front of the shop before he softly closed it behind him. Dupont noted the sheen of perspiration that coated the man's face. Tremblay was rubbing his jaw like he had just been walloped.

"What's wrong, Julien?"

Tremblay slid out a battered café chair and let his entire body weight hit the seat. "I think I was followed. Not completely sure. Roget's men, I think. But—"

"You took the necessary precautions?"

Tremblay wiped his brow with the sleeve of his faded blue jacket. "Of course. It is why I am late."

Dupont understood his nervousness now. "Is that the only reason for your…agitated state?" Tremblay took a moment before mustering the words for an answer. "Julien?"

"The police. They are angry. They have rounded up many. So far, there is no need to worry. But if they don't back off soon, there is no guarantee that one of us won't be brought in for questioning."

"About?"

"Surely you heard about the Coq Hardi attack?"

"Of course. But we have no involvement. Rogues with no relationship to our people."

"Yes. That is so. But if they look deep into the attack, they may learn something."

"What are you talking about? Learn what?"

Tremblay leaned over the table; the joints of his chair cried out in distress. "Our man Michel Chrétien, you remember him?" Dupont did. What he first recalled was that Chrétien was not his choice to have the group's packet of records taken to the basilica for safekeeping until the authorities had moved on from the Darlan assassination.

"Has Roget rounded him up?" Dupont could detect the rising alarm in his own voice. Chrétien was to leave for Oran after depositing the archive in the basilica with his mother's help.

"No."

"Has he reported to you through our friends in Oran, as was the plan?"

"Not as of yet. I assume he has had some…challenges with travels. That and he is possibly taking extra precautions before contacting us."

Dupont dwelled on Tremblay's explanation. It unsettled him. There was so much at stake. His future business interests with the Allies and his relationship with the American Robert Murphy chief among them.

"There's more. Michel's father was killed in the attack on the café. He was there with his wife and another man."

"Do we know this man?"

"We do. The head waiter is a friend. He only knew his name… Antoine Brunel…nothing else." Tremblay pulled a pack of Gitanes from his jacket pocket and fumbled for a moment while he shook a cigarette from the pack. He stopped short of lighting it. "We are asking for information about this…this Brunel. Our waiter friend says that he and Michel's mother escaped out the rear of the café after the attack." Dupont watched Tremblay light the Gitanes with a shaky hand. Dupont didn't need to hear any more.

"Do you know where the archive is hidden in the basilica?"

"Not yet," Tremblay said, exhaling a stream of gray smoke through his nostrils like a raging bull in a cartoon. "He was to communicate the location once he was settled in Oran." Tremblay took another deep drag. This time, his hand was steadier. "We felt that his mother would help us when we decided to…reclaim our property."

Dupont didn't like not knowing where exactly the archive was. But he was convinced that paying off the hotel's pool worker for information—that the American and British agents were searching for the archive but knew less than he did—offered up some solace. He'd hoped that the cemetery attack he'd ordered would slow down their efforts, so the failure of the attack had been a setback. "Find the archive as soon as possible." Tremblay's eyes widened. "Then destroy all contents. Two people must witness this, you being one. Do this immediately. It was a mistake not to have done so earlier. Before the day of the assassination."

"Why? They are safe. You shouldn't be—"

"Well, I am concerned. And you should be as well. The Allies are searching for them," Dupont said. He could feel the throbbing of a vein in his neck. "We cannot be linked to the admiral's death. If it is leaked that there is a connection between us and Bonnier, no matter how close Robert Murphy is to Giraud or Eisenhower, it won't be enough to save our skins. Our futures in a liberated France are tied to a spotless relationship with the Allies. Do as I say as soon as possible. And, Julien, do not make a mess of it." Dupont rose from his chair and donned his overcoat.

"Where are you going, Jemond? In case I need to find you?"
"To meet with Murphy. I must find out what he knows."

CHAPTER THIRTY-ONE

1630 Hours, Thursday, January 7, 1943
DuBois Home/Office, 5th Arrondissement, Lyon

René DuBois's mind slipped from third gear to fourth as it raced around his head, trying to make sense of Maggie Thorn's appearance.

"Lucie, go back to the storeroom and fetch the tin of Vaporole, quickly," DuBois said, his composed voice masking the calamity that his brain was dealing with. Villard beat a path to the storeroom and returned promptly with a small rectangular tin box with the name *Aromatic Ammonia* in black block letters placed above the Burroughs, Wellcome & Co name. DuBois flipped the lid and pulled out a single silk-covered glass capsule, almost letting it slip from his fingers. He positioned the capsule one inch below Maggie's nose and snapped the glass. The burst of ammonia worked instantly and had Maggie moaning and thrashing her head back and forth as if she were fleeing what it had released.

DuBois pulled back. Maggie quieted but didn't open her eyes. He made a move for another capsule just as her eyes sprang open. She started to prop herself up on an elbow as she took in her surroundings, only to be pushed back by DuBois.

"Maggie, lie back. I need to examine you. You've had a hard time of it, according to Yves."

Maggie opened her mouth, but before words formed on her lips, DuBois held up his hand to shush her. "And when I'm finished, you can tell me why you have…dropped into my life."

When DuBois was finished suturing and dressing two deep gashes, one to her left outer thigh and another five inches below her left armpit, he aimed the narrow beam of light from his ophthalmoscope at one eye, then the other. Not seeing any signs of hemorrhaging, he stepped back. "Not bad for someone who jumped out of a plane and landed dab smack into a tree."

"It's smack-dab, René. Now, can I sit up?"

"Yes," DuBois said, stepping closer to help her.

Maggie softly slapped his hand away. "I got it."

"How's the headache?"

"Out of control. But I'll survive it. Not sure if I would have if you used another one of those smelling salt things. Nasty stuff," Maggie said as she tussled with the tangled mess of her hair. She sat upright with some difficulty and dangled her legs over the table. She gave her cheeks a tweak that brought some color to her skin. The tense atmosphere in the office faded at Maggie's lighthearted reaction to the smelling salts. Villard busied herself with cleanup, and Yves and his young friend took the two chairs that were set before the desk and turned them around to face the examination table. DuBois faced Maggie, driving his hands deep into his pockets.

"This can't be a coincidence." DuBois glanced at Yves and the young woman, both seated with their attention riveted on him and Maggie as if they were watching a stage drama. "Can it?"

Maggie cleared her throat and dipped her chin toward Villard as she finished tossing bloodied gauze pads into the trash.

DuBois nodded in response. "Feel free."

"A few seconds after I hit the first tree limb, I don't remember anything. Yves and Hélène pulled my fat butt out of the fire, so to speak."

"I got most of that story already from Yves, Maggie. What are you doing in France? I thought you were bound and determined to be the next Dorothy Thompson, the next most intrepid journalist to come out of the United States."

"While I still count her as one of my heroes…after all, how can you not after being kicked out of Germany for calling out Nazism for what it is?"

Villard stopped fussing about and stood on the other side of the exam table, awaiting another request from DuBois.

"Answer my question."

He saw a slight glimmer in Maggie's eyes. Not a foreign look for her. "Are you married?" A surprise of some sort always followed glimmering eyes. DuBois noticed his nurse hike her eyebrows at the question. He had been married. He didn't want to deal with her questions. Her name? What was she like? How did she die? Were there any children? Why couldn't he ever forgive the Jewish butcher who ran her down on the street?

"No. And you?" DuBois saw peripherally that Villard had raised a hand to cover her mouth. He realized he should have excused his nurse. Too late.

Maggie studied him as if she were dealing with an unexpected answer. "After you left me, I found out I…I mean, I was close a few times. But don't tell my brothers."

He knew what she was going to say before she stopped herself. He was pleased she did. What DuBois never knew was where he stood with Johnny and Conor, the intrepid Thorn brothers. They were both fiercely protective of their younger sister, as they should have been. But Conor took his protective role more seriously than Johnny. Conor was supremely better at holding grudges—that he remembered. "Left you? Maggie, you well know that we both felt that the circumstances we were facing weren't very favorable for a lasting relationship."

"Maybe you felt that way more than I did."

"Well, that's not what you led me to believe."

Maggie shrugged and studied her ankle-high laced up shoes. "Maybe so."

"You've not landed on my doorstep to rekindle a relationship. What did bring you here?"

Without raising her gaze to meet his, she spoke. "To bring you and your mother out of France and back to England. They have plans for you."

DuBois retracted his hands from his pockets and stepped toward Maggie. His quick movement startled her. So, Maggie was the someone Gilbert mentioned. How much did London know about his past? He was adamant that their relationship be kept out of the society pages of the local newspapers, much to Maggie's dismay. "England? When?"

"As soon as I deal with one other matter. Then we travel, with the help of Yves and Hélène, to Switzerland, then to England, with a little luck."

"You're SOE. How long have you worked for them?"

"Don't spread this around, but this is my first mission. I've been loaned out by the OSS to the SOE." Behind Maggie, DuBois noted a startled reaction from both Yves and the young woman. Obviously, they didn't know everything about the woman they found in a tree.

"One other matter, you said. What does that mean?"

"That's something that I can't share. At least not now."

Before DuBois summoned the words to his next question, the door to his office opened. His mother, Sarah, stood in the doorway, transfixed on the seated Maggie. "Red. I…I thought I was light-headed, dreaming when I heard your voice. A New Jersey accent isn't heard often in Lyon."

Maggie's mouth opened, then shut just as fast. She slipped off the table with a grimace and took unsteady steps toward DuBois's mother. "Sarah. You are a sight for this sore Jersey girl's eyes. Let me give you a hug so you can keep me from falling on my ass."

After a warm embrace, Sarah put Maggie at arm's length while she studied her face. "Why are you here? Not to see—"

"No, Sarah. That's not the reason." Maggie motioned for Yves to hand her the travel bag in his lap. She pulled out a package wrapped in brown paper and held together with twine and handed it to Sarah.

"And what's this?" Sarah said.

"A new dress. Something nice for a trip to Switzerland."

While Maggie and his mother shared whispered conversation, the notion that the other matter might play havoc with the unfolding of the next few days nagged him. If he didn't discover what the other matter was, it would fester like a nasty wound.

CHAPTER THIRTY-TWO

1700 Hours, Thursday, January 7, 1943
Robert Murphy's Office, rue Michelet, Algiers

On the quick trip from the hospital, Butcher gave up the lowdown on Robert Murphy that Conor hadn't already known from his days working for Colonel Eddy in Tangier. His title, head of the Civilian Affairs Section, didn't convey what role he played currently or in the lead-up to Operation Torch. Butcher explained Murphy worked clandestinely, forming relationships with a prominent fifth column that all but secured Algiers on D-Day. It seemed to Conor that Murphy was a jack-of-all-trades sort of diplomat.

Not the type he and Emily had run into at the US legation in Stockholm on their mission to track down the secret-peddling traitor Gunnar Lind. The head of the legation, a guy named Ramsay, wanted nothing to do with the dealings of the OSS—too ungentlemanly for him and a bunch of State Department old-timers.

What Conor wasn't aware of was the depth of Murphy's connections in North Africa. Especially with the former *Sûreté Nationale.* Connections that Conor felt would need to be tapped if they were to pick up the pace of their quest for the archive.

When Butcher explained to Murphy's assistant that he needed to see his boss right away, Butcher was told that Murphy was meeting with police Captain Roget, but that he would let Murphy know he was waiting. While the assistant disappeared into Murphy's office, Butcher shook loose a cigarette from a Philip Morris pack.

Conor turned to Emily, who displayed signs of dogged exhaustion.

"How are you feeling?" Emily said.

"About as bad as you look." *Shit. What a dumb thing to say. That confirms it. My brain is scrambled.* Emily lifted her chin, showing her displeasure at his comment. "Sorry, I mean, I feel shaky. Downright ready for bed at the worst. I am sure you feel the same."

"Nice save," Emily said, tacking on a shaming shake of her head.

Murphy's assistant returned, his face a mask of alarm. "Mr. Murphy said he wants you to join him and the captain right away." He extended his arm toward Murphy's office door.

The modest size of Murphy's office surprised Conor. Given his reputation and close ties to Eisenhower, Conor expected something more impressive than what appeared to be the office of a lowly diplomatic underling. A dark-haired man approaching six feet in height stood behind the desk, towering over a uniformed man, cap nestled in the crook of his right arm, with broad shoulders and an impeccably trimmed mustache. Murphy's head was lowered and tilted to his left, as if he was lending an ear to the officer. Murphy's pinched face signaled he had just heard something extremely unwelcome.

Murphy raised his head along with a hand to cut off the officer. In his other hand, Murphy held a photo. "Commander, this is Captain Roget of the French police. He has brought news that I'm not sure how concerning it might be. But it involves Charles Brunel. I believe you have been made privy to our...position regarding Mr. Brunel?"

There's that name again. Butcher told Emily that the French police had photostats of letters between the Germans and Brunel, appointing him as an industrial agent for the Nazis. Another way of saying he was their spy. It did not help Brunel that he was a naturalized US citizen.

Murphy reached across his desk and handed the photo to Butcher. "What am I looking at, Robert?" Butcher said.

"That, Commander, is the son of Charles Brunel. Antoine Brunel," Roget said, his voice sharp—sure. Conor expected to hear his heels click after he finished. "And who are these people, Commander?" Roget said.

Butcher handed the photo to Conor and made the quickest introduction Conor ever heard. "This is Thorn and Bright."

Conor moved shoulder to shoulder with Emily and narrowed his gaze on the partial image of a young man's face. The back of the head of another person seated at the table obscured a small portion of his face. A tall thin waiter was placing a dinner plate in front of Antoine Brunel.

"We're aware the police released the son. May I ask what else the captain has to report concerning the son, Mr. Murphy?" Emily asked. She was so good with the dulcet approach. A yin to Conor's ham-fisted yang.

"Captain, please share your earlier report to me with Commander Butcher's friends."

Roget turned forty-five degrees to face the three of them and rambled off a series of facts. He started with the date and time the photograph was taken, the location, and the others at the table.

"One guest of Brunel's cannot be seen in the picture. It is, besides Brunel himself, the one person we are most interested in finding. It is Liliane Chrétien, the wife of Charles Brunel's assistant. Minutes after that photograph was taken, the café was attacked. I lost three men. I barely escaped." Roget paused, puffed out his chest, and looked at each of them like he was waiting for a *we're glad you made it* response, which didn't materialize. He pressed on. "The man facing Brunel…her husband…was killed." Roget paused again, searching out reactions to his report. Besides some soft shuffling of feet, there was none.

"Why are you looking for the wife?" Conor said.

It was Roget's turn to shuffle feet. "That, I cannot share with you."

"And why is that, Captain Roget?" Emily said.

Roget looked at Murphy for a lifeline. "Our friend, Captain Roget, has not been authorized to report that," Murphy explained. "He told me earlier that Antoine Brunel escaped the café after the attack, with Mrs. Chrétien in tow. The police have circulated the photograph of Brunel throughout Algiers hoping to locate him and possibly Liliane Chrétien."

"Why are you looking for the wife?" Conor immediately saw his question startled everyone. He wasn't sure why. There was a midgrade buzzing in his head.

"That's been addressed, Conor," Butcher said, shooting a glance at Emily.

"Right." Conor waited a beat and took a deep breath. "What am I missing here? This seems like French police business. Why let us in on this saga?"

"Mr. Thorn, I am here to ask for assistance from you Americans. We believe that harm has come to the woman at the hands of Brunel. If we find him, we may find her. And we have more questions to ask her," Roget said.

"Butch, the captain here has asked for Allied help in tracking Brunel down," Murphy said. "A fisherman down on the waterfront has identified Brunel as someone he saw there earlier this afternoon. He was seeking a way out of Algiers."

When Murphy finally related that Brunel was seen boarding the *Cadiz*, a Spanish-flagged steamer that left for Marseille three hours earlier, Conor was the first to glance at his watch. "Commander, we'd have some interest in chatting up Brunel. The freighter has a top speed of...maybe twenty knots. Shouldn't be a big problem to track them down with the help of a PBY teamed up with a destroyer escort."

"No way we can free up any naval assets. The general just won't buy into it. As far as a PBY goes, I just came from a briefing where it was reported that all air assets have been grounded due to heavy weather that has skies over the western Med socked in. Could be for days."

Murphy cleared his throat. "Captain Roget, let me confer with the commander and his friends." Murphy placed his hand on Roget's back and steered him to the door. "I'll get back to you soon with specifically what we can do to help our French allies." Murphy opened the door and finished depositing Roget on the other side.

Through the door opening, Conor spied another man speaking with Murphy's assistant. When he saw Roget being deposited by Murphy just feet away, his jaw slackened. Roget responded with a stiffened back.

"Hello, Jemond, I'm running a bit late. I'll let you two chat while I finish my meeting with the commander," Murphy said as he closed the door. Murphy turned to face his three guests. "I'll get a report a bit later from my assistant about the snake-and-mongoose show that the curtain just went up on out there."

Conor turned to Butcher. "Commander, I have an idea." He expected it would take five-plus minutes to sell his idea about hitching a ride on the *Casabianca* and convincing the sub's commander to transit on the surface to make up time, but it took less, because Conor himself didn't have all the details worked out in his scrambled brain.

"How do you know if this French sub is even available?" Butcher said.

"Well, from what I hear, it's being prepared for a joint OSS and SOE resupply mission to Corsica." Conor carefully parsed out the few details he gleaned from Bobby Heugle about the impending mission of the *Casabianca*, leaving out the comment about the *lucky bastard* that was going to be dropped on the French coast. "We know a little more, but I think it best you don't know what we know. It might put you in a compromising position, if you get my drift."

"Yeah, lying to General Eisenhower is something that will get me sent Stateside pretty damn quick. You've probably told me too much already."

Conor didn't think so, but the *what the hell are you thinking* look on Emily's face told him she did. "We're on a deadline. I say we assume we can't find the *Cadiz* on its way to Marseille and make our way there," Emily said.

"Answer this. How do we know he has what we're looking for?" Butcher said.

Conor tried to form the words for his answer, which was banging around in his head. It must have been banging around in Emily's head also because she responded.

"Why would he be headed into occupied France? He's carrying something of great value," Emily said. "Leverage to be used in some way with important people with influence. If the archive details any OSS or SOE involvement in the assassination, it could trigger high-level anger and indignation about the Allies interfering in French political matters. It could possibly lead to pressure on American officials to release Charles Brunel, to smooth over their anger."

"It's still a bit of a reach, don't you think?" Butcher said.

"Commander, we can't just let this man reach France, even though we're not sure one way or another if he has what we want. As a backup plan, when we do track him down, if we don't find the archive, we come back and pick up the search. Maybe we pound on Brunel to give up what he knows," Conor said.

"All right," Murphy said. "If you're headed to France, there's a gentleman outside, someone I've been working with for many months, who has plenty of connections with the Resistance, or so he tells me. He could be a source of valuable insight on how to get where you need to go. And stay alive."

#

Jemond Lavigne Dupont's face lost its color when he first glimpsed Murphy's guests. He was a tall broad-chested large-fisted type who seemed to be suddenly overcome with the jitters. In Conor's experience, most people who were physically imposing didn't exhibit the nervous vibrations that Murphy's friend gave off during their introductions. The clammy handshake confirmed his assessment.

After the quick name-swapping, they all settled onto the couch and the odd assortment of straight-back chairs that filled most of the office. Murphy kicked things off, reciting a big piece of Dupont's résumé. Dupont, a well-connected businessman who owned vegetable oil companies based in France and in French-controlled territories in North Africa, was a go-between that Murphy dealt with often to conduct business with General Giraud. Pre–Operation Torch, given his status with German and Vichy authorities, travel permits were not a problem for the consummate businessman.

What Conor found hard to believe was Murphy's account of the early stages of their relationship. Dupont told Murphy that he devised his own police record that described him as a pro-German collaborator in the late thirties and found a way to make this phony police record available to the Nazis. It was his record that convinced the Nazis to ensure he had all the necessary travel permits needed to move around the whole of France and in North and West Africa. Murphy touted this freedom of movement as key to Dupont having established relationships with the Resistance. Dupont kept staring down shyly at his shoes as Murphy went on.

"It was from Jemond that I first learned about a group of powerful business leaders in France—technocrats, he called them—who in effect thought aligning themselves with the Nazis would best serve them in a postwar economic environment. They sought a new world order."

"Money makes people do stupid things," Conor said, prompting Dupont to raise his gaze and zero in on him. Murphy grinned and then shifted to address what he was asking Dupont to assist with. He laid it out in ultra-vague terms that even confused Conor. It was, Conor mused, a skill that most successful diplomats had to master if they were to survive in the cutthroat environment of the Department of State. While Murphy was laying out the murky reasons for the need of his experience and contacts inside France, another sign of Dupont's skittishness appeared in the form of a bouncing right leg.

Conor gave Dupont some credit though—he pressed Murphy more than once for more specific reasons for the need of Allied operatives to infiltrate southern France. Butcher aided Murphy's efforts to deflect by trading on the name of General Eisenhower and his need to prosecute the war now that most of North Africa had been secured.

"I see. Yes, I most certainly understand," Dupont said, his voice carrying an ample measure of *no, not really*.

"Do you see any way that you can help our operatives, Monsieur Dupont?" Butcher said.

Dupont's piston-like leg movement kicked up a notch while he cracked his knuckles. The dry snapping sounds made Emily flinch.

"Yes. I believe I can assist...but limitedly. The German occupation of southern France cut off my level of contact with the Resistance." He placed his hands on his knees, which quelled the right leg's jitter. "Two months ago, I made arrangements to meet with some known members of a Resistance network in southern France."

"Which one?" Conor asked.

Dupont looked to him, then to Murphy for, Conor presumed,

consent to respond. That came as a single, almost imperceptible nod.

"The Combat Network. They are the most active and organized network operating in the south. Someday, the time to land on French soil in the south would arrive. We attempted to establish a method to contact the network."

"Where would this have happened?" Emily asked.

"In Avignon."

"And the method?" Conor said.

Dupont sat back, freeing his leg to resume bouncing. He again cracked his knuckles as if to give himself time to think about his response. "All that was agreed was that contact would take place at a café. Le Chat Noir Café." Conor eyed Emily as she mouthed the words *the Black Cat*. "The specifics of how were never established. Time ran out."

Conor didn't buy it. It was like leaving out the most important ingredient to a recipe. *Were they supposed to sit around the café and hope the Resistance would wait on their table?*

"Who would be the contact?" Conor said.

Dupont's mouth opened, then closed.

"Jemond, a name would be helpful," Murphy said.

"Yes, of course, if I remember accurately, it was... Beaugard."

"Who is this Beaugard? Is it his real name?" Conor said.

"That is doubtful. I know nothing more."

"You're sure there's nothing else you can add that will help once they arrive in France?" Murphy said, his voice calm.

Dupont cleared his throat. "France is a dangerous place for anyone not a German or a member of the police. Trust is a scarce commodity in France." Dupont paused a beat. "Is it the two of you who are—"

"Sorry, Jemond. That's classified," Butcher said.

#

Dupont was surprised and annoyed that Murphy briskly escorted him out of his office after he made his attempt to find out if Thorn and Bright were headed to France. True, his brusque manner of asking questions often produced strong reactions, but he should have assumed that Thorn and the woman were the ones being infiltrated. Murphy was one man Dupont did not want to be on the wrong side of.

Murphy's assistant handed Dupont his hat and overcoat, and he had taken his first step onto the rue Michelet when a harried Julien Tremblay almost knocked him to the ground. To Dupont, his associate looked peeved and indignant, as if he were the victim of a robbery. He motioned Dupont to follow him. After a woman and three children passed, Tremblay snapped his head toward a narrow alley that connected to a neighboring street. The air in the alley was a strange mixture of sewage and roasting Deglet Nour dates. Tremblay shook a cigarette from a pack and tapped it against the back of his hand. He didn't light it. Dupont pulled a lighter from his pocket, but Tremblay waved him off.

"I have come from the convent. I went there to talk to Michel's mother. To ask where the archive was hidden and if she had heard from her son. The news is not good."

"Go on, Julien. Tell me."

"She is dead."

"*Bon Dieu.*" Good God. Dupont snatched the cigarette from Tremblay's hand and lit up. He blew a thick stream of smoke up in the air. "Are we even sure the archive made it to the basilica?"

Tremblay drew in a deep breath and expelled it through bulging cheeks. "No."

Dupont knew it was due to his vanity that he hadn't ordered the archive to be destroyed earlier. He cursed his conceited plan to have the French postwar press use the contents as proof of his and his associate's patriotic cunning.

"The father. He was shot...in the café, was he not?"

"Yes."

"He worked for the financier...Brunel. The one the Americans wanted arrested?"

"Yes." Tremblay ran his hand through his hair. "I don't understand. You think there is a connection?"

"I don't know. But ever since we lost touch with Michel Chrétien, I have not had a sound night's sleep. But here's what I fear." Dupont flicked his cigarette down the alley. It hissed when it hit the surface of a foul rivulet that trickled down the center of the alley. “Thorn and Bright. They do not have the archive. But they know who does. I am sure they are headed to France to recover it. They seem to be chasing someone who must have taken it from the basilica.” Dupont’s jaw slackened. “And we have not a clue who.”

CHAPTER THIRTY-THREE

2045 Hours, Thursday, January 7, 1943
At Sea Aboard the Spanish Freighter Cadiz

Antoine Brunel's stomach was a repository of churning, burning acids that were determined to free themselves from the confines of his stomach. They eventually won out and Brunel retched in violent spasms into the crew compartment's sink. The roars and howls from his bunkmates drove him out onto the ship's heaving main deck, still wiping his chin clean with the sleeve of his gabardine short coat. The coat was a gift, a loan, she said, from his self-appointed seagoing mentor, Josefa, the nearly two-hundred-fifty-pound Catalan cook, the de facto bully overseer of the *Cadiz*'s crew. She took a liking to Brunel, which initially saved him from being picked on by the experienced crew, but had quickly become unwelcome when he couldn't seem to escape her constant leering disguised as, in her words, *maternidad benevolente*, benevolent mothering.

The *Cadiz* was making headway to Marseille in six-foot seas with leaden skies delivering a steady windswept rain. Antoine Brunel's sole experience with sailing on a large seagoing ship was when his mother and father had taken him on the maiden voyage of the French-flagged liner *Normandie*. It was a present marking his eighteenth birthday. He had no more luck tamping down a roiling stomach then than he did now. The difference was the quality of the food sent down sinks and over railings then, as compared to his current circumstances.

Contending with his seasickness was, on one hand, a welcome distraction to his nagging concerns about the security of his satchel that hung around his neck and down his back under the gaberdine coat. He asked to place the satchel containing his newly acquired six-round Modèle 1892 revolver and the papers belonging to the seditious group in the ship's safe. When his request was rebuffed with a round of mocking laughter, he was left with the satchel in his possession while he went about his duties as a deckhand and on watch topside.

If his father was correct in his thinking that the information in the papers, which implicated the Americans and the British in the assassin's training, would prove valuable enough to trigger his mother's release, he must protect the satchel with his life. He would have to put up with the questions and taunts from the crew, who had already received a profane-filled reprimand from Josefa. But the taunts continued whenever she wasn't around.

After a series of dry heaves, Brunel left his position along the rail and returned to his bunk, where, he was sure, sleep would elude him. Upon entering the crew compartment, he took in the sight of four members wearing tweed flat caps and moth-eaten sweater vests sitting around a rectangular table playing a card game, each with a cigarette in various stages of being smoked dangling from their lips. Cigarettes. Brunel felt in his front right pants pocket for his lighter and only found some loose coins. Then he remembered tossing it to the old man on the felucca earlier that day. Lighters could be bought. But not those with an inscription from a father to his son.

None of the crew was talking. Three crew members stood behind the players, studying their faces and cards. Two single exposed light bulbs swung above them, mimicking the movements of the ship and producing shadows of the crew that danced about the compartment. A pet cockatoo in a small bamboo cage emitted ear-piercing shrieks at unpredictable intervals. Only one player looked up at Brunel as he shed his coat, repositioned his satchel to lie across his chest, and hoisted himself into the top bunk, which overlooked the table. From his bunk, Brunel could see through a thick layer of smoke that the pile of pesetas signaled a long round of wagering. The player who had looked up at him earlier sent the crew member opposite him a sly glance and then jutted his chin toward Brunel's bunk. Both men sneered and exchanged muffled asides that Brunel couldn't make out.

Brunel lay back on the black-and-white-striped mattress, which smelled of perspiration and piss. He rested his head on a length of metal tubing that acted like a small railing along the sides of his bunk. Just after his arrival, someone snatched the rolled-up blanket that stood in for a pillow. The porthole to his left had been painted over with a heavy black paint to keep interior light from signaling their presence to neutrality-ignoring German or Italian ships. He closed his eyes to the muted sounds of the game, punctuated by an occasional accusatory shout. The acid in his stomach took advantage of his prone position and crept up his esophagus. Heavy eyes and a fit of drowsiness washed over him.

The night Alain's wife, Liliane, took him to the crypt of the Basilique Notre Dame d'Afrique, never once did her deep-set deadpan eyes shed a tear about the death of her husband during the attack at the café. Adding the news from the French officer Roget that their son was found dead would have emotionally crippled any other mother. But the woman complied with all his demands without pushback. More than once she said that she wanted to rid herself of the satchel, the cause of so much painful heartache. She fell silent on the way to the crypt, as well as inside, as Brunel retrieved the satchel from its hiding place.

When they left the basilica behind, they made their way back in darkness to the convent where she worked. Liliane was two steps behind Brunel as they headed down the rue de la Basilique. The hoarsely barked order to stop froze Brunel. He slipped his right hand into the jacket pocket and put a firm hold on his revolver's grip. At that moment, the realization that he'd never shot a gun before exploded in his head.

He turned back to see Liliane stepping into a shadowed doorway, out of the line of sight of a single uniformed officer a hundred yards behind them. Brunel prompted her to follow him. She uttered a guttural no. He backtracked to the doorway, and with his left arm stretching into the darkness, he grabbed her shoulder, then slipped his hand down to her upper arm and pulled her out into the street.

The policeman shouted again to stop. Brunel yelled at the woman to move. She resisted, which confused him. Had she just given up, having lost her family? He yanked with some force, and he heard fabric ripping.

He gave another yank but lost his grip. She fell. The officer was seventy yards and closing.

Brunel swore at her and bent down to pull her back to her feet. She was dead weight. As he rose with her arm in a tight grip, a shot ricocheted off the building's facade, just above the doorway, driving large chips of stucco into the air. He struggled to get Liliane to her feet. She looked up at his face. Her emotionless stare told him she was done with it all. Another shot. Liliane fell to her knees, Brunel still holding her left arm. He let go, and she fell face down in the street.

Brunel turned and ran, hugging the walls of the buildings as he did so. He ran for a long time, then stopped and hid in the dark recess of a garage door. He tried to calm his heavy breathing but failed, making it difficult to hear if the officer was still in pursuit. The running made his legs ache. He began rubbing his right thigh. The firm strokes brought minor relief. Then he felt a firmness growing...in his crotch.

Brunel jolted upward, banging his head against the compartment's ceiling. Through the burst of stars in his eyes, he saw her. Both hands rubbing his thigh.

"What are you doing?" he said, slapping away her hands.

"I sent them away. You were...having a bad dream. Your legs were like they were in motion. I...I only tried to calm you, bring you comfort."

Brunel rolled off his bunk and landed on his feet. He stood inches from the corpulent cook. She was of equal height, and he detected the odor of that evening's paella on her breath. It activated a fresh bout of churning stomach acids. Brunel brushed past the woman with difficulty given the cramped space. "I am reporting this to the captain," Brunel said. "Your advances are entirely unwelcome."

Josefa snorted and gave a dismissive wave. "The captain. He is a spineless excuse for a man. He and others have tried to control me. They all failed."

Brunel stopped, turned, and took another look. She was picking her teeth, like she had just finished a feast of a meal. He pressed the satchel close to his chest and left to find a place to hide for the rest of the voyage.

CHAPTER THIRTY-FOUR

2050 Hours, Thursday, January 7, 1943
Hôtel Saint-George, rue Michelet, Algiers

Conor and Emily sat at a table five feet from where he and Stevens had gone at it. Not his most bright and shining moment. He was about to mention the fun fact to Emily when she leaned in toward him.

"How are you feeling about…all this? You haven't said much."

"I could say the same about you. Not that we've had much time alone."

"Yes. Of course. It's…it's just unsettling…the way this is all unfolding."

Before Conor could dig into what was unsettling her, Commander Butcher glided into the bar. The brass buttons on his double-breasted uniform jacket sparkled, his black tie slightly askew. An out-of-breath Staff Sergeant Billings, holding a manila file, was a half-step behind him. Butcher unbuttoned his jacket and pulled out a chair. "Sergeant, track down some coffee for the three of us, and don't forget to add some special flavoring. Then have a seat and take some notes." Billings had half turned to the bar when Butcher told him to leave the file. "How's the head, Conor? Still bothering you?"

Conor, whose head hadn't stopped its dull throbbing pain since the firefight in the cemetery, wasn't above lying when it came to making sure he wasn't going to be left behind on any mission that came up. Especially if it meant that Emily would have to go on the mission alone. "Fit as I'll ever be, Commander. Ready to go hell-for-leather after this Brunel character."

"Hopefully, you don't mean carelessly."

"Never careless. But maybe a little reckless abandon thrown into the mix." Sure as shit that got the expected reaction from Emily, in the form of a shaming shake of her head.

"Yes, well, that seems to have worked for you in the past." Billings returned with four mugs of steaming coffee and took a seat at the table. Butcher glanced at the mug in front of Billings.

"Just black, Commander. Just black."

Butcher chuckled and said, "Notes, Sergeant."

"Sir," Billings said, then took a hearty swallow of his coffee.

"So, where are we, Commander? Did you get us on the *Casabianca*?" Conor said.

Butcher nodded. "You leave tonight. Murphy and I pulled some strings. Or I should say, Murphy did. He has quite a bit of sway with General Giraud, who assured the sub's commander that he was to cooperate. I briefed the commander. He's none too happy about the surface transit. You'll have to win him over on that once you meet him."

Conor looked at Emily. "Commander, if we could get Bobby Heugle sprung from Colonel Eddy, that would make us feel a lot better. This is all coming together really quick."

"No can do. If I go to Eddy, he'll ask too many questions that I won't be able to answer truthfully. Just make the best of it."

"Once we finish dealing with Brunel, how do we get back out?"

"I had no time to figure that out. Deal with the *Casabianca*'s commander. He seems to be pretty resourceful. If he can't get you back here, head for Spain."

Conor and Emily served up reluctant nods. "Commander, after the cemetery attack, we're low on supplies. Can you let us run up a tab somewhere?" Conor asked.

Butcher pointed to Billings. "Sergeant, pave the way for these two with the quartermaster of the thirty-fourth infantry unit. Any pushback, throw General Eisenhower's name around, with some finesse. Understood, Sergeant?"

"Fully, Commander."

Conor passed a list to Billings, who peeked at it, then shoved it into the breast pocket of his uniform blouse.

"Anything else?"

Conor and Emily exchanged glances, then shook their heads. As Butcher rose from his chair, Conor was already compiling another list…of things that could go wrong.

CHAPTER THIRTY-FIVE

2215 Hours, Thursday, January 7, 1943
DuBois Home/Office, 5th Arrondissement, Lyon

After René had finally convinced his mother, Sarah, to retire for the night, Yves and Hélène took their leave after Maggie conferred with them for several minutes. They agreed that Yves or Hélène would come back the next night to check on her and bring any information on the priest Alves. They told her not to expect much. She did anyway.

Maggie lay on her back on the table as René, his tall frame bent over her exposed side, sleeves rolled up to his elbows, took his time inspecting his handiwork while speaking softly in French. The scowling nurse took notes as he spoke.

Maggie couldn't ignore Villard's presence if her life depended on it. The woman stood just behind and to the left of René, scribbling on a clipboard. She made her presence and ticked-off disposition known with her guttural mumbling and repeated bumping into the exam table for the past several minutes. Maggie tried to dissuade the nurse from further displays of nastiness by directing several of her best stink-eyed looks in her direction, which all fell short because Villard refused to look at Maggie.

"Does your nurse speak English?"

René paused his inspection of her wounds and raised his head. "Limited. Her brother is a professor of languages at a local university." René's lips formed an inkling of a smile. "Don't think I didn't notice your famous Thorn stink eye you have been sending in her direction." He turned to Villard and asked her to place the notes on his desk, then excused her for the night.

"Not the warmest person, is she?"

René laughed. "I will say that is a quality she isn't known for. Loyalty to my father. Well, that's another story. But I must admit, she seems to be somewhat colder than normal. I'll have to ask her why."

"Well, don't on my account." She paused; her lips moved slowly into a smile. "So, am I going to live, Doctor?" Maggie asked playfully.

"Yes. But you were lucky. Those branches could have punctured a lung, or worse."

"Good to know." Maggie was drawn into René's dark-green eyes. Familiar eyes. But there was something missing. Something also familiar. The scent of his cologne. The first time he wore it was as her guest at Conor and Grace's wedding back in 1938. They had only been dating for a handful of weeks. He said it was a gift from his mother—Old Spice. After they broke up, she bought a bottle of it at Bamberger's. When Conor asked who it was for, she lied and told him it was a birthday gift for their father, but she kept the oddly shaped bottle with its ivory-colored stopper for herself. She took it with her when she spent two semesters in France after they broke up. Snatching whiffs of the cologne when the numerous episodes of melancholy swept her up. Much like René had swept her up the first time they met.

"Maggie, your wounds will heal nicely, but any movement will bring on more bleeding. You must give them time to heal. Any physical exertion will pull at the stitches."

"That's my problem, not yours." René went to the sink and began washing his hands. The silence between them brought Maggie's thoughts back to her mission, which had set a record for hitting the skids. She stared up at the vaulted tin ceiling. "Have you ever run into a priest, someone by the name of Alves?" When the water stopped running, the silence returned. "René?" She rolled over on her right side, thinking that he had left the room.

But there he stood, taking his time drying his hands on a dingy white towel. Staring at her.

"Did you hear me?"

"Yes. Yes, I did." He draped the towel over the side of the sink and returned to the table. His brow creased. "You said Alves? Robert Alves?"

Maggie lay back. "I said Alves, René. But I didn't mention his first name. So, it seems safe to say that you know him."

He ran a hand through his hair and blew out a long breath. "Yes. Just in passing, though. Can't say I know much about him." He rolled down his sleeves as he stepped to his desk and began shuffling papers.

Maggie rolled onto her back and turned her head toward him. "What can you tell me about him? Anything would help."

"Well, he's close to the mother of a patient of mine. As a favor, he calls on her son, checking on him," he said without making eye contact. When he stopped moving papers on his desk, he looked up. "Would this priest be the subject of the other matter you mentioned?"

Maggie returned her gaze to the ceiling, a familiar intuition telling her he was holding something back. "Yes. He's working for the Germans. And I'm going to…put a stop to it."

"I see." Maggie heard René rise from his chair and come closer. "What can you tell me about the plans London has for me?"

The change in subject surprised Maggie. "It involves Paris. That's all I know." A lie of omission. But she was okay with that, given her nagging intuition.

CHAPTER THIRTY-SIX

0100 Hours, Friday, January 8, 1943
Aboard the French Submarine Casabianca, Algiers Waterfront

A thin line of blood coursed down the shin of Emily's right leg. The blood seeped through the woolen pant leg, creating a circular dark-forest-green patch the size of a pound sterling coin. Emily sat in an undersized metal chair in the *Casabianca*'s wardroom, one hatch down from the control room, waiting on Conor's return from his search for the submarine's lavatory. She surveyed the cramped space and took note of the aircraft and surface ship identification charts, their edges slightly curled, pinned to a corkboard on the bulkhead. The black silhouettes of the Me-109 and a German submarine chaser were circled in pencil.

She was waiting for the commander Jean L'Herminier to make an appearance. Their initial encounter, just after Emily and Conor had come aboard, was in the submarine's conning tower, where she'd smashed her shin on the ladder as she descended into the low-lit depths of the Redoutable class submarine. L'Herminier, after a quick welcome aboard, asked if she was all right and, not waiting for an answer, told her he had scars on both shins from repeated disagreements with the sub's ladders and hatches.

Every spare inch of the wardroom, as well as every compartment she and Conor were led through by the *Casabianca*'s second-in-command, was crammed with cases of supplies, from foodstuffs to ammunition, explosives, radio parts, and medical supplies. Most of the crates were labeled in English and accompanied by the initials *U. S. A.* seared into the soft wood. Some crates of food were identified as coming from various places in and around Algiers.

Emily looked down at her sore leg as she heard footsteps pounding on the metal grating in the passageway outside of the quarters.

"I've been on one sub in my naval career. And let me tell you, it was memorable." Emily looked up at Conor, who stood in the doorway, his hands plunged deep into his pockets. "And do you want to know why?"

Emily shifted her gaze back to her shin and began to massage the area surrounding the point of impact. "Something tells me you're going to tell me, even if I don't want to know."

"The smell. Even with the deck hatches open while this sub's been tied up, the smell is something damn hard to get used to. Diesel fuel, hydraulic fluid, cooking oil, sweat, cigarettes, and… sewage. It's why the surface navy called the crews of these subs sewer pipe sailors." Conor shook his head. "God bless any sewer pipe sailor who volunteered for sub service, that's all I can say."

"I never liked that term." Emily looked up and could only make out the top of an officer's cap tilted back. The once-white stretched cotton material had given way to numerous grease and oil smudge marks.

Conor spun around, allowing Emily to see Commander L'Herminier, his pale clean-shaven face and prominent droopy nose seemingly pointing to an impish grin.

"Unless it came off the lips of another sewer pipe sailor," L'Herminier said.

"Commander, I was just sharing some…some—"

"Colorful history about the cadre of brave submariners worldwide," Emily said.

The slim-built L'Herminier's grin grew into an unabashed smile as he squeezed past Conor. He took a seat at the metal table attached to the bulkhead. A red-faced Conor took the other chair in the compartment beside Emily. "So, Mr. Thorn, do you know the story about the submariner who, as he returned from shore leave, quite drunk mind you, was spotted by the topside watch officer? The officer observed the sailor stop on the pier, bend down, and remove a manhole cover, and, to the watch officer's surprise, drop down into it. The watch officer ordered another crew member to inspect the manhole. When he reported back to the watch officer, he told him that one of their crew, a long-serving *officier marinier*—a first-class petty officer in your navy, Mr. Thorn—who was assigned to the engine room, was fast asleep, curled up at the bottom of the sewer with his head resting on his rolled-up shirt."

Conor exchanged a glance with Emily, who responded with raised eyebrows and a slight shrug.

"At some point, I'd like to introduce him to you. He's the absolute best engineer sewer pipe sailor in the Free French Navy."

"Commander, I meant no disrespect. Please believe that," Conor offered. "It takes a special man to want to serve as a submariner. I lost a couple of classmates from the academy on the *Grunion* last year." The sub was overdue from patrol, and all hands were assumed lost. Not knowing what happened stuck in Conor's craw.

L'Herminier laughed, then removed his cap and ran his hand through his thinning hair. "Aah, don't worry, he'd be the first to tell you he was a sewer pipe sailor. That's just before he directed a raging right hook into your jaw." The commander's laugh was throaty, and Conor realized that the commander had a healthy sense of humor.

A steward, spotted apron wrapped tightly around his tapered waist, entered the wardroom and placed three mugs of steaming coffee on the metal table, then withdrew. "Thanks to your OSS, we have been granted special stores, including real coffee. Enjoy." After they each imbibed, L'Herminier trained his gaze on Conor. "I will tell you what I have been told by Colonel Eddy. Then you will tell me what Commander Butcher and Robert Murphy have chosen to withhold that may contribute to getting my crew killed." L'Herminier paused. "*D'accord?*"

"Agreed, Commander," Emily said.

L'Herminier slapped the metal table with an open hand. "Good." After another sip, he said, "Commander Butcher was too tight-lipped for my taste. All I know is that besides the two missions previously assigned by Colonel Eddy, I am to make sure you two make it safely ashore."

Conor caught Emily's attention. *Two missions from Eddy?*

"And I have been told to alter the sequence of my missions to accommodate your pressing schedule for a reason Butcher wasn't interested in explaining or couldn't."

Emily beat Conor to the punch. "Commander, you said two missions. We were only aware of a mission to Corsica."

"Yes, one is a resupply mission to Corsica; the other I will get to in a minute." After another swig from his mug, L'Herminier continued. "To expedite matters, I have been ordered to travel on the surface in the daytime. An order that, if followed, will heighten the odds that we will all be killed before we even get close to the French coastline." He paused as if to detect any signs that they agreed the order was as crazy as he thought it was. "So, we are good so far, are we not?"

"Good as we can be," Conor said.

"I am not going to risk this boat and crew to transit on the surface in the daytime. Are you both good with that?"

Conor shook his head. "That's a no. A long-range forecast has predicted a low thick ceiling. No air threats. That was something that Commander Butcher passed along to us," he said and leaned in for emphasis. "Commander, we can't afford to spend time submerged. Even twenty percent of the trip submerged would add about five hours to the transit across the Med. The *Cadiz* has too much of a jump on—"

Emily darted a look at Conor, her shoulders slumping at the mention of the *Cadiz*. He was digging a hole for himself...and her. Before she turned back to the commander, she noticed Conor's pallid face. He was sweating.

"What is this...the *Cadiz*? Is this a ship? Butcher said nothing—"

"Commander, this has been a very fluid situation. Since Commander Butcher briefed you, there has been news," Emily said. "We need to apprehend someone on a Spanish-flagged vessel, the *Cadiz*." Conor sat back and gave Emily a nod of thanks. She needed to close the door to any further probing by the clearly peeved Frenchman. "We are under strict orders not to divulge anything beyond what we have thus far. I'm sure you understand."

"I am sure I don't understand why elevating the danger beyond what already exists for this submarine and crew, just so you two can apprehend some individual, makes sense to General Eisenhower." L'Herminier scooped up his mug and drained it.

Conor started to speak, but Emily's hand on his forearm stopped him. She wanted to let the commander stew on her last response for a moment. "You mentioned two missions," she finally said. "What was the other one?"

L'Herminier accepted the change in subject and massaged his forehead. "Colonel Eddy has ordered us to drop off another agent. It will be the same location you two will be sent ashore—east of Les Saintes-Maries-de-la-Mer, in the Camargue area, which is all marshland and étangs. Briny lagoons, you call them. But there are spits of land throughout. We're banking on the Germans thinking marshland wouldn't be a likely landing spot for the Allies, and they would forgo mining the area."

"Is this agent aboard?"

"Yes. Just before you both arrived. The agent, code name Jacqueline, is in the forward crew quarters checking his equipment. I suggest you both do the same. We shove off—" Conor snatched a small metal wastebasket from under the table and let loose an explosive charge of vomit, prompting Emily and L'Herminier to push away from the table, both wide-eyed in shock.

#

Emily put her left hand firmly on Conor's chest, which kept him pinned to the thin mattress of L'Herminier's pull-down bunk. Emily and L'Herminier had locked their eyes on him.

"Never seen a guy lose his lunch before?"

"Stop with the jokes, Conor. You have a severe concussion."

"Maybe you should go ashore for bed rest," L'Herminier said.

"You're a danger to yourself. And to this mission," Emily said with a tone of finality for good measure.

"Listen, Em—"

"I will let you two work this out. And, Mr. Thorn, I would listen to this young woman. She seems to be sensible." L'Herminier donned his officer's cap. "We shove off in thirty minutes. Come to an agreement in fifteen." With that directive, he withdrew.

"We don't need to. It's settled," Conor said to the fleeing commander. He turned to the glaring Emily. "Right?"

"Wrong. As I said, you are a threat to this mission. I can't be taking care of you and track down this Brunel character."

"I don't need taking care of. So get that through that pretty head of yours." He started to free himself from the bunk, but it only fueled the stamping press that pounded away in his head. He shut his eyes tightly to keep the pain from leaking out his eyes onto the compartment's deck.

"Pretty head? What the hell, Conor? You are one thick-headed child."

"Good. That's settled."

CHAPTER THIRTY-SEVEN

0200 Hours, Friday, January 8, 1943
At Sea Aboard the French Submarine Casabianca

Leaving the rank smell from Conor's vomit behind, they moved forward and stopped at the sub's galley. There was a group of men numbering around twenty who sat at narrow bird-egg-blue Formica-topped tables. Few were talking. Those who did spoke through mouths crammed with food. When two officers stood and scooped up their plates and forks, Conor and Emily took their seats. None of the remaining crew paid him much attention. As for Emily, that was another matter.

The crew's heads were on a swivel. From their plates, then to Emily, then back to their plates. When their plates were empty, Emily received uninterrupted stares until a twig of a cook shouted something that goaded the men into clearing the tables and, in a clatter of noise, dumping their plates into a tub that held two inches of cloudy water. Conor and Emily talked in hushed tones as another section of men appeared from both forward and aft and proceeded to settle in for a quick meal. They received the same treatment from the new section.

"Are you as uneasy about all this as I am?" Not getting an answer, Emily leaned in. "Well?"

"Em, it's not like we spent months planning the last three missions. Hell, the last one…that whole mission developed almost overnight. Real seat-of-our-pants style. We need to trust L'Herminier and his crew."

"Oh, I do. It's what we are expecting once we get put ashore. No meetup. Just a meeting place. What if we have to wait hour after hour before anyone makes contact with us? Brunel is so far ahead of us."

"Whoa, lady. Slow down that train, will you?" His response to Emily's anxiety-driven concerns netted a few stares from the new diners. It was Conor's turn to lean in. "We'll figure it out. We'll get to Lyon, and with your language skills and my—"

"Reckless, impetuous behavior."

"Yeah. I would have put it another way, but yeah—that and some luck thrown in…we'll figure out a plan."

Emily narrowed her eyes and gave him a stare that Conor could almost feel. "You're not well. If you must know, that's a big part of what's driving my train, to use your phrasing."

"Enough with the concussion stuff. I'm fine. A headache that won't go away, that's all. I've had worse ones after academy football games."

"Now that's a relief." Conor was surprised by her sarcasm. But he deserved it. His head felt much worse. His vision wasn't much to talk about either.

"Let's head forward and meet this Jacqueline. Maybe you two can commiserate about the men in your lives."

"You know, I'd really like to smack you one, but I'll spare you the embarrassment."

Emily was quick to take the lead through a berthing compartment that seemed to be more populated with food stores and ammo boxes than with the boat's crew, then through a hatch into the forward torpedo room. At first glance, Conor saw two people on their knees, stuffing a rubberized duffel with what looked like a suitcase radio. Propped up alongside a stored gleaming black torpedo was a folding wood-framed canvas kayak, first used in the war by British commandos. It was their mode of transport to a French beach. His eyes shifted to four torpedo tubes, their hatches open, revealing the gleaming brass propellers of the loaded torpedoes. Along the sides of the room, he counted six more torpedoes painted in glossy black, stored on ready racks. Below and on either side of the decking were two additional stored fish. Their waiting tubes were hard to make out, but he was sure they also were preloaded.

Emily pointed to the berths that lined the inner hull above the stored torpedoes. Conor could hear the muffled sounds of snoring off-watch sailors. Emily bent over the two kneeling figures and tapped one on the shoulder. The tap startled the person whose head snapped around, revealing the weathered face of a thirtysomething man, an unlit cigarette dangling between bloodless lips.

"Sneaking up on me, are ya? Couldn't hear you for the rattle and hum of this blasted submarine." He uncoiled his frame, rising to his feet, and stood a head taller than Emily.

The other man who had been helping also rose. He was dressed in sharply pressed khaki pants and an open-collared shirt, its sleeves rolled up to his elbows. Conor didn't see an insignia anywhere. A degree of familiarity made his gaze linger on the second man's clean-shaven face. His stare was met with one just as focused on him.

"So count us as a little confused. We're looking for Jacqueline," Emily said.

"That'd be me." The weathered face broke into a smile. He snatched the cigarette from his lips and extended a hand. "Code names are silly, don't you think?" Emily shook his hand. "The desk jockeys back in Algiers thought a woman's name would create a bit of a headache for the Jerries. They didn't seem to think it would confuse the good guys also. Just call me Jackie."

"I'm Emily and this is Conor."

Conor looked at Mr. Khaki, expecting a name, but none was forthcoming. "And you would be…"

Mr. Khaki bit at his lower lip before dropping a name. "James Stones. SOE."

"Is this a pleasure cruise or more one of a business nature?" Conor asked, then shifted his eyes to the port-wine stain on his neck the size and color of a plum just below his left earlobe.

"I'm what's called the conducting officer. Last-minute assignment. You two headed to France?"

Conor continued to study the skittish Stones's face, letting Emily jump in.

"You said last-minute assignment. What happened to the regular conducting officer?" she asked. Conor noted she didn't respond to the question about France.

"That's Wallace. Came down with a resurgence of malaria. Something he first caught on a previous mission in the jungles of Burma. I was next up." Conor watched Stones give his deep-purple birthmark a buff with his fingertips.

"First trip into France, Jackie?" Emily said.

Jackie nodded and ran his fingers through his thinning hair. "Affirmative. I mean since the Germans steamrolled the French Army in forty."

Conor shifted his gaze to Jackie. "Assuming you have gotten more training than us, can you spend some time with us? Some dos, some don'ts? Things have come together pretty damn quick for us."

"Be happy to, Conor. I spent quite a bit of time in France before the war. Things have changed for sure, but quite a bit hasn't."

"Wonderful, Jackie," Emily said. "Say, I can't accurately place your accent. You're not a Brit. You're—"

"Canadian. Spent the last decade in Algiers. Been helping the OSS establish radio communication chains. Bit of an engineer. My wife says I can't pass by a radio without trying to take it apart."

"Could you take a look at the set we brought along? It's an SSTR1," Emily said.

"My pleasure. That's a reliable unit. Where's your gear?"

"Aft crew quarters," Conor said.

"No time like the present," Jackie said. "I'll lead the way."

Jackie headed aft to the compartment's hatch, and Emily followed right behind. Conor and Stones looked at each other. "Will catch up with you later, Jim."

"It's James. No one calls me Jim."

"Well, I just did." Conor turned and caught up to Emily just as she cleared the hatch. "Em…Stones. The night I butted heads with Stevens…Stones was the guy having words with him."

"The night he was killed?"

Conor nodded. "The night he was killed."

CHAPTER THIRTY-EIGHT

0900 Hours, Friday, January 8, 1943
Hôtel Terminus, Gestapo Headquarters, Lyon

Steam from three locomotives parked on the tracks just outside the open-air Lyon Perrache train station crept toward the hotel, hugging the ground like an animal seeking its prey. Major Kurt Eklof watched as the stealthy vapor neared the set of four sidings closest to the Gestapo's headquarters. It camouflaged the cattle cars on the two farthest sets of sidings and dissipated before it reached the cattle cars on the siding closest to the hotel.

His breath was fogging the window. He cleared a circular patch on the glass with a swipe of his hand so he could watch a group of people as they crossed over the closest siding and were prompted at gunpoint to climb up into the railcars. The ones who tripped over the rails or were too slow were introduced to the butts of rifles in their necks and backs. One woman, who was the first to fall, remained on the ground face down, her legs and arms splayed out in four directions. She did not respond to numerous rifle butts. Two soldiers stood over her, talking animatedly.

"Shoot the damn woman," he said to himself.

One soldier bent down and stretched his arm toward her. Before he could touch her, the other soldier placed the barrel of his rifle on the base of her skull and fired. The blast knocked his comrade to the ground.

"What was that?" The question came from behind him. He

turned and saw a woman twisted in her chair staring at him, looking frightfully pale.

"Nothing you should be concerned about, Fräulein. Unless you have thrown in with the Resistance or"—Eklof turned away from the window and strode back to his desk—"happen to be a Jew."

The woman—Lucie Villard was the name she gave to his adjutant—resettled herself in her chair. Eklof dropped into his high-back leather chair and studied her. He placed her in her early forties. She had dyed blonde hair, which was under siege by a surge of black roots. Her wide face and quivering chin betrayed her nervousness. But Eklof wasn't sure if he should give the woman credit or criticize her for her stupidity for voluntarily coming to the Hôtel Terminus. He was sure that the woman had heard stories. Most of which were probably true.

"I am neither, I can assure you, Major." The woman's voice was gravelly as if choked by mucus.

"So you say. I am told that you have information. That makes you, as a Frenchwoman, a collaborator. One who wishes to turn in another Frenchman. Is that correct?" The woman nodded. "Well, out with it, then. I haven't all day."

She cleared her throat, then swallowed twice. "I am a nurse. I assist a doctor in the Vieux Lyon. He is a good man. But..." She cleared her throat again.

"Stop that," Eklof shouted, startling the woman. "But what?"

"His mother, she is an American. She was married to a French doctor... He's dead now. She has been helping Jews get out of France."

"Hmm...name?"

"Sarah DuBois."

"How do you know this?"

"I have seen them...the Jews. They come with their suitcases to the house when the doctor is out treating patients. But I never see them again." Her blue eyes narrowed to slits. "And she has given refuge to another American, a woman. She was dropped near Lyon by parachute some days ago and was injured."

Eklof sat up. "Go on."

"I heard this American say that she came to Lyon to take Sarah DuBois to Switzerland."

"Why? Why is she so...special?"

"I do not know, Major."

"The son. The doctor. Besides helping this American spy, is he also helping Jews?"

"Hardly. He is loyal to Vichy. Which has driven him and his mother apart. He hasn't treated the American spy's wounds. Only the mother has. And..." Villard lowered her eyes.

"And what? Out with it."

"I can't be sure, but I believe he is working for the Abwehr."

"That is hard to believe." He hoped casting doubt on her disclosure would prompt a more thorough explanation. "How do you know this?"

Villard raised her gaze. "I saw him once. It was Tuesday. I was in the Place Saint-Jean with friends. He was near the Fontaine Saint-Jean. He was getting into a car, a black Citroën. Everyone knows the Abwehr drives those black cars."

"Hardly unquestionable proof," Eklof said, deciding not to press the issue more. He would have Hauptmann Krupp look into it. "The spy. What is her name?"

"Maggie. That is the only name I heard, Major."

Eklof, processing what he just heard, adjusted the patch over his right eye and then ran his hand over the hair that covered what was left of his left ear. His failure to bring in Thorn and the engineer, who was to sell to the SD top-secret documents concerning British code-breaking, was a black mark on his record. But perhaps one that was not indelible. A black mark that two spectacular arrests—Americans, no less—could wash away.

CHAPTER THIRTY-NINE

0930 Hours, Friday, January 8, 1943
DuBois Home/Office, 5th Arrondissement, Lyon

René DuBois recognized the knock. It was always a rapid, impatient double rap. Very American, he thought each time he heard it. And each time, his mother entered without waiting for a response.

"René, where's Red?"

He looked up from Henry Gray's *Anatomy of the Human Body* he had his nose buried in, then shut it and pushed it aside. "She's in the attic, regaining some strength. Why do you ask? Is there something wrong?"

"No. Nothing's wrong. I told her I would look in on her. I want to make sure she is comfortable. Don't be alarmed."

"Well, I am alarmed. She can't be found here."

"She won't be. As long as we can trust Yves and that woman who brought her here."

"That has me worried. Yves. He and I don't get along."

"And why is that, René?"

"Ask him, Mother." DuBois rose from his chair and moved toward the bay window that overlooked the courtyard. He parted the drapes with his forefinger and took in the scene below. He glimpsed three rats scurrying across the courtyard. Two rats were chasing the lead rat, which had a crust of bread in its mouth. He turned back to his mother, who stood in front of his desk, arms folded across her chest. "What? Let me guess. You want to talk about Switzerland."

"You know I can't leave. Not now. But I don't want to talk about that. I want you to see someone. Actually, a couple. The wife. She's pregnant and feeling poorly."

"Fine." René saw a look that he took as *there's more*. "What else?"

"They have no money."

"That's nothing new. Are they here?"

"Just outside."

He rolled up his sleeves and headed to the sink in the corner of the office. "Well, let's get on with it. I have a house call in thirty minutes. Someone with money."

Sarah left without a thank-you.

As he turned off the tap, he heard rustling behind him. He grabbed a towel and turned toward the door. There stood a couple in their twenties. The husband, holding a tattered cardboard suitcase, had sunken eyes and an unshaven face. He was malnourished. The wife was showing. Tight auburn curls framed her tear-streaked face. She positioned her right hand under her belly to support her unborn child. DuBois flung the towel into the sink.

"Are you Jewish?"

The husband started to answer but stopped and exchanged a glance with his wife. "Yes…yes we are. But the kind lady said you could help us. My wife, she's—"

"I don't treat Jews. My mother…she knows that. Not that she agrees with me. It will invite trouble." The husband again opened his mouth to respond, but DuBois raised his hand to stop him. "Leave. Do not come back. And do not contact my mother. If you do, I will report you to the Gestapo."

CHAPTER FORTY

1000 Hours, Friday, January 8, 1943
At Sea Aboard the French Submarine Casabianca

Emily sat alone in the wardroom, thumbing through a French-to-English dictionary she found tucked away on a packed metal shelf just above a fold-up stainless-steel sink. She had just paged through the entries for the letter *D* when L'Herminier stepped in and took a seat at the table. His officer's cap was pushed back on his head, revealing a patch of thinning salt-and-pepper hair. He took out a handkerchief and wiped his brow.

"*Vous étudiez de notre langage riche et mélodique?*"

"*Oui*, Commander. And yes, your language is, indeed, rich and melodic. I haven't been to France since my days in finishing school in Switzerland."

Before L'Herminier could respond, a sailor entered, a clipboard in his severely burned right hand. The sight gave Emily an involuntary start. She directed her gaze to the sailor's face. The right side closely resembled the appearance of his hand. A long road back, Commander Butcher said of her brother. It seemed this sailor had been on that road for some time. The molten, almost translucent skin seemed pulled tight across his cheekbone and jawline. He spoke in a clipped manner as he waited for the commander to sign for the message he slipped from the clipboard.

When the sailor left, L'Herminier read the message, folded it, and stuffed it into his breast pocket. "That was Graduate Seaman

Brun. His previous posting was on the destroyer *Fougueux*, which, I must point out, the Americans sank during the invasion of Casablanca."

Emily shifted in her seat. "The losses there were sad, Commander. And so unnecessary."

"I think there was much…confusion leading up to your Operation Torch. Loyalties in many cases were aligned… mistakenly."

"Which led to losses on both sides."

"Yes. But don't try to explain that to Seaman Brun. He sees things differently."

"I am sure he does." The sight of Seaman Brun's injuries saddened Emily. The war affected all lives, even those without physical manifestations like those of Richard or Seaman Brun.

A silence fell between them that Emily broke. "How's the weather, Commander?"

"Just to our liking. Thick cloud cover delivering a driving rain complemented by a heavy chop. A distant thunder completes the picture. We have made good progress…despite the risks." L'Herminier again fell silent but only for a moment. "Speaking of risks, your husband—he is stubborn, no?"

Emily chuckled. "That might be an understatement of understatements, Commander. I assume that his refusal to stand down because of his concussion prompted your question?"

"Yes. I assume anyone sent to France, such as the two of you, have a crucial mission. But his condition is far from what is necessary to guarantee success." L'Herminier rubbed his temples with his fingertips and closed his eyes for a second as if to tame a headache of his own. "So many risks and so few people to trust. Don't you agree, he himself is a risk to the mission?"

Emily agreed with everything he'd said but replied, "No, Commander. If Conor believed he was putting the mission at risk, he would admit it." She locked her eyes on L'Herminier, but she knew she would not stake her life on her own words—except, she already was.

CHAPTER FORTY-ONE

1000 Hours, Friday, January 8, 1943
DuBois Home/Office, 5th Arrondissement, Lyon

Eklof glared at the unconscious body on the floor. When he'd slapped the wailing woman with the back of his right hand, she'd fallen to the floor as if her entire skeletal structure had been vaporized by some hellish power. The heap of clothes that covered all but her hands and head seemed to still float in the air, then softly they settled on DuBois's mother's feeble frame. Eklof shook out his right hand; it stung sharply from the blow. At the far end of the foyer, he spotted the nurse, Villard, peering through a crack in the door. When she made eye contact with him, she vanished, leaving the door ajar.

"Two of you, take her to the van. And wait there. We won't be long," Eklof said to the trench coat–wearing police officers who stood over the woman. He motioned to the third officer with the hand that still pulsed with pain. "Follow me, Krupp. But be quiet."

As Eklof brushed past, the two police officers pocketed their Ruby semi-automatic pistols, then picked up the old woman, one by the arms and the other by her ankles. Hauptmann Krupp, his mouth curled up in an ever-present sneer, was on his heels.

The stairway to the attic was narrow. A thin layer of dust coated the steps, and in the center were at least two sets of footprints. At the top of the stairs, both men waited and listened. Hearing no sound from the other side, Eklof tipped his chin toward the door. Krupp nodded once and rammed a foot into the doorknob.

Splinters of wood launched into the dim room as the door slammed into the wall, then bounced back, smashing into Krupp's shoulder as he burst through the doorway. Eklof followed him into the air-starved attic. His own Walther PPK held loosely in his right hand.

A folding campaign bed along the wall to the right of the doorway was empty except for bedclothes that seemed to have been hurriedly tossed off. A small embroidered pillow lay on the floor at the far end of the cot. Gauze, a roll of bandage, and a half-drank glass of water sat on top of a nightstand alongside the cot. Eklof again signaled Krupp to wait quietly. Krupp swept his Walther pistol around the room. Eklof shook his head. Then he heard a shoe or boot scrape across the wood plank floor. It came from the corner of the attic farthest from the cot's location, where some furniture in disrepair had been stored.

"Is that you, Maggie?" Eklof paused and took steps in the direction of the noise. He picked up labored breathing. "That is your name, is it not?" Eklof pointed to the corner of the attic.

Krupp covered the ground to the corner swiftly and disappeared behind two matching chests of drawers, one set missing all of them. There was a scuffle, highlighted by a squeal from Krupp, something he'd never heard before. Eklof waited in the center of the room. He'd made sure his instructions to all the officers were clear—do not allow the American to make any sudden movement to a hidden capsule. The scuffling continued.

Making his way around the discarded furniture, he was treated to the sight of Krupp lying against the wall, holding on to his crotch, a chain with a locket also clutched in his hands. The American, a grunting redhead, was clawing at the hand that held the locket. Eklof fired off a round from his PPK into the floor inches away from the American's head, delivering the effect he wanted. The scuffling ceased. Krupp slowly rose to his feet. Eklof saw a pool of blood forming on the floor beneath the woman's left side.

"She went for this," Krupp said, his words a bit choked. He held up the chain, its locket dangled from it half-opened.

"Of course she did. As they trained her." Eklof holstered his PPK. "Get her up and put her on the cot."

It took the physically hampered Krupp long moments to get

the wounded and uncooperative American to the cot. For his efforts, blood smeared across the lower portion of Krupp's trench coat.

The American's face was contorted in pain and anger. "Leave her with me," Eklof said, his eyes glued to her. "Search the house. Make sure the doctor isn't in a closet or a corner of the cellar. If you find him, bring him and the nurse to me." He dragged a wooden chair closer to the anguished face of his prisoner. "You need a doctor, no? Your wound has reopened." He reached across the woman's body and lifted the hem of a bloodied heavy wool sweater. Underneath, the left side of the pale-blue shirt had turned maroon in color. The American had closed her eyes so tight that the skin above and below them was wrinkled. With his finger, he poked at the center of the blood pattern. The woman's involuntary reaction shocked Eklof even though he'd expected one.

"Bastard," she said, the word hissed more than spoken. Her eyes were narrow slits. He dropped the sweater's hem and sat back.

"Aah...she speaks, even though minus any respect. But speaks nonetheless." Eklof heard heavy footsteps on the stairs and turned as an out-of-breath Krupp entered the attic.

"There is no sign of the doctor. Nor the nurse. I have looked everywhere as you instructed, Sturmbannführer," Krupp said, running a hand over his stubble-covered head.

"You searched the entire house?"

"*Ja*. The house...it is small."

"Go down to the street and bring back one man to help take our prize down to the van." He turned back to the American. "Maggie, where is the doctor?"

Maggie's cheeks flamed. "Go—"

"No, no, no. Don't go there. You already have started out on the wrong foot. Wouldn't you say?"

"Fuck yourself." Maggie gave a forced smile. "But by the looks of your face...that eye and, heavens, that ear, it looks like someone already had a good go with you."

Eklof felt the heat of a flush move up his face. He punched the American's left side once, twice, aiming dead center for her bleeding wound. The sound the American made was one he'd never heard before—it was as if she was strangling her own scream.

CHAPTER FORTY-TWO

1030 Hours, Friday, January 8, 1943
DuBois Home/Office, 5th Arrondissement, Lyon

René DuBois clutched the cloth bag with the lone baguette close to his chest to shield the cooling bread from the light mist that floated down into the courtyard. The visit by the young Jewish couple earlier that morning delayed his trek to the boulangerie, resulting in being short-changed his normal two loaves. At the sound of someone sweeping, he stopped and looked at his neighbor Monique Latard, a sixty-year-old pensioner with a prominent case of osteoporosis, where she stood at the top of the stairs that led to the second floor. She stopped sweeping and looked down on him. Her face around her eyes was puffy and red, *as if she's been crying*, DuBois thought. He saw the silhouette of her husband in a window next to the apartment's door.

"It was not us, Doctor." The declaration triggered a fresh wave of tears. The woman's husband cracked open the door, grabbed her upper arm, and nearly dragged her off the stoop into the apartment. DuBois's mind raced. Citizens of Lyon learned quickly that one could not place their trust in anyone. Neighbors and even extended family members seeking favored treatment from the Germans and Vichy officials were not to be trusted. He took a deep breath and approached his front door.

The first thing he noticed when he stepped inside was the silence. Customarily at that point in the morning, his mother would have the gramophone turned on, playing the songs of

Glenn Miller and his orchestra. "At Last" was the one song that his mother would repeat several times before he would have to ask her to vary her selection.

He shouted for his mother and heard no response. He then hollered for his nurse, Lucie, and again, no response. It was strange that both were absent, leaving Maggie alone. He climbed the stairs, heading to the attic to check on his patient. The door to the attic was open and the cot empty. A sheet with a fresh bloodstain was visible from just inside the doorway. A wooden chair, brought close to the bedside, held the blanket he'd given Maggie. His heart hammered against his ribs. Maggie wasn't fit to travel, and his mother rarely left the house, except on her missions to assist escaping Jews. He turned to head back down the stairs. The sight of Lucie Villard standing at the top of the stairs surprised him.

"Lucie! You startled me. I called for you. Do you know where Maggie is? And Mother?"

Villard brought a hand to her mouth and bit down on her index finger. She was breathing hurriedly, which matched the rapid flutter of her eyelids. She was fighting back tears. "They're gone. The Nazis…they came and took them." Villard lost the fight against her tears. "Oh, Doctor, I am so sorry."

Monique's words echoed in his ears. *It was not us.* Then the thought hit him. "You. You were the informant?"

Villard crumpled to the floor and buried her face in her hands. She uttered not a word but nodded.

DuBois kneeled and pulled her hands from her face. "Why? Why did you do this?"

Villard looked up at him through swollen eyes. Her cheeks shimmered with her tears. "Your mother always hated me. She was jealous. She never trusted your father. And that American. It's obvious that she meant something to you. Once. Maybe still. But you continue to ignore the advances of my own daughter. She's in love with—"

"Stop this at once." DuBois released her hands, and she dropped to the floor. Before he could get to his feet, Villard reached up and grabbed his forearm, pulling him toward her. He yanked his arm free and stood over the broken woman. "Who took them? Just answer that."

The crying continued, but between sobs, Villard squeezed out the name Eklof. Then, "He's a Gestapo major. I don't know where they took them."

"Did this Eklof ask about me?"

Another nod. He stared at her; her shoulders heaved as she sobbed, then she turned her head. "I told him you knew nothing. That you were a good doctor…and I said that you were loyal to Vichy. Believe me, Doctor. I speak the truth."

"Get up. Collect yourself. You will take a message to someone, then never come back here. If you do, I will kill you."

DuBois turned away and headed down the stairs, formulating what he was going to say in his message to Colonel Henri.

CHAPTER FORTY-THREE

1035 Hours, Friday, January 8, 1943
At Sea Aboard the French Submarine Casabianca

As Conor and Jackie made their way aft to the wardroom, Jackie wouldn't give a rest to his running monologue about the merits of the M1941 Johnson Light Machine Gun versus the 9mm British Sten Gun. His blathering was just another noise vying for superiority inside Conor's wounded head.

When he parted the curtain to the *Casabianca*'s wardroom, he found Emily and the commander sitting in silence, each staring at empty mugs. "Okay. What did I do now?"

Emily looked up. "Oh, stop, Conor." She looked at the commander. "We were just having a brief discussion about our mission."

"Yeah? Anything I should know?"

The French commander didn't hesitate. "I expressed my concerns about your physical condition. Specifically, your compromised—"

"Can it, Commander. Subject closed."

"No need to be rude, Conor. The commander—"

"Just needs to get us to the coast of France," Conor said, angry at himself for not controlling his annoyance. He needed L'Herminier on his side.

"Conor," Emily said with a look of exasperation.

"Sorry, I just..." Conor wanted to say that the donnybrook taking place in his head made the jump to irritability damn easy, but he held back.

"I just need some sleep, I guess. A bit keyed up too."

"Well, that makes two of us," Jackie said as he brushed past Conor and took the chair next to Emily. "I'd rather be keyed up, as you say, than a bit laid-back. The Nazis like to kill spies. After they pull out your fingernails."

"Oh, good Lord. The two of you should get some sleep," Emily said.

"That is a sound idea, gentlemen. You, too, Emily," L'Herminier said.

"Later. Say, that Brit...the one who said he was the conducting officer. What's his name?"

Emily shot Conor a confused look. "You mean, Stones? You're the one who told me his—"

"Yeah, Stones. It was on the tip of my tongue. I haven't seen him lately. It's not like we're sailing on an aircraft carrier. Anyone seen the guy?"

"He may be back in the aft crew quarters," L'Herminier said. "He seems to have something in common, background-wise, with the boat's corpsman."

"Why do you ask, Conor?" Jackie said.

"Nothing major. I had a few questions for him. It can wait."

"Well, this question can't wait. It seems to me that you two didn't know a few days ago that you'd be heading to Nazi-held France on a submarine. Do I have that right?" Jackie said.

"More right than wrong, I guess," Conor said.

"Any experience behind enemy lines?" Conor could see L'Herminier betray a look of shared curiosity.

"Yes. Italy," Emily said, jumping in before Conor could answer. "We got by."

"How good is your French?" L'Herminier asked.

"I spent two years at finishing school in Switzerland. Geneva. They speak a great deal of French in the city and surrounding area."

L'Herminier turned to Conor, who then noticed that all three had zeroed in on him. "I can comprehend it. And read some. I admit, I don't sound like a Frenchman. I know when to play the role of a mute."

"You better work on that, Conor. You come across to me like a guy who doesn't like anyone speaking for you," Jackie said.

"I'll survive." Conor looked at Emily, a sheepish grin breaking out on her beautiful face. "We'll survive." Jackie gave a halfhearted nod and took his leave.

"Something tells me that Jackie has his doubts," Emily said.

Conor swallowed his response when he heard the muffled booms of naval gunfire followed by the sub's claxon and the shouts of "*Plongée...plongée...plongée.*" Dive...dive...dive.

#

By the time L'Herminier, Conor, and Emily arrived in the control room, two lookouts were sliding down the ladder from the conning tower, their boots riding the ladder's side rails. An orderly chaos enveloped the confined space as orders were being shouted and echoed. After the lookouts, two limp bodies were passed down through the hatch. Emily helped lay the first sailor, then the next one on the deck, and tended to them.

"Fifteen-degree down angle, take her down to periscope depth," L'Herminier said, his voice carrying a healthy dose of calm borne out of experience. The *Casabianca*'s deck tilted downward, the control room's crew instinctively leaning in the opposite direction. Five or six crew members ran through the control room, bumping the shoulders of the crew manning their positions as they headed to the bow to aid in the sub's descent. The order acknowledged, L'Herminier flipped a switch above his head near the periscope. "Engine room, secure the diesels, shift to battery power, make for five knots, set course zero two five."

The executive officer, his heavy rain gear still shedding water, had both hands wrapped around a steel cable connected to the hatch leading to the conning tower and, with a grunt, let his full weight drop to the deck while a seaman scurried up the ladder to seal the hatch. Before it was fully sealed, buckets of seawater showered down on the seaman, XO, and Emily as she bent over the two wounded sailors.

"Henri, *rapport*," L'Herminier said as four seamen arrived and carried the wounded from the control room, heading aft.

The XO wiped seawater from his face. "Commander, a fog

rolled in. Out of nowhere, a convoy…shallow draft coastal steamers…maybe *quatre ou cinq*." Four or five. "I'm not sure…" The XO took a deep breath. "One German flak lighter and a sub-hunter trawler escorted the convoy. Before we could return fire, they raked the top deck with machine-gun fire, wounding the deck gun crew."

"What's a flak lighter?" Emily said.

"It's a barge-like landing craft outfitted with two 88 millimeter guns and plenty of 20 millimeter antiaircraft guns, which could tear up the top deck of any sub crazy enough to take it on," Conor said. It was the eighty-eights that scared the shit out of him. Between the flak lighter and the trawler, the *Casabianca* was outgunned. He backed up and leaned against a narrow section of the bulkhead to keep out of the way.

"Did they detect us first?" L'Herminier said.

"Eighteen meters…periscope depth, Commander," the planesman answered.

"Up periscope," L'Herminier said.

"I don't know. I think we surprised them, maybe more than we were."

The gleaming steel tube rose, the cable hoists screeching, as L'Herminier pushed back his cap and nested his left eye into the rubber eyepiece. A stream of seawater seeped from the periscope's collar above the commander's head and drenched his cap. "The sub-chaser has pulled away from the convoy. The flak lighter is staying with the convoy." L'Herminier slapped the handles back up into place. "Down periscope. XO, flood all tanks…make depth forty-five meters. Quiet the boat. Make turns for three knots." The XO repeated the orders.

"Commander, we're picking up heavy cavitation." The voice was from the other side of the control room, from where Conor was standing. He had smelled fear before. But he detected none from the men who manned the control room. "Splashes in the water. Multiple splashes." He knew these men wanted to fight. And that was the problem.

Conor stepped toward L'Herminier, who had trained his sight upward, as if he could see the depth charges coming at the sub. The first depth charge was off target, as the sound was suppressed, but the sub still shook. The next explosion was closer; lights in the control room flickered, then held fast. Conor saw the rest of the control room's crew also looking up. The next four depth charges were finding their mark, and each successive explosion rattled the sub more violently.

Above Conor's head, a pipe fitting gave way and water gushed from it, dousing him. Two lamp lenses and bulbs inside wire cages shattered, darkening the room until Conor could only make out the commander. When auxiliary lighting kicked in, Conor saw the control room crew holding tightly to anything near them, except for the XO, who had been knocked off his feet. Conor knew what a destroyer attack on a sub looked like from the surface. He never thought he'd experience what it felt like from below. "Commander, what's the plan?" he asked.

L'Herminier lowered his gaze onto Conor. "I have orders to avoid contact with any enemy shipping...if at all possible. We'll see how persistent our pursuer is. If he grows impatient and thinks the convoy is more important than us, then we'll be on our way. But..." Conor hated buts. L'Herminier redirected his sight upward. "It would seem that this Boche is looking for a fight." He turned away. "XO, order depth changes of ten meters every sixty seconds. I don't want to give the trawler a static target."

Conor thought back to Butcher telling him and Emily that there was a deadline they needed to meet. He regretted not voicing his feeling that people made stupid mistakes trying to meet deadlines. "Commander, I know enough about anti–submarine warfare to know that the cat-and-mouse game can take quite a long time to play out. Time we don't have. We need to get to France yesterday."

"I am under attack, Mr. Thorn. No matter how silent we hope to run, we still make much noise. I believe our only hope for survival is to attack."

Before Conor could respond, a series of four explosions rocked the boat. The pressure hull groaned and popped. One of the two planesmen was knocked off his seat and hit his head on the deck. The glass face of a depth gauge in front of the other planesman fractured. Conor's feet slipped out from under him, but he held tight to the periscope hoist cables. Sparks spit from port-side mounted electrical panels. Some sparks fell on soaked shirts, causing smoke to mingle with the smell of fried wiring. The XO, who had been glaring at Conor, hit the deck again when he lost his grip on the chart table. Another pipe fitting gave way and was swiftly pounced on by two damage-control team sailors. Conor regained his stance, but his hands felt sticky. The smell of blood was unmistakable.

"XO, place us under the trawler's stern. He will not hear us for his own engine noise and prop wash." The XO repeated the order to the crew.

Another four explosions, each separated by three seconds, seemed to send a shock wave rippling down the length of the hull. More pipe fittings burst, resoaking the crew. The glass faces of three gauges shattered in quick succession. The sound of the sub-chaser's props permeated the pressure hull. Two sailors appeared out of the spraying water and began to furiously close valves along pipes suspended from the ceiling. Conor slipped alongside one sailor and took his turn at tightening valves. He followed the lead of the crew because he knew they knew how to survive underwater in a steel sewer pipe, and he didn't. The cascading water slowed, and he turned back to L'Herminier.

"Commander, you and I both know the sub-chaser has a shallow draft. I don't think it's losing sleep over a torpedo attack. That leaves your four-inch deck gun, which is no match for the firepower they have. I have an idea." Conor wrapped his left arm around the periscope to steady himself, and L'Herminier mirrored him. "How well do you know the currents in these waters?"

"The Golfe du Lion is our backyard. We know it well."

"Strong currents in the area?"

"Aah...yes. But at lower depths. They are southerly."

"How far down?"

Before L'Herminier could answer, two more charges exploded in quick succession, plunging the control room into complete darkness. The XO appeared behind his commander with a lantern, its beam blinding Conor briefly. He heard L'Herminier call for a damage report from all departments. They slowly trickled in. Most were managing any damage, but the engine room reported a bearing on the port-side electric motor was heating up and emitting a squeal. Never good for a submarine to be noisy when being hunted.

"Commander, the Boche, they have stopped," a seaman shouted.

"All stop," L'Herminier said. Lights flickered back on, and L'Herminier looked at Conor. "They're strongest at sixty meters. Close to ten knots. Why?"

"That's about two hundred feet. You need to get there. Quickly. And stop all motors."

"I can't. To stay submerged, I need some forward motion. You should know that."

"I do. But once you're at two hundred feet, the current will push you south. At ten knots, it won't take long to be a fair distance south. By the time your natural buoyancy takes you near the surface, you should be—"

"Out from under our Nazi friends. Maybe two to three miles south." L'Herminier nodded and began rubbing his chin as if he was running the scenario through his brain, looking for points of failure. "That's how you lost the U-boat? They drifted away?"

"As far as we could figure out, yes. Losing them hurt for a long time." Conor paused to see if L'Herminier was done looking for holes in the plan. "Once the sub-chaser loses contact, they'll head back to the convoy. You kick the motors back to life and head north, submerged until we're a safe distance from that convoy, which, I assume, was headed south."

Two rapid explosions were followed by an equal number of burst pipe fittings, one port side, the other starboard, pouring more water into the control room and knocking L'Herminier's cap to the deck. He bent to pick it up, and Conor went down with him. The XO followed with the lantern.

L'Herminier looked at Conor and wiped his face with his left hand. "Yes. Headed south. Okay. We'll try it. If they figure out what we're doing, we fight. As long as it takes." L'Herminier stood. "Fifty-degree down angle. Take us to eighty meters." L'Herminier had just gotten the words out when two more depth charges exploded, straddling the *Casabianca*. More sparks flew across the compartment, momentarily blinding Conor as he was rising from the deck. Before he could widen his stance to steady himself, another explosion detonated above the sub's conning tower. The downward hydraulic shock drove him back down onto the deck. Then blackness enveloped him.

CHAPTER FORTY-FOUR

1045 Hours, Friday, January 8, 1943
Hôtel Terminus, Gestapo Headquarters, Lyon

"Sturmbannführer Eklof, I am very impressed," Barbie said, earning a tight smile from Eklof. "And when I report to Obergruppenführer Oberg, I am sure he, too, will be pleased, if not a little surprised, given your past performance." Eklof's smile faded, which pleased Barbie. "Where is this American spy now?"

Eklof stood, back straight, eyes transfixed on the wall behind Barbie, who sat imperiously behind his desk. Eklof had his hands clasped behind his back. "I have put her in interrogation room three. Second floor. I will start interrogating the American spy first. With your permission."

"Yes, of course. Have your fun. One would say you've earned it." Eklof's bloodless lips stretched into another tight smile. "I shall give you your time with this spy. But expect me to observe in good time. Oh, and a suggestion. You must let Hauptmann Krupp have some practice in the art of interrogation. We must...spread the wealth, so to speak."

"Yes, Hauptsturmführer."

"And what of the old woman, the Jew lover? She was nursing the American?"

"According to my source, yes. The mother is in the room next to the spy."

Barbie nodded. It brought to mind the day Barbie was proudly told by the hotel manager, when the Gestapo's Section IV first took over the hotel as its headquarters, that groundbreaking soundproofing techniques were employed when building the hotel, including the use of cork and double bricking between rooms. A pity, Barbie remembered thinking, noting that it would have been useful if those being interrogated could hear the sounds of others going through the same process. The Gestapo's experiences to date, however, proved that the builders weren't as successful in deadening the sounds of guests as they'd thought. "The son, he wasn't aware of his mother's activities?"

"Again, my source says he was not involved."

"What else do we know about him?"

"Little, Hauptsturmführer. My source tells me he is a loyal Vichyite. And that he has been seen meeting with a suspected Abwehr member."

"This doctor…an Abwehr agent?"

"I have Krupp looking into it, Hauptsturmführer."

The news annoyed Barbie. Anything concerning the Abwehr annoyed him. The intercom on his desk buzzed. He looked at his watch, then flicked his hand at Eklof. "That will be all, Sturmbannführer. Tend to the American."

Eklof turned, pivoted on his heel, and made for the door. When he opened it, standing in the outer office was Ambassador Abetz. He was five minutes late.

Barbie let the antsy diplomat settle into the chair along the left side of his desk. He let the man sit while he read from a file about the preparations for the impending raid on the headquarters of the Union Générale des Israélites de France. It was to be the beginning of a concerted effort to round up the preponderance of Lyon's Jews. Barbie had spent hours poring over the plans. At the sound of the ambassador clearing his throat, Barbie raised his eyes, shut the file, and let it drop to the desk.

"The next time you request a meeting with me, Ambassador, it would serve you well to be on time."

"Apologies, Hauptsturmführer Barbie. My driver…he was taken ill. I drove myself, and I admit, I do not know the streets of Lyon as well as he."

"How unfortunate for you both. Now, what is the reason for this meeting?"

"I have been sent as an intermediary. I am good friends with Pierre Laurent, the head of the Lyon branch of Worms et Cie."

Barbie was well aware of the financial institution. It held great sway with Nazi officials in Berlin. "Why isn't this Laurent here himself?"

"He is quite ill, Hauptsturmführer. His doctor, René DuBois, insisted that Pierre needed bed rest. Pierre told me that his information should be passed on to you as soon as it was possible."

Barbie cocked his head at the name DuBois. As Abetz rambled on about an ex–Worms et Cie officer who had violated the bank's code of ethics and put the bank in a less-than-positive light with the German officials, all Barbie could think of was René DuBois, son of the American Jew lover whom he held just one floor below. René DuBois—suspected Abwehr operative.

"Pierre wanted the Gestapo to know that this official, a Henri Babin, is married to a Jew. This Jew has not been seen in over two weeks. Pierre has it on good authority that Babin has planned to have her taken to Spain."

"What do you know of Dr. DuBois?"

The question startled Abetz, who made no effort to hide his shock. "Excuse me?"

"Laurent's doctor. What do you know of him?"

Abetz took a moment to formulate an answer. "Very little, Hauptsturmführer. Pierre was in the care of René's father before he died." Abetz paused, then leaned closer. In a low soft whisper, he said, "A Jewish butcher killed René's wife. Run over. He was drunk, Pierre says."

"Does Laurent know that we have arrested DuBois's mother for conspiring to transport Jews out of France?"

Abetz's jaw slackened, his lips parting. "I…I am sure that Pierre did not know that René's mother was such a scoundrel. Although he did once say that he didn't like the brash American."

Barbie held back his next question for the time being: did Laurent know his doctor was a reputed Abwehr agent? He would find the answer himself.

CHAPTER FORTY-FIVE

1235 Hours, Friday, January 8, 1943
At Sea Aboard the French Submarine Casabianca

When Conor forced his eyes to open, busting through the crud that seemed to have glued his eyelids shut, his eyes drew their focus on the bottom of a bunk ten inches from his face.

"How the hell…"

"It's about time you woke up."

Conor could barely make out Emily's voice over the constant hum of machinery, or was it the pulsating headache that made it scarcely audible? Before he could decide, Emily rose from below the edge of his bunk, her hair mussed and tangled, her right cheek showing a crease mark from the seam on her shirtsleeve. "How long have I been out?"

Emily grabbed a look at her watch. "About ninety minutes." She felt his forehead. "Temp feels normal. What about the rest of you?"

"Absolutely nothing feels normal." Conor rolled onto his right side. "So, the decks aren't awash. We came through in one piece?"

"The short answer is yes. I'll let the commander fill in the details."

Conor swung his legs over the side of the bunk when the sub's corpsman entered the compartment, an open book balanced in his left hand.

"Hold on there. I have some questions for you, so lie back, please," the corpsman said in faintly accented English. He slid past Emily and pulled up alongside the head end of the bunk, then rested the book on the edge of the mattress. Conor lay back as the corpsman pulled out his ophthalmoscope and peered into both of his eyes, a process he was getting damn tired of. The man then dabbed his index finger on the tip of his tongue and flipped one page of the book, then another. "Questions for you. Yes or no."

Conor knew where this interrogation was going. He decided to play along nicely. No one was going to keep him from going ashore anyway.

"Questions? Are you with me?"

"I'm all ears, Doc."

The corpsman ran his finger down to the middle of the page. "Headaches?"

"Yep."

"Dizziness?"

"Yes. Comes and goes."

"Irritability?"

"Hell yes."

"Loss of memory?"

"Not really."

"Yes, really," Emily said, getting a nod from the corpsman.

"Ringing—"

"In the ears, oh, yeah."

"Nausea?" the corpsman continued.

"The new normal."

"Fatigue?"

"Plenty. Who can sleep on this thing?"

"Anxiety?"

"On that count, no."

"I have plenty for both of us," Emily said, prompting the corpsman to snap shut his book.

"Your head hitting the deck during the attack has worsened your post-concussive symptoms. I have been reading about a condition...a serious one called second impact syndrome."

Conor shook his head and waved him off.

"Conor, listen to the man," Emily said.

"That's right, listen to me. What can often happen is a swelling of the brain when you receive a head injury before your brain has a chance to heal from a previous impact." The corpsman looked at Emily, then back at Conor. "Or impacts. It can be fatal."

"Thanks for the appraisal. I'll take better care of my noggin from here on out."

"You joke too much," the corpsman said. He turned to Emily and shrugged. He grabbed her hand and dropped a vial into her palm. "Aspirin. I can do no more."

"Thank you, Édouard," Emily said. "Your English is quite good."

Édouard smiled and nodded. "Thanks to the American films that my older sister took me to in Paris. She was in love with Clark Gable. We must have seen *It Happened One Night* fifty times. As for me, I was in love with Claudette Colbert."

"I was quite smitten with Mr. Gable myself," Emily said, then made room in the narrow aisle for him to exit the compartment. She turned to face Conor; her demeanor was one hundred eighty degrees from the person who was chatting about heartthrobs. "You did hear him use the word *fatal*, did you not?"

"With the ringing in my ears, I could make out only every other word." The attempt at humor elicited a reproachful look like none other. "Sorry. I heard him, Em. But I'm not letting you go on this mission alone. It's just not going to happen. When we get back to friendly confines, I'll stand down for as long as it takes my head to get back to normal, or something close to it."

Emily took his right hand in hers. "I'll hold you to it, Conor. No matter what it takes. I'm not going to lose you. Not after all we've been through."

Conor was about to pull her toward him and land a wet one on her lips when the sound of footsteps on the deck made Emily look away. L'Herminier entered the compartment and leaned against the stack of bunks across from them. He wore rain gear that still trickled the soggy topside elements.

"My corpsman thinks you are a fool. He says he is done with you."

"He's doing his job, Commander. Just like I plan to do," Conor said. "What did I miss?"

L'Herminier slipped off his rain slicker and wide-brimmed hat and snapped both free of the rain. "Thanks to your idea, we escaped from under the sub-chaser's nose, surfaced down current about where you thought we would." L'Herminier chuckled. "Not bad for a destroyer sailor."

"Thanks, Commander. You were pretty cool under fire. I could see your men put a lot of trust in you. I hope I didn't play too heavy a hand."

"I'm sorry. Explain this heavy hand," L'Herminier said.

"Besides being stubborn, Americans can be a bit…indelicate. Forceful. I believe the French word that fits best is énergique," Emily said. Conor let her have her fun.

"Aah, yes…pushy," L'Herminier added.

"You two about done?" Conor asked. Emily and the commander shared a sly smile. "It feels like we're back on the surface. How far from the coast are we?"

"Ten minutes ago, we were about three hundred and eighty kilometers south."

Conor crunched the numbers. A little more than two hundred and forty miles. At the sub's flank surface speed, he calculated they were approximately eleven hours from the coast. "How's your boat?"

"Normal damage reports. Pipe leaks, valve failures. A dive plane that seems to have been mangled some. The bearing issue in the port-side electric motor is a concern. We are affecting repairs while we are on the surface."

"And the crew?" Emily said.

"Plenty of bruises and head stitches. Nothing serious. Your friend Jackie has a nasty gash on his forearm. Overall, we were lucky."

"Lucky is good," Conor said.

"Now, my turn. Are you still set on going ashore given your condition?"

"Commander, that is still being discussed," Emily said.

"Well, decide. If he stays, say your goodbyes now, while you have a little privacy. Some of the crew will occupy the rest of these bunks in the next fifteen minutes." The commander took two steps to leave, then turned. "And the answer is no, if you're wondering if the bunk can handle two people. At least not in the way you might be thinking."

CHAPTER FORTY-SIX

1300 Hours, Friday, January 8, 1943
Abwehr Headquarters, Fort Saint-Irénée, Lyon

Hugo Bleicher looked at his watch. It was the second glance in the last fifteen minutes. His Junghans 86 told him that time had not passed. A closer look at the small sweep hand confirmed it. The art deco–style watch, a well-regarded German-made timepiece, had been acting erratically for the past few days. The victim of excessive winding, Bleicher figured, because of a jitteriness that he couldn't explain. He wanted to be in his Lyon office before the twenty-four-hour deadline imposed by Colonel Rudolf on their recalcitrant priestly agent had run its course. But the weather, equal to Alves's obstinacy, wouldn't have it. His repeated demands that his driver increase speed were met with repeated explanations of hazardous road conditions.

When he entered his modest office, he was both surprised and annoyed, more annoyed than he had to admit, to see Alves sitting in his desk chair, digging under his fingernails with gusto. The sleeves of his black cassock were pushed up on his forearms. On his right wrist—hard to miss—was a Swiss-made Patek Philippe watch. Bleicher was sure that not even Pope Pius XXII owned such a sought-after timepiece. This added fuel to his annoyance.

"Sergeant Bleicher. I have been waiting…" Alves looked at his Patek Philippe—*for much too long,* Bleicher thought. "For over an hour. Bad weather slow you down?"

Bleicher flung his trench coat toward a square table covered in stacks of files, regretting the action before the coat settled on its surface, spilling one entire pile to the floor. "Get out of my damn chair," Bleicher said as he closed the distance to the slow-moving priest.

"Apologies. Your guest chairs are rather uncomfortable."

"They're supposed to be," Bleicher said, reclaiming his seat. "Staying away from the Gestapo, Alves?"

"Most certainly, Sergeant. As per your and the colonel's wishes."

Bleicher narrowed his gaze at the priest. He knew Alves was lying to him, but he couldn't prove it. "Because your deadline has passed and you've invaded my office, I can only assume that you have what Colonel Rudolf has so patiently waited for."

"I have names. Yes. I do not know if it is a complete list as recruitment, from what I understand, is an ongoing activity."

Alves made no move to hand over the list of Heckler Network names. "The list, Alves?"

"These names. They did not come cheaply, Sergeant. In fact, it cost more than my monthly…fee. Surely you can make things right."

"The list, Alves," Bleicher said again, his hand extended palm up.

Alves hesitated, then unbuttoned the top button of his cassock and reached inside. He pulled out a gray envelope and placed it in Bleicher's waiting hand. "I wish you'd properly consider my request," Alves said.

Bleicher opened the sealed envelope and pulled out a card. It depicted an iconic image of a blue-eyed Jesus Christ. Below the image he read the words *En Tendre Mémoire*. In Loving Memory. Bleicher, a lapsed Catholic, knew he was holding a Mass card for the deceased. He looked up at Alves, who was smiling.

"Quite ironic, wouldn't you say?" the smirking priest said.

"You are a cruel bastard." Bleicher opened the card and saw a list of names, some accompanied by code names. "Colonel Rudolf will be pleased."

"I expected he would have wanted to be here in person," Alves said.

"Were you not paying attention in our last meeting? The

colonel is quite disgusted with you. He has left dealings with you to me." Bleicher paused and considered revealing something that might lessen the priest's hubris. "He is, as we speak, meeting with Cardinal Gerlier." The mention of the name of the archbishop of Lyon seemed to soften Alves's brashly self-confident facial features. Alves cleared his throat and started to speak when Bleicher's adjutant hurriedly entered the office.

"Sir, this letter was delivered just before we arrived. I found it underneath some files. I inquired about who sent it and was told it was a woman. Staff described her as being quite distraught."

Bleicher set aside the card and took the letter. He recognized the handwriting as being DuBois's.

He ran his index finger underneath the flap and pulled out a note card. There were three short lines of bold, partially smudged text written with a heavy hand. He felt his face flush as he read. "God damn them to hell."

CHAPTER FORTY-SEVEN

1310 Hours, Friday, January 8, 1943
At Sea Aboard the French Submarine Casabianca

Conor, from the shoulders down, felt as close to normal as he had in months. From the head up, now that was a completely different story. The act of simply taking in air through his nose made his head pulsate with pain.

Emily convinced him that spending more time with Jackie would be the best use of their remaining time on the *Casabianca.* They'd set off toward the aft crew quarters when they came upon Stones, who, given his reaction as a man who just came upon his mistress's scorned husband, wanted to be anywhere but bumping shoulders with Conor.

"Stones. You've been missing in action since we shoved off. What have you been up to?" Conor said.

"Aah…nose to the grindstone, Thorn. Keeping close to Jackie. These operations are all about minding the details. I'm sure that's no surprise to you two."

"You'd be correct, Lieutenant," Emily said. Clearly not interested in a chat fest, Stones brushed past Emily, then Conor.

"Stones, wait up." Stones stopped and turned back. "Did you know a guy back in Algiers named Stevens?"

Stones's eyes darted up, as if the answer were scrawled on one of the myriad pipes that ran the length of the compartment. "I recollect that name. Not sure I can recall a face, though."

"It's still a bit foggy, but I thought I remembered seeing you in the Saint George's bar the night that I had a run-in with Stevens. You two looked like you knew each other."

"No, not really. Just a passing conversation about a shared acquaintance." Stones started to turn away.

"Yeah, I remembered hearing you say something about a cock-up," Conor said. "That's Brit slang for a mistake, right?"

"I have no such recollection. We just had a brief conversation about a shared acquaintance, like I said. Someone we both knew from our time at Massingham." The mention of the SOE base outside of Algiers, where the OSS shared some space, made Emily's eyes light up.

"Who would that be?" Emily said.

"Oh…" Stones stammered. "Let me think…someone named Barney. Bent as a nine-bob note. Took us both at pinochle, the pincher. That's all I remember." A hasty exit from the compartment followed Stones's realization that he ran his mouth more than he'd wanted.

Conor turned to Emily. "Now, correct me if I'm wrong, but that didn't sound like someone who only had a passing conversation about a shared acquaintance. In fact, it sounded like—"

"They were quite acquainted," Emily said. "That thought occurred to me as well."

CHAPTER FORTY-EIGHT

1400 Hours, Friday, January 8, 1943
Hôtel Terminus, Gestapo Headquarters, Lyon

Eklof sat in a weak-legged chair similar to the one the unconscious blonde woman sat in across from him. Yet another chair, used for interrogations, was upside down in the corner of the room, tossed there by Krupp after he broke off one of its legs. The leg, now covered in blood, was in his right hand. Like Eklof, Krupp rolled his sleeves up to just below his elbows. Unlike Eklof, he was sweating and bloodstains darkened his shirt. Eklof didn't want to touch the bloodied woman. Not now. Maybe later, when he sent Krupp away.

"Water," Eklof said. Krupp laid the chair leg on a nearby table strewn with various tools needed for thorough questioning of suspected French Resistance members. And Jews. Sometimes they were one and the same. Krupp grabbed a rusted tin that once contained butter cookies and dipped it into a tub of ice water four feet behind the woman. Krupp, always wanting the full effect of any interaction with the woman, didn't pour the water over her head but threw it in her face. The frigid water hit her with a force that snapped her head back. Her revival, the reaction both men were seeking, was achieved. The green-eyed woman slowly stuck out her tongue and caught a few drops.

"You made us hit you. Why did you do that?" Expecting no answer, Eklof finished his bluff. "You did talk. Finally. But why not answer our questions sooner? It would have been so much easier for all of us."

"I made you hit me? That's preposterous and you know it." The blonde woman shifted in her chair and chuckled, which sounded more like a gurgle. "What I do know is you did make your minion put his finger inside me. And slap my breasts with his rubber truncheon. And here I thought you saved those measures for yourself."

Eklof admired the woman's pluck, which he was about to admit when she let loose a wad of spit in his direction. It fell somewhat short of its target and landed on his left boot. "I told you nothing. And do you know why?"

Eklof pointed to his boot without taking his eye off the woman. Krupp made quick work of the spit, swiping it with a cloth.

"Because I know nothing. No names of Resistance members. No addresses. Someone leaves a note under my door with names of Frenchmen who would rather collaborate with the likes of you than defend their own country. Then, I seek them out and put a bullet in their head or a knife across their throat before they can do more harm to France."

Eklof was growing tired of the woman's bluster. He averted his eye from her to Krupp, an unspoken order. Krupp crept behind the woman, reclaimed his chair leg from the table, and delivered a blow to the back of the woman's head. The impact drove her head forward. She moaned and blood spilled from her mouth. Eklof thought it more than likely came from a bit tongue. Appropriate, he thought, for such a glib woman.

"You were seen entering the home of Dr. René DuBois with a man and another woman. An American spy. Tell us why you brought her to meet this doctor. And we know it was not just because she was injured. There was another reason."

The woman couldn't form words. Her lips moved; blood continued to seep between them.

"Give her some water." Krupp went to retrieve the cookie tin. "In a cup. We need her to talk."

"Of course, we do."

Eklof twisted around in his chair, startled by Barbie's discreet arrival. Barbie stood just inside the cell's doorway. Cradled in his left arm was a black cat, which he stroked softly with his free hand. "But why has it taken so long, Sturmbannführer? I'm so, so disappointed. In both of you."

"Hauptsturmführer, I need a little more time. She was unconscious for several minutes, and we couldn't revive her."

"Which confirms to me you have much to learn." Barbie stepped to Eklof and handed the cat off to him. "Krupp, be a good man and fetch me the blowtorch. I have a meeting and I don't have time for games with this beautiful blonde woman." Krupp, for some reason, delayed any response to Barbie's order. "Krupp, are you, by chance, deaf? The blowtorch…and be quick about it."

#

Eklof followed Barbie into his office suite on the third floor, where his superior headed straight for the bathroom in the far corner to wash the blood from his hands. Eklof considered pointing out that there was a blood spatter on one side of his face but thought it would have been unnecessary. As long as Barbie would look at himself in the mirror.

Eklof stood at near attention in front of the desk with his back to the bathroom. The thick, almost meaty smell of burnt flesh clung to his tunic. When Barbie finally emerged from the bathroom and then passed Eklof, the blood spatter was untouched. Barbie sat staring off into space. Eklof hesitated a long moment before he removed a handkerchief from his front pants pocket and placed it on the desk. Barbie stared at the offering.

"Hauptsturmführer, there is some blood…" Eklof's voice trailed off as he gently brushed his face with his fingertips. When Barbie didn't move for the handkerchief after Eklof's prompt, he thought Barbie didn't hear him. Then Barbie seemed to snap out of a trance and snatched his own handkerchief from his tunic's breast pocket. As he wiped at the blood, he slid Eklof's handkerchief back across the desk.

"That one…the longer she held on, the stronger she became. That is quite unusual for these French people. Especially the women. And for all that, we still don't know where this DuBois is."

"I will reach out to Alves. He is deeply connected. Threats of exposure seem to be most effective in convincing him to dig deeper for information as to the doctor's whereabouts."

"Tell him to use the money we pay him as an incentive. He will complain, but so be it."

"I will do so—" Eklof's choked response hung in the cold air of the room with the double doors slamming into the walls.

"You fucking excuse for an officer of the Third Reich." Two men entered, one he recognized from his wanderings in and around Lyon—a low-ranking Abwehr operative decked out in a ridiculous-looking French beret—the other a colonel in a smartly tailored Abwehr uniform, his hands still gloved and his cap sitting firmly on his head at a rakish angle. The Abwehr man was the one who had brazenly called out Barbie, who, no surprise to Eklof, sat nonplussed in his chair, replacing his stained handkerchief into his breast pocket.

"Colonel Rudolf, what brings the Abwehr's finest midranking officer to Lyon from the cushy surroundings of Paris? It seems it is something that has you…quite distressed."

"You and your heavy-handed thugs have damaged, irreparably, a major Abwehr operation. One that has been planned for many months, goddammit," Rudolf said, his face glowing bloodred.

"What operation is that, Colonel?"

"You must release the mother of René DuBois immediately," Rudolf said, avoiding a direct answer to Barbie's question but giving him a meaningful clue.

"Aah, the doctor. You do know that his mother has been helping Jews escape France? Jews, Colonel." Barbie paused to take in a deep breath like a boxer did before going another round. "And her son must be involved." Barbie stood. "Tell me what you know about him. And tell me where he is," Barbie said, slamming his hand on his desk.

"Only the Reich suffers from this duplicity. It must stop. The Abwehr does not interfere in Gestapo operations. But it seems the Gestapo has no such inclination. Admiral Canaris, who has full knowledge and oversight of our operation, will get a thorough report of your bumbling and interference." Eklof realized Rudolf stepped in dog shit when he mentioned the head of the Abwehr. So did Barbie by the amused look on his face.

"Well then. If I have disrupted a Canaris plan, then award me the Iron Cross." Rudolf and the beret-wearing underling both snapped their heads back as if slapped. "Come, come, Colonel Rudolf. We both know that Canaris is a traitor to the Third Reich. You would be wise to do the opposite of what the old man orders you to do." Barbie sat down and took in Rudolf like he was sizing up the carcass of a vanquished animal. "Now, where is this doctor? This son of a Jew lover?"

CHAPTER FORTY-NINE

1500 Hours, Friday, January 8, 1943
Home of Pierre Laurent, 5th Arrondissement, Lyon

DuBois approached the front entrance to the walled compound of Pierre Laurent's estate. As he opened the oak door, heavy with the moisture of a drizzly day, he struggled to regain a sense of calm. He would settle for even a fleeting sense. Slow, deep breathing failed him. He would have to enlist Laurent to secure Sarah's release. DuBois could not depend solely on Bleicher and the Abwehr, given their deeply fractured relationship with the Gestapo. He swallowed a curse and knocked. The sleepy-eyed butler opened the door enough to reveal a sliver of his creased face.

"Hello, François. I know I am unexpected, but I must see Pierre. I…I—" DuBois stammered, damning himself for not thinking about how to explain why he was there without a scheduled appointment. "I have some test results for Pierre. We must discuss them without delay."

The butler didn't challenge the explanation and opened the door an additional three inches, making DuBois pay the price for not providing prior notice, he thought.

When DuBois entered Laurent's bedroom, he found his patient dressed in a shimmery silk or satin bathrobe. He couldn't tell which. Laurent was prone on a brocade-covered divan; his slipper-covered feet stuck out from the bottom of the robe, revealing vellum-colored skin. A pair of half-moon glasses was perched on the end of his nose. DuBois's entrance interrupted Laurent reading the contents of a file. When Laurent looked up, a pair of watery red eyes looked back at him.

"René, I wasn't expecting you today. Is anything wrong?"

DuBois drew closer. "I come because I must ask a favor. It is not a trivial one."

Laurent shifted and lowered his legs to the floor. DuBois noted a slight grimace. "Yes, René. What is it?"

"It concerns my mother. The Gestapo has arrested her. It is..." DuBois hesitated. He was unsure how much to share. "It is unclear why the Gestapo have targeted her."

"This is terrible news, René. But...what favor are you asking of me? Certainly, you can't be asking me to intercede on her and your behalf."

"That is precisely what I am asking. I hold no sway with the Gestapo. But you, given your position and contacts, there must be something you can do." Laurent opened his mouth to respond, then stopped. The minute that followed was long. "Pierre, please say something."

Before Laurent could summon words, François cracked open the bedroom door. "Sir, Ambassador Abetz has arrived. He says it is important." DuBois perked up. Abetz, a close ally of Laurent, was exactly the type of person DuBois was referring to just now.

Abetz entered the bedroom with purpose. His attention was not on Laurent, but DuBois.

"I didn't expect to see you. But now that you are here, explain this news about your mother. Is what the Gestapo's Barbie reports true?"

"What has Barbie said?" DuBois said.

"Don't be coy, Doctor." DuBois didn't respond, nor did he look at Laurent. "The Gestapo arrested your mother because she was responsible for helping Jews escape France. That is what Barbie told me. And I find it impossible to doubt Barbie's revelation given his standing in the Gestapo." Abetz shifted his gaze to Laurent. "Pierre, are you listening? It is quite possible that the Gestapo is looking for René as I speak. He cannot care for you if he is held by the Gestapo." Abetz turned to DuBois.

"The Gestapo is misinformed, Ambassador," DuBois said,

hearing the deceitfulness in his own voice. "My mother has no contacts with the Jewish community. I came here to ask Pierre to apply his influence to see that she is released. It is a gross error."

"Are you sure, René?" Laurent said. "Your father...he told me more than once that she was brash and, on top of that, was anti-fascist. A dangerous combination. The Gestapo is not known for making mistakes."

Regret overpowered DuBois's thinking. He should never have called upon Laurent. He was about to take his leave when he heard heavy footsteps just outside the bedroom door followed by a voice. All three men turned, and when the door opened, DuBois heard Laurent inhale sharply.

"Antoine. What are you doing here? Is your father with you?" Laurent said.

"No. He is rotting in an Algerian prison. As for why I am here, it is to make a deal with you."

#

A weakened Laurent fell back on the divan, having lost what was left of his color. DuBois went to his side and took hold of his wrist to check his pulse. Abetz and the young man stood by silently.

"My business is with you, Monsieur Laurent. And you alone."

Laurent waved his free hand at the young man. "Nonsense. As you can see, I am not well, and I am in need of my doctor. And this is a dear friend, German Ambassador Abetz, whom I trust without reservation. Now explain yourself." His voice lost strength as he talked. "I know nothing of this...this *Synarchique*. It sounds quite preposterous," he said when Brunel finished laying out his demands.

"I think...no, I know you're lying. Even the look on the ambassador's face confirms it," Antoine said.

"Don't be ridiculous," Abetz said. "Pierre is a true Frenchman who values a healthy relationship with Germany. Nothing more."

"That being said, I have no overt influence with the Germans. I have just told my doctor here the same thing," Laurent said. "And claims that your father helped cover up fraud he says I initiated is equally preposterous." Laurent took a deep breath. "Your grandiose scheme is not worth entertaining one more second."

"Where is the archive?" DuBois asked, triggering a look of shock on Laurent's face.

"Stay out of this, Doctor," Abetz said.

"Pierre, if this archive is as valuable as this man claims, you could possibly use it to have his mother and my mother released," DuBois said. "While I doubt his claim of your involvement in bank fraud, we all know there is truth to claims about involvement in the *Synarchique*."

"Damn you, DuBois," Abetz said. "You know nothing."

"On the contrary. My father was well-informed about the *Synarchique*. Most of his knowledge was gleaned from Pierre himself." DuBois looked at Brunel. "The archive. Is it in Lyon?"

"Do we have an agreement?" Brunel asked.

When no one answered, Brunel said, "If there is no agreement, a detailed letter will be sent to the Banque Worms that will fully explain the fraud I mentioned and your involvement."

"Antoine, your mother is Jewish. Even if I knew Hitler, or Goering, I do not have the influence to have a Jew released." Laurent's voice betrayed a shakiness. "Pétain himself couldn't secure a release."

"Figure it out, Pierre."

"Where is the archive?" DuBois said.

"Hidden, of course, Doctor." Brunel smiled, seemingly pleased that Laurent did not refuse outright. "I will be at the Hôtel Normandy. I await your answer. Do not delay, Pierre. There is much at stake for you."

CHAPTER FIFTY

1610 Hours, Friday, January 8, 1943
At Sea Aboard the French Submarine Casabianca

Splayed out across a forest-green cloth that covered the wardroom table were the components of two Colt M1911A1s, a Walther PPK, and a Colt M1903. In front of Conor was one M1911A1 and the smaller M1903; the other M1911A1 was broken down in front of Jackie, while the Walther PPK's parts were neatly laid out in front of Emily. Three flask-sized containers of Ballistol gun oil sat uncorked in front of each sharply focused agent. The wardroom's air, already a concoction of various scents, now included the pungent odor of the gun lubricant.

While Jackie regaled them with details from his last mission to Corsica, Conor's hands, one clutching a well-oiled cloth, glided over the parts to his two weapons as if guided by a second brain. His conscious thought process was locked on Stones and an overpowering feeling that the man was misleading at best and outright lying at worst.

Conor picked up the M1911A1's slide when L'Herminier popped into the wardroom, a sheet of paper attached to a clipboard flapping in the sub's odorous air. All three agents lifted their heads and took in the commander.

"I bring news. For Emily. Commander Butcher sent a brief message a few moments ago." He handed the clipboard to Emily, who wiped her hands before taking it. A moment later, she looked up from the message with eyebrows raised in muted surprise.

“That’s…that is wonderful news,” Emily said as she handed the clipboard to Conor.

Conor read the message. All eight words. *Brother Richard has made his way to England.* Conor handed the clipboard to L’Herminier. “I’ll take that as a good sign. For us, I mean.”

“I hope *us* includes me,” Jackie said.

“Of course, Jackie. The timing couldn’t be better,” Emily said halfheartedly. Conor guessed she was thinking about the long road back she said Richard would face, both physically and mentally.

“I see you are continuing with your preparations. Good. We should be off the coast just after midnight. Be ready to disembark one hour before.” L’Herminier tucked the clipboard under his arm and turned to leave, but Conor stopped him.

“Commander, speaking of messages, I need to send a message to Butcher before we go ashore.”

“And the nature of this message?”

“It concerns Stones. I can’t go into detail, but when you return to Algiers, Stones needs to be questioned by Major Campbell Stewart. I think he has knowledge about a murder that he is withholding…for some reason,” Conor said, knowing full well that the reason was that he was involved in a major way. He was about to continue when the corpsman—Emily called him Édouard—filled the doorway to the wardroom. He held out a small glass vial.

“Salt tablets, Commander. Take as needed.” The corpsman then turned to the three of them at the table. “With the weather on the mainland, you shouldn’t be needing them.” And just as abruptly, he exited.

“I will send your message, as disturbing as it is. But, now is time for a mission brief. Are you ready, Mr. Thorn?”

“Ready for a while, Commander.”

Once three of the *Casabianca*’s crew and Stones were present, Conor ran through the mission plan methodically.

He started with the role of the *Casabianca*, which was to provide fire support with its deck gun for the three teams until all inflatables had returned to the sub. “Because of our surface transit, Jackie’s contact who was supposed to meet him won’t be there because we’re early. So, we’ll need scouts to swim in and secure the landing spot. That will be me and Jackie.”

Jackie nodded. Emily didn't. Conor knew she wasn't happy about his selection of scouts. She'd get over it. *Maybe*, Conor thought.

"The three rafts will head in. I'm with one crewman and gear, Conor and Emily plus another crewman with more gear, and Stones and another crewman with the rest of the gear. All boats will hold fifty meters from shore," Jackie said.

"Jackie and I will deploy and hit the beach. Assuming it is secure, we'll signal—"

"Two long flashes, one short," Jackie said. "Once the inflatables hit the beach, first thing—"

"Emily takes a Sten gun and moves inland as a lookout while Jackie and I help get the boats unloaded and change into a dry set of clothes. The rafts push off and head back to the sub. From that point, we're on our own.

"Then we start to bury the gear that Emily and I need to leave, including the radio to signal the *Casabianca* that we're ready for pickup." Conor looked around the crowded wardroom. No one looked confused or overly anxious. Stones looked surprisingly calm. Conor always felt a little anxiousness was a good thing.

#

1630 Hours, Friday, January 8, 1943
Vieux Lyon to Hôtel Normandy

Antoine Brunel took his time as he, seemingly without aim, coursed through Vieux Lyon's streets and traboules. He made several stops along the way to take in the contents of shop windows and the occasional menu posted at the few cafés that were open. DuBois, who had been following the man since he left Pierre Laurent's home, was close to being detected when Brunel stopped to smoke a cigarette halfway through the traboule at 27 rue Saint-Jean that connected with 6 rue des Trois-Maries. DuBois, wearing a high-collared raincoat and a wide-brimmed rain hat pulled low over his face, feigned being lost and hurriedly exited the traboule when he glimpsed the smoking Brunel. Giving the man a minute to finish, DuBois reentered and spied his target exiting the traboule.

For the next ten minutes, Brunel picked up his pace to the extent that DuBois found himself a bit winded. The two men covered a great distance, which took them over the River Saône and eventually into Place Bellecour, a sprawling pedestrian square in the Presqu'île district. The packed red clay spread out before him like a plush rug spotted with dozens of puddles that reflected the low rain-filled clouds. Brunel hustled across the square, making no effort to avoid the puddles, and headed south toward the Perrache train station.

The young man's startling pronouncement, or "deal," as he called it, was the single subject of DuBois's thoughts as he trailed him. The value to him specifically, of an archive containing information about those involved in the Darlan assassination, ran a circuit in his head. He realized he needed something to trade if he was to get his mother out of the Gestapo's hands.

Brunel turned down a narrow side street off a thoroughfare that fed into the Perrache station and disappeared through the entrance to the hotel. DuBois waited less than a minute and then followed. He found himself in a courtyard. The space amplified the sound of the rainfall. At the far end, a circular structure looked like it held a spiral stairway. It was open air, with openings scaling up the structure, toward its roof. He heard heavy footsteps, but the covered walkways on each floor were unlit. DuBois, craning his neck, could make out a dark figure entering a doorway into a room with a dim interior light. He was considering checking for a room number when he felt a tap on his shoulder. DuBois whirled around to see the face of a troubled Hugo Bleicher.

"Doctor, are we now making house calls at hotels?"

"Why are you following me?"

Bleicher grabbed DuBois's elbow. "Come, our voices carry too well in this dreary courtyard. Join me in my car." After Bleicher herded DuBois into the back seat of his Citroën, Bleicher lit a cigarette. "Just what are you doing in the courtyard of this hovel of a hotel?"

"You received my letter?" DuBois said, extracting a look of annoyance from Bleicher for ignoring his question.

"Yes, of course—"

"You have done nothing to see that my mother is released."

"Nonsense, Doctor. It is being dealt with at the highest levels. You do understand that we are dealing with the Gestapo."

DuBois sank deeper into his seat and weighed if it was the right time to bring up the news of Brunel's archive. Bleicher's mention of the Gestapo convinced him that time was of the essence. He sat up and rapidly recounted what Brunel had revealed about the archive. "Would this archive be of value to the Abwehr?" Bleicher took a moment to think, but when he opened his mouth to answer, DuBois went on. "What I mean is, could the Abwehr use the archive to help secure the release of my mother?"

"That is not for me to answer. It is for Colonel Rudolf and Admiral Canaris to decide."

"Then you will advise them as soon as possible?"

"Yes. But tell me. Where is the archive?"

DuBois sank back into his seat and took a deep breath, held it, then released it. "I don't know. At least not yet."

CHAPTER FIFTY-ONE

0030 Hours, Saturday, January 9, 1943
Shoreline of the Camargue

The selected landing spot on a spit of land was quiet, eerily so. The briny scent was a shade below overpowering. Partly cloudy skies and a half-moon provided scant light. Small pebbles and larger rocks covered the shoreline, their surfaces worn smooth by the surf. The beach's composition wouldn't make an easy chore of burying their gear or their radio. A massive dune loomed forty feet from the water's edge, giving them precious cover. Above the dune was a dike built of rounded stones. On top of the dike was a low wooden structure. Conor crouched beside Jackie as he signaled the inflatables offshore.

Emily's raft was the first to arrive followed in quick succession by the two others. Conor and Jackie pitched in to unload their rafts, while Stones and his boatmate unloaded theirs. Emily, with Sten gun already in hand, headed inland to the grassy, sandy dune and made her way up. As Conor and Jackie began to change into dry clothes, Conor saw the first two inflatables push off the beach and head back to the *Casabianca*. Conor zeroed in on the third raft and saw that it was headed back also, but without Stones. *Not part of the mission plan. What gives?*

"Go, Conor, start digging," Jackie said, handing him a shovel. "And be quick about it." They both started burrowing.

Conor kneeled, head down, which brought on a bout of

dizziness. He put his back into it, hitting a waterlogged mixture of rocks and sand. The deeper he went, the sandier the mixture became, which made the going easier. As he dug, he tried to make sense of Stones's decision not to return to the *Casabianca*. He'd deal with that later. His head still down and both hands on the shovel, he paused and took a short breath. Then he heard a grunt, followed by a smothered shout. Jackie's body fell forward into the hole, knocking Conor down with him. Blood gushed from Jackie's slit throat. Conor grappled with Jackie's body, pushing it aside.

He sprang out of the hole, stumbling over a pile of freshly dug sand, the shovel raised above his head. Stones lunged at Conor with his knife in his right hand.

Conor swung the shovel, striking Stones's wrist and knocking the knife out of his hand. Stones, his face contorted, grabbed his wrist and dropped to one knee. Conor thought to make a run for his duffel and his Colt but didn't want to turn his back on Stones and give him a chance to run.

"What's the plan, Stones? After you get rid of us, that is. It must have changed at some point." Stones stood and looked at Jackie's body, his upper torso concealed by the hole in the ground. Holding his wrist, Stones began to move in a circle around Conor toward Jackie's body. Conor's eyes were locked on him. "Let me guess. A neutral country. East to Switzerland or west to Spain? From here, you've got mountains to deal with in either direction. You up for that?"

"You Americans, so cocksure."

"There's that word again—*cock*. Just like I heard you use that night at the hotel bar with Stevens—a cock-up. So why mutilate your victims? What's that about? Could you be queer and just can't stand to be rejected?"

"So many questions. Unfortunately, it's time you shut up."

"Maybe you're on a crusade to rid the world of homosexuals? Or maybe you did it that way to throw off investigators."

The beam of a flashlight pierced the darkness from the top of the dune and found them at the dune's base. Conor turned briefly and saw Emily bounding down with an older man in tow.

"*Allô...Allô?* Jacqueline? Is that you?" the old man said.

Stones craned his head toward the raspy voice of a man.

"Conor, what's happened? Where's Jackie?" Emily said.

The flashlight's beam danced around both men. Conor was momentarily blinded. He blinked and heard heavy footsteps on the rocky beach. Then a handful of wet sand hit his face, blinding him again. He dropped the shovel to clear his eyes of the sandy muck.

"Emily, shoot!"

A short burst from Emily's Sten gun filled the nighttime air. Conor's compromised vision captured Stones cresting the dune. The man was gone, swallowed by darkness.

#

He called himself Théo. He was shy of fifty years, Conor estimated. Théo was without a midlife paunch, but a noticeable stoop gave away his age. A thick head of gray hair complemented a full brush mustache. He told them he was a *gardian*, hired to watch over the wild horses found in the Camargue near his home. Théo explained he was to meet Jacqueline at that location at some point between midnight and one a.m. over the next three days. If Jacqueline didn't appear, he was to wait for further instructions.

"I did not expect him tonight. I was only here to become familiar with the area." Slung across his shoulder was a rifle that looked to Conor to be well over twenty years old. Conor took him for a veteran of the Great War. "He's a day early. Why have you killed your own man? Was he a traitor?"

"No. He was nothing like it. Nothing," Emily said, her voice wavering.

Conor was about to ask a question when the loud sound of flapping wings from beyond the dune filled the air. Emily drew a bead on the sound with her Sten.

"It is the birds. They have taken over the duck blind."

Emily stood down.

"The other. The one who ran. Who was he? Was he a traitor?"

The smug image of Stones's face flooded his mind. "Yes. The worst kind. One who is not afraid to kill his fellow men in arms," Conor said.

Théo watched as Emily and Conor finished burying Jackie's gear, then their own radio. When Conor started to dig Jackie's grave, Théo spoke up again. "Please, let me help. Save your energy. You two must have something important to do. When I finish, we will go."

CHAPTER FIFTY-TWO

0430 Hours, Saturday, January 9, 1943
In Transit to Avignon

Their trek into the town of Les Saintes-Maries-de-la-Mer went slowly. It reminded Conor of their escape from the deep woods where Henry Longworth had taken them both, along with his sister, Maggie, to put an end to Conor and Emily's pursuit of him. Their long walk out of the woods south of Bristol had dragged on because Maggie had badly twisted her ankle. This time, Emily was still unsteady on her feet after the thrashing she'd received from Stones on the beach. More than once, Conor stumbled for no good reason other than having, what did the corpsman call it? Second impact syndrome. *I wish it had been only two.*

The path they traveled was a hard pack gravel single track. As they neared the town, they left the gravel road. Théo carefully guided them behind and between houses avoiding, he said, frequent German foot patrols. It was half past four in the morning when they arrived on the cobbled main street of town, avenue d'Arles. Théo pointed out a truck parked in front of what appeared to be a general store. "The owner, he makes regular runs north to Avignon. He normally leaves around five in the morning. Look for a plump man in his sixties, no taller than five feet, with a thin scar. He will have a cigarette in his hand, or mouth, or possibly in both. He will also have a couch-sized seat cushion. He needs it to see out the truck's windshield."

Conor and Emily parted ways with Théo and headed across the street. The negotiation, once the driver got over his initial shock at seeing an American and Brit standing before him, was brief. No names were exchanged, but a roll of French francs was. The driver, who guarded the cushion tucked under his left arm as if King Louis XIV had sat on it, pointed into the darkened cargo bay of the old Renault delivery truck. Conor helped Emily aboard, then started to pull himself up. Before he got to his feet, the driver was up and pushing past both him and Emily. He headed toward the cab, past two rows of wooden barrels with a symbol of a fish branded into the sides. He then pulled free a false wooden wall from the bulkhead. The driver pointed inside a space two feet deep and the width of the truck.

"*Allez.*" Go.

Conor didn't need to be told twice; he slipped into the space and prompted Emily to join him. They sat facing each other. Their legs intertwined. Before the driver replaced the false wall, he rambled on for a minute, pausing twice, once to rap on the wall with his child-sized hand, then the second pause, followed by two more knocks. Emily nodded at what sounded like instructions and threw in a couple of *oui*s. The driver ended the exchange by slamming the wall back into place, plunging them into darkness. Their home for the next two hours.

"Was he explaining his warning system?" Conor said.

"Ha. If you could see me, you'd see that my face looks like someone who is shocked."

"Are you poking fun at me because I might have understood someone speaking French?"

"You would be correct," Emily said, tacking on a snort for emphasis.

Conor smiled. Emily mocking him was a good sign. "Good. I hate to be wrong." He folded his arms across his chest. They spent the next several minutes in silence.

Conor broke the stillness. "Jackie. Great guy. He didn't deserve that."

"No one does."

"No, there you're wrong. Stones does."

"Why did he do that? I get it he was involved in Stevens's murder in some way. But—"

"Probably a few more murders if Campbell's suspicions about multiple cases sharing some similarities are correct."

"So his plan was to wipe us out and head for...where?" Emily said.

"He couldn't stay in Algiers or North Africa...too many people asking questions. Campbell would have caught up to him at some point. No, the timing of the *Casabianca* heading to France, that gave him an option to head east or west to a neutral country, sit out the war."

"If the Nazis come across him and he talks, we—"

"I know. Besides Jackie, that's all I've been thinking about. We need to find this archive and get back to the *Casabianca* pronto." Conor yawned. "Let's get some sleep. We'll need it in the next few days."

From the level of numbness in Conor's ass, he thought they could be as far north as Paris. Their sleep was interrupted once. A two-knock interruption. A roadblock, according to Emily. The driver cut the engine and launched into a shouted explanation for his travel. There were many intermingled voices, shouts in German, the sounds of revving motorcycles going up and down the road. Conor heard the truck's canvas flap land on the top of the cargo area. Boots hurriedly stomping on the cargo bay's floor, followed by the sound of the barrels being forced open with a pry bar. "*Mein Gott. Oh, mein Gott!*" My God. Oh, my God! The overpowering smell of fish filled the cargo area. The cargo wasn't fresh fish—not even close. Conor preferred the exhaust he had been breathing from the Renault's leaky manifold for God knew how long. The Germans rammed the barrel tops back into place and beat a path off the truck. A minute later, they were back on their way.

The next time the truck stopped, approximately thirty minutes later, the false wall came down. Conor looked at his watch and saw that it was a few minutes before eight in the morning. and rain was beginning to fall. Both he and Emily had some trouble even adjusting to the muted sunlight.

Standing behind the truck, they watched the driver, his cushion under his arm, shove the wall back into place. Conor looked around and saw that the driver had parked alongside two other trucks in a square. Across the square, there were more trucks loading and unloading cargo.

Conor whispered something to Emily, who nodded back. The driver jumped down, landing in a shallow puddle, shedding the dangling ash from the tip of his cigarette. Emily engaged him in hurried French. Conor picked out the words "Le Chat Noir." The driver pointed off into the distance, toward the center of Avignon. Satisfied, Emily said, "*Merci beaucoup*," and added a kiss on both cheeks for good measure. The gesture caught the driver off guard. His cigarette fell from his mouth and landed in the puddle at his feet, hissing for a long moment.

#

0815 Hours, Saturday, January 9, 1943
Place de l'Horloge, Avignon

The driver had given Emily directions to Le Chat Noir that he said would be nothing more than a fifteen-minute walk, first heading down the rue de la République, then heading east to the Place Saint-Didier. Bordering the square was the café. It took them twenty-five minutes, which included the time they spent ducking into an alley when two motorcycles, followed by a scout car with two officers in the rear seat, approached them.

The square was empty, and as they walked across it to get to the café, Conor noticed a waiter at the establishment to their right, his long white apron tied around his slim waist. He was standing under an awning riddled with holes, smoking a cigarette. The rain picked up in intensity, urging them into a jog. Twenty feet from the café's entrance, Conor noticed the interior was dark. He stopped and tugged on Emily's sleeve to stop her.

"Shit. I think they're closed."

"We've nowhere else to go. We can knock. Maybe the owner lives in the back or on an upper floor. Maybe they open up late."

"That's a lot of maybes, Emily." She didn't respond because she was already fifteen feet ahead of him. Five seconds later, she was knocking firmly on the front door of the café, loud enough to wake up any black cats inside. When no one came, Emily backed up ten feet and looked up toward the second floor. No one came to any of the three windows. She turned to Conor. All he gave in response was a shrug of his shoulders.

"*Il sont fermés.*" They are closed. The voice was that of the smoking waiter at the café behind them. "*Vous* êtes *aveugles?*" Are you blind? The waiter's acid tone was unmistakable.

"Let's go around back." Before they could round the corner of the café, the thin hollow-cheeked face of a man peered out of a sliver of an opening in the front door and confirmed, in as few words as possible, that Le Chat Noir was closed.

Emily ran up to the man with surprising speed before he could relock the door. "*Monsieur, on vient voir Monsieur Beaugard.*" We come to see Mr. Beaugard.

The door reopened a crack. The thin-faced man studied the drenched visitors top to bottom. Satisfied or not, Conor didn't know, but he then stuck his head out farther and surveyed the entire square. The waiter across the square was gone, leaving Conor and Emily as the sole inhabitants. He made a *come here* signal, opened the door wider, and waited for them to enter before shutting and locking it. The man's rail-thin frame mirrored the gauntness of his face. But he moved deeper into the darkened café with a spryness that surprised Conor.

He glided through the interior, leading them into a cracker box–sized kitchen that was slightly better lit. He sat at a table in the corner strewn with newspapers and an ashtray overflowing with ash. The blade of a butcher's cleaver peeked out from under the newspapers. When he took his seat, the chair made no sound, his weight nothing to a piece of furniture that looked like it was made at the turn of the century. The masthead of one newspaper read *Combat*. Alongside the ashtray was an empty glass; a reddish residue ringed its bottom. Conor sat at the table after Emily took the chair opposite the owner. He took off his coat and hung it on the back of the chair.

"*Parlez-vous anglais?*" Conor said, breaking the ice.

The man didn't answer immediately but ran a finger through

the ashes in the ashtray, maybe searching for a butt that still had a puff or two left in it. Then he spoke. "*Un peu.*" A little.

"Closed? Why?" Conor said.

The man drew a deep breath. When he exhaled, it came with a rasping sound. "Germans. They take workers. Kitchen help. Waiters." A pause followed by a deep inhale. "My son."

Emily said something to encourage him to fill in the whys. He wasn't stingy with his words in reply to Emily. His response in French went on for over a minute, his face getting redder with each passing second. From Conor's view, he seemed to run out of breath, but not words, as his drawn face registered a burning frustration. Toward the end, he feigned spitting on the floor when he mentioned Pétain.

"He says most of his staff were taken to Germany to work camps. Forced labor to replace German workers who were conscripted into the military. He called it STO, *Service du travail obligatoire*. It was too much for him and his wife to remain open."

"What did he say about Pétain?"

"That it was Pétain's decree that created the work service program. As you saw, he was angry about that."

"I definitely get that," Conor said.

"But there's more to it. I read about the program last year. For every three workers who volunteered to work in Germany, the Nazis would release one French prisoner of war. But as time passed and the need for workers grew, it became compulsory for men and women in certain age groups."

"Another sign things aren't going well for Adolf," Conor said.

"Beaugard. What business do you have with him?" the owner said.

"Can you get word to him?" Emily said.

"Only for something..." The thin-faced man searched for a word.

"This is important. We need help to get to Lyon. And we need to ask some questions about someone he may know," Conor said.

The owner gave thought to their request as he shuffled his feet and wrung his hands for a short interval before letting them come to rest. "I will get word to him."

CHAPTER FIFTY-THREE

0830 Hours, Saturday, January 9, 1943
Hôtel Lutetia, Abwehr Headquarters, Paris

Hugo Bleicher knew well Colonel Rudolf had few face-to-face dealings with Admiral Canaris, the head of the Abwehr. None of them went well. Rudolf blamed his misfortune on the fact that he was more of a spit-and-polish soldier than the officers Canaris had working for him at his headquarters in Berlin.

When Bleicher was shown into his superior's top-floor suite to wait for Rudolf and Canaris's arrival from Le Bourget Airport, he first noted the potent scent of furniture wax mixed with the pine odor of a floor cleaner. He was sure that Rudolf missed nothing in his preparation for the admiral's visit. Rudolf appreciated Bleicher's suggestion that he pay particular attention to Canaris's two wirehaired dachshunds, Sabine and Seppel. Frequent travel companions, it was joked about at higher levels in the Abwehr that Canaris preferred their company to that of his staff and family. When Bleicher reminded Rudolf of this, he scoffed and shook his head but dared not voice his disdain for his superior's odd behavior.

Bleicher looked at his broken watch out of habit. While he waited, he stared across the street into Boucicaut Square, which sat leafless and doleful under a dreary, leaden sky. A numbness in his right thigh set in, as it often did these days whenever he stood motionless for extended periods of time. He was walking in a circle around Rudolf's desk when the gilt-trimmed doors that led to the private elevator opened and in strode Rudolf, his heels clicking loudly on the shiny parquet floor. With much less pomp, the diminutive gray-haired Canaris followed, dressed in a blue-pinstripe double-breasted suit.

From behind his desk, Rudolf gestured to Canaris to take one of the Louis XIV chairs in front of the desk. Canaris's face displayed his familiar frown before he accepted Rudolf's invitation. After sending for coffee, Rudolf made a quick introduction of Bleicher, who stood off to the side.

"Admiral, I know you are expecting a full report of Abwehr activities in France, but I feel I must start with the most important issue facing the Abwehr at present."

"And what is that, Colonel?"

"Sergeant Bleicher and I have recently returned from Lyon, where we attempted to overcome a setback to *Unternehmen Maulwurf*. Operation Mole."

"Setback? This is news to me," Canaris said, his voice barely rising above a harsh whisper.

"One of two of our agents, whom, as you know, we instructed to ingratiate themselves with a Resistance network in Lyon, has become uncooperative. This is extremely unfortunate, for he had been chosen to be sent back to London, with his mother, for training before being sent to Paris to reestablish the Gloria Network. Being sent to London, I don't need to tell you that development would mean literally infiltrating the Secret Intelligence Service at a high level."

Canaris settled deeper into his chair. "As we discussed, that would be quite an intelligence windfall for the Abwehr."

"Agreed, Admiral," Rudolf said.

"Is it the priest or the doctor?"

"The doctor. Code name Columbia."

"You say uncooperative. Why is this?"

"The Gestapo has arrested his American mother for assisting in the escape of Jews from Lyon, along with another American who was sent to take him and his mother back to England. The mother's actions are an act that the Gestapo's leader in Lyon, Hauptsturmführer Barbie, has taken quite an exception to, putting it mildly, Admiral." Bleicher noted that mentions of the Gestapo elicited a series of fidgets. "We have a valuable opportunity, one that has fallen into our laps, that we cannot squander," Rudolf said, his tone sounding more like he was pleading. "We must have the British think that the mission to have the mother and her doctor son taken back to England is still on track."

"And how do you propose to do that?"

Rudolf darted a look at Bleicher, then said, "The American agent must be allowed to escape." Canaris snorted. "And the Gestapo must release his mother." The latter request was met with silence. "Otherwise, her son refuses to go."

Canaris turned his head and shot an incredulous look at Bleicher. "Is that all?"

"Surely, Admiral, you can convince Polizeiführer Oberg to order Barbie to comply."

"I agree. It would be quite a coup if Columbia were to find himself amid the SIS. But, Colonel, what you ask could very well see my remaining leverage with Oberg expended. That will not bode well for the Abwehr or myself." Canaris rose from his chair. "Once my leverage is used, it is Oberg who will have the leverage."

Bleicher heard the complaint from many of his fellow Abwehr operatives that Canaris let the Gestapo, particularly Oberg, manhandle and outmaneuver the Abwehr at every turn. It surprised Bleicher to hear that Canaris had any leverage at all.

"I must feed my dogs," Canaris said, then turned to leave. "I will let you know the outcome of my talk with Oberg, but do not let your hopes get the best of you," he said without looking back.

#

0845 Hours, Saturday, January 9, 1943
Hôtel Terminus, Gestapo Headquarters, Lyon

Emotionally, Maggie Thorn felt nothing. Physically, she felt everything. She sensed the skin on her face tighten. Swollen for sure. She tasted blood on her lips. The skin around her wrists was raw. She lowered her head and saw bluish-purple bruises running up and down her legs. She was sure a mirror would have revealed that her eyes were blackened, and her hair matted with her blood. And the pain. Lowering her head alone was enough to bring on a near blackout.

It was her second day of captivity. The first day had been bad. But the second day was just beginning. They left her alone for the past ten minutes. It could have been longer, for time became a warped, unreliable measure. When Barbie stormed out, it was easy to see she had frustrated him. She called it a victory—one that could very well lead to more bloodshed. Hers. She had been sitting, bound and tied to a chair, for the entire day. She had asked for nothing. Not that she would have been given anything.

Steel yourself. Take your secrets with you. Maggie kept Virginia Hall's parting words at close reach. *Steel yourself, Maggie. Take your secrets with you.*

The door to the interrogation room flung open. Klaus Barbie marched in with the one called Eklof two steps behind. Two guards, tall and as Aryan-looking as one could be, followed, one on either side of an armless wooden chair that was hoisted in the air between them. Seated in the chair was Sarah DuBois. Except for the age difference, Maggie thought she was a mirror image of herself—bruised, battered, and bloodied. Sarah's head flopped up and down and side to side in concert with the movement of the chair.

"Here," Barbie said, motioning with a crooked finger to a spot on the blood-spattered floor three feet from Maggie. The two guards dropped the chair and it landed hard. Sarah's violated body bounced in her restraints. "Awake, I see. That is good. You must do better at staying awake, Maggie. When you don't, how could I be anything but offended?" Barbie stood to Sarah's left and Eklof on the right. Both wore the steel-gray-and-green uniform of the SS. Their suit coats with their wide lapels led to large collars that featured the runes indicating their rank. For Maggie, it was the uniform that struck as much fear as the men wearing them.

"Sarah. Sarah?" Maggie whispered. Sarah's head hung low. Her auburn hair, matted like Maggie's, covered her face. Better that Maggie didn't see her face.

"As you can see, Maggie, we've been spending some time with

your friend. When she displayed some reluctance to tell us about you, it forced us to take steps," Barbie said as he began pacing in a tight circle. Maggie picked up the smell of cigarettes as he passed close by. "She was very forthcoming about what she has done for her Jew friends. But there was nothing new that we learned. Imagine our disappointment."

Up to that point, Maggie thought it best to maintain her silence when with Barbie, lest she slip up while in pain. *But what is the fun in that*, she thought.

"I'll take a cigarette. Two actually. One now and one for after-dinner cordials." Her chatter halted Barbie's pacing.

"Aah…nice to hear your voice. Cigarette, you say? I'll give you an entire pack. Just tell us what brings you to Lyon. A simple exchange."

"No…on second thought, that's okay. I'm trying to quit."

Barbie was having nothing of it. He locked a searing stare on Maggie and didn't disengage for a full minute. When he finished staring a hole into her skull, he turned to Eklof. "Take them both to Montluc Prison. I have matters to attend to." He marched out the same way he had marched in.

"Hauptsturmführer, what of Obergruppenführer Oberg's orders?"

The question stopped Barbie's exit. He turned and looked at Maggie. "Take her back to Montluc for now. I am not done with her. As for Oberg, at some point, I might make sense of his orders." He turned back and resumed his march.

CHAPTER FIFTY-FOUR

0950 Hours, Saturday, January 9, 1943
Le Chat Noir, Avignon

When Conor heard two sets of footsteps on the wood floor above their heads, he looked at his watch. An hour and a half had passed. A single set of footsteps from the top of the narrow stairs quickly followed but stopped near the top.

"Come. He hasn't much time." It was the owner's voice, this time a harsh whisper.

At the top of the stairs, Conor and Emily found a nattily dressed man in a dark-blue suit, a few years over fifty. What stood out was his height. Beaugard was every bit as tall as Charles de Gaulle. He was peeking out through the swinging door that led from the kitchen into the empty dining area. Conor assumed he was confirming through the café windows that he was not followed.

Beaugard turned to face them as they entered. He held on to his brimmed felt hat in one hand and a cane in the other. He approached Conor and Emily with a limp. A pencil-thin mustache skimmed along his upper lip so precisely it looked as if he drew it with a sharp-tipped fountain pen. He extended his hand to Emily with a smile, then to Conor with a bit more caution. Conor wondered if Emily could hear the man wheezing or notice his short, shallow breaths. If he was a veteran of the Great War, Beaugard had some experiences with mustard gas.

"Your names?"

"I think it best, monsieur, for you and us if we remain nameless," Emily said.

"You leave me at a disadvantage." Beaugard shrugged. "But if that is what you prefer, so be it." He went back to the swinging door and took a prolonged look. "Now, tell me why you called for me."

Conor summarized their meeting with Jemond Lavigne Dupont back in Algiers. The mention of Dupont's name prompted Beaugard to turn back to them.

"He told you to contact me?"

"He said that you two were to meet at some point. Here at this café. But the German occupation of the south prevented it," Emily said.

"He mentioned wanting to coordinate with the Combat Network," Conor added.

The mention of the Resistance network made Beaugard inhale with a start, which then triggered a coughing fit. When the fit ran out of gas, his wheezing was more pronounced. Beaugard took a chair at the table and rested his cane across his lap. He placed his hat on top of the edition of *Combat*, the network's underground newspaper.

"What is it you want?"

"We need help with transport to Lyon." Conor pressed on when no response was forthcoming. "And we need to know about a prominent businessman, a banker, named Pierre Laurent."

Beaugard pulled a handkerchief and, following a shorter fit of coughing, spit into the cloth. "*Excusez-moi.*" Excuse me. Beaugard held on to the handkerchief and stared down at it as he spoke. "I will help with your trip. The roads between here and Lyon are busy. Much more so than roads to the south—many Nazi convoys, as the Wehrmacht is very active in this area. Travel will have to be by river barge. I will need time to make arrangements. I suggest you leave in darkness."

"We need to get to Lyon as soon as possible," Emily said. "We can't afford to wait for darkness."

Beaugard nodded and raised the handkerchief to his face but stopped and turned to Conor, then Emily. "Those Nazi convoys. They make for choice targets. I will help you two, but I ask in return that the British and the Americans send us arms, ammunition, explosives. Many here have the desire to fight, but we have no means to do so. Will you see to this?"

Conor exchanged a glance with Emily. "Sir, all we can promise is that we will relay your request to our superiors in the most effective way possible," Emily said.

"We all want to see the defeat of Germany, and France back in the hands of the French," Conor said. Beaugard lowered his head, clearly disappointed, but Conor felt sure he wasn't surprised. "What can you tell us about Laurent?"

"Nothing. I know no such man." Beaugard rose from his chair and replaced his handkerchief in his breast pocket. "I will ask some people. In the meantime, stay here, out of sight, and wait for my return." Beaugard, cane in hand, made for the swinging door in a slow, limping gait. Before he reached the door, another fit overcame him.

#

The first surprise was that Beaugard returned sooner than Conor expected. The second was the woman he brought with him. She was thinly built with beet-red shoulder-length hair pulled back and tied off at the nape of her neck. Fair skinned with a smattering of freckles that ran along the top of her blushed cheeks and across the bridge of her nose. She wore the dark-colored nondescript clothes of a workman. What made him stare was her uncanny resemblance to Maggie, right down to her freckles.

Beaugard took the same seat at the kitchen table he had earlier. Conor and Emily joined him. Beaugard asked the café owner for a glass of water. When the owner brought it, Beaugard downed it in one go. "This is Anick. That is not her real name. It is necessary to protect her family." He pointed to Conor, then to Emily. "These are the two who need help to travel to Lyon."

Anick nodded solemnly and remained standing. "Let me see your papers. Both of you." Anick's tone resembled that of an imperious Nazi official. Possibly like the voice she had heard often since the Germans occupied Vichy-controlled France back in

November. *Her command of English is quite good,* Conor thought, but the request caught him off guard. He reluctantly handed over his papers, as did Emily. She rifled through the pages, stopping at a few to study them more closely, all without indicating her opinion. She tossed them back to each of them. "Those papers will get you killed. You must hope no one asks for them."

"What's wrong with them?" Conor asked.

"The stamps. The ink has run on some of them. They are not clear and sharp. The Germans will question the imperfections." Conor took a quick look at a couple of the stamps. She was right. They didn't look official. "How is your French?"

Emily responded straightaway with a cover story about why they were traveling to Lyon. Anick didn't betray any sense of approval or disapproval. When she looked at Conor, he reeled off an explanation of what village he was from and what he did—a farmer.

"Ça *n'va pas, non!*" It is not okay! "Do not open your mouth except to say *oui* or *non*. Shrug when in doubt. And that should be often."

"Listen to Anick. Take her words to heart," Beaugard said, then tapped his empty glass. The owner left and Beaugard turned to Conor and Emily. "Anick will take you from here to a chapel on the Pont Saint-Bénézet. It is a historic bridge that has just a few spans remaining. It stretches out into the Rhône, where it is close to river traffic."

The owner returned with another glass of water, and Beaugard promptly downed it. He wiped his mouth with the back of his hand. Conor heard his wheezing return. "You will wait in the chapel until a barge, scheduled to pass the bridge at approximately five o'clock, approaches. Anick will signal the barge. The barge will slow as it approaches and come close to the last span. There are stairs that lead you down to the last pier. You will have to jump onto the moving barge. Once you are aboard, they will hide you both somewhere safe. Oh, one other item…the captain requires compensation. He won't be satisfied with anything less than five hundred francs."

Beaugard burst into a bout of coughing. They waited for it to subside, then Conor spoke up. "Have you any information about Pierre Laurent?"

"As I said before, I do not know him. But I know someone who knows many people. He has lived in Lyon his whole life. Go to this address." He shoved a slip of paper across the table toward Emily. "It is Soie Sainte-Geneviève, a silk shop in the Vieux Lyon. Ask to see Maurice. He is the owner. Say this to him, '*Allô*, the weather, it is quite awful today.' Use those exact words. His reply should be, 'For several days now.' If he cannot help, he will know someone."

"*Merci*, we are indebted to you. To you both," Conor said.

"Yes," Emily said. "We have funds, francs. May we leave some with you? Maybe it will help with needs from the black market."

Beaugard began coughing, a deep-in-the-chest cough.

"What we need are weapons, radios, as he has mentioned," Anick said. "Ammunition, guns, explosives, anything that can be used to drive the Nazis from France. Things in France are only getting worse with time."

Time has a habit of doing that, Conor thought.

CHAPTER FIFTY-FIVE

1130 Hours, Saturday, January 9, 1943
Hôtel Saint-George, rue Michelet, Algiers

"Commander, Major Stewart has arrived." Butcher jumped when Sergeant Billings entered his office undetected with his announcement. He was lost in thought about Ike's nagging subpar physical condition, brought on by a persistent cold that had sucked the energy from his body.

"Show him in, Sergeant."

Butcher hadn't met Stewart and was marginally up to speed on the investigation that he was heading up regarding the string of murdered Allied personnel that had been occurring over the past couple of months. The message he had received from the commander of the *Casabianca* made little sense to him.

"Commander, sorry for the delay. I was across town tracking down some leads. I got here as fast as I could."

"Take a seat, Major. Feel free to light up. Coffee?"

"No, sir. Thanks though."

"I'll get to the point. I received a message thirty minutes ago from Conor Thorn. You remember him?"

"Sure do. Concerning me, Commander?"

"Yes. It concerns the Stevens's murder and, I assume, possibly the others that you've been looking into." Butcher slid a clipboard with the message across his desk toward Stewart. "I think it will make more sense to you than me."

Stewart's lips moved ever so slightly as he read the message. When he looked up at Butcher, his eyebrows were hiked. "Stones. The name…not the least bit ironic."

"Sorry, I don't catch your drift."

"Excuse me, Commander. Just mumbling to myself." Stewart passed the clipboard back to Butcher. "Any idea when this Stones will get back to Algiers?"

"It will be a few days. All I can do is send word when I know more."

Stewart nodded and stood. "Thanks, Commander. This could be a big development in this case. I'll be waiting—"

"Commander," Billings said as he took long hurried strides to Butcher. "We just received another message from the *Casabianca*'s commander."

Butcher looked the message over. It was brief. He folded it and laid it on his desk. "Major, it appears the subject in question won't be returning to Algiers after all. He has, with no authorization, landed in southern France and, from what we understand, won't be returning anytime soon."

CHAPTER FIFTY-SIX

1430 Hours, Saturday, January 9, 1943
Hôtel Terminus, Gestapo Headquarters, Lyon

When Barbie's lead goon, Eklof, intercepted him before he could leave for Abwehr headquarters, DuBois's primary concern was Bleicher's infuriated reaction to his absence. A more visceral fear percolated as he stepped into the office of Klaus Barbie and recalled his last visit to the hotel.

"Aah, Dr. DuBois. Thank you for joining us," Barbie said. He sat behind his desk, his legs, crossed at his ankles, propped up on the desk's corner. A spotted Egyptian Mau cat sat in his lap, eyes closed, purring rhythmically.

With his coat draped over his arm and hat in hand, DuBois took a chair in front of Barbie's desk. In a shadowy corner of the office, he glimpsed Abbé Alves seated in a club chair. Seeing him in Barbie's office threw him. The thought that a priest would consort, possibly be collaborating with the Gestapo, unnerved him.

"And where did you find the doctor, Eklof?"

"He was escorting a patient out the door." Eklof took up a position behind and to the left of Barbie. "He looked like he was going somewhere. He won't tell me where."

"A patient? Was he a Jew, Doctor?"

"I am sure you are aware that I have done some work for the Abwehr," DuBois said.

Barbie shoved the Mau from his lap and lowered his legs. "I'll take note that you didn't answer my question." He picked up a letter opener. "The Abwehr. Yes, of course. That's the reason I am being so…deferential to you."

"I want to see my mother."

"And I want you to tell me what you know about Pierre Laurent. He is a patient of yours, yes?"

"Yes."

"What is wrong with him?"

"I can't tell you that. It's against—"

"He has prostate issues, according to his mother," Alves said from the corner of the room.

"Is he a member of the Resistance or is he a loyal Vichyite?" Barbie said.

DuBois looked over at the slouched figure of Alves, his hands held in front of his face, steepled, as if praying. "A loyal Vichyite," DuBois said.

Barbie cut his glance in Alves's direction. Alves nodded.

"Now tell me about this American redhead found in your home. And the people who brought her to you. Only then will I allow you to see your Jew-loving mother." Barbie's calm tone said he had all day to toy with him.

"I don't know who the woman is."

"Do you let people you don't know stay in your attic?"

"Listen to me," DuBois said louder than he intended, allowing Barbie's game-playing to get to him. "Someone unknown to me brought the woman to my office. She was injured. I'm a doctor. I cannot and will not turn someone in her condition away."

Barbie turned and nodded curtly at Eklof, who withdrew a short stack of photos from inside his tunic and tossed them onto DuBois's hat, which was perched in his lap. The top photo was of Maggie Thorn. She had been brutally tortured. She was almost unrecognizable given the swollen, bruised facial features. Dried blood caked her matted hair. The other pictures were close-up images of individual wounds, one being her original wound, which looked as if it had been prodded by a sharp instrument. DuBois's stomach churned, and he became lightheaded.

"The black-and-white photos don't do the results of our interrogation justice, wouldn't you agree, Eklof?"

"Agreed, Hauptsturmführer."

DuBois put the photos on the edge of the desk.

"Doctor, it is your turn to listen to me," Barbie said, the toying tone replaced with one full of anger and arrogance. "You have twenty-four hours to tell us all you know about this American and those who brought her to you. If you fail to do this, we will question your mother again, and our methods will be more drastic than those employed on the redhead. And given your mother being old and infirm, she will be unlikely to survive." Barbie paused.

DuBois swallowed hard to hold down the boiling acids; he was sure it was audible.

"You are listening, are you not?"

DuBois nodded and stood. Before he turned to leave, he looked once more at the top photo on the desk. The face, so contorted and mangled, it could have been anyone. But it was Maggie Thorn. He turned and stopped, looking directly at Alves. "Are you here as a private confessor for the Gestapo, or might you be thinking about trading professions?"

CHAPTER FIFTY-SEVEN

1545 Hours, Saturday, January 9, 1943
Prison de Montluc, 3rd Arrondissement, Lyon

In between the involuntary jolts, the pain that wracked Maggie's body pulsated at a steady voltage. Despite the pain, she felt like she could hang on a while longer. But the jolts and any other movement of her body brought more pain, as if she had thrown a bucket of gas on a roaring bonfire.

Her cell was on the top floor of the prison. She was next to Sarah's cell, from which she had heard nothing in the past two hours. When she had been brought to her cell after the last interrogation at Gestapo headquarters, a bit of weak, beaten sunlight filtered through the soot-covered skylight that ran down the center of the mezzanine—a slight contrast to the darkened cell she now sat in. There was a constant opening and slamming of cell doors mixed with the pleas and sobs of the prisoners as they were shuffled past her cell.

As a jailer stomped past, she held her breath until she could determine that they were after someone else. She ran her unbound hands over her face lightly so as not to put an ounce of pressure on her distended skin. She felt dried blood, lacerations, and a gash above her left eye. She ran her fingers down each arm, both their own field of bruises sensitive to the slightest pressure.

Several sets of boots pounded the mezzanine's floor. The metal railing that ran down both sides of the opening to the floor below rattled noisily. Sarah's cell door opened and slammed against the wall. Maggie's door then flew open, and a light that had all its brightness sucked out of it filled her cell. One guard stood at the door while another bound her wrists together with a thin wire. He yanked her up from the wood bedframe. Her body screamed out in pain and anguish; her heart hammered against her ribs.

They pushed her out of her cell and directed her past Sarah's. She slowed as she did and darted a look inside. There was a stretcher on the floor holding a body covered with a soiled, bloodied sheet. A guard shoved her to keep her moving. Maggie swerved to her right and vomited over the railing onto the floor below. Angry shouts floated upward.

As the two guards marched her outside into the yard inside the massive wall that surrounded the main building, she knew she was headed back to Gestapo headquarters for another interrogation. *Steel yourself, Maggie.* The fear that she would break this time reared up and shook her. She had to make a move to escape. She couldn't risk another session with the butcher. As they led her to the waiting panel van, she frantically calculated the best opportunity for an escape. There were so few, it didn't take long to run through them. She settled on making a run as they unloaded her in the front of the hotel. If she could make it into Lyon's traboules, she might disappear. Virginia Hall mentioned they were a good place to get lost—but also never found .

CHAPTER FIFTY-EIGHT

1550 Hours , Saturday, January 9, 1943
Pont Saint-Bénézet, Avignon

Anick, bundled tightly in a blue peacoat, led Conor and Emily through the maze of streets that wormed through the old section of Avignon. She carried a soft cloth bag, its straps looped over her shoulder. She took long strides, which put her a step or two ahead of Conor and Emily. They turned a corner and found themselves on a cobbled lane. A light layer of mist made the stones shimmer like sequins.

The lane led to a set of stairs that brought them to the Pont Saint-Bénézet's gatehouse inset in the city's ancient wall. Four remaining spans of the bridge jutted out over the fast-moving Rhône River. The gatehouse was open, and the drawbridge connecting it to the bridge was down, its permanent position, according to Anick. "We must move along, or we will draw attention to ourselves," Anick said, motioning with her hand for them to catch up.

One hundred fifty feet ahead, across a crushed stone pathway that traversed the first two spans of the bridge, sat a structure on the north side—the Saint-Bénézet Chapel, once the resting place of the saint's remains. As they crossed the pathway, a firm wind rose off the river and buffeted them. Conor didn't spot anyone on the bridge, which was a comfort.

Anick's long strides again put her in the lead as they covered the distance to the chapel. On the exterior stone wall, someone had engraved a Cross of Lorraine. The wind rushing past his ears muted any other sounds as they progressed toward the doorless chapel. It was why they didn't hear the two Wehrmacht soldiers, their rifles resting against the set of steps that led to a stage where a modestly sized altar sat. The soldiers sat on the steps, their helmets at their feet.

Conor counted two wine bottles—one on the altar and one in the hand of a soldier, who was the spitting image of Joseph Goebbels. Goebbels hurriedly placed his bottle on the altar, almost tipping it over, and followed the other soldier as he reclaimed his rifle. Standing there with rifles pointed in their direction, Conor detected a slight sway. The reddish bloom on their faces confirmed they had a good load on. The second soldier, the one who looked like he could have been the stout younger brother of Rudolf Hess, the crazy Nazi who flew to England looking for a peace deal, shouted, "*Papiers!*" Papers!

Anick was quick to respond, shoving her papers in Hess's shaky hands. Hess looked them over, having a noticeably difficult time focusing on the documents. He handed Anick's papers back. Conor was the next to get a hand signal from Goebbels for his papers. Then Emily got her own signal from the chubby Hess.

Hess was the first to speak. "*Diser Mann konnte nicht mit einer Frau umgehen, aber mit zwei?*" A hearty round of mocking laughter that lingered too long for Conor's taste followed this comment, though he understood perfectly.

Conor couldn't help himself. "*Die nadelschwänze sollten es wissen.*" That seemed to add a notch to their sober belts as their smiles faded just as quick as their laughter. Hess shoved the butt of his rifle into the center of Conor's chest. Ever since he was a kid, he hated being pushed. He'd rather Hess took a swing at him. So Conor repaid the push with a right cross. He connected with Hess's jaw, which sent him stumbling backward. Goebbels grabbed Emily by the upper arm and separated her from the rest of the group.

Conor, his knife now in his right hand, took a long stride to Hess. A blur of motion to his left distracted him. It was Anick, a length of pipe in her left hand. She swung it and landed it on the side of Hess's head, just below his helmet. He landed in a heap of grayish-green wool. Conor and Anick looked up from Hess and saw that Emily had Goebbels in a headlock. He was spitting and gurgling, struggling for breath. Wordlessly, Anick took three steps, removed the helmet strap from under Goebbels's chin, and brought the pipe down on the crown of his head.

"We need to kill these goons," Conor said, "and drop them into the river."

"*Non*. The Boches will seek reprisals. Very unwise. We have no weapons to defend ourselves." She placed the pipe in the small of her back. "Drag them both over to that sealed doorway. They will be out of view until they wake up. They will not want to report that two women got the better of them."

Conor felt a little left out of that story but understood her point. Emily grabbed Goebbels by the back of his collar, and Conor dragged Hess by the ankles to the sealed doorway.

"What did you say to them?" Anick said.

"Nothing important."

"The guard said that Conor couldn't handle one woman, let alone two," Emily said. "That right, Conor?"

"I believe that is correct."

"And you said what to them?" Anick asked again.

"I said you needle dicks should know."

Anick turned her head away, looking downriver, and seemed to be stifling a laugh, her shoulders shaking somewhat. But it was only for a moment. "*Merde*," she muttered. "The barge, it is coming."

Conor looked out the entrance of the chapel and spotted the barge over a mile downriver, moving at less than five knots. He glanced at his watch. Their transport north was early to the tune of one hour. Anick reached into her bag and pulled out a flashlight.

"Come, move to the end of the bridge."

They had taken just two steps toward the entrance of the chapel when they heard a commotion behind them. Conor turned. Hess was struggling to his feet, a sidearm in hand. Conor grabbed for his knife but quickly opted for his gun. He pulled his Colt from its shoulder holster and snapped off a round, landing dead center in the advancing Hess's forehead. The man dropped, his sidearm clattering across the worn, smooth floor. Conor opted for the head shot over a chest shot. He decided Hess's uniform would come in handy.

"Em, help me get his uniform off," he said.

Anick opened her mouth, probably looking to protest, but Emily began peeling off his tunic and shirt while Conor worked on his boots and pants. They made quick work of the process. Conor, with a firm hold of Hess under his armpits, dragged his body out of the chapel and draped him over the railing like a wet rug. Then he lifted Hess's legs and tipped him into the swirling muddy water of the Rhône, causing quite a ruckus among four white swans milling around below.

As they ran down the crushed stone path toward the last span, Conor stuffed the uniform into his musette bag. Arriving at the bridge's last span, Anick kneeled on one knee and began signaling the barge, which responded by maneuvering toward the pier. Conor, followed by Emily, took the stairs two at a time, landing on the pier's cobbled surface; dormant limp weeds poked through the cracks.

Emily and Conor looked up the stairs, and Anick looked down at them, then downriver. She turned back to them and cupped her hands around her mouth. "It's coming. But it hasn't slowed much. Get ready."

Conor and Emily inched to the far edge of the pier and watched the barge, some hundred fifty feet long. It was sitting low in the water. Its uncovered holds contained six mounds of what appeared to be gravel or sand. The pilothouse, open to the elements, was at the stern. Conor made out the profiles of two men. A square-shaped structure, its walls streaked with rust stains, sat behind the pilothouse. Life preservers hung on the wall on the bridge side of the barge. At the bow, the Rhône, churned white by the barge's progress, rippled outward in a calm wake. Conor estimated that they would have to leap five feet from the edge of the pier over the gunwale of the boat.

"We're going to have to jump aboard. Put your musette on your back. When you jump, try to target one of the piles of gravel or sand. Better than landing on the hard deck. I'll go, then you. Maybe I can soften your landing. Got it?"

"Yes. The piles," Emily said. "This is a first for me. You?"

Conor snorted, then kissed her hard on the mouth.

They stood side by side on the pier's edge. The barge plodded toward them. Conor held Emily's hand. The barge was slower now but not getting as close as Conor thought they needed to come. "He's not getting closer. We have to get a running start to make it."

Emily nodded.

They both backed up. Conor squeezed her hand, then sprang forward. The barge passed ten feet ahead of him, surprisingly quiet. Conor flailed his arms and raised his feet into the air like a long jumper. When he landed, he hit a mound of gravel hard. The mound was more like a hard-packed road base. His legs took the brunt of the landing, then he looked back at the pier.

Emily was starting her run toward the edge. She leaped, gaining more height than Conor, and seemed to move through the air at a faster clip. But midair, a gust of wind hit her and sapped some crucial speed from her jump. Her feet landed short of the barge's deck, directly on top of the gunwale. She teetered there for a horrifying moment. Conor reached up to grab her hand, but her arms were gyrating in a circular motion, trying to keep whatever balance she had. He snagged the belt of her trousers and yanked her toward him.

Her torso snapped back with the tug, and she lost her footing on the slippery gunwale. Out of nowhere, another hand caught her arm. Between the arm pull and the tug on her belt, Emily tumbled headfirst into a mound of sand with a grunt. Conor kneeled at her side and gently rolled her onto her back.

A young man in a black rain slicker, his face broken out in acne, stood looking down at Emily. He turned to Conor. "Come quick. You can't be seen on deck. Follow me."

Conor helped Emily up. Her breathing was still recovering. "I thought you were about to join that German floating down the river in his underwear."

Emily tried to answer but gave up. As they followed the young man aft, Conor noticed Anick running down the bridge's span toward the chapel, then disappearing inside.

CHAPTER FIFTY-NINE

1555 Hours, Saturday, January 9, 1943
Hôtel Terminus, Gestapo Headquarters, Lyon

"Thank you, Hauptsturmführer Barbie, for taking the time to meet with us on such short notice," Ambassador Abetz said, nervously twirling his trilby in his hands. He sat on the edge of his chair, looking as if he were readying himself to have it yanked unexpectedly from under him.

"And on this occasion, you're on time, Ambassador." Barbie smirked. Abetz was actually fifteen minutes early, but Barbie had elected to make the man wait. "Make your introductions."

"Yes, of course, this is Pierre Laurent, of whom I've spoken," Abetz said with a wave of his arm toward the seated Laurent. Barbie was not totally surprised that the man looked ill after the priest Alves confirmed the prostate condition. But Laurent's extreme, ghostlike pallor still took him aback. "And next to Pierre is Antoine Brunel. It is he who is the reason for my request to meet with you." A jittery Brunel gave off the smell of fear. A smell all too familiar to Barbie.

"Get on with it, Ambassador. The Gestapo has business to address, even on a Sunday."

"Permit me, Ambassador Abetz. I will get to the point." Laurent spoke up, to the apparent relief of Abetz. "Monsieur Brunel has brought to our attention a proposal that, we feel, has great value to the Reich."

Barbie allowed five ponderous minutes to pass while Laurent explained before he held up his hand to shut up the sallow Frenchman. "What use would the Reich have for this archive? And please state your answer in an economical fashion."

"You must understand, being a Frenchman, it galls me that the British and Americans could have been involved in the assassination of Admiral Darlan. If true, it would deeply displease many other Frenchmen, even if they were not fully behind Marshall Pétain. If these documents in the archive were to include information...proof that they were involved...it would poison the alliance formed since the invasion of North Africa." Laurent paused and cut his gaze toward Brunel, who was nodding in agreement.

Barbie loathed the politics of war. It didn't interest him. The victories were never as clearly defined as they were for those hunting down Jews and Resistance fighters. He admitted the defeats were also more easily determined. But this Laurent made sense. It would be a mistake not to follow up on this potential opportunity. Of course, he would place it in the hands of Oberg, who relished the intrigue of the political arena.

"Where is this archive?"

"Hidden, Hauptsturmführer," Brunel said.

Barbie was losing his already thin patience. "Where?"

Brunel looked at Laurent, who leaned forward and mirrored Abetz's pose on his chair. "Monsieur Brunel has made a proposition, Hauptsturmführer. He seeks the release of his mother, an American, from an internment camp. Only then will he reveal the location of the archive."

Barbie threw his head back and cackled. "Ambassador, it seems the Americans are everywhere I turn." He snorted; his face lost its momentary amusement. "Some are quite stubborn, these Americans. Others are quite easy to break." He riveted his piercing look on Brunel. "I wonder how stubborn Monsieur Brunel would be after spending an afternoon with me and my staff of experts."

CHAPTER SIXTY

1610 Hours, Saturday, January 9, 1943
Prison de Montluc, 3rd Arrondissement, Lyon

As the guards shunted Maggie toward the waiting panel van, she pushed back at the rising fear in her gut. Her heart pounded, her tongue felt like sandpaper against the roof of her mouth, and her wrists throbbed with a dull pain as the wire burrowed into her skin. Angry clouds that changed their appearance every few seconds filled the sky. They threatened…something. She wished she could stand there and wait for the show, but the tip of a baton in her back had other ideas.

As she passed the cab of the truck, she saw Eklof sitting in the passenger seat, smoking a cigarette. His one eye squinted at her as the guard shoved her past him toward the rear of the van. Whether he squinted because of the thick smoke rising from his cigarette or just plain poor eyesight, Maggie didn't know. She also didn't know why she was mulling such a mundane thought. She was ten minutes away from another round of torture.

She rounded the back of the van as the rear door opened. There was someone already inside. All she could make out was a slumped figure in dark clothing seated in the right corner nearest the cab. Before she took a step on the van's bumper, it hit her. The stench of burnt flesh.

Eklof yelled something in German that Maggie couldn't make out. The guard muttered something, put a hand on the small of her back, and shoved her into the van headlong. She landed on her stomach, her face inches away from a pair of bare feet, their soles covered with blisters weeping a reddish puss. Maggie rolled onto her side and looked up into the contorted, scarred face of the man whose cell was across from hers. The rear doors slammed shut, and they threaded the lock and chain through the handles. She didn't blame the guard for not riding in the back with them.

The man raised his head halfway. "*Allô*, our American friend. Please excuse my feet. It seems I have forgotten my shoes and socks."

Maggie struggled to her knees and sat across from the man. "No worries. I often forget where I put things since I arrived here," she said, pinning on a snort at the end. The van's engine turned over, and it crept ahead. The engine noise shrouded their voices.

"I told them nothing. This did not make them happy. Especially the one with the cat. He would take off his watch before each session. To keep it dry during the water torture. Did he do that to—"

"I'm going to run. The first chance I get." He stared at her, parted his lips, and seemed about to say something, but abandoned the idea. "As they take us from the van before we go inside the hotel. The trains are close by. I won't have far to run before I think I can hide in an empty rail car."

"*Non, non, non.* You must not hide there. Those rail cars are going to the place you will never survive. Just keep running, past the rail station and all the tracks. Head south toward the confluence of the Saône and the Rhône. They won't think you'll head in that direction."

All Maggie could do was nod. Her throat was tight and constricted. She was crying. The last time she'd cried was when she and René broke off their relationship.

"I will do what I can. Which is not much." He raised both feet. "As you can see, they made sure that I could not run."

Maggie's tears dried on her cheeks. A short while later, the van stopped, and the cab doors opened, then shut. Her friend was lying on his back, his feet toward the rear doors. The doors swung open. One guard stood there, confused. The man drove his blistered feet into the guard's chest. The sound of a rib crack, a sputtered exhale, and her friend's muted yelp of pain all filled the air nearly simultaneously, mixed with the sound of locomotives releasing streams of steam.

Maggie bolted from the rear of the van, jumped on the guard's chest, and drove her bound hands into his windpipe, crushing it. Eklof shouted impatiently from the front, and Maggie sprang to her feet and ran for the Perrache station's network of tracks that spread out before her. Breathing hard, she crossed several tracks, hearing no sound behind her.

Then came the shouts, clear and unmistakable, from Eklof. They were not the shouts of a panicked man. They were from someone who knew how this scene was going to end.

A shot pinged off a rail. Another shot drilled into the gravel near a rotted wooden tie. The third shot ripped through her lower back and dropped her to the ground just as a train passed between her and her pursuers. She drove her bloodied bound hands into the gravel and rose to her feet. Searing pain rocketed up her spine, into the base of her skull. She thought she was running, but looking down at the maze of rail tracks, they passed by as if her legs were in slow motion. The train behind passed, opening a clear sight line, and she risked a look. Eklof was thirty yards behind her, the driver of the van on his heels. She tried to crouch to minimize the size of his target, but her back wouldn't allow it.

Phht. Phht. Two shots split the air. One on either side of her head, sucking air from her ears. Blood rushed down the right side of her head from the grazing shot. Another shot rang out. Then a pure silent darkness consumed her.

CHAPTER SIXTY-ONE

2315 Hours, Saturday, January 9, 1943
Quai du Docteur Gailleton, Lyon

Twenty minutes before they were to dock in Lyon, the captain of the barge instructed them to wait at the stern and look busy coiling lines and stowing shovels and brooms. They were to look like part of the barge crew to lessen any suspicion from curious eyes. Conor liked the *hide in plain sight* plan. Conor and Emily could have been told to stand on their heads and bicycle kick their legs for an hour, and they would have done it. They both were feeling pretty…fulfilled at that point.

Just after they landed on the deck of the barge, and after forking over five hundred francs to cover their clandestine passage to Lyon, they were led to a cramped compartment aft of the pilothouse and told to remain there until they approached Lyon. The space was used for storage. In one corner, there was a bunk bed, the upper bunk minus a mattress. The bottom had a thin mattress covered with a single blanket with several cigarette burn holes and a pillow the size of a small seat cushion, which was what it was. Emily and Conor had exchanged charged glances. The sparkle in Emily's eyes seemed to reflect a series of white-hot fireworks. He didn't know what his eyes reflected, but he felt something in his stomach that he had been tamping down ever since they left Algiers—a bourgeoning lust.

"Well, my father always said, don't put off to tomorrow what you can do today."

"Conor, I adore your father, but your mention of him is certainly not the image I want popping into my head right this minute. Do you want me to tell you what Bertie says?"

"I see what you mean. I love Bertie like my own mother, but—"

"Shut up, Conor." Emily had grabbed his hand and nudged him to the side of the bunk. The first piece of clothing that hit the deck was their shirts. They both bent over, heads almost colliding, to untie their boots. Then both pairs of pants settled on the deck at the same time. Conor's lips pressed against hers. They stood there exchanging warm moist kisses until Emily pulled him down toward the bed, where they lay side by side for a long quiet moment. He started to say something, but her finger on his lips put an end to that. She reached down and found what she was looking for. And that ended any thought of talking. For both of them. For two hours, their long, trancelike lovemaking was the only thing in their world.

Exhausted, their bodies glistening with sweat, they lay there, pressed against each other, breathing in each other's breath. The thought that he loved Emily more thoroughly and deeply than he did Grace saddened him. Then the realization scared him. To lose her after losing Grace would kill him. He shook his head with a snap to rid his mind of the thought.

"What is it?"

"Nothing. Really." He paused. "How do you feel?"

"Hmm. How do I feel?" Emily smiled. "So this is what love feels like."

"Yeah. My thought precisely." A sleep like none that they had experienced for some time engulfed them.

The barge's bow nestled against the bulwark of the quay and two crew members handled the chore of securing the bow to the quay by casting mooring lines from barge to shore. Conor looked up and down the quay. Their playacting as crew members seemed unnecessary, as there weren't any guards or officials in sight given the hour. Conor and Emily, along with the crew, climbed the ladder to reach the top of the quay. He surveyed the river. North, some two hundred yards, three patrol boats were tied up bow to stern. No crews were in sight. As most of the barge's crew dispersed, the captain approached.

"You remember how I told you to get to this shop?"

"Yes," Emily said. "Head west. Travel through Place Bellecour, cross the Saône into Vieux Lyon, and turn north. When we arrive at the Court of Appeals building, then head west again to rue du Bœuf."

"Perfect. Good luck. Be careful who you trust."

#

0015 Hours, Sunday, January 10, 1943
Soie Sainte-Geneviève, 5th Arrondissement, Lyon

To no one's surprise, the front door to the silk shop was locked. The street was empty except for two stray cats that were pawing through a pile of trash trapped in a corner of a doorway across from the shop. Conor considered breaking a glass pane in the door but didn't want to announce their presence so boldly.

"There's got to be a back way in that isn't so exposed." The shop was a short distance from the end of the street, which made quick work of getting to the back of the row of buildings that lined the street. Down both sides of the alley were trash bins, all overflowing with soaked trash. The back door to the shop had four panes of rippled, imperfect glass that was close to impossible to see through. Conor wrapped his right hand in his handkerchief to protect it from the soon-to-be-shattered glass when he was rudely interrupted by Emily turning the knob and sliding the door open.

"That works too," Conor said. Emily lifted her chin in a show of gumption.

The narrow room was lit by a single banker's lamp seated on a worktable located dead center. The air was heavy with a mix of cigarette smoke and the burnt acorns used to make ersatz coffee. Conor and Emily carefully moved about the room. Along the right wall was a double pedestal desk piled high with swatches of fabric, ledgers, and files. The desk's chair was tucked under it, a knee-length white smock draped over the back. Along the side of the desk was a leather nailhead chair on three feet, the leather cushion faded and cracked. In one corner was a circular wrought-iron stairway.

"I'll go find our man, Maurice. Hopefully, he's not entertaining anyone," Conor said. "Watch the door." Emily nodded and Conor headed up the staircase.

It didn't take long to find Maurice. He was in a deep sleep, the top of his head poking out from under a patchwork quilt. When he shook the man's shoulder the third time, Maurice woke, completely unfazed by the interruption.

"*Allô*, the weather, it is quite awful today," Conor said in faltering French.

"*Quoi?*"

"Damn," he said under his breath, wondering why he didn't send Emily on the hunt for Maurice. Conor repeated the coded greeting slower and used his hand to accent his terrible command of French.

"Aah. For several days now," Maurice said in French.

He let Maurice head down the staircase first. Emily was standing to the side of the back door, looking out. In the low light, Conor noticed Maurice was dressed in silk pajamas. So French. A closer look at him revealed he had the same shaped nose as Jimmy Durante—the Great Schnozzola. A closer look showed that Maurice was clean-shaven with bloodshot bug eyes. His most unusual feature was a crop of wiry black hair protruding from his ears and nose, complemented by the biggest set of bushy eyebrows Conor had ever seen.

"Do you speak English?"

Maurice took a seat at his desk and swiveled in his chair to face them. "I do. But not often. So I'm not so good."

"Good enough for me," Conor said, even though his thick French accent was hard to cut through. "Why is your back door open? Isn't that a little foolish?"

"I get visitors at all hours. Like you. They know they can hide here. And I don't want them to break the glass. You cannot get glass here." Conor looked at Emily and was greeted with an annoying smirk. "I don't see many British and fewer Americans. What do you want?"

"We need some information about a Pierre Laurent. A banker here in Lyon. Do you know him?" Emily asked.

"*Oui*. What of him?"

"He might be involved in something of great interest to the Allies," Conor said.

"Is it his involvement with the *Synarchique*?"

Conor and Emily exchanged looks, both noting the second mention of the fascist-leaning pro-German group. "That's something we can't get into. What else do you know of him?"

"Not a great deal. He is a very private man. He used to be seen about but not since his sickness."

"Is it serious? Is he about to kick the bucket?" Conor said, immediately seeing Maurice struggle with his question.

"Maurice, is Laurent about to die?" Emily said.

"Aah. No. From what I hear, at least." He paused and took in his guests. "I have a friend. He is a doctor. He is one of us. Laurent is his patient. You may learn more from him."

"Who is he and where can we find him?" Emily said.

"Dr. René DuBois. His office is on rue des Trois-Maries here in the Vieux Lyon."

Conor's head jerked back. *DuBois? Maggie's French boyfriend? Ex-boyfriend.* Conor remembered that he had shipped back to France after they split. It devastated Maggie. He'd never seen her so low and hurt. It had taken her several months to get over the breakup.

"This DuBois…did he once live in America?" Conor said.

Emily gave him a confused look.

"*Oui*. For several years. With his father and mother."

Conor remembered not liking DuBois. He never paid enough attention to his sister, which, surprisingly, Maggie put up with. "Take us to him."

"Not now. No, no, no. The curfew makes it too dangerous. We must wait."

CHAPTER SIXTY-TWO

0800 Hours, Sunday, January 10, 1943
Hôtel Terminus, Gestapo Headquarters, Lyon

Eklof wasn't sure if the Englishman's head tic resulted from his gloomy predicament or something that he dealt with for a large part of his life. Eklof knew that the purple blotch below his left ear was a lifelong trait. He thought to ask about the tic, but he really didn't care what the answer was.

After Krupp had worked over the Englander, he was barely conscious. Eklof had told Krupp not to be too excessive and to keep the loss of blood to a minimum. Eklof remembered his own mistake when interrogating a British Royal Marine while stationed in Stockholm. Stuben, his superior, was apoplectic when the marine, working for the British Legation, suffered a heart attack while under questioning about his spying on the German Legation. How was he to know the marine had a weak heart? Krupp was able to pry the Englander's name, rank, and unit out of him: James Stones, a lieutenant assigned to the SOE base in Algiers.

When Eklof stepped in to relieve Krupp, he ordered him to hold Stones's left hand on the table, palm down. Looming over the man and without asking for any information, Eklof crushed his hand with a short-handle sledgehammer. Stones's screams lasted for thirty seconds, then trailed off. Stones pulled his mangled hand and let it rest in his lap. When Eklof threatened to do the same to his other hand, Eklof had learned about an Allied mission to land three agents along the southern coast of France.

"What was the mission of these agents?" Stones's head hung low, his chin resting on his chest. Eklof noted the head tic had ceased. When no answer was forthcoming, Eklof nodded at Krupp, who slammed his truncheon into the side of Stones's head. Stones's eyelids fluttered, then shut. Still no answer. Another nod from Eklof, and Krupp yanked Stones's other hand and slapped it on the table. Eklof picked up the sledgehammer.

Stones's eyes opened. "One agent…he's dead. He was to set up communication networks. That's all I know about him."

Eklof could barely hear the SOE agent. "How did this agent die?"

"I killed him."

It was Eklof's turn to jerk his head. "Why?"

Stones began to drool a mixture of blood and saliva. "Because I wanted to escape and didn't want anyone left behind alive."

"Escape? From what?"

Stones lifted his head halfway. "I killed some people. In Algiers. I wanted to get to France so I could make my way to Switzerland."

"You killed people…for what?" Eklof said.

"Does it matter?" Stones stared at his hand, which was still being held down by Krupp.

"No, it doesn't really. The other two agents… What was their mission?"

"I never found out. They only spoke to the submarine's commander."

"Names and descriptions?"

"A man and a woman. American and British. Names Thorn and Bright. He was—"

"Stop," Eklof shouted. He reached up to his left ear—or what was left of it after Thorn ripped it from the side of his head after Eklof chased the insolent American across Sweden. Thorn had humiliated him more than once. "I know what they look like." Eklof palmed the head of the sledgehammer three times. "Where were they going?"

"The corpsman on the sub…told me they were headed to Lyon."

Eklof's slit of a mouth broke into a sneer as he drove the sledgehammer onto the Englander's outstretched hand.

CHAPTER SIXTY-THREE

0800 Hours, Sunday, January 10, 1943
DuBois Home/Office, 5th Arrondissement, Lyon

Conor and Emily held back inside the covered passageway that led into the courtyard of DuBois's building, while Maurice climbed the steps to the second floor and knocked. Shortly after the series of knocks, the door opened. The slender frame of René DuBois filled the partial opening. Maurice turned and signaled them to come forward as DuBois retreated inside the home, unaware someone from his past was about to pop back into his life.

Inside, Maurice waited for them in the foyer, then led them to DuBois's office. DuBois was seated at his desk, studying a thick textbook. When he looked up at his guests, Conor was sure he could see the blood drain from his face.

"These are the people I spoke of, René," Maurice said.

DuBois didn't rise, nor did he speak. He did nothing but stare at Conor.

"Hello, René. It's been a while."

"Aah, excuse me. Mind telling me what's going on here?" Emily said.

"The doctor here once dated my sister. Pretty seriously, if you ask me," Conor said.

"Well, that's quite a coincidence. And here he is in Lyon," Emily said, her words dripping in sarcasm. She was getting good at that.

"Are you here to find your sister?"

"What?" Conor asked, his brow lowering in confusion. "She's in England."

"No, she's not." DuBois rose and came around his desk. He'd aged little, except for some gray hair around his temples and a more prominent set of laugh lines. Conor didn't notice the slight bags under his eyes and a shaving nick on his neck below his jawline until he came around his desk. "She arrived in Lyon three days ago, badly injured from landing in a tree after jumping into France."

"Holy shit," Conor muttered. She made it in theater much sooner than Conor had expected. *Did she get enough training for an operation this soon*, he wondered.

"Where is she?" Emily said.

"She was arrested. Taken to Montluc Prison. She's—"

"What the hell was she doing here?" Conor said.

"She was to take my mother and me back to England. Through Switzerland. And..." DuBois's voice trailed off.

"And what," Conor snapped.

"There was one other part of her mission. She was to track down and kill a German spy."

"Who?" Emily asked.

"Robert Alves. He's a priest. He works closely with the Abwehr. And the Gestapo."

"Is he here in Lyon? Now?" Conor said.

"He comes and goes. As of today, I do not know."

"Maggie. You said she's in this Montluc Prison?" Emily said.

"Yes. Some of the time. They take her back and forth between there and Gestapo headquarters. No set timetable."

Emily headed to the bay window and snuck a peek out into the courtyard. "There's someone lurking in the passageway to the street. We can't stay long." She turned back and looked at DuBois. "We are trying to track down someone...Antoine Brunel. Have you heard of him?"

DuBois's posture stiffened. He looked confused. "Brunel? As a matter of fact, yes. He has met with my patient, Pierre Laurent. He is negotiating a deal with him." DuBois paused and began to rub his chin. "What do you want with him?"

Ignoring his question, Conor said, "What sort of deal?"

"He has some valuable documents. He thinks he can exchange them for the release of his mother. The Germans have her in an internment camp."

"Do you know where we can find him?" Emily said.

"Yes, he is staying at the Hôtel Normandy."

"It isn't far from here," Maurice said.

"Do you have transport?"

"Yes. An old Peugeot. I haven't driven it in a while. I hope it starts."

Emily was about to speak when there was a vigorous knocking at the back of the house. DuBois left the office and returned less than a minute later. A thickset jowly faced man close to fifty with a large flat nose followed him. He was breathing hard.

"This is Yves. He was the one who brought Maggie here for treatment," DuBois said.

Yves took a seat on the examining table. His legs dangled toward the floor and his boots dripped. "You must leave. There is much bad news for you." Yves sucked in a breath, and when he blew it out, words came with it. "Your mother. They have killed her."

What little color that had returned to DuBois's face vanished. He leaned against the desk, the knuckles on both balled fists a yellowish white.

"Why?" Emily asked. "What did she do?"

"The Jews. They went to her for help to get out of France. They wouldn't leave her alone." DuBois turned to Yves. "Where did you learn this?"

"We have informants in the prison. I am sorry to bring this to you. She was very brave," Yves said.

"Did your informants say anything about another American?" Conor said.

"You mean the redhead?"

"Yes. A redhead. She's—"

"She was shot yesterday in front of the Hôtel Terminus, trying to escape."

CHAPTER SIXTY-FOUR

0815 Hours, Sunday, January 10, 1943
The One-Eight, 5th Arrondissement, Lyon

Germaine held the message she'd just decoded from London between her thumb and first finger as she flicked open her St. Dupont lighter and thumbed the side igniter. The flame sprang to life and lit the edge of the paper. Two heartbeats later, a white-hot flame consumed it. She let the ash fall into the fireplace, where she mixed it in with the dormant ashes of the prior evening's fire. She mulled over the contents of the short message.

We are anxious to receive Atlantic Wall intelligence. It is of growing importance.

It was early for Germaine. She had been lounging in a silk robe with a white fur collar, smoking her first of many Gauloises, when her bodyguard, Louis, brought her the message. Her stomach was uneasy, dashing the thought of eating her customary slice of quiche Lorraine. Was it the caviar from the night before that stroked the pangs of uneasiness, or could it be the contents of the message she just set afire? She wound up the phonograph and played some Josephine Baker to calm herself while she sat on the cranberry settee. Her cat, Baker, leaped onto her lap and settled in a ball of coal-black fur.

Germaine needed to talk. "Louis, be a dear and find Dr. Russier for me."

Before Louis even reached the door, she heard firm double

knocks. A second after Louis finished the process of unlocking the door, Russier barged into the room.

"There is news. None of it welcome."

Germaine held up a hand. "Louis, go down the back stairs and check on the girls." As Louis exited, Russier wheezed, slipped off his wire-rimmed glasses, and ran his handkerchief across the lenses as he nearly collapsed on the end of the settee. The news of Sarah DuBois's death and the demise of the American sent to take them out of France jolted her. Germaine picked up the cat and gently placed her on the floor. "Does René know?"

"I don't know," Russier said, slowly shaking his head. "Poor René."

Her stomach churned. She dropped her smoked Gauloises into the ashtray and fumbled through the process of lighting up another. "The timing…it couldn't be worse. London is impatient for the Atlantic Wall information. What might be the reason for their impatience?"

"Could it be plans for the invasion of France have been moved up?"

Germaine gave thought to that possibility. It helped quell her nerves, but she waved the thought off with a flick of her hand. "If only that were true."

"Then why?"

"It is a waste of time to even think about reasons. I will take the place of the American. I have impeccable papers, money, and I am French. I will take René and the intelligence as far as Switzerland. Then the English will have to figure out how to get René to London."

CHAPTER SIXTY-FIVE

0815 Hours, Sunday, January 10, 1943
Hôtel Normandy, 3rd Arrondissement, Lyon

After dropping Yves and Maurice off at Place Bellecour, Conor and Emily headed for the hotel. Two minutes later, they pulled up to a five-story structure at the end of a block. A wind-beaten narrow awning barely covered the entrance. On the front edge of the roof was a sign with capital letters attached to a metal framework. The letter *E* was missing from the word *HOTEL* as was the *Y* from *NORMANDY*.

Conor told DuBois to pull around to the rear, where they entered and headed up the staircase in the courtyard. Conor wanted to take a boot to the doorknob of Brunel's hotel room and shatter the doorjamb, but Emily voted for a less conspicuous approach. It didn't fit Conor's mood, but he relented. Emily knocked softly and said something flirtatious. Conor made out something about it being cold and the words *may I come in*, which sounded so much more alluring in French.

Brunel opened the door, and his smile faded abruptly when he saw Conor standing before him, his Colt M1911 raised. Conor grabbed Brunel's collar and dragged him out of the room. Brunel protested, but Conor shoved the tip of his Colt in his open mouth. "You can talk when we get to the roof."

"Conor, where are you going?" Emily asked. "I thought we were going to take him away."

"We need him to talk. Fast." Emily and DuBois followed, Emily in the rear, looking over her shoulder. Once on the roof, Conor shoved Brunel toward the edge overlooking the rear entrance. "Emily, head over to the front. I could have sworn we had a tail. A black Citroën. Look for it." Emily withdrew, and Conor turned his attention to Brunel. A jumpy DuBois stood nearby and kept his eyes on the door to the stairway. "We'll make this quick, I promise. I need to know what you've done with the archive you brought from Algiers."

"Go to hell," Brunel said, his English quite good.

"I probably will, given the things I've done, but not today. And since you didn't say *I don't know what you're talking about*, I'll assume you do know what I'm talking about. Just know this, I am very much in a killing mood. Tell me where it is, and our business is done." Conor put his left hand in the middle of Brunel's chest and pushed him toward the edge. There was a foot-high retaining wall, and Brunel's feet were now mere inches away from it.

Brunel's jaw slackened now that he saw what Conor was threatening to do. "I brought nothing but the clothes on my back from Algiers. Nothing."

"Let's try this again," Conor said, adding a light shove in the chest. The back of Brunel's shoes met the wall. Conor waved his Colt in his face. "Up here, this gun will sound something like a truck backfiring. Probably won't cause too much concern. But when I put a gag in your mouth and tie your hands behind your back, and you scream after I push you off this roof, no one will hear you or the thud your body will make in the alley when it meets the pavement." Conor put his hand on his chest. "One more time—where's the archive?"

Brunel looked over his shoulder. And then reached to grab Conor's wrist. Conor brushed it away and raised his Colt to eye level, three inches away from Brunel's face. Then the full weight of his predicament hit Brunel. "It's buried. In Pierre Laurent's front yard. Under an old Linden tree."

CHAPTER SIXTY-SIX

0830 Hours, Sunday, January 10, 1943
Outside Hôtel Normandy, 3rd Arrondissement, Lyon

Back down the stairs, they headed out of the service entrance to their car. Emily reported a black Citroën parked in front of the hotel with one man inside, smoking.

"We can't have them follow us to Laurent's house. And we don't have the time to lead them around Lyon in the hopes they get lost. We don't have the fuel for that, right, René?"

"Yes."

"All right. Emily, you get in the back with Brunel. Make sure he sees your Walther. René, you're up front with me. I'll drive around the side of the hotel and leave you and the car just out of sight. Then—"

"Then what, Conor?" Emily said, her hackles up.

"I'm going to pay our tail a visit."

"And do what exactly?" Emily said, clearly exasperated.

"Something I did back in Tangier in a very similar situation. It worked. Can't see why it won't again. The best defense is a good offense." Before Emily could mount any further protests, he said, "Let's go. The clock is ticking."

After coasting up to the corner of the building and stopping, he got out of the Peugeot and walked calmly around the corner of the hotel, taking long strides to the Citroën. Exhaust was streaming from the tailpipe, and the windows were partially fogged up. At the sight of him, the driver dropped his cigarette in his lap and started flopping around to put it out. Conor tapped on the driver's side window. The driver, a blue-eyed blonde-haired man in his late forties with a prominent scornful look, found his cigarette, then, with wide eyes, rolled down his window.

Conor recalled the exact words he'd said to the two Gestapo agents sitting in a Mercedes in Tangier one early afternoon. They had been following him and Booth as they were taking a key informant back to OSS headquarters. Conor was on a tight deadline and needed to put the Gestapo thugs out of action. "*Ihr Motor klingt wie Scheifse. Aber ich werde ihn reparien.*" As was the case in Tangier, his German about a bad-sounding engine surprised the agent. Conor reached in and felt for the hood release, then pulled on it. He stepped to the front of the car and lifted the hood. The driver got out and reeled off a string of profanities, pulling out his weapon. Conor raised his right leg and drove it down the agent's left shin, landing on top of his foot like a piston, crunching several, if not all, metatarsals. Then he snatched the handgun from his hand.

The agent hopped around on one foot, then leaned against the Citroën's rear door as Conor pulled his Fairbairn-Sykes from its sheath and slit the spark-plug wires in one smooth motion. He lowered the hood and realized he could have saved some time by just slitting his throat. In Tangier, the Gestapo agents in the Mercedes were smart enough not to kill an American on a busy street in Spanish Morocco. It was another story in occupied Lyon. He hadn't thought this through. His head and heart were still wracked with pain and white-hot anger at the news of Maggie's murder.

Conor turned to the Gestapo agent. In German, he asked him if he killed a redhead in front of the Hôtel Terminus yesterday. The agent, through gritted teeth said, "*Nein*...*nein.*"

"I don't believe you." Conor lurched toward the Gestapo agent and shoved the blade of his knife into his chest. In his head, he heard Anick say, *The Boche will seek reprisals.* Let them seek their reprisals. Which he just did for Maggie's death.

CHAPTER SIXTY-SEVEN

0905 Hours, Sunday, January 10, 1943
Pierre Laurent's Home, 5th Arrondissement, Lyon

The house was located where a main thoroughfare vectored into a street that was narrow, more alley-like, wide enough for a small car or motorcycle. A twelve-foot stone wall surrounded the house. The side that ran along the narrow lane was more crudely built. The stones were set more haphazardly, some indented and others jutting out. Some stones were even missing. It provided a scalable solution to getting inside the walls of the property.

Conor looked at the Peugeot that he'd left parked on the side of the main road, still within sight of the front entrance to the house. He gave DuBois his M1903 Colt to keep trained on Brunel. Emily wanted to wait for darkness, but Conor pressed the issue, saying the longer they were in the city, the more the odds favored the Germans. It was her turn to relent. The poor morning weather did its part in keeping people off the streets. An occasional pedestrian, head down, looking at the cobblestones, or on a bicycle heading up the steep main street, were all they saw. Scaling the wall from the narrow alley side shielded them from the main street, but once at the top, they would be plainly visible, like a star atop a Christmas tree.

"I'll go first. Once inside, I'll signal you with a stone over the wall if it's okay to climb over," Conor said in a voice just above a whisper.

"Fine. Be on the lookout for dogs. You still have your knife?"

"Wouldn't be without it," Conor said.

"No gunplay. Too risky."

"Agreed."

Conor tugged on the shoulder straps of his musette bag and started his climb. He wasted no time, and inside a minute, he was at the top of the wall. He looked inside the property and saw that the entire wall was ringed by low leafless shrubs about three feet high. It was a drop of somewhat less than the exterior height; he thought around ten feet. He dropped, purposely missing the shrubs, fearing a sharp branch in the eye or, worse, up the ass.

He hit the ground and rolled. The ground was thankfully soft from recent rains. He sat on his haunches and surveyed the front of the house. No dogs, no people. One problem. There were two mature Linden trees, a thick carpet of leaves at each tree's base. *Shit.* He found a small rock and, after one more look around, tossed it over the wall. Emily appeared at the top of the wall in less than thirty seconds.

He pointed to the spot where he landed, and after nodding, she landed on her feet, then lowered to one knee.

"There's two—"

"Linden trees. I know," Conor said.

"I'll take the one on the left side of the path to the door. You take the one right across from it."

With that, they moved quietly to their assigned trees. They both stabbed at the ground with their knives. The blades, sharp and strong, pierced the ground easily but moved little earth with their slim blades. Conor used his hands to push the dirt aside. He dug one hole after another. Conor thought there would be telltale signs of previous digging, but the wet weather had made that difficult to make out. He was on his fifth hole when a stone landed near the edge of the hole. Looking up, he saw Emily holding up a leather-bound satchel with a strap. He filled the five holes he dug, swinging one arm after another like a plow to replace the dirt. He crab-walked over to Emily's position and watched over her shoulder as she thumbed through the sheaf of documents.

Emily held up one page, then another. "These mention the OSS and the SOE. Names of Coon and Captain Michael Gubbins of the SOE. It mentions training and the provision of some weapons for the training. On those documents…wait." Emily paused while she held one page closer to her face. "I don't see any mention that there were any plans to assassinate Darlan with the help of the Allies." She pulled another page from the sheaf. "There are several pages containing names of a Group of Five. Other pages are biographical information about members of the Corps francs d'Afrique. One name is a Bonnier de la Chapelle."

"That's the guy," Conor said.

"What now?"

"Like we discussed, we destroy the documents. I'll take care of that. You go over and make sure I covered our tracks under the other Linden tree."

Conor gathered the documents into a pile and sifted through them one more time. He pulled his lighter from his pants pocket just as he heard a vehicle outside the wall on the main street side. They both paused. Conor looked over at Emily, whose back was toward him. *Go ahead. Do it. Now.* Fifteen seconds passed, then Emily crept over to his position as he lit the pages. The dampness made for a delayed ignition, and Conor fanned the pile. Once it caught, they watched as ashes floated upward. They let the pile come close to extinguishing before they shoved armfuls of earth over the smoldering ashes and the leather satchel.

When they returned to the Peugeot, they found DuBois agitated. Beads of sweat had broken out on his forehead. He handed over the pistol Conor had given him as soon as Conor sat in the driver's seat. "We can't go back to my home. It's too dangerous."

Conor looked at Emily in the dashboard-mounted rearview mirror and met her eyes. "We need to get out of Lyon."

"We could use the help of the local Resistance," Emily said. "Can you—"

"The One-Eight," DuBois said. "It's a brothel. The owner is heading up the local network. Her apartment above the brothel should be a safe place…for a while, until you can figure out how to get out of Lyon."

Conor started the Peugeot and shifted into first gear. "The One-Eight. Call out directions, René," he said as he popped the clutch.

Conor kept the Peugeot in second gear, so the roar of the engine would alert any people on foot headed up the steep grade. Near the bottom of the street, a black Citroën appeared a hundred feet in front of them. Conor slowed to carefully navigate the Peugeot past the oncoming Citroën. His front left fender came close to grazing the Citroën's, but both cars squeaked through. At the bottom of the street, he caught a glimpse in the dash mirror of the Citroën turning a corner and disappearing. "I hate to break it to you, but I could have sworn there was a Nazi officer in the back seat," he said.

They continued on, Conor pushing the Peugeot hard. Up ahead, a tram tangled up with a string of German troop carriers jammed an intersection of three streets. The gap between the tram and the troop carriers allowed other German trucks on the third street to pass through, alternating with vehicles heading in the same direction as the Peugeot. Conor slowed, watching the tumult ahead.

The sound of the back door opening broke the silence inside the car. Brunel jumped from the Peugeot as it crept along. Emily followed suit and ran for Brunel. Conor punched the accelerator, but he had a mere car's length he could travel. As Brunel was about to round the corner, he looked back at Emily. What he didn't see was the three-ton Wehrmacht troop carrier coming at him. It slammed into Brunel, propelling his body into the air as if he hit an electrified fence. He landed in the street, sliding to a rest on the cobblestones. Emily slowed as she drew close. After a quick look, she turned and slipped back into the car.

"It's my fault. I took my eyes off him. Just for a second."

"He's—"

"Dead. Skull split open," Emily said.

CHAPTER SIXTY-EIGHT

0905 Hours, Sunday, January 10, 1943
En Route to Pierre Laurent's Home, Lyon

Discovering Krupp in the back seat of his car, his tunic soaked with his blood, was upsetting enough. Finding out that Brunel wasn't in his room put a sharper edge on Eklof's anger, his face heating, which had dissipated little since they left the Hôtel Normandy. Barbie would not be pleased if he couldn't locate the conniving Frenchman.

"You're going too slow. Pick up your speed," Eklof shouted to his driver.

"Sturmbannführer, you must learn to manage your emotions. I am confident we will find Brunel." No sooner had Abbé Alves spoken than Eklof spied a Peugeot headed toward them. Both cars slowed to navigate the narrow street, allowing both him and Alves a good look at the occupants. Eklof picked out the unnerving sight of a familiar face—Thorn—quickly followed by the target of his search.

"Turn around. Turn around immediately," he shouted, his voice cracking at the higher octave. For the past two months, not a day had gone by that he didn't think of his last encounter with Conor Thorn on the stern of the British gun boat in the waters of Lysekil Harbor. He wasn't going to let Thorn escape again.

"You see, we have found Brunel," Alves said.

"You're sure?" Eklof said. "You saw him?"

"Yes. And blessed be God, we have also found him together with René DuBois. But, why are they together? My, my, this is getting interesting, is it not, Sturmbannführer?"

The driver pulled a quick three-point turn and then they were advancing down the steep street at great speed. Eklof sat on the edge of his seat and held on to the back of the passenger seat. He elbowed aside the Gestapo agent sitting there to improve his view out the windshield. When he saw the traffic congestion up ahead and no sign of the Peugeot, he swore under his breath. As they slowed, he looked for a way through the tangled mess of trucks, a tram, and a gaggle of onlookers. "Stop the car."

Eklof popped the rear door and slipped out, followed by Alves. He trotted up to where the group of gawkers had gathered and barged through, sending an elderly woman to the pavement. The body of Brunel lay on the street with a massive head wound. Gray matter seeped from a fracture and coated the cobblestones near his head.

"Care to administer last rites?" Eklof said.

"Not really," Alves answered to no surprise to Eklof.

As he and the priest walked back to the Citroën, he realized revenge may be within reach. "The driver—he's an American agent. But I don't know why Brunel would be linked to the American. Could he be conspiring with him?"

"Another question is why was Dr. René DuBois with them both?" Alves said.

"You are sure you saw DuBois?"

"I told you. Yes. Next to the driver."

Eklof and Alves settled into the back seat, but Eklof gave no orders. Lyon was a big city. Where would they go? "Driver, head to number ten rue des Trois-Maries—DuBois's home."

Alves considered Eklof's answer for a moment. "Hear me out, Sturmbannführer. I don't believe DuBois would go back to his home. Your last visit there would convince him it is not safe for him…and certainly not for the American."

"Go on."

"I believe a visit to the One-Eight might prove to be… productive."

CHAPTER SIXTY-NINE

0930 Hours, Sunday, January 10, 1943
Germaine Gilbert's Apartment, 5th Arrondissement, Lyon

Just outside the door to Gilbert's apartment, Conor heard a female voice singing in French. DuBois knocked twice, then twice again. The music abruptly stopped, replaced by the sound of locks and deadbolts releasing and the door opening cautiously. Before he entered, Conor looked over the staircase railing. The gap that ran down the center of the spiraling staircase allowed him to see down to the first floor. He listened for footfalls and heard none. Satisfied, he followed DuBois and Emily into the apartment. A statuesque woman locked the door.

At first, the plush and color-saturated surroundings were a heavy dose of visual stimulation. But it suddenly occurred to Conor that it was perfectly suited for a French madam. A pink silk robe was wrapped tightly around Gilbert's slender frame, its hem brushing the surface of the Persian rug. The tip of pointy silver slippers peeked out from the bottom of the robe. Her face was fully made up, her nails long and painted a shimmery red. The apartment, however, was cold. Heavy drapes were drawn, but slim shafts of sunlight managed to knife through gaps. The air was smoky and carried the strong smell of cigarettes. But not the smell of American cigarettes—more pungent, bordering on being caustic.

"René, I'm glad you're here. But tell me, who are your friends?

No, no, no, how awful of me." She approached DuBois and gently placed her hands on his shoulders. "I must first express my sympathies for the loss of your mother. It is so tragic. The Boches, they are inhuman," Gilbert said and placed a soft kiss on each cheek.

"I haven't had a chance to grieve. I won't until I can see her body. It is horrible," DuBois said but appeared to shake off his pain.

"Tell me, any more harassment from the Abwehr?" Germaine said.

Abwehr? What the hell?

"No, thankfully. Just the one time, and just some questions about Laurent," DuBois said. He turned from Germaine to look at Conor and Emily. "Germaine, this is Conor Thorn and Emily Bright. They are Allied agents. And they need our help."

Gilbert looked both him and Emily over. Emily approached and extended her hand, which was swallowed by two hands and held for a long moment.

"*Bienvenue en France.*" Welcome to France. "To you both," Gilbert said. "Now, tell me, how can we help our Allied friends?"

"Madam, we need access to a radio. We hid ours when we landed, but it is urgent we send a message now. Then we need help to get back to our rendezvous location. By the fastest means possible," Emily said.

"But before we leave Lyon, I need help in locating an abbé named Alves—Robert Alves. Do you know him?" Conor said.

The question seemed to catch Gilbert off guard. Her pencil-thin eyebrows arched into the shape of two mountain peaks. "Why, yes, I do. What do you want with him?"

"I plan to kill him." The only sound heard in the room was the ascending trill of a cat. "In case it's not clear to you, he's a spy for the German Abwehr."

"No, it's not clear, or wasn't until now. I'm shocked." Gilbert shook her head, then picked up a pack of cigarettes and shook one free, bringing it to her lips with a shaky hand. DuBois did the honors. "He visits the One-Eight from time to time. It truly unnerves the girls. But he appears harmless. The Abwehr you say? I am truly shocked. A priest working with the Abwehr..." she said, her voice trailing off.

"According to what my sister told René, yes."

"Your sister?"

"London sent her to take René—"

"Yes, yes, I know that."

"They also sent her to eliminate the priest. I plan to finish her mission."

Gilbert stared intently at Conor, maybe sizing up his chances for success. "Your sister, we heard that she betrayed no information to the Boche. Were you aware of that?"

"No, I wasn't. I'm not surprised though." Conor paused. "Thanks for mentioning it," he said, his voice thick with emotion.

A double knock, then another, sent Gilbert to the door to unlock it. A middle-aged man wearing wire-framed glasses and a neatly trimmed mustache entered. Gilbert introduced Dr. Russier and then settled on a swanky red divan. She looked exhausted.

"Paul, I have just received utterly devastating news that Abbé Alves is working with the Abwehr," Gilbert said, fixing a steely gaze on Russier, whose face betrayed his own shock. She started tapping her foot on the rug and held her stare on Russier.

"Yes, Germaine, I did vouch for him. Had I known—"

"Of course, Paul. I should have paid more attention," Gilbert said. The tension created by the Alves news lessened.

"What will happen now?" Russier asked.

"His time is coming to an end," Conor said.

Russier reluctantly nodded. "Germaine, I have a pressing medical matter. Might I take René downstairs to help me with one of the girls? She is highly agitated, and I need someone to calm her while I examine her."

"Who is it?"

"Sophie. She was—"

"I need a few more moments with René," Gilbert said.

"I'll go," Emily offered. "I might be of some help."

Russier bowed slightly and Emily followed him out.

"René, I am making arrangements to take you and the intelligence London wants to Switzerland myself. I hope to be ready to do so in a day. Two at most."

"Intelligence?" Conor said.

"Yes. Critical information and photos about the German

project to build defenses along the northern French coastline," Gilbert said.

Now that is highly prized intelligence. If it did get to Switzerland, it could take weeks to get back to London.

"We'll take the intelligence with us," Conor said. "It will get into the hands of General Eisenhower faster." Gilbert and DuBois gaped at him but said nothing. "Good. That's settled."

DuBois shook his head in protest, then opened his mouth just as the door and its jamb exploded, sending splinters and shards into the room and stopping him from speaking. Two men in Gestapo uniforms, both holding machine pistols, burst in. Kurt Eklof strutted in behind them. "Tell me, Conor Thorn, you impudent American, what is it you all have settled?"

Conor's mouth fell open as he jerked his head back. *Kurt fucking Eklof, eye patch and missing ear and all.* Eklof casually waved his Walther P38 at the group. A scrawny man in a black cassock followed Eklof. *Alves. With the Gestapo. He doesn't care who he betrays France to.*

"Disarm the American. And search the doctor and the famous Madam Gilbert. Do so carefully."

"I thought maybe you might have drowned when I kicked your ass off the gunboat. I guess it was you who alerted the Luftwaffe and e-boats after we had slipped through your fat fingers." Once they found his M1911A1, he hoped they would relax. But no such luck. One guard pulled the compact M1903 Colt from the small of his back and then located his knife in the side of his boot.

"Look for the pill. Check all his pockets," Eklof ordered. The third pocket checked yielded Conor's small case containing his cyanide pill. The guard handed it to Eklof who pocketed it and exchanged it for a set of handcuffs. It was when they were wrapped around his wrists that Eklof felt safe approaching Conor. He shoved the end of his Walther inches from Conor's face.

"The past is the past, Thorn. You should be very worried about the present."

"And you and all of your Nazi friends should be worried about the future."

"Ha. Such false bravado. So American." Eklof withdrew his Walther and took a step back. "I almost forgot, the Englander, the one with the birthmark on his neck. Stones. He was quite helpful in filling in some details about your soon-to-be tragic visit to France. I thought you would want to know."

Regret for not finishing off Stones on the beach surged in Conor. "I hope you fucked up his interrogation like you did the Royal Marine's in Stockholm. Stones deserved to die."

"You bore me, Thorn."

"Who's the priest, Eklof? Let me guess. Alves, maybe?"

"Were you involved in my mother's death?" DuBois said.

Eklof looked at DuBois, showing little interest in answering his question.

"I'd take that as a yes," Conor said. Eklof turned back to Conor. Conor's heart rate quickened. "How about the American redhead?"

"Aah. The redhead. She was quite stubborn. She is dead too. You see, escaping is never a good idea. People lose their lives doing it. Even you Americans." The ballsy response shot a thousand volts through his legs, and Conor hurled himself headfirst at Eklof's chin. A foot from making contact with Eklof, a heavy blow to the back of his head dropped him to the floor.

A shower of stars blanketed his vision. He didn't lose consciousness, but he felt he lost something. Like the ability to make sense out of the sea of shit he was in.

CHAPTER SEVENTY

0945 Hours, Sunday, January 10, 1943
Germaine Gilbert's Apartment, 5th Arrondissement, Lyon

Conor heard footsteps coming up the stairs. It had to be Emily and Russier returning from treating one of Gilbert's girls. Eklof and his men heard them too.

Conor raised his head to shout a warning, but the kick to his rib cage made sure the words never made it out of his mouth. He was laid out on his side on the Persian rug, the side of his damaged head brushing the colorful but blurry fibers of the rug. A swell of nausea engulfed him. Conor didn't see what happened next. He heard a commotion as black boots passed by his head, and a general rustling of bodies was accompanied by orders shouted in Eklof's voice. When he could raise his head, he saw Emily on her knees, a Gestapo guard holding a gun to her head.

Russier was led over to the divan and roughly positioned next to Gilbert, who looked amazingly sedate. Conor struggled to his knees, which, luckily for his head, Eklof and his men permitted. Just as a sense of order was established by the Gestapo thugs, all hell broke loose when Gilbert pulled a small revolver from between the cushions on the divan and started shooting.

One Gestapo thug took a round in the face; the other, slow to react, took one in the chest. Alves hit the floor behind Emily, using her as a shield. Eklof wasn't slow to react, and before the second Gestapo goon hit the floor, he shot at Gilbert, but Russier leaned in front of her, and the round blew out his left eye. Conor lurched to his feet as a shot buzzed by his head. He swung his handcuffed hands like he was swinging a baseball bat, targeting the gun in Eklof's hand. The back of his left hand contacted Eklof's gun hand, his Walther flying across the room.

Conor wrapped his right leg around both of Eklof's and thrust his bound hands into his chest. Eklof tumbled backward, landing on his back. Conor jumped on him, straddling his chest and pinning both arms into the rug with his legs. As he whipped the man's face with his hands, an image of Maggie floated in his mind's eye, fueling his attack. Eklof's eye patch came free, just like during the last time they battled. Blood oozed from the eye socket, whose surface again reminded him of a dried-up peach pit.

Eklof arched his back, pushing off the floor with his legs and lifting both men. He was trying to topple Conor, but Conor landed two more blows to the face and Eklof's legs gave way. Conor used his bound hands, bloodied and bruised, to nudge the cyanide pill case up to the opening of the pants pocket Eklof placed it in. He grabbed it, opened the case, and held the pill in his fingers. He pried open the nearly unconscious Eklof's mouth and placed the pill between the man's teeth.

Eklof must have felt it, as he tried to tongue it out. But Conor rammed the man's gaping mouth shut. The scent of burnt almonds wafted up into Conor's face, and a white creamy froth leaked out the corners of Eklof's mouth, then across both lips. Eklof writhed and thrashed for ten seconds, his face turning red. Conor stole a look at Emily, who sat on the floor, her back against the wall. She had Alves's arms pinned behind him; he was practically sitting in her lap.

Conor looked down at the now-still Eklof. His left sky-blue eye had remained open, staring back at Conor. He slipped off Eklof's chest and saw DuBois tending to Gilbert. He had pushed aside Russier's body to work on the woman.

Conor frantically searched Eklof's tunic pocket for a key to his handcuffs. The first pocket yielded nothing but a magazine for his Walther; the second produced the key. But a flurry of motion in the corner of the room distracted him, and the key slipped from his fingers as he looked up. Emily's head was tilted back, her nose spewing blood. She looked dazed.

Alves was on his feet, headed out the door. But he didn't head down the stairs. Emily rose unsteadily and followed Alves. Conor picked up the handcuff key, freed his hands, then grabbed Eklof's Walther and flew out the door.

He saw Emily as she headed up a short stairway to a door. He knew they were on the top floor of the building, so it had to be an access door to the roof. Emily shoved it open wide and took one step out onto the roof. A shot rang out and Emily collapsed, her right leg draped over the threshold. Conor raced to her. She was holding her shoulder, her lips and chin still showing fresh blood from Alves's headbutt.

"Go," she said. "Finish Maggie's job."

Conor looked out over the roof. Beyond was a sea of slanted, canted, and peaked roofs, all showing a tiled surface, which was slick with a coating of morning mist. "I won't be long. Go down and see DuBois." He hated to leave her, but Maggie's mission had to be dealt with.

He couldn't see where Alves had fled. The brothel was located near the end of a block. Five distinct rooftops to his right, the block ended. In between the last house and the next block, Conor saw a cable car, part of a funicular—a cabled railway—ascend the steep mountainside the neighborhood was built on. He did not know where Alves went, but he was sure that if Alves made it to the funicular and could make his way down to the base of the railway, he may never see him again. And they had already overstayed their welcome in Lyon.

He crouched and skulked along the slanted roof of the One-Eight toward the funicular. Gun in his right hand, his left hand outstretched to aid his balance, his fingertips skimmed the slick terracotta tiles. His boots couldn't get a firm grip because of the curved shape of the tiles. He stopped to listen for any movement but slipped toward the roof's edge. He had to keep moving forward, sound or no sound. Conor angled his pursuit upward to fight off the downward force of the steep slope.

He reached the roof's edge and squatted. As he battled a strengthening sense of vertigo, Conor took in a full 360-degree view and saw nothing, but what he heard confirmed he went in the right direction. It was the sound of a terracotta tile smashing into the cobbled street below. Conor scrambled ahead, keeping low, his boots slipping, sliding, his ankles being torqued in all directions. He covered three more buildings before he heard several more tiles shatter on the street. Conor pulled up to a brick chimney and stood, then peered around its side. He stared at the last building on the block. It ran lengthwise, parallel to the funicular rail line. Loud metal-on-metal clanging and screeching signaled that the rail line was on the building's far side.

Conor slid down the roof on his back, digging his bootheels into the roof's surface to slow his descent. His right hand, his gun hand, slid into a hole where a tile was missing, dislodging his gun. Two tiles, freed with his boots, along with the Walther, slid down and over the edge of the roof. He stopped just before the gutter and snapped his head back in disgust, regretting it immediately. He took deep breaths to calm himself, then rolled to his left, to the bottom of the next and last roof. He scampered up the incline to its ridge. Crouched low, he popped his head up and saw nothing. *Damn it.* Then, he heard a grunt and saw it—a hand. A white-knuckled grip on the edge of the gutter.

He hoisted his legs over the peak and slid toward the hand, putting as much braking pressure on his feet as he could muster. His descent was slow but controlled. Stopping at the gutter, inches away from the left hand that belonged to Alves. His right hand, still holding the gun, had a loose grip on the gutter. He was swinging in a slight breeze, the priest's face red with the strain.

"First, drop the gun. Then, and only then, I'll help you up." Alves looked at the ground below. "You don't need the gun. You don't want to shoot the person who can save your life, do you?"

"Why...help?" Alves said through gritted teeth.

"You are a Nazi spy after all." Thinking that a little false hope was in order, Conor said, "You know things that I want to know." Conor slotted his left boot in the gutter and applied some pressure to see how secure it was. Satisfied that he had some leverage, he extended his left hand. "Drop it."

The gun clattered, then bounced on the ground, settling between the two rails. Conor reached down and grabbed the priest's left wrist, then his right. "Push off the wall with your feet...work your way up. And don't stop." Conor dug his left boot deeper into the gutter for more leverage. It slipped in the muck of wet decaying leaves. He took a deep breath and yanked both wrists, flinging the priest up, and he landed on Conor's chest. Alves rolled off.

Conor reoriented himself. A blur of an arm swung and landed below Conor's chin near his throat, stunning him. Alves struggled to his feet. He lunged for the priest's left leg and yanked him back down onto the roof and pulled him closer. Conor wrapped his hands around Alves's neck, his thumbs finding his Adam's apple. Alves swung his arms, pummeling Conor's head and the sides of his face. The blows were powerful. Conor pulled his shoulders up, but the blows lessened in power as his thumbs drove deeper into the priest's throat. Then they stopped.

Conor lay there, the blow to his throat making it difficult to swallow. He rolled off the dead priest and looked up into a roiling cloudy sky. Then he heard thunder. Was God pleased?

Don't care one way or another. I am.

He heard the screeching and rumbling of a cable car below. Looking over the roof's edge, he saw it was descending and would be right below him in less than ten seconds. That was all the time he needed to shove Alves over, onto the rails.

CHAPTER SEVENTY-ONE

1010 Hours, Sunday, January 10, 1943
Germaine Gilbert's Apartment, 5th Arrondissement, Lyon

Emily watched as Conor wrapped his right hand with his handkerchief. A portion of his palm was scraped free of surface skin.

"Alves?"

"Dead. Details later."

Emily nodded and watched DuBois, kneeling next to her, as he tended to her wound.

"How bad?" Conor said.

"The bullet went through cleanly. The bleeding has stopped. It will be painful to move it," DuBois said. "I have some aspirin in my medical bag."

"Not unlike the shot you took a few months ago," Emily said as a chill ran up her spine. A sign of shock hitting her system. Conor had received a similar wound from the gun of Henry Longworth, the Abwehr-connected traitor who occupied a seat on Churchill's War Cabinet.

"Em, we've got to get on the move. The circus up on the roof is sure to catch the attention of someone. And if not, Alves's body on the funicular's track surely will. Think you can manage the pain?"

"Well, I'm not staying here. That's your answer."

"Thought so." Conor turned to DuBois. "Did Germaine have a radio hidden somewhere? I need to get a message back to Algiers before we leave."

"I believe so. But I never knew where." DuBois shut his medical bag and stood, giving Emily a clear view of Germaine's body draped over the divan, a rivulet of blood dripping down her left arm onto the oriental rug. Russier's body lay face down on the rug. His wire-framed glasses, bent at a ninety-degree angle, lay beside his head. "The bedroom. She never let anyone in there. She was quite adamant about that."

"The intelligence about the German coast defenses, could it be there too?"

"Possibly," DuBois said.

"Where—"

"Down the hall. The last door on the left," DuBois said. Conor sprinted from the room. "Good chance that it's locked." Emily wasn't sure Conor heard DuBois's last words.

DuBois poured a glass of water from a cut-crystal pitcher and handed it to Emily, along with two aspirin tablets. As she popped the pills into her mouth and washed them down, they heard a loud bang. The sound of a door being kicked in. Emily watched DuBois move toward a small writing desk in the corner. He lifted the folding top to reveal six pigeonhole compartments stuffed with papers and packs of cigarettes. DuBois pulled out a piece of notepaper and wrote a message, folded it, and stuffed it into an envelope. He scribbled something on the envelope's face.

"Leaving a message?"

DuBois turned around. "Yes. On the way out."

That struck Emily as odd, given the circumstances. "To whom?"

"Sophie. One of the girls."

"She's gone. She was the one the doctor and I went to see. He sent her home for bed rest."

DuBois looked puzzled, as if not sure what to do. He stuffed the envelope into his suit coat's breast pocket. Conor walked back, stopping beside the two uniformed Gestapo men Germaine had shot, then pulled his two Colts and knife from their pockets. He kept the M1911A1 and shoved the M1903 into his bag, along with a bundle wrapped in newspaper that Emily assumed was the prized intelligence regarding the German fortification project.

Conor bent and helped Emily to her feet. The move brought on slight dizziness. "Let's put some distance between us and this place," Conor said. "And fast."

CHAPTER SEVENTY-TWO

1055 Hours, Sunday, January 10, 1943
Aboard Germaine Gilbert's Yacht, Lyon

The back of Conor's head pulsed with pain. His vision was losing its grip on clarity. It was why, when DuBois pulled his Peugeot up to the wharf, he was sure his eyes were playing a nasty joke on him.

"That's not a boat. It's a goddamn yacht." It was covered stem to stern by a brown canvas tarp streaked with stains from the winter's rains. A grimy soot splattered the hull. From the front passenger seat, Conor rolled down the window and took in the sight of it. "There's no way we can sail downriver in that. It's too damn conspicuous. And too damn risky. We wouldn't get out of the city limits."

"I'm sure it drinks petrol like it's the *Queen Mary*," Emily said.

"We have to get out of sight. We'll stay on board for the night. After it gets dark, I'll seek out another transport." He rolled up his window and turned around to look at Emily. "It will give you some time to rest." Conor turned to DuBois. "Get rid of the car. A back alley or a wooded lot somewhere. While you do that, I'll figure out the best way to set this monster on fire."

"Why do that?" DuBois said.

Conor looked back at the yacht. "Germaine's sailing days are over. And we'll need a diversion to mask our escape."

#

Once nightfall came, Conor took his leave in search of some other form of transportation while Emily and DuBois rested in the yacht's salon. The odor of wet canvas was strong but not offensive. A single end table lamp to Emily's left shed a minimal amount of light. They had peeled off bedsheets from a club chair and a couch, which left another dozen or so pieces of furniture covered, ghostlike.

A good forty-five minutes had passed, which gave Emily some time to rest. She thought she even fell into a light sleep for part of that time. DuBois spent some of the time rummaging around in his medical bag and closing his eyes for some respite. The aspirin she had taken earlier was wearing off. She called out to DuBois and asked for more. He rose and handed two more tablets to her then inspected her shoulder wound's dressing. Satisfied, he turned away. She said, "Tell me about your mother."

DuBois settled back into the felt-covered club chair across from her and replaced the aspirin bottle in his medical bag. "She was one reason the British were going to get us both out of France. They knew I wouldn't leave without her. I loved her. She was the only family I had left."

"You said Jews went to her for help in getting out of France. Did—"

"She was going behind my back to help Jews leave France."

"Behind your back… You mean you didn't help her?"

DuBois looked at her with tired eyes accented by droopy eyelids. "No. I am not…partial to Jews." He waved a hand, then said, "I mean, I kept quiet. That's what I did."

Emily pushed herself more upright, about to challenge DuBois's admission, when Conor appeared at the stern end of the salon.

"Em, let's have a chat about how we're going to get out of Lyon. Outside on the deck." Once they were outside, Conor said, "He's not partial to Jews?"

"So, you heard." Emily paused, shook her head. "Quite a…"

"Confession? Yes." Conor blew warm breath into his cupped hands. After laying out his plan to get out of Lyon, Emily had a few questions, which he answered to a weak level of her satisfaction. Conor blew more breath into his hands. "Getting back to the doctor…running into DuBois…it got me thinking." He took the next five minutes to describe a dinner that he, DuBois, Maggie, and his father, Jack, had at their home in New Jersey. It was 1938. DuBois had gone on and on about how Germany was the new economic and military power in Europe. He heaped most of the praise for their resurgence after their defeat during the Great War on the shoulders of Hitler.

"DuBois pissed off Jack, who brought up the book burning and the persecution of Jews and intellectuals. DuBois just waved him off and blamed it on the overreaction of the press. When Jack brought up how Hitler was looking to take over more of Europe after successfully marching into Austria, DuBois laughed it off. And now we hear that he's not partial to Jews. Are we sure he didn't turn his own mother in?"

"What a horrible thought. But there were people, many in my own country, who praised Hitler as a remarkable statesman."

"He was a despot then and now."

"DuBois…1938 was a long time ago. People can change, can't they?" Emily said.

"Some do, Em. Many don't."

CHAPTER SEVENTY-THREE

1130 Hours, Sunday, January 10, 1943
Robert Murphy's Office, rue Michelet, Algiers

"Commander, fancy meeting you here," Colonel Eddy said. "And here I thought I was going to butt heads with Murphy."

Butcher cracked a smile. "Thanks for coming, Colonel. Robert was kind enough to act on my behalf. I wasn't sure you would warmly receive a request to meet me."

"Now what in heaven's name gave you that idea?" Eddy said, making no effort to dampen the cynicism, confirming that Ike's reading the riot act six days before about OSS involvement in the Darlan assassination was still a sore subject.

Butcher ignored the disparagement and handed a slip of paper to Eddy.

"What's this?"

"A message from Conor Thorn."

Eddy cut a sideways glance. "Conor's working for you? Well, I'll be damned. I wondered where he disappeared to. Let me guess, Bright is working for you also?"

"Read the message, Bill."

Butcher watched Eddy's face for telltale signs of how the information was received. He noted a slight parting of the lips when Eddy got to the end of the message—the part about Maggie Thorn's death.

"Wild Bill…have you told him about Maggie?"

"No, I'm asking you to do that," Butcher said.

Eddy nodded. "So he found the archive. Where, if I may ask?"

"I don't have the details. But I assume somewhere in or around Lyon." More head nodding from Eddy. "Any idea why Conor didn't mention what was in the archive? You've worked with him for some time. You know him better than me."

"Well, what I can tell you is he's done that before. He had his reasons then, and I'm sure he has his reasons now." Eddy passed the message back to Butcher. "But it could be he was rushed. Plenty of Nazis in the Lyon neighborhood." Eddy lit up a Chesterfield and extinguished the match with a fanning hand. "Any idea what the critical intelligence is that he mentioned?"

"No. Not one clue. Icing on the cake after finding the archive."

Eddy chuckled. "He mentioned a request for a pickup three days from now. How is that going to happen?"

"Sub. The *Casabianca*. The same way we got them there."

"Yeah, that makes sense." Eddy took a drag and calmly picked a speck of tobacco from the tip of his tongue. "So, you and Ike in the spy business these days?"

Butcher ignored the question. "You knew, didn't you?"

"About Thorn and Bright working for you? Now, how would I know that, Butch?"

CHAPTER SEVENTY-FOUR

1300 Hours, Sunday, January 10, 1943
Hôtel Terminus, Gestapo Headquarters, Lyon

"*Mein Herr?* Sir, did you hear me?" Barbie stared out the window of his suite. Another train with a string of boxcars was leaving the Perrache station. It carried over two hundred Jews, Resistance members, and other lowlife targets of the Reich. A haul that made him gush with Nazi pride. That was moments before his adjutant broke news of the deaths of Eklof, Alves, and two other Gestapo agents.

"Go on," he said, stomping down his roiling anger.

"We found the priest on the tracks of the funicular. The others in an apartment above the One-Eight brothel. The madam and one other were found there as well."

"How did Eklof die?" Barbie asked, his gaze still fixed on the slow-moving train. When there was no reply to his question, he turned to face the adjutant. "Well?"

"It was death by cyanide poisoning." Barbie walked to his desk and began tapping his forefinger on its surface while he gave the Gestapo's response some thought. It seemed that the American and British agents Eklof learned about from the captured SOE agent had made their presence known. In a manner that he would not forget. "Your orders, Hauptsturmführer?"

The tapping stopped. "Round up forty people. I don't care what their ages are. A ten-for-one exchange. Take some from Montluc

Prison. Line them up in Place Bellecour and have them shot at noon tomorrow."

"Aah...children, *mein Herr*?"

"Didn't you hear what I said? I don't care what the ages are."

"*Jawohl*, Hauptsturmführer, right away."

"I want roadblocks set up on all roads leading in and out of Lyon."

"Who are they searching for, Hauptsturmführer?"

"An American male and British female. I don't have descriptions...just find them." Barbie paused; he felt his face flush with anger. "And I want patrols on both rivers."

"There are already patrols on the rivers, *mein Herr*."

"Increase them," Barbie shouted. "Now go carry out your orders." He returned to the window overlooking the maze of rail lines below. The train with its human cargo was gone.

CHAPTER SEVENTY-FIVE

2215 Hours, Sunday, January 10, 1943
Aboard Germaine Gilbert's Yacht, Lyon

"How do I look? One of Hitler's finest?" Conor smoothed out the tunic of the Wehrmacht uniform that he'd pilfered from their entanglement with the two Germans on the bridge in Avignon. It wasn't a perfect fit. It was shy on room in the crotch, and the sleeves were also short. But beggars couldn't be choosers.

"Walk through the plan again," Emily said.

"Oh, I know that tone. You don't think it's going to work, do you?"

"It's just not fully thought out. Let me go with you. Maybe the odds will be better."

"No. You have a bad wing, and you need to take care of the diversion. And keep an eye on DuBois. He's making me nervous. That's a lot."

"All right. But don't get carried away with the heroics." Conor gave her a single nod. "So run through it."

"The patrol boat is tied up about a hundred twenty yards just south of here. It has been out on the river patrolling, probably looking for us. It looks like they're about to take on a new crew of two. And they're refueling. So now's the time to move. I'll approach, put on my drunk soldier act, and call up some obnoxious behavior, and force myself aboard. Some quick knife work and... we own a patrol boat. I'll give you three flashes with the flashlight, and you set the plastic explosive. I checked the detonator and the time pencil setup. The location of the PE on the fuel tank should do the trick."

"You're sure there's enough fuel in the tank?"

"Yes. And I checked the time pencil. It's black, meaning you have ten minutes after you remove the safety strip to get off the boat and head south to me. Remember, these time pencils are not always precise. You could have less than ten minutes. Or more. But it's what we have to work with. Okay?"

"Yes, but I hate to destroy this beautiful boat. Is there—"

"No. We need something to—"

Emily bracketed his face with both hands and kissed him. It was one of her best. "Good luck," she said.

Fifty yards from the patrol boat, Conor heard one of the Germans shouting at the other. The response to the shouting was laughter, followed by more shouting. The night's darkness was lessened by light from a half-moon, which sparkled on the Rhône's surface.

Twenty yards from the boat, Conor started belting out a song he learned from his high school German language teacher, "*Ein Prosit der Gemütlichkeit.*" A well-known German drinking song.

"*Ein Prosit, ein Prosit, der Gemütlichkeit.*" Conor made sure there were some slurred words, enough to convince his audience that he was in the tank. "*Ein Prosit, ein Prosit, der Gemütlichkeit.*" As he drew even with the boat, both crewmen stopped making the boat ready for the next patrol in order to take in the sight of a drunk soldier. Conor repeated the verse and took a step onto the boat's gunwale. The unexpected move rocked the boat and knocked the two crewmen off-balance, prompting a string of profanities.

Conor lurched toward the one closest, his Fairbairn-Sykes knife's handle in his right palm, its double-edge blade hidden under his forearm. As soon as he could smell the German's breath, he shoved the knife in his gut and yanked it up toward his heart. Conor pulled the knife out and shoved the dead German into the path of his oncoming crewmate, who shoved the body aside and went to draw his sidearm from its belt holster. Conor planted his left hand in the German's face. The sidearm made it halfway out when Conor repeated the motion with his Fairbairn. But this time, something was blocking the blade's entry. Conor withdrew the knife and wrapped his left arm around the man's neck and spun the German, who tugged his arm downward.

Conor relented, which gave him an opening to slide the Fairbairn across his neck. Blood gushed from the wound, coating a control panel on the starboard side. He let the body drop to the deck. It fell face down, blood spewing from the neck. He turned the body over and ran his hand across his waist, above his belt line. He tore open his shirt, buttons flying in all directions. Tucked under the German's belt were two issues of a French magazine called *Paris Sex-Appeal* from 1939.

"Son of a bitch." *No one's gonna believe this story.*

Conor signaled Emily. Three flashes, then a quick look at his watch. "Ten minutes," Conor mumbled to himself. As Conor finished topping off the fuel tank, he looked back at Germaine's yacht. He made out two dark figures coming toward him. Another look at his watch told him eight minutes remained. He started the patrol boat. Just as the engine sprang to life, the yacht erupted in a massive explosion, thrusting the tarp that covered it two hundred feet in the air. Shards of teak and glass flew in all directions. Soon flames lit up the night.

Time pencils are not always precise—sometimes I hate to be right.

CHAPTER SEVENTY-SIX

0715 Hours, Monday, January 11, 1943
Le Chat Noir, Avignon

They traveled through the streets to the café in silence. Conor and Emily, shoulder to shoulder, led DuBois at a quick pace. Few people were about as they traveled down the boulevard. Occasional shafts of light pierced the wooden shutters of apartments above the closed ground-level shops and cafés. The sight of the Le Chat Noir was unchanged from their previous visit. When she knocked on the front door, as expected, there was no immediate answer. Nor was there a waiter watching them from across the square this time. Emily knocked again. A long moment later, the slender face of the owner appeared in the crack of the door's opening. He said nothing this time but nodded when he recognized his two visitors from two days before.

Once inside, while they stood in darkness, the owner said his name was Albert. He led them once again to the cramped kitchen. The table in the corner was still covered with newspapers. This time, there were two plates, a small crust of bread on each. On another plate was a small knife alongside the rind from a slice of cheese.

They sat at the table, and Emily introduced DuBois, adding that they needed transport to the coast. Before the owner responded, a figure emerged from the far shadows of the low-lit kitchen. It was Anick. She looked over at Conor, who seemed to be, once again, transfixed by the young redheaded Frenchwoman. Her haunting resemblance to Maggie Thorn spawned a sad, heartbroken look from Conor, whose eyes welled up with tears. He ran his hand down his face and wiped it on his thigh.

"We didn't expect you so soon," Anick said, staring at DuBois.

"Events have unfolded quickly," Emily said. "We arrived by stolen patrol boat. We can't risk using it any longer."

"Is there any chance that you could arrange travel back to the coast by truck, perhaps?" Conor said.

"At this hour, it is very doubtful." Anick jutted her thumb in DuBois's direction. "Is this the reason for your mission?"

"That's a long story," Conor said. "And what of Beaugard? Is he—"

"He's been arrested. Yesterday. After your departure."

"Were we the cause of his arrest?" Emily said as she sat up straighter in her chair.

"We do not know." Emily, somewhat relieved, sat back. "But I would guess it was."

"I'm sorry we had to tangle with the two Wehrmacht soldiers, but it couldn't be avoided," Conor said, getting no reaction from Anick.

"I know someone who might be convinced to take you. Do you still have francs?"

"Yes. But a limited supply," Emily said, looking at Conor.

"Five hundred francs. That's it," Conor said.

Anick again locked her gaze on DuBois. "What makes him so important?"

"Top secret," Conor said and added a smirk.

Anick shrugged. "I will be back soon, if successful. If I am longer than thirty minutes, you will know that I am having no luck. Then you should leave. Understood?" Anick received a single nod from both Conor and Emily.

She disappeared into the kitchen shadows she had emerged from, leaving Albert and his three guests sitting silently at the table. Albert stood and went over to a wood cabinet in the dimly lit rear of the kitchen and returned with three small baguettes and three slices of cheese, a bottle of red wine tucked under his arm. He placed the bread and cheese on one plate on the table, then uncorked the wine. Conor beat Emily in reaching for one baguette, while she gratefully thanked Albert, who left and promptly returned with four glasses and a cloth bag he said contained more bread, cheese, and a bottle of wine.

DuBois looked glumly at Albert's offerings. Emily took the glass of wine Albert handed her and sipped while she watched Conor tear off a piece of the baguette and pop it into his mouth.

"So, what *does* make you so important that London sent Maggie to get your ass out of France?" Conor said.

The question seemed to snap DuBois out of his doleful trance. "London wants me to reestablish the Resistance network in Paris. After some necessary training, of course. Germaine and Virginia Hall recommended me. Then the German fortification intelligence came into the picture, as you have already heard."

Conor exchanged a furtive glance with Emily. "What makes you the right guy for that…reestablishing a Resistance network?" He took a sip of wine.

"I don't know. I do know people there. Friends of my father. He was raised there. The contacts would be an advantage. Beyond that, as I said, I don't know." DuBois sat up, back straight as if the chair had just sent an electric charge through the seat. "Albert, *toilette*?"

Albert nodded and waved his hand to follow him. Both men rose. DuBois slipped off his suit coat and draped it across the back of the chair, then they headed to the rear of the café. Their previous conversation about DuBois's mother and Conor's dinner story had been preying on Emily's mind. The lack of empathy for the plight of the Jews and his early affirmations about Germany troubled her. *Was Conor right? Some people didn't change?* As Albert returned and took his seat, she set her glass on the table and reached into the left pocket of DuBois's suit coat, finding a ring with two keys.

"Em?"

Emily placed her finger across her lips to shush him and reached into the right pocket. There she found the note he wrote while in Germaine's apartment. Sophie's name was on the envelope's face. She ran a thumb under the flap and pulled out the single piece of notepaper. She detected a scent of lavender. It took her less than five seconds to read it.

Colonel Henri,

Heading to the south coast with the Allied friends I spoke of earlier. If our plan is to succeed, we must have no interference to our journey.

Columbia.

A shiver ran up her spine; her shoulders slumped. She hurriedly placed the note in her musette bag. Conor was about to say something when Anick reappeared from the shadows. DuBois was three steps behind her.

"I found someone. He will take the five hundred francs. But he says you must leave now."

CHAPTER SEVENTY-SEVEN

0900 Hours, Monday, January 11, 1943
Hôtel Terminus, Gestapo Headquarters, Lyon

In Barbie's mind, surprise visits by one's superior only served to disrupt the important work he and his men were tasked to complete. He had quotas that must be met. The timing of an unexpected visit by Oberg was especially troubling given the rash of unsettling news that had transpired over the previous twenty-four hours. The murders of Eklof and Alves and the unfortunate demise of the Frenchman Brunel were more than enough to trigger Oberg's wrath. Barbie thought the loss of the Allied agents, surely responsible for the deaths of Eklof and Alves, would send Oberg into an emotional realm Barbie had never experienced.

He was right.

"You mean to tell me that another agent…no, two agents…have slipped through your fingers?" Oberg's face turned bloodred. Barbie saw a vein above his left eye throb. Something he hadn't seen before. Oberg paced behind Barbie's desk, the heels of his knee-high boots digging into the floor, his hands clasped behind his back. "And now you have the gall to report the loss of a Gestapo officer and an undercover agent. This is…this is unacceptable. You must be the most incompetent officer in the entire Gestapo." Oberg ceased his pacing and his eyes bore into his underling. "And what have you done about the loss of Eklof?"

Barbie's explanation of measures taken to send a message to the population of Lyon did little to quell Oberg's high-voltage fury. As did the report that there was a massive search for the escaped agents. The vein continued to throb. Oberg continued to berate him. And he continued to listen, showing no repentance, for he knew that his service to the Reich would not be summed up by what happened in the last twenty-four hours. His contribution would be lauded given the vast numbers of those he and his men had sent east.

Oberg unbuttoned his collar. There was a sheen of perspiration across his forehead. "Now tell me about this archive that I am hearing about. Is it in your possession?"

Barbie's pulse quickened. The beat echoing in his ears. The surprise visit was almost over.

#

0915 Hours, Monday, January 11, 1943
The One-Eight, 5th Arrondissement, Lyon

The visit to DuBois's home was fruitless, as was his stop at the home of Pierre Laurent, his most important patient. Bleicher's next move was to visit the One-Eight and ask questions, perhaps rattle the nerves of its madam. He was at a loss as to what else he could do to find his absent agent. He carefully piloted his Citroën through the narrow streets of Vieux Lyon, a rain shower making the cobblestones slick. As he approached the brothel, he spotted another Citroën, newer and cleaner than his, parked in front. Not unusual in and of itself, but what was odd was the two Gestapo men, both smoking cigarettes, seated inside. *Men don't wait outside a brothel. What is the sense in that?* Bleicher wondered.

He nosed his Citroën to a spot inches from the grill of the Gestapo vehicle, which, as he hoped, annoyed the two men enough that they exited their car. He opened his door and heard their first question.

"What the hell are you doing? Are you mad?" the taller sneering agent said, flicking his spent cigarette into a puddle.

"Just paying a visit to my favorite bordello. Is this where the line begins?"

"We know you. You're Abwehr," said the one with a horse-like face sporting a ruddy complexion.

"And you're Gestapo. And if you're done with the stupid questions, I think I'll go inside."

"It's closed. Now get back in that piece of junk and go back to—"

"By whose order?"

"None of your fucking business," the sneering agent said.

"By order of Hauptsturmführer Barbie," his partner said, drawing an exceptionally pronounced sneer from the tall one.

"For what reason?"

"He doesn't need a reason. Now go somewhere else and get fucked."

Bleicher didn't move. He looked up at the upper floors of the building. All the windows were shuttered. Its facade drenched. In front of the building next door was a woman, old and waif-like, dragging a broom over the cobblestones. He walked toward her as the Gestapo men got back into the car. The woman stopped her sweeping and looked up at Bleicher.

"What goes on here, old woman?"

"Ha, you surely know what. Why have you come?"

"To see a friend. A doctor."

"You are too late. The doctor is dead. So is the madam." The woman made the sign of the cross and mumbled something. "One of the girls told me before they locked the place up."

"Who is responsible for this?"

"How am I to know? I'm not the police!" she nearly shouted. "But I hope whoever killed the priest is caught." She paused and looked up at the sky. "Why would anyone kill a priest?" She shook her head in disgust. "Tossed his body on the tracks." She looked down the street and pointed to a funicular cable car that was passing above the street, heading up the steep grade to the city's basilica.

Bleicher wondered if he could have lost two agents in one day.

CHAPTER SEVENTY-EIGHT

0915 Hours, Monday, January 11, 1943
On Board a Truck Headed South

The truck cargo area stank of a mixture of several smells, all equally offensive. There was no false wall in this truck. All three of them were seated on the floor. Conor and Emily leaned against the side walls of the cargo area near the cab, facing each other. DuBois leaned against the cab's back wall. They were told by the driver that the wooden crates stacked around them were filled with ice for the transport of fish from the coast northward. The leaked ice melt made the floor a slippery mess.

The six-by-six truck was fueled by coal gas. A cylinder the size of a home water heater was attached behind the driver's side door. Conor could feel the heat through the thin metal wall. A supply of coal and wood was included as cargo in the rear. The truck's operation would have, in normal prewar times, fascinated Conor. But reading the note that Emily slipped him as DuBois was boarding the truck sapped any curiosity he would normally have had.

Once they were settled, Conor passed the note to DuBois. The expected shock didn't materialize at first. Conor and Emily waited and watched. When DuBois's hands began to shake, Conor waded in.

"Interesting note. Who is Colonel Henri?" Conor asked. "And why was the note addressed to Sophie?"

DuBois's head bobbed from Conor to Emily. "It's a code

name… He's…he's in the Resistance," he said, his brow deeply furrowed.

"And Sophie?" Emily asked.

"She would know how to get it to him."

"Why did you tell this Henri character about us? The Resistance already knew we were here," Conor said. DuBois looked blankly at Conor. "Okay, no answer noted. Try this one: interference from whom? The Resistance, the Nazis, or the police?"

"The Resistance, of course."

"Why in hell would the Resistance interfere with our transit south? They're helping us," Emily said.

"There are different Resistance factions. Henri would spread the word to them."

Conor took another note that he hadn't actually answered the question. "When we were in Gilbert's apartment, she asked if you had any more contact with the Abwehr. You said no and that they asked a few questions about Laurent."

"Maybe it was more than a few questions. Maybe it was a meetup with your contact within the Abwehr," Emily said.

"It was only a few questions. Trust me, I told him nothing. It would be a betrayal of ethics to reveal patient information," DuBois said in a haughty tone.

Conor recalled the advice from the driver who took them to Avignon: *Be careful who you trust.* And Murphy's friend, Dupont, said something about trust being a scarce commodity.

"You mentioned the plan. Tell us, what would that be?" Conor said.

"To reestablish the Gloria Network. I mentioned this earlier, don't you remember?"

"Nothing more than that?" Emily said.

"That's quite enough, don't you think?"

This guy seems to have all the answers. So why doesn't it feel right?

"Do you remember a dinner you attended at my father's house with me, Maggie, and our father, Jack? Back in thirty-eight?" Conor said.

The change in subject caused DuBois to smile, probably out of relief. "No. I don't believe I do. Why do you ask?"

"Conor tells me you were very impressed with Hitler's handling of Germany's resurgence after the Great War," Emily said.

"And you casually dismissed the persecution of Jews and had no issue with book burning and other Nazi storm trooper strong-arm tactics," Conor added.

"I attended a few dinners at your father's home. I don't remember that conversation."

"Do you deny that you felt that way?" Conor said.

"No. I did at one time."

"Yet you've admitted that you are not… How did you put it? Partial to Jews, which explained why you did nothing to help your mother in her efforts to help Jews find freedom."

"As I said, I did not get in my mother's way," DuBois said, pulling a handkerchief from his breast pocket with a shaky hand and wiping his forehead free of sweat. DuBois's answers and nonanswers settled nothing for Conor.

The driver pounded on the back wall of the cab. "Quiet. Too much talking. You want to give us away?"

#

1415 Hours, Monday, January 11, 1943
In the Camargue near the Coast

To avoid German patrols, they trekked in silence along a drainage ditch that ran along the side of the hard-packed gravel road. A half hour into their march, Conor picked up the Camargue's briny scent. During the walk from Les-Saintes-Maries-de-la-Mer, where they were dropped off, Conor spent the time mulling over variations of the plan DuBois could have been referring to in his note. He wanted to run some of them past Emily, but there wasn't any opportunity. He was sure she had her own ideas. Probably more plausible than his. The last hour of the trip south, DuBois appeared to be more at ease. Conor even heard him humming some tune. Maybe DuBois thought he had passed a test.

When they reached the beach, it looked much more expansive than he remembered it. Their infiltration had been in the early-morning darkness. The beach ran for a long stretch northward along the étang, covered entirely in a blanket of small rounded stones and smaller pebbles. The place at the base of the sand dune where they buried Jackie was marked by a cairn-like pile of stones, probably placed there by the *gardian* Théo, the old man sent to meet Jackie.

They took refuge in the duck blind where they had hidden their radio. All three sat in the sand and rested. Conor wanted to mount one more attempt at getting more info from DuBois about his note.

"There's something sticking in my craw about your note, René. It's about the plan."

DuBois let out a long breath, confirming for Conor that he'd thought all this shit about the note was in the past. "Ask your questions. As if I can stop you."

"You wrote 'our plan.' Who were you referring to?"

"I would think the plan to revive the Gloria Network would be initiated solely from F Section," Emily added.

DuBois's gaze bounced from Conor to Emily. He ran both hands over the patch of gray hair at his temples, thinking of what to say. "Yes, of course. A poor…a poor choice of words."

Conor looked at Emily and cocked his head faintly. "Let me tell you what I think the plan is." Conor looked at DuBois. "Listening?"

DuBois sneered at him.

"I think you are a well-regarded doctor, pro-German, who hates Jews and who quite possibly is or was a member, like your patient Pierre Laurent, of the fascist group called the Synarchy, the group of high-ranking people who were rooting on and doing the bidding of the Nazis early in the war—"

"And has had," Emily said, "at least one meeting with the Abwehr—"

"That we know of," Conor said. DuBois looked from Conor to Emily, then back at Conor. "I would put money on the claim that Colonel Henri is your Abwehr contact. You made inroads into the local Lyon network, made friends, did some good things, and, in return, Gilbert and Virginia Hall vouch for you and"—Conor snapped his fingers—"you're on your way to London to get trained, with my sister as your travel guide."

"It was all a plan to get to Paris, a ruse to flush out Resistance members still in hiding after the Abwehr shut down the Gloria Network," Emily said. Conor saw Emily had buried her right hand in her jacket pocket where she normally kept her Walther.

"That's literally what I was thinking. Of course, you had nothing to do with Maggie's murder. After all, she was going to get you and your mother out of France. Lucky for you, I believe that. Because if I didn't, I would have slit your throat yesterday."

DuBois sat motionless, hands draped over the medical bag in his lap. "You…you have no proof of any of that."

"Oh, I think we are definitely onto something," Conor said. "So much so I have to say that we're going back to Algiers…alone. We can't bring a Nazi spy back to Allied territory…unless—"

"You'd agree to be a double agent. We have quite a few of them," Emily said.

Conor and Emily drew their sidearms and trained them on DuBois. He gripped the top of his medical bag tightly, revealing white knuckles. He cleared his throat. Twice. "That's out of the question. I cannot betray my beliefs."

And there it was. "Of course not. Your loyalty to the Reich and its policies, especially toward the Jews, wouldn't allow that," Conor said.

"I would guess that at some point, probably right here on this beach, you were going to make sure we didn't make it back to Algiers," Emily said.

"And the Atlantic Wall intelligence was going to fall into the sea," Conor said. A pause. DuBois kept his cool, which impressed Conor. "How were you going to kill us?" Another pause with no response. "Emily, check his medical bag."

Emily yanked it from his white-knuckled grip and opened it. "Hmm, maybe a rock to the head when we weren't looking, huh, René?" She reached in and pulled out a round tin and held it up like a trophy. "Strychnine."

"How 'bout that," Conor said. "Mix it in with some food when our heads were turned or mix it in with that wine Anick gave us back at the Le Chat Noir."

"I want to bargain," DuBois said.

"With what?" Emily asked.

"Maggie." DuBois narrowed his gaze on Conor. "She had a baby. A girl. I will tell you where you can find her."

Conor's head jerked back, and his mouth fell open.

"What the hell are you talking about?" Emily said.

"In 1939, she became pregnant. I didn't want her to have the baby. She ignored me. That's when I broke it off. She traveled to France. My mother went with her. To help make…arrangements." Conor remembered Maggie went to Paris to study for several months. It was while he was serving on the USS *Somers*. "My mother helped place the baby for adoption with a doctor in Paris. A Jew." Conor easily detected an air of disgust in his voice. "I will tell you where you can find the baby if you let me go."

"You are one classic piece of shit, DuBois." Conor looked at Emily.

"Tell us," Emily said.

DuBois's eyes brightened. "You'll let me go? Unharmed?"

"Yes," Emily said.

"Em, we're not—"

"Tell us, René," Emily said. Her words had an insistent, hard edge.

"The doctor, his name is Rothbard. He lived on Avenue Foch. Across the street from the Gestapo headquarters. I don't know if he is still there. It's unlikely, I'm afraid. That's all I know."

Conor, still reeling, stared at DuBois. "What is the baby's name?"

"She named it Maguire, after herself."

And after our mother.

Conor reached into his left pocket and pulled out his M1903 Colt and tossed it to DuBois. It fell in his lap behind the medical bag. Emily shot an alarmed look at him. "I'll let you take the easy way out."

"But she said…" A puzzled DuBois hesitated, then reached for the Colt and fired at Conor. A click, then nothing.

Emily raised her Walther and pointed at DuBois's chest. The sound of the round was deafening. It took a long minute for Conor's ears to stop ringing.

CHAPTER SEVENTY-NINE

1015 Hours, Friday, January 15, 1943
Hôtel Saint-George, rue Michelet, Algiers

"Any idea where my murder suspect made off to?" Major Campbell Stewart was the first familiar face Conor and Emily ran into when they arrived in the bustling lobby of the hotel. Given all that transpired since that dark day on the beach, Conor had managed to shove some of the details of the whole James Stones affair to the back of his mind.

"No idea, Major. Traveling alone with no Resistance contacts in occupied territory, that's a sure recipe for capture by the Gestapo or the police," Conor said.

"Did he admit to killing Stevens?" Stewart said.

"No. But when Conor probed, Stones didn't deny it. I think he had been working on his plan of escape well before he boarded the *Casabianca*," Emily said.

"Well, it's still an open case," Stewart said. "What's next for you two?"

Before Conor or Emily could respond, Staff Sergeant Billings was waving his arms to get their attention from across the lobby as he made his way toward them. "Sorry, Major. Commander Butcher has sent for us, and we don't want to be late," Emily said.

"This way," an out-of-breath Billings said. "The commander said to tell you both he apologizes for not meeting you when the *Casabianca* docked. He's been holed up with the general. Another meeting about a big conference all the bigwigs are attending."

Emily looked at Conor and winked. They both were aware of the conference—Emily had been part of the advance team—that would take place in Casablanca. The same conference where Eisenhower was prepared to tell General Marshall that he was stepping down due to the involvement of the OSS and SOE in Darlan's assassination.

"The Commander also wanted to make sure that you had been seen by Doc Tompkins about your shoulder," Billings said.

"Yes, Sergeant. All is good except for some stiffness." A nodding Billings led them out to the familiar pool deck. The weather was warmer than in southern France, which was a welcome change.

"I'll get some hot java and try to scare up some grub. Maybe some powdered eggs, if that's okay?" Billings said.

"That would be lovely, Sergeant," Emily said.

As Billings made for the door to the lobby, Butcher came through it and whispered something to Billings, who saluted, then disappeared into the lobby.

"Welcome back to Allied territory. Are you both rested from your French holiday?" Conor and Emily each offered a soft smile in response to Butcher's attempt at humor, which Butcher picked up on. "Sorry. I'm sure it was no picnic."

Billings arrived with the pot of coffee and some mugs. "Eggs coming up," he said, then did an about-face as he headed to the lobby.

"Conor, please accept my condolences for Maggie. I know it hit Bill Donovan hard. He feels responsible. Says he shouldn't have approved of her being seconded to the SOE."

"Commander, I am sure Maggie was all for it. It got her into the fray sooner. She didn't like being on the sidelines," Conor said.

"Sounds like someone I know," Butcher said.

"Sure does, Commander," Emily said.

"So…your last message… You gave just enough information to allow me some sleep. But—"

"The OSS and SOE *were* involved…but only in the training of the Corps francs d'Afrique," Conor said.

"There was nothing in the archive that describes their role as any more involved than that. No mention that either organization was aware of what the conspirators had been planning to do," Emily said.

Butcher's chest seemed to deflate as if he had been holding a deep breath. He sipped from his mug. Then came the slow affirming nod. "Do you have any proof for me?" Conor gave a sideways glance at Emily. "No…no, I don't want proof. I'll take your word for it. Both of your words."

Conor reached into his breast pocket and pulled out a single piece of paper. The piece he had taken from the archive just before setting it on fire when Emily was distracted by a passing vehicle. Conor heard a soft gasp from Emily. He passed the sheet to Butcher. Conor watched Butcher as he read it. Fifteen seconds later, Butcher pulled his Ronson from his coat pocket and lit the corner of the document, then held it for a moment before letting it fall to the pool deck. With the sole of his shoe, he ground the ashes into the rough surface of the concrete.

"Well done. Anything else you want to tell me? What about Stones?"

"We've already given Major Stewart a quick briefing. We can elaborate later, if necessary," Emily said.

"Commander, what about that offer you made? About us getting back with our outfits. That still stands?" Conor said.

"It does, and it still includes reinstatement in the navy for you, Conor. If that's what you want."

Conor looked at Emily, then turned to Butcher. He had rehearsed his response for a good part of the trip south on the *Casabianca*. "I'm going to stick with the OSS, Commander."

"Reasoning?" Butcher said.

"You've heard about the 'tip of the spear'?"

"I have."

"That's the reason."

Butcher nodded. "Wait here. General Eisenhower wants to shake your hands and thank you for bringing the Atlantic Wall intel to us. You don't know how critical having that in our hands this far out will be." Butcher got up and looked down at what was left of the ashes on the pool deck, then strode off toward the lobby.

"It would have been nice if you'd let me know you pilfered a piece of the archive. That was quite a surprise," Emily said, her words at first scolding, then softening.

"I thought we would need proof, thinking that higher-ups

might not believe us given how the Majorana mission played out."

"Actually, that was good thinking. I approve."

"I wasn't sure you would. Therefore, the subterfuge."

"Hopefully there won't be any more of that, Conor Thorn."

EPILOGUE

1115 Hours, Monday, January 18, 1943
Claridge's, London

On the drive south from RAF Tempsford to London, they continued to feel the cumulative effects of ebbing adrenaline. A shroud of fatigue and listlessness had overcome them. The long flights from Algiers to Gibraltar, then to Tempsford, had done little to mitigate their malaise. Bill Donovan had sent his driver, Anne Hollis, a familiar figure to them both, to pick them up. It shocked her when Conor relented and allowed her to drive. Her normal role was to sit in the back and read a tabloid or two while Conor piloted the Buick Roadmaster around England. For much of the drive, he held Emily's hand, until they both gave in to sleep.

As soon as they passed through the revolving doors of Claridge's into the lobby teeming with guests and staff coming and going, Conor heard his name shouted above the din.

"Over here, Conor." The Irish-accented command unmistakably belonged to Father Sean Sullivan. A longtime friend of the Thorn family and a willing participant in two of his and Emily's last missions, both to Italy—one to track down the traitor Henry Longworth and the other to find and recruit Ettore Majorana. It was Sean who had convinced him and Emily to let Majorana go free, instead of forcing him to work on the Allied atomic bomb project. An outcome that got them booted from the OSS and SOE.

Sean stood in the middle of a grouping of plush chairs and a long couch set before a roaring fireplace. First to rise was Conor's father, Jack, followed by an officer in the uniform of the British Merchant Navy. One side of his face was badly burned. His right hand was as well. It seemed that his first two fingers were fused together.

"Richard," Emily gushed. She stood in the middle of the lobby's tumult and stared. Beside Richard was a tiny woman, her hair in a short blonde bob. Cradled in her arms was a baby.

Conor and Emily, arm in arm, strode over to the group. "Finally, you've arrived," Sean said. "David Bruce passed along to me you'd be arriving this morning. So I thought a little greeting party to welcome you both back to friendly shores was called for."

"Wonderful idea, Sean," Emily said, wiping a tear from her cheek. She went to Richard, and they embraced each other warmly and for a long silent moment.

"Bertie, your mother, she thought I could be of some help to Richard. And to Catherine," Sean said.

"We are to be married," Richard said. "And Sean has agreed to do the honors." Emily wiped another tear away. "We waited until you returned. Seemed like the right thing to do." Emily went over to Catherine and silently motioned if she could hold the baby. Catherine nodded and handed over a blanketed bundle.

"It's a girl. Her name is Emily," Catherine said. A cherub-like face peered out from deep inside the blanket. Catherine brushed away several tears as she looped her arm through Richard's.

A somber-faced Jack extended his hand to Conor. "Son, so glad you both made it back."

Conor thought it was a slight reference to Maggie. "You heard?"

Jack nodded. "Bill Donovan reached out. Said it was the worst part of his job. And I believe him." He went on saying he thought he was prepared for such news, with all three of his kids doing their part in the war. "But, lo and behold, I find out I wasn't. Not one bit."

Emily joined them, still holding the baby. Conor steered the small group toward the window overlooking the busy street fronting the hotel. "There's something else, Dad."

"Not more bad news…is it?"

Conor could hear fear creep into his father's voice. "No…I… we found out…Maggie had a baby." Conor wasn't sure what to expect, reaction-wise, from his father. What he saw was complete confusion.

Jack's eyes darted about the lobby, out to the street, then back at Conor.

"It was back in thirty-nine. When she left—"

"For Paris," Jack muttered as he nodded. "Right after she broke up with that doctor, DuBois."

"Yes. She had help finding the baby a home. With a doctor, in fact," Emily said.

Jack appeared to have gotten a grip on the news as he locked his eyes on Conor. "Boy or girl?"

"A girl," Emily said, fresh tears rolling down her cheeks. "She named her Maguire."

"After herself. That's so Maggie," Conor said.

"And after her mother. *That's* so Maggie," Jack said.

The three of them stood there in silence, Richard and Catherine's baby munching on her balled-up fist. All three staring at the baby.

Conor placed his hand on his father's shoulder and gave it a squeeze. "Dad, I'll find her. Trust me." Conor could only hope that, when he did, she would be alive.

DID YOU ENJOY *TRUST NO ONE?*

You can keep reading by grabbing a free short story that pits Winston Churchill against the leader of the Soviet Union, Joseph Stalin, when you join my newsletter. You'll also get the Prologue and Chapter One of *THE TORCH BETRAYAL*, the first book in the Conor Thorn Series, and notice of upcoming releases, promotions, and personal updates.

Sign up today at:
https://www.glenndyer.net/#subscribe-form

You can help other readers (and this author!) by leaving a review for *THE TORCH BETRAYAL, THE ULTRA BETRAYAL, THE UNQUIET GENIUS,* and *TRUST NO ONE* on Amazon.

Don't worry—it can be short and to the point.

But if you didn't get a chance to read
the first three books in the Conor Thorn Series,
THE TORCH BETRAYAL, THE ULTRA BETRAYAL, and
THE UNQUIET GENIUS, you'll find them at Amazon.

You can connect with Glenn Dyer at:
www.instagram.com/glennduffydyer
www.facebook.com/GlennDyerAuthor
www.twitter.com/duffy_dyer
www.glenndyer.net

AUTHOR'S NOTE

If you've read the previous books in the Conor Thorn Series, you are well aware that the storylines were inspired by actual events that occurred prior to and during World War II. What I like about this approach is that it gives me a chance to introduce a bit of history that might have been overlooked. Many events and participants have been, in fact, overlooked, which is not hard to understand given the mind-boggling scope of the conflict. To this day, there are new works of fiction, nonfiction, memoir, and films released on a regular basis detailing aspects of WWII that were little known and then become valuable additions to the archive of the history of the war.

The initial idea for *Trust No One* was born after discovering the existence of a secret archive. I am getting ahead of myself here. I began the search for a story by researching the Casablanca Conference that took place January 14, 1943, between Prime Minister Winston Churchill and President Franklin D. Roosevelt. While I was reading about the conference in Meredith Hindley's excellent and deeply researched book *Destination Casablanca: Exile, Espionage, and the Battle for North Africa in World War II* (Public Affairs, 2017), passages concerning French Admiral Jean Darlan piqued my interest.

Hindley delved into the role he played in the early stages of the war, his dealings with Nazi Germany and the Allies and his assassination on Christmas Eve in 1942 by Fernand Bonnier de la Chapelle, a member of the *Corps francs d'Afrique* and a group of conspirators intent on eliminating the admiral, who was a former

Nazi collaborator. Bonnier was a monarchist and passionate anti-Vichyite. The assassination led me to a book by Peter Tompkins entitled *The Murder of Admiral Darlan* (Simon and Schuster, 1965). One fact jumped out at me immediately. The group of conspirators had an archive. He didn't detail its contents. Tompkins went on to state that the archive was hidden in the convent of the Sisters of the Notre Dame d'Afrique. Tompkins made no further mention of the archive. But he did mention that, before an inquest into the assassination had begun, rumors began to swirl that Allied secret services had organized the murder of the double-dealing admiral.

Further research along this line led me to an article by T.C. Wales entitled "The 'Massingham' Mission and the Secret 'Special Relationship': Cooperation and Rivalry Between the Anglo-American Clandestine Services in French North Africa, November 1942-May 1943" (*Intelligence and National Security*, 20:1). In the article, Wales states that AFHQ (Allied Forces Headquarters), essentially General Eisenhower, warned that "any Allied agency plotting to liquidate the Admiral would be expelled from North Africa." Add this revelation to Tompkins's research, and the story rapidly developed. In Warren Tute's *The Reluctant Enemies: The Story of the Last War Between Britain and France 1940-1942* (William Collins and Sons, 1989), he mentions that Eisenhower initiated an investigation into the assassination and stated that "if this (investigation) revealed the slightest British or American complicity in the plot, he would ask to be relieved of his command."

At this point, I felt I had the backbone of what would be *Trust No One.* What if the archive detailed some involvement in the assassination of a high-ranking French official by the OSS or the SOE and it fell into the wrong hands? The hands of those who wanted to drive a wedge—or worse, destroy the alliance—between the British and Americans and their French allies, an outcome Nazi Germany would be all too eager to help facilitate.

If you've read the previous three novels in the series, you know I employ real people as characters in my stories along with the fictional ones. Putting words in their mouths is a creative process that I don't take lightly. Those words and actions must accurately reflect their role in history and their personality. Doing so properly adds authenticity and allows me to highlight their role in the war and hopefully, along the way, keep their contributions from fading from history. This goes for both sides of the conflict. That said, their actions and words herein are products of my imagination.

A short list of the real people that deserve to be remembered and read up on include Virginia Hall, Carleton Coon, Commander L'Herminier, Commander Harry Butcher, Hugo Bleicher, Maurice Buckmaster, and Vera Atkins. With reluctance, I also add the name Klaus Barbie, known as the "Butcher of Lyon." Barbie's actions during the war, however horrific, should never be forgotten.

Lastly on this subject, in *Trust No One,* there are several characters that are composites of real people. One character in the novel, Abbé Robert Alves, was based on a real person. His name was Abbé Robert Alesch. Reading about this priest, who earned the sobriquet *Rasputin of the Abwehr* in Sonia Purnell's *A Woman of No Importance* (Viking, 2019), was quite shocking. Raised Catholic, I was astounded as I learned about a priest siding with the Nazis who lived a double life, complete with mistresses. His work for the Abwehr did, indeed, lead to the shutdown on August 13, 1942, of the Paris-based Gloria Network, which led to the capture of approximately eighty people, many who did not survive the war. After the war, Alesch was taken by French authorities and tried beginning on May 25, 1948, and found guilty of collaborating with the Nazis by the Court of Justice in a three-day trial. Some surviving members of the Gloria Network witnessed the trial. An ironic twist to Alesch's story was that his handler, Hugo Bleicher, testified against him. He was shot by a firing squad on February 25, 1949.

Another character that is inspired by a real person is Germaine Gilbert. The owner of the One-Eight is based on a brothel owner by the name of Germaine Guérin. She worked closely with Virginia Hall. As a member of the French Resistance, Guérin was known for harboring Jews and assisting downed Allied air crews escape capture by the Germans and protecting SOE agents passing through Lyon. Guérin purposely promoted the spread of sexually transmitted diseases among the German patrons of her brothel. She also was betrayed by Abbé Alesch but survived her internment in Ravensbrück concentration camp. She later testified against Alesch at his trial.

A few words on the city of Lyon. My wife, Chris, and I traveled to France in December of 2022 in order to do some research. Nothing beats putting your boots on the ground for getting a good feel for a setting that your characters will find themselves in. Lyon has a rich history dating back to Roman times. On September 14, 1944, General Charles de Gaulle proclaimed Lyon as "the capital of the Resistance." Traveling through a few of the city's traboules that Resistance fighters had traveled decades before was a spine-chilling experience. If you are ever so lucky to travel there and you wish to learn more of its history as a major setting for the Resistance's struggles against the Nazi occupiers, you must visit the Centre d'Histoire de la Résistance et de la Déportation, a museum dedicated to those members of the Resistance that fought and died to free their country from the grasp of Nazi Germany.

Lastly, I'd like to add some background on the *Synarchique* organization that is first mentioned in Chapter Three. My research shed light on the tumultuous political landscape that existed in France in the 1930s. First, I must mention *La Cagoule,* The Cowl. This was a fascist-leaning, anticommunist, violence-prone organization that was formed circa 1936 to overthrow the Popular Front government. In November 1937, when police infiltrated the group, approximately seventy men were arrested. In the 1930s, there was a ground swell of anticommunist sentiment that existed throughout Europe. *La Cagoule* directed its members to generate suspicions of communists in order to destabilize the French Republic.

In former OSS officer William Langer's book, *Our Vichy Gamble* (Alfred A. Knoff, 1947), he cited that during the 1930s, Hitler's doctrines had many admirers in France. Germany's stature in Europe was rising. There were high-placed, wealthy industrialists that saw Germany as a bulwark against communism. This sentiment led to the establishment of, according to Anthony Cave Brown's *Wild Bill Donovan: The Last Hero* (Times Books, 1982), "an association of French financiers and industrialists who have organized themselves into a political pressure group for the maintenance and extension of their power in the new order," as quoted in one of the reports entitled "Bank Worms and Synarquisme" that Bill Donovan, chief of the OSS, sent to FDR June 26, 1942, which I mention in Chapter Twenty-Three.

Donovan went on to say that their political aims were to "advocate maximum political and economic collaboration with Germany" and "to facilitate a negotiated peace between the Axis and the Allies" against Russia. As I mention in Chapter Twenty-Three, FDR didn't respond to Donovan's reports. His concerns about the Synarchy's status in France were replaced by the numerous issues that Bill Donovan and the OSS faced as the war ground on.

ACKNOWLEDGMENTS

As it was with the previous three novels in the Conor Thorn series, I traveled down the road to completion alongside many people. The journey is always a challenging one, and my family, friends, and associates were largely responsible for me getting to the finish line sane and satisfied that I had done the best I could in writing the most compelling, accurate, and entertaining novel. While the actual writing process is a solitary one, the overarching process of creating the novel from the ground up couldn't be done without the guidance of people that are so much smarter than I.

First up, my wife, Chris, and our children, Tom, Mike, and Riley. Chris was the first to read a very early draft of *Trust No One*, and her feedback saved me from completely running the story into the ground. Some of you may not be aware how much goes on behind the scenes when it comes to marketing a book series. Tom, Mike, and Riley are always available to lend advice, tend to a technological issue, comment on social media posts and author newsletters, and sometimes just offer simple, sincere support to a writer who always needs it. Their contributions keep me from embarrassing myself and running my writing business off the rails. I have to mention Ethan Eisenbarth and his company Splitnotch, who is my right-hand man when it comes to managing my presence on various social media platforms. He's one creative guy!

To Gretchen Stelter, my primary editor, I owe a great deal to her for her wise counsel as a developmental editor. Uncovering plot problems early on saved a tremendous amount of time and drafts.

To Kimberly Hunt from Revision Division, who did a manuscript evaluation as well as a couple of edit passes, thanks for your feedback and keen eye for the weak spots in the story. I can't fail to mention Cayce Berryman, and Richelle Braswell, who did a copyedit and final proof and provided many thoughtful comments.

To Genevieve Montcombroux, a fellow member of the Second World War Author Facebook group, who so patiently answered many questions about the French Resistance, life in France during the occupation, and nuances of the French language. Genevieve read an early draft of *Trust No One* and provided invaluable guidance that added a considerable amount of authenticity to the story. *Merci, Genevieve!*

Speaking of authenticity, I have author colleague Phil Yates to thank for his suggestions and advice regarding the passage of the French submarine *Casabianca* across the Mediterranean Sea. Phil's command of tactics, material, and facts concerning WWII is jaw dropping.

While I'm on the subject of military tactics and terminology, I have to send thanks to my brother Mike. A veteran US Navy lieutenant, Mike's sharp eye was critical in making the key dream scene aboard the USS *Reuben James* flow more accurately, tensely, and concisely.

For further assistance with the layout of the USS *Reuben James*, the Clemson class destroyer that Conor Thorn served aboard, I have to thank Brian Siela who provided numerous pictures and detailed captions that I relied on greatly. The Facebook group Flush Deck Four Stack Destroyers that Brian is a part of is a wonderful place if you're interested in the preservation of the history of the Clemson, Wicks, and Caldwell class destroyers.

To Chris Grall from Tactiquill, who provided additional military, firearms, and action scene comments, I am so grateful for his willingness to spend an enormous amount of time on the phone and via countless email exchanges with me. Chris's vast knowledge in the above-mentioned fields has helped so many other authors and screenwriters keep out of trouble as they craft their stories. I am no exception.

To doctors Krista and Craig Lauer, many thanks, dear friends, for your medical guidance when it came to injury-prone Conor and Emily Thorn. It's my job to put them in life-threatening situations, and your job was to make sure I didn't go over the top in doing so.

I am indebted to Jane Dixon Smith, who has applied her impressive graphic talents for all the books in the Conor Thorn series. From covers to marketing materials to manuscript formatting, she is always a joy to work with. Even when I change my mind so many times. Thanks, Jane, for your professionalism and patience.

Thanks to Randy Harris for his help on the subject of OSS agents Frederick Brown and Carleton Coon, and thanks to Ben Major from WW2 US Medical Research Centre for some answers to questions about military hospitals in active operational theaters during WWII.

And thanks to author Peter Dixon, who was generous in providing information about the OSS's and SOE's activities in North Africa. I also relied on his well-researched book *Setting the Med Ablaze: Churchill's Secret North African Base* in order to get comfortable with the feel for the period in late 1942 and early 1943 as the Allies were in the late stages of ridding the Axis from North Africa. Thanks, Peter.

Family and friends that wander into my office can't miss the table beside my desk that holds my stacks of "To Be Read" books. Needless to say, they are quite impressed with the size of the stacks. As for myself, the stacks of books intimidate me. There are some unbelievably talented writers represented in those stacks. I have read previous works of a vast majority of them, which has served as long-lasting inspiration to me as I continue to hone the craft of fiction writing. I am indebted to this group of storytellers.

Topping my list is Steve Berry followed by Mark Greaney, Jack Carr, Lee Jackson, L. T. Ryan, Chris Glatte, Robert Dugoni, Daniel Silva, W. E. B. Griffin, Lee Child, James R. Benn, Kate Quinn, Elizabeth Wein, David Baldacci, fellow Livingston, New Jerseyite Harlan Coben, Brad Thor, Don Bentley, David Poyer, Alex Finlay, and P. T. Deutermann. This group of thriller and mystery writers are at the top of their game. Thanks to you all for being so inspiring. If you're looking for a heart-pounding read, sample some of their work. You won't be disappointed.

I have mentioned the OSS Society (OSSSociety.org) in

the acknowledgments in previous novels in the Conor Thorn Series, and I will do so again. This organization exists to honor the accomplishments, heroism, and sacrifices made by so many people who were the "tip of the spear" for the OSS during WWII. The OSS Society continues their efforts to establish a National Museum of Intelligence and Special Operations (NationalIntelligenceMuseum.org). The motto of the museum is *Honor, Educate, Inspire, Serve.*

As you can see, I called on many people for feedback and advice as I pounded out the drafts of *Trust No One.* But, because I don't always listen, any errors herein are mine.

PRAISE FOR THE TORCH BETRAYAL

"The disappearance in 1942 of a page from a secret document concerning Operation Torch...drives Dyer's suspenseful espionage thriller... Jack Higgins fans will find a lot to like."

—*BookLife/Publishers Weekly*

"Atmospheric and tense, with plenty of treachery and a heavy dose of history. What more could you ask for in a thriller? Take a walk on the perilous side and check this one out."

—Steve Berry *New York Times, USA Today* & Internationally Bestselling Author

"Welcome to 1942. Glenn Dyer is your tour guide to the world of spies and betrayal in the lead-up to the Allied Invasion of North Africa. You're in good hands, so settle back and enjoy the fireworks."

—James R. Benn, author of *Road of Bones,* A Billy Boyle World War II Mystery

"...what sets Dyer's book apart from the others in the genre is his unfailing attention to historical detail and great writing."

—The BookLife Prize

"...a classic spy story in the vein of John Le Carré or Daniel Silva..."

—BlueInk Stared Review

"*The Torch Betrayal* is the best mix of genre standards from a fresh voice...crisp writing, plot reveals that pop like firecrackers, and cinematic excitement..."

—Foreword Reviews

"A well-crafted espionage tale set during World War II."

—*Kirkus Reviews*

"In this highly entertaining tale...Dyer has hit all the notes in the thriller genre."

—IndieReader Five-Star Review

PRAISE FOR THE ULTRA BETRAYAL

"Brilliantly researched and filled with fascinating characters from the pages of history, Glenn Dyer once again brings World War II espionage to life in his latest Conor Thorn thriller. *The Ultra Betrayal* exceeds all expectations. I'm a fan! Read it today!"

—Jack Carr *New York Times* bestselling author of *Savage Son*

"A tantalizing premise set among the ominous atmosphere of World War II, there's sizzle and plot twists galore—more than enough to satisfy any thriller reader. Enjoy this latest in the Conor Thorn series."

—Steve Berry *New York Times, USA Today* and #1 Internationally Bestselling Author

"*The Ultra Betrayal* is blessed with a plot that zings along like a ricocheting bullet that finds its mark in the last electrifying pages. Meticulously researched and filled with fascinating characters, this one is sure to please."

—James R. Benn, author of *Road of Bones,* A Billy Boyle World War II Mystery

"Dyer's series, which started with *The Torch Betrayal*, is one of the more underrated spy franchises set during WWII, and a perfect fit for fans of Alan Furst. And Conor Thorn is a really fantastic hero, who doesn't get the attention he deserves."

—The Real Book Spy

"Conor Thorn is back with a vengeance in Glenn Dyer's compelling new World War II thriller, *The Ultra Betrayal.* This time out, Thorn is on the hunt for a missing cryptographer before the Nazis get their hands on his secrets. But the enemy may be closer than Thorn thinks. History and thriller lovers alike will stay up reading late into the night until the final breathtaking twist. Don't miss this one!"

—Anthony Franze, author of *The Outsider*

PRAISE FOR THE UNQUIET GENIUS

"A tantalizing premise with a plot to savor. Settle back and enjoy this one."

—Steve Berry, *New York Times* and #1 Internationally Bestselling Author

"Glenn Dyer does it again with *The Unquiet Genius*, his third work of World War Two historical fiction. With characters both familiar and obscure from the pages of history, Glenn weaves a fascinating story of action and espionage that has become the hallmark of his must-read Conor Thorn series! Not to be missed, this one will blow you away!"

—Jack Carr, *New York Times* Bestselling Author of *The Devil's Hand*

"Glenn Dyer's *THE UNQUIET GENIUS* has it all—action, suspense, and the endlessly fascinating World War II era and makes a worthy addition to the author's gripping espionage series."

—IndieReader

"From beginning to end the story enthralls with its crisp action, high stakes, and clever twists and turns. Dyer's like a puppeteer pulling the strings of readers' imaginations."

—BookLife/*Publisher's Weekly*

"*The Unquiet Genius* is a well-written, suspenseful, and deeply researched thriller that thrusts you into the atomic arms race during the critical days of WWII. You'll find yourself deeply invested in the mission, urging the Allies forward to beat the Nazis and Russians to the punch. Buckle up and get ready for the ride."

—Steven Netter, Best Thriller Books

"Dyer has taken a relatively unknown but fascinating piece of WWII history and vividly brought it to life."

—BlueInk Reviews

PRAISE FOR TRUST NO ONE

"*Trust No One* opens with an adrenalin-packed flourish and continues in a similarly tense fashion throughout… This book functions well on multiple levels and will attract readers who yearn for an enthralling yarn. It is hugely immersive."
—The Book Commentary

"Dyer immerses readers in daring infiltrations, military secrets, dirty politics, and the unexpected… Crisply told, alive with intrigue and telling detail, *Trust No One* will please espionage fans who favor historical accuracy but also a ripping yarn."
—Booklife Reviews

"Actual historical figures, who played critical roles in intelligence operations with both the OSS and SOE during World War II, are part of Dyer's stories, and the realism he spins within his novels is pure genius… You may promise yourself you'll only read one chapter before bed, but you'll find you can't put the book down. Before you know it, you've read another 50 pages! This story keeps you guessing right up until the end."
—J. R. Olson CDR, US Navy (ret.) Co-author with David Bruns of the WMD and *Command and Control* Series

"*Trust No One* is a propulsive, masterfully crafted WWII thriller. If you like the Conor Thorn series, you will love his latest adventure."

— Chris Wallace, veteran journalist, CNN anchor and best-selling author of the *Countdown* series

"A gritty and visceral historical thriller laced with international espionage amidst a rich tapestry of suspense, *Trust No One* by Glenn Dyer offers a well-crafted and calculated spiral of intrigue… Every line in this novel is steeped with intention and tension, as Dyer continues to expand the dimensionality of his characters and demonstrate his narrative mastery as this series pushes confidently forward."

—*The Independent Review of Books*

Made in the USA
Columbia, SC
04 November 2024